ALPHA

ALPHA

T. D. RAMAKRISHNAN

TRANSLATED FROM THE MALAYALAM
BY PRIYA K. NAIR

MACMILLAN

First published in English 2022 by Macmillan
an imprint of Pan Macmillan Publishing India Private Limited
707 Kailash Building
26 K. G. Marg, New Delhi 110001
www.panmacmillan.co.in

Pan Macmillan, The Smithson, 6 Briset Street, London EC1M 5NR
Associated companies throughout the world
www.panmacmillan.com

ISBN 978-93-89109-89-4

1 3 5 7 9 8 6 4 2

Typeset in Fairfield LT Std by R. Ajith Kumar, New Delhi
Printed and bound in India by
Replika Press Pvt. Ltd.

1

1 January 1973

THE ISLAND CAME INTO VIEW LIKE A GREEN DOT IN THE grey sea. The boat was at a distance of nearly one nautical mile from it. Everyone in the group started peering into their binoculars intently just as the island came into view. It was the fourth day of their journey to this island, about seventeen square kilometres in size, located 409.827 nautical miles south of Sri Lanka in the vast Indian Ocean. After spending four nights and three days at sea, the small motorboat, although enervated, continued to chug over the rising waves as it gradually made its way towards the island. Now, with the destination within reach, all thirteen members of the team began to feel a sense of nervousness. They were on the brink of a great experiment.

Alpha. That was the name Professor Upelendu Chatterjee had given to the island. It was the Professor who had selected this island that could not be found on any published map and had not been claimed by any country as its territory. Theirs was an experiment that was to last twenty-five years. He was a professor of anthropology at the Jawaharlal Nehru University. The twelve members of his team were from different Indian states.

Anthropological experiments are quite unlike the ones conducted by chemists or botanists. In this particular instance, the investigators also happened to be its subjects. In other words, this group of thirteen intended to carry out an experiment on their own lives. They would have to bear the gains or losses. The Professor was gazing at the island, stroking his grey beard; he could see that they would reach the island in very little time.

The passengers were to get off the boat at a point where the water was neck-deep. Then the experiment would begin.

They would have to give up all knowledge gained since the uncertain emergence of their lives. Go back to zero – the beginning – and from there start once again. In other words, alpha, beta, gamma.

Everyone in the group was under great duress. They were aware of all aspects of the experiment. The Professor had discussed everything with them alone and in groups. He had not pressurized a single one of them to participate; on the contrary, he had told them frankly not to expect much from the outcome of the experiment and warned them that the lives they had lived up to that point would be completely lost to them.

Everyone wanted to say something; they had questions for the Professor. But they could not utter a single word. It cannot be said that they were sad; rather, they were anxious. Most of them were in their thirties, well educated; some were researchers in various disciplines. The knowledge they had acquired, the positions they had gained in society, the money they had made would all be lost in the next few moments. Once they stepped off the boat, they had to obey the rules of the experiment – live as primaeval beings, for twenty-five years, uncontrolled by the norms of society, without rules or laws. They were to have no language, clothes, weapons or houses; in fact, anything that modern life offers would be unavailable to them. They knew very little about the hitherto uninhabited island. Maybe it was the fear of their fast-approaching reality that had robbed them of their ability to speak.

The boat slowly came to a stop a short distance from the island. Christopher, who had been quiet during the boat journey, came and stood in front of the Professor. There was complete silence on the boat. Nobody moved. At last, the Professor spoke, 'We have arrived. If we get down at this spot, the water will only reach up to our necks. Once everyone gets off, we will burn the boat. If any one of you has the slightest inclination to withdraw from this experiment, you can return by this boat. If you are willing to comply with the rules we had agreed upon, let us alight.'

No one moved for a while. Each one of them was struggling to curb the desire to return home rising within them. Memories of the luxuries of life they had been enjoying until then prompted them to rethink their decision. At last, Pradeep Mehta, a journalist, turned to the Professor and said:

'Sir, can I ask you something? All of us had agreed wholeheartedly with this scheme when we started this journey. The question of whether we want to go back doesn't arise at all. But I have a doubt. How will the outside world come to know of this twenty-five-year-old experiment as we would have given up our knowledge of languages? How then will the world outside know of our thoughts and findings? What is the purpose of an experiment that will not be useful to society?'

'Pradeep, please listen. This experiment seeks to reveal the hollowness and the futility of concepts like society, family and morality and to prove that these concepts retard the freedom and progress of the human species to a great extent. And thereby, establish that we have no obligations to society. And there is one person other than us who knows of this experiment. Do not ask me who that is. Exactly twenty-five years from this day, he will come here. It will be then that we will analyze the results of this experiment.'

The members of the team started discarding their personal belongings one by one. But they all hesitated before taking off their clothes. They were reluctant to get naked before jumping into the water. They looked at the Professor, hesitant to relinquish the knowledge gained over a lifetime and the culture passed down through ages. The Professor, assuming complete responsibility for this experiment, had already taken off his clothes and entered the sea. He half-swam and half-walked to the shore.

The white sands of the island raised a question in the Professor's mind. At that time, everyone in the boat was looking at him in wonder. He was no longer the Upelendu Chatterjee they had known till then. The great Professor Upelendu Chatterjee who had presented papers at international seminars was standing before them, completely nude – a primaeval man. They realized they had nothing more to think about. Pradeep, Urmila, Shweta, Christopher, Anwar, Rajesh, Santosh, Malini, Hari, Merlin, Aruna, Anjali … everyone stepped off the boat into the sea. Anwar, as had been decided beforehand, doused the boat with petrol and set it on fire. The thirteen of them looked on, as their last viable link with the outside world burnt to ashes. And so begins the story – the story of a magnificent experiment.

2

1 January 1998

BEFORE EMBARKING ON THE JOURNEY, WE WERE besieged by doubts. Will this boat be able to carry us over six hundred and ninety-five nautical miles? I did not have much experience in sea travel. I only had the information that Professor Banerji had given us about the island. The only consolation was that my friend Michael Peter, from Goa, was a seasoned sailor and knew how to handle a boat. We travelled for three days and with the help of a map and a compass, we were finally able to locate the island Alpha.

Is there more to this experiment? What must have happened to the thirteen people Professor Banerji had told us about? Would we find a highly evolved society of human beings living on Alpha within the space of twenty-five years as Professor Chatterjee had believed? Would human intellect have progressed faster and attained more strength once the shackles of societal taboos had been removed?

As Professor Banerji had warned us not to approach the island suddenly, we anchored the boat some distance away from it. We wanted to observe the inhabitants of the island without being seen. But we could only see thick, green woods full of trees. There were no traces of human society. I wondered if we had reached the wrong island. But Michael insisted that it was the same one we had directions for. After waiting a long time, as daylight began to fade, we saw a group of creatures approaching the shore. It was difficult to believe that they were humans. They reminded me of the sketches of primitive men and women one saw in history textbooks. Is this the great breakthrough they had gained after twenty-five years? Are these the same people whose biographies I have with me? We slowly guided the boat to the shore. When we neared the shore, we saw that the people on the island were fairly young and not the people on my list. There were women, men and children among them. I felt oddly repulsed when I saw their wild hair, matted beards and nude bodies.

They looked at us startled when they heard the sound of the boat. As our boat drew closer, they ran back into the island to hide as if in fear of alien creatures. We could not comprehend the sounds they were making.

Covered with trees, flocks of birds and multi-coloured butterflies flying all over the place, Alpha lay before us like the beginning of human civilization. We felt as if we had reached a new world. There were trees I had never seen before, some of them really huge. Amidst this wilderness, where would we find the world-famous anthropologist Professor Upelendu Chatterjee? And the twelve men and women who had travelled with him to this island? We started making our way into the island. The ground was covered with bushes and creepers.

'Careful! There may be snakes,' Michael warned me.

As we were wearing clothes and shoes suitable for rough terrain, we moved forward, cutting down the plants that blocked our way. For a long time, we didn't come across another soul. Later we could hear the sounds we had heard earlier somewhere on the other side of the trees. The new generation, that was born here on the island, looked at us with dread as if we were strange beings. Not one of them came close to us. But if Professor Banerji were to be believed, wouldn't the thirteen of the first settlers be waiting for someone from the outside world after twenty-five years? Or were they all dead?

Michael secretly clicked a few pictures of them. It was nearing twilight. We had carried with us some food and a few weapons as well in case we faced any danger. When darkness set in, we were suddenly gripped by a fear that we might get attacked. The strong beams from our headlamps had kept the islanders at bay so far. Might they be cannibals? We were quite confused, but Michael's eyes shone with the light of courage.

Finally, we found a cave. It was small and only one person could enter at a time.

'Let's go in. There is bound to be someone inside.'

I had a gun in one hand and a long, sharp knife that I'd used to cut down the foliage in the other. As our headlamps beamed around, a woman came running towards us. Overcome with emotion, she said, 'Oh God! You have finally arrived. I was sure that you would come today. I have been waiting for you.'

I couldn't guess the age of this emaciated, sunburnt, naked woman. Her body was wrinkled and dry as she had not worn any clothes for a long time. But her eyes were glittering with hope. I took a candle from my bag and lit it. The three of us sat around the glimmering light of the candle.

She continued, 'I am Malini Desai, one of the thirteen experimenters who came to this island. Two more of us are still alive. They are lying unconscious in the next room.'

'I am Avinash, Professor Sathish Chandra Banerji's student. Years ago, your Professor had entrusted Dr Banerji with the responsibility of coming here to meet all of you on this very day. Unfortunately, he fell ill and is now paralyzed. This is my friend Michael. Malini, now tell me, where is Professor Upelendu Chatterjee?'

'Professor Chatterjee? Oh, he died fourteen years ago. Only Santosh and Urmila are left. Have you brought anything with you? It's been twenty-five years since I ate proper food.'

I took the food out of my bag and we ate together, speaking through the night, about Alpha, about their experiment over the years and then about the primitive life the new generation was leading. In the dim light, when I saw her shrivelled breasts, I asked, 'Can I give you a shawl?'

'No. I'll remain this way till we leave this place. You feel bad when you look at me. But I don't think this is unnatural.'

As we spoke, the other island-dwellers peered at us. They all respected Malini and probably thought of her as a grandmother. The next day we departed from the island, taking Urmila and Santosh with us on the boat. Malini spoke to the islanders in a strange language. They listened to her attentively and accompanied us to the boat as if to bid farewell.

Michael plucked a lot of plants from the island and a few big leaves off the trees. He attributed the physical strength of the island-dwellers to the medicinal properties of the plants.

As the boat moved, I gave Malini some clothes. And with great difficulty, we dressed the unconscious Santosh and Urmila. At times, Malini would behave in a very strange manner. She would speak continuously for a few minutes and then suddenly fall silent for a long time. Then her eyes would fill with tears. Initially, she greedily ate the food we had brought. But later on, she would look at the food in silence and refuse to eat it. Then she spotted my binoculars.

'I too had one when I came here. I gazed at Alpha through my binoculars for a long time. Alpha looked beautiful then. Alpha … pure and untouched by humans. When I discarded all my belongings, the binoculars were thrown away as well. Avinash, everything was destroyed in this madness. The other creatures had lived so peacefully on the island.'

The boat moved forward slowly. Alpha gradually disappeared from our view. When the island was no longer visible even through the binoculars, Malini held her hand to her forehead and started weeping. 'Twenty-five years … twenty-five years have been lost. Just think about it! So little is left of my life. I was a fool. Not just me, all of us. Did you really want to come looking for us, Avinash? Or were you merely doing your duty?'

'Well, not just out of a sense of duty but also an eagerness to know. Think of me as a seeker of truth.'

Finally, after a journey that lasted for three days, we reached the shore. By the time we reached Michael's house with the three people from Alpha, I was completely confused.

3

The Story as Narrated by Malini Desai

SEATED IN A CANE CHAIR ON THE BALCONY, MALINI started talking to me with great difficulty, in a mixture of English and Hindi. There were unfathomable silences between her broken sentences. It was difficult to piece everything together. She was the only other anthropologist on the Professor's team. She was twenty-five years old when she went to the island, the youngest in the group. And now, twenty-five years later, she had changed beyond recognition. It was difficult to believe that this thin, emaciated, dull-complexioned woman sitting in front of me, was the centre of attraction at JNU twenty-five years ago. The same girl who used to speak at great length at various seminars and would mellifluously recite Ramakant's verses at gatherings. Even her language had changed. Though she attempted to laugh, her efforts only resulted in a mechanical movement of her facial muscles.

I was in the throes of confusion. Professor Upelendu Chatterjee who had left to conduct an experiment twenty-five years back was no more. And here I was, listening to Malini Desai, who was seated in front of me, narrating her strange and unbelievable stories, shifting between facts and imagination, interspersed with inexplicable revelations that lay somewhere between reality and illusion. I was struggling to understand her ... Was this emaciated lady conversing with me on an evening in January 1998 or was it an evening in 1973?

'Initially, all of us were scared and shy. We often felt that it was sheer foolishness to have come to the island with the Professor. Even on the boat journey, I had been tempted to return. I could have turned back when the Professor offered us one last chance to go home before the boat was burnt. But I couldn't do so. Don't ask me why. I had this passionate, insane desire to be a part of this experiment. But I've lost my life to it. Where will all my friends be now? My mother must have been devastated.'

I listened in silence. I did not know what to say to a woman I had known for barely three days.

But I had to piece the story together from her disjointed sentences. Looking at her, I wondered how vociferously she might have argued about the basic theories of anthropology in Professor Upelendu Chatterjee's classes. In 1973, India was a young lady of twenty-six, under the reign of a prime minister fresh from the victory over Bangladesh. A time when she was burying capsules containing bits of altered history. A defining time when the country stood perplexed, not knowing which of the many truths to choose and uphold.

Malini was quite interested in the Harappan culture. She believed that civilization in the Indian subcontinent originated on the banks of the Indus River. In an article she wrote for *Natural*, she argued that it was on the banks of the Indus River that the human jawbone became smaller, and the nose gained its current shape. For Malini, who selected her Kolhapuri slippers with great care, life was all about research, studies and seminars. The one question she repeatedly asked, whether she was in the corridors of the library or the courtyard of Upelendu Chatterjee's house, was, 'Why does this society need so many rules and laws, so many taboos?'

She never received a satisfactory answer. But later, the Professor started asking her the same question. During those arguments with him, she wondered whether she was slipping from sanity to insanity. Those questions finally culminated in their experiment that was 'Alpha'.

Malini continued, 'We decided to absolve all laws, discard all knowledge gained till date and begin afresh. That is why the project was named Alpha. The Professor argued that the human intellect was strong and tenacious. And that if we let it be free for twenty-five years, unhindered by societal norms, we would be able to gain more than what we would lose. I initially argued against it. But finally, I was satisfied with his responses. But the poor Professor died of malaria in a small cave on the island. He was not willing to use any escape route. Self-sacrifice. What a mad idea! Do you know whom he did all this for? When he came with us to Alpha, he left behind a weeping family in Chanakyapuri. A mother, a daughter and all the birds and animals he had reared in his home. How are you going to present him to the world? As an eccentric? Avinash! Can birds and animals weep? You must be thinking that I am mad. But they do weep.

They have a language of their own. We discovered that during our life on the island. When we gave up the many languages that we had learnt until then and lived only by communicating through gestures and dreams, we began to understand the language of birds, animals and trees. As you are a writer, can I ask you something? What is language? If language is only meant for communication why does Sanskrit have such a complicated structure?'

I couldn't help but answer, even though I had earlier decided not to argue with her, a person who had probably lost her sanity after years of such intense research. I'd decided to let her talk freely, to listen to her silently and then think about it. Maybe the others will have different things to say. But when the existence of a writer had been questioned … For me, language is my raw material – from letters to words. How could I, who was trying to create empires with language, agree with her?

'I am sorry but I cannot agree with you. For us humans, language is a medium through which we convey the sum total of the knowledge we have gained over centuries to the new generation. But the language of the crow and the cuckoo has not developed along these lines. They are just sounds representing love, anger, happiness and sorrow. The beginnings of human language can be traced to these representations of sound. But then tens of thousands of years back, we were able to give shape to these sounds and transform them into letters. It developed into different scripts of various modern languages which became one of the most important achievements of human civilization. I feel that the fact that you discarded language is one of the greatest failures of your experiment. Even though visual media like TV has been able to communicate without language, it has its own drawbacks. Have you read Kalidasa's *Meghasandesham*? In it, you can see how language is not inhibited by the constraints of time and can convey ideas to different generations.'

Malini interrupted, 'That is not what I wanted to say.' It seemed as if her argumentative abilities were returning.

'I have no disagreements about the infinite possibilities of language. But what I meant was that though the language of animals is not structured like that of humans, it is a clear and beautiful language. Have you heard the squeaking of a squirrel? Even in that feeble voice, we can discern the variations in tone and rhythm, which leads us to believe that even the squirrel has complete mastery over its language. All animals are like this. But we must be able to distinguish between these sounds. In the initial days after casting off language from our lives, we felt quite suffocated. We were all people who read and spoke a lot. It took us weeks to develop a stock of non-verbal signals to address one another. I would inadvertently use an English or a Hindi word. And then I would immediately say "Sorry". Both actions were against the laws of the experiment. I think it was in the third week that I said "O God" without thinking. Not because I was a believer. It was just a force of habit. But the Professor didn't forgive me. He slapped me across my face. From that moment till the time I met you, I didn't use language.'

An uneasy sea breeze blew through my balcony as I thought about the forty-seven people living on Alpha. They are the progeny of this experiment. Forty-seven human beings without a proper language or a script, who are the children of some of the most educated people in India.

'My father is in Bhopal. He used to have a good business there. I was his sole heir. Wonder what has happened to that. They must have all forgotten me. After all, how long could have they kept the memories alive? In our living room, there used to be a photograph of me as a child … a five-year-old in a white dress with yellow flowers on it and a toothy grin on her face. My parents loved that photo.'

I could see that she was struggling to speak of the past. She started weeping, overcome by her memories of her home.

'If you wish to, we can go to Bhopal,' I offered.

'No. I don't want to go there. What will I tell them? That I have lived for twenty-five years on an unknown island ungoverned by any social norms? That I was a wife to seven men and mother to four children? This is material for you to write stories about, but will the public be able to accept these truths?'

I did not have a response for her. I felt that aeons separated Malini from Bhopal. It was impossible to bridge the distance she had put between Bhopal and herself. Was the freedom, that they had gained by destroying all fundamental institutions like family and society, actually a poison that tasted like nectar? Only three of them remained to share the memories of the anarchic lifestyle they had chosen; two of them were still unconscious. They were breathing so we knew that they were still alive, but their faces had lost all signs of life. Santosh Bhatnagar with a wild grey beard, and Urmila Shanker who lay still, resembled an Egyptian mummy. I hoped that modern medicine would revive them.

Malini continued, 'I have lots more to say, but later… I feel dizzy. No, I'm not ill. And even if I am, my body has the strength to overcome this illness without the aid of medicine. I just need to sleep. I feel like a long-distance runner who has reached the finishing point. We will speak tomorrow.'

4

The First Day on the Island

'AFTER THE LAST OF THE FLAMES THAT ENVELOPED the boat had died down, we walked over the sands on the shore into the island. The geographical terrain reminded us of a village in Bengal covered in greenery. There were trees we had never seen before and different kinds of birds flying over them. A salt-tinged breeze wafted in from the sea. There were no clear paths before us. The ground was a carpet of plants and dead leaves. Many sorts of creatures moved through the dense foliage – worms, butterflies, chameleons and squirrels. We didn't know whether snakes were crawling underneath it. The fact that there could be leeches in swamps filled us with fear. Barefoot, we were hesitant to even step on the soil. The Professor walked ahead, and after a while, he waved us forward. We obeyed. Feet that had been protected by a variety of footwear, bodies that were used to clothing suited for changing climates, were readying themselves to face the wild realities of Alpha. I was revolted. I used to hate it when insects flew into my hostel room. I couldn't bear the feeling of insects crawling over my body. The thought of having to spend my life with these creatures was upsetting me. Suddenly, Christopher who had wandered away from us clapped his hands to draw our attention. He wanted to show us a rainbow created by sunlight falling on a huge spider's web. The web was spun between two trees and was nearly 1.5 metres long. A big spider waited for its prey on the edge of the web. Our lives were also about to be trapped in such a web, or weren't we already trapped? A web from which escape was impossible. I had never imagined that I would be able to speak to you after spending twenty-five years in that web. Only I, who was initially reluctant to even join the experiment, am left to narrate the story of our experience. Couldn't Harikrishna Sarkar, an adept storyteller, or Urmila who was garrulous by nature, have narrated this story? I don't know if she will be able to regain the language she once discarded.

'Oh! I was speaking about the spider's web, wasn't I? I gazed at it for quite some time. Christopher had studied and taught zoology. He was a taciturn man from a modest family in Goa and had done his research at Bombay University. So he was the luckiest amongst us. Only those people who use language often feel troubled when they have to give it up.

'By noon we had split up into groups of twos and threes. Some sat on the beach. Christopher who had been wonderstruck by the spider's web was alone. Hari and I walked deep into the island. The Professor sat alone under a huge tree. We did not disturb him. After walking for a long time, we realized we were the only ones there. Everyone else had wandered away. I knew Hari had a lot to tell me. I had many things to tell him too. But we remained silent.'

'Why? I thought you didn't agree with all the rules of the experiment.'

'We could have talked if we wanted to. We had spoken to each other for years. But we had nothing novel to share. We could have spoken about the end result of our experiment, about the island, the sights around us or about the changes that had come over all of us after reaching the island. Some unknown force held us back. Was it our respect towards the

Professor or his power over us? We finally sat down on a sand dune. Hari rested his head on my naked lap. I don't know how long we sat there. I was scared that I would start speaking. But after a while, we started communicating with our eyes. We learnt to assign meanings to our changing glances. 'Do you know what Hari's eyes were telling me ...?

"'Malini, we are centuries back in time. We are at the beginning of human evolution. The wheels of time have moved backwards. This island might have been a part of Africa or Asia or Latin America. A piece of land torn apart by tectonic explosions. That is where we are. Those early days when human beings were good. It is on the highway of progress that they learnt deceit and selfishness. With multiple forms of power and arrogance began the days of sin. All of that has been abandoned and we are beginning a new age, enjoying the pinnacle of freedom. Think of the freedom that is gained without feeling regret or loss for what has been lost. Here we decide what we must do. We need not satisfy anyone else. No obligations. We can begin a life of truth."

'I don't know what he read from my eyes. It was twilight. We were hungry. We searched for food but couldn't find anything edible. We finally went to the

Professor. Urmila was with him. They gave us some wild fruits that intoxicated us. We fell asleep after eating those fruits.'

When I heard about their first day on the island I got a sense of the beginning, yet a lot of questions arose in my mind. Was Malini speaking the truth? Or merely some aspects of the truth that were beneficial to her? Why did she, who did not agree with all the rules of the experiment, decide to join the project? To answer these questions, one must read Malini's biographic sketch that Professor Banerji had written three years ago. He had entrusted me with thirteen biographies and a route map to the island. Leaving Malini to sleep, I started reading the biographies.

5

Malini Desai's Biography

AFTER I READ MALINI'S BIOGRAPHY, I WAS CERTAIN of one thing. The issue was far more complex than what she had told me. There were crucial factors other than her interest in anthropology that had persuaded her to join the experiment. That was true not only for Malini but for many of the others too. Most of them yearned for a taboo-free, lawless life. They only agreed to discard knowledge and language because the rules of the experiment mandated it. The seventeen-page biography detailed Malini's drug dependency and nonconformist lifestyle. Though she was a good student, she rebelled against living a life controlled by norms. She had undergone rehab for it twice and had seven or eight love affairs during her seven years at university. For Malini, this experiment was an escape from unpleasant realities. But she had carefully concealed all of this during her conversations with me.

I read each of the biographical sketches. What an assortment of individuals! Urmila, who lay unconscious today, was from Karnataka. She had a master's in English literature and special training in investigative journalism. At the time she was the Delhi bureau reporter of *The Statesman*. For her, this experiment was an episode of adventure journalism. An assignment no reporter had dared to undertake. A girl who wrote poems sitting under the trees in Lal Bagh, Urmila had seen peaceful days in her early life. Her father was an engineer in the IIL. Her mother taught in a college. She too wanted a career like her mother's, but her life changed when she won an essay writing competition conducted by *The Statesman* during her second year of post-graduation. Urmila's story and her use of uncomplicated language earned her a job even before her results were out. And that is how she became a journalist.

She had met the Professor for the first time when she was in Delhi to cover a history conference. The Professor's answers to her questions on anthropology gained wide publicity. He had said that the social norms and taboos of society were destroying the youth. Many people disagreed with the Professor's view that the youth in the West had progressed more, as they had more freedom of choice. During the storm of these attacks, Urmila had called the Professor from Bangalore and asked him, 'Can you prove this?' In reply, the Professor wrote to her about this experiment and the scientific challenges it raised. His letter ended with a question: Was she interested in being a part of the experiment? After spending days in deep thought, she rang the Professor and said only one word: 'Yes'.

I went to Urmila's room. There was no change. She was still unconscious. A doctor had visited her that evening. Medicines were being administered to her intravenously. But even her eyes were not moving. We would hear faint grunts and sometimes her breathing would become very rapid.

'This is a complicated stage of coma. We don't know when she lost consciousness. We can only hope for the best. It may take time,' the doctor gave us some hope and left. I wondered how long we would have to wait. What will Urmila speak about when she wakes up? What information would she have collected for *The Statesman*?

When I went to the next room I was surprised. Santosh was sitting up, looking around in bewilderment. What should I ask him? Or maybe it was better to let him talk. We were silent for a while. Then hesitantly Santosh asked, 'Who are you? Where am I now?'

'Santosh, I'm Avinash. Satish Banerji's student. Your Professor had entrusted my teacher with all the details about your experiment. Unfortunately, he couldn't come as he is ill. I brought you back from the island. We reached this place from Alpha three days ago. Malini is in the next room, and Urmila is in a coma.'

Santosh listened to me quietly. I could see a faint ray of hope in his eyes. He was slipping into the memories of the past twenty-five years.

Finally, he found some words, 'I want water. I am terribly thirsty.'

6

The Story as Narrated by Santosh Bhatnagar

'THERE WERE BIG, BLACK LIZARDS ON THE ISLAND. They would fall suddenly from the trees. They were extremely poisonous too. Merlin fell unconscious after being bitten by one of these lizards. We later discovered an antidote for its poison.

'The island was filled with such strange animals. Different types of lizards, butterflies and so on. Life on Alpha had only reached the initial stages of evolution. There were no dogs or tigers or elephants or leopards around. I liked the island's yellow-coloured birds with long beaks. Once Shweta said that she wished there was an island only for these birds; an island full of yellow birds. I didn't like the idea much. Yellow birds that suddenly darted between trees and plants, living among the other animals on the island, that is what I wanted. The first few days were quite comfortable. Feeding on the strange fruits that grew on the island, we slept on the shaky steps of a cave we had discovered three days after our arrival. We were slowly adapting to life on the island.'

'Was it easy to adapt? Were you able to cast away the artifice and rituals of urban life?'

'No, it wasn't easy. From the beginning, we suffered each time we broke the rules of social life. The women were more troubled than us. These women who had argued vociferously at seminars in favour of the emancipation of women were deeply uncomfortable when they had to remove their clothing. Malini was the first one who was ready to try anything new. But even she was unable to accept complete nudity. Don't you know the restrictions our society places on women? A lot of rules are imposed on them on the pretext of safeguarding their bodies. The West is far better in these matters. They don't admire beauty by covering it up. As for us – a five-metre saree and what not!'

'Santosh, you were completely mad. Instead of doing research that would benefit humanity … what if all the intellectuals in a country go mad?'

'Insanity! What are you saying? All the great discoveries were made by challenging the norms of society. It is because Columbus sailed west instead of east that he discovered America. Most often it has been the insanity of a few that has led to achievements that benefited many.'

'And what have you gained? Ten deaths in twenty-five years. Three people drained of health and forty-seven people devoid of language or culture. You have been so unjust to them. You've held them away from the light of knowledge and reared them like animals. They are your flesh and blood. Don't you think they too are entitled to enjoy the fruits of the development and discoveries made after centuries of hard work? Do you think you have the right to deprive them of it? And now they live like wild animals, screaming and tearing each other apart. How many of them are your own children? How did you find the courage to do this to them?'

Santosh fell silent. It was as though he had lost something somewhere. As if he was struggling to justify his decisions, or maybe it was a moment of longing for the son or daughter he'd left behind on the island. Shweta's first baby girl, Urmila's second son. He had always thought that they resembled him. Just them? No, definitely not. And even those two he couldn't claim as his own for sure. In the first few weeks, Shweta was solely his. And in the last days, it was Urmila who was his companion. But all that was against the rules of the experiment. Among the original thirteen, everyone belonged to everyone else.

'Avinash, I can understand your feelings. But a scientist does not have any sympathy for the guinea pigs and the rabbits that he conducts his experiments on. What you think of as the progress of mankind is actually a result of the sacrifice of many human beings and animals. Science does not speak the language of love and sacrifice. Science itself is cruel at times. The achievements of science are the sum total of man's ambition, which is a combination of selfishness and cruelty. Therefore, a scientist never succumbs to emotions. Wasn't it cruel of me to leave my wife and two children in my home in Cuttack without telling them where I was going or when I would return? My children would have assumed that I was dead. Suicide, murder … they must have considered all these options. It is indeed unfortunate that a man seeking truth has to experience these cruelties.'

'They are educated and intelligent. Your children would have found their own way. Maybe even your wife. But the forty-seven people on Alpha – they have nothing. They are innocent victims of a crime they did not commit. They are the living martyrs of your crazy experiment. Is that justifiable?'

'Yes, definitely. Only the mind can analyze the distinction between right and wrong. Your sense of what is right or wrong may not be mine. You have taken a stance that is sanctioned by the society in which you live, or perhaps your mind analyzes things based on the norms generated by your society. Shake off those norms and analyse this problem from a perspective other than that of the family or society. Then guilt does not come into the equation.'

'Terrible! That's the only word I can think of.'

'It might be terrible for you, Avinash. But for us, this became a matter of routine in the twenty-five years that we spent there. But we were speaking of something else. Yes, the mental turbulence one feels at discarding clothing. I felt it too, freeing my body which had been wrapped in layers of clothing for thirty-five years. We were reluctant to even look at one another. Initially, we communicated only through our eyes. We were careful to not let our eyes wander down below eye level. We were after all educated, dignified people. But for how long? We couldn't control ourselves for even a day. Within a few hours, the facade of morality slipped. The wild and bestial urges rose from the subconscious mind. But even then, the softer emotions that governed our former lives came to the fore. I used to like Shweta Dasgupta.'

7

The Essence of the Experiment

TODAY, MALINI SEEMED A BIT MORE RELAXED AND pleasant. We sat on the beach in a secluded corner. It was the first time that all three of us were speaking to one another in a group. Santosh had bathed and shaved. Though he was very gaunt, there was a glow on his face. Malini was wearing a light yellow khadi saree. She started talking.

'The Professor had asked me to codify and publish all the details of our experiment. But I don't think that I'll be able to do it. Avinash, maybe you'll be able to after talking to us. Unlike in other conventional experiments, we did not record any data. The Professor believed that the new generation on Alpha would gain knowledge quickly and that they would be able to analyze and conceptualize on a higher level than us. But as you saw for yourself, that did not happen. So we can only tell you about our lives and experiences. I have done proper research before. I do remember how an anthropology experiment should be conducted. But now I find all that impossible to do. My brain has frozen. Perhaps the only reason I am still alive is to give you these details.'

Santosh added, 'Avinash, I too have the same thing to say. I used to be a geologist at TIFR. But I have lost all my research abilities. I can only tell you what I remember from my own experiences of Alpha.'

'Okay. Tell me everything. Openly. I will listen to you no matter how long it takes. But I want to know the truth without any sort of filters or cover-ups. Not merely to write a book, but to understand the base nature of human beings. And to comprehend the results of your life-altering efforts to change these characteristics of human nature.'

Santosh went first. 'Well, we tried to move back to zero. But we were never able to completely empty our minds. We were merely acting as if we were at the beginning of time. We were characters in a play that we were directing ourselves. All the knowledge we had acquired still filled our minds. Moreover, the feeling that all this was an experiment put some of us in peculiar frames of mind. Some people like Malini were able to push away the thoughts of the result of this experiment and were able to convert it into an experience. Such people were more relaxed.'

Malini explained, 'No, you don't quite know the tension I experienced. Certain secret desires lay hidden beneath my passionate enthusiasm; the desire to know about the wild reality of human life, the desire to float through life without being attached to anything, to break all the rules and norms of society. When I was young, I had decided that other people shouldn't dictate one's life. When we discarded everything and started from the beginning, I felt a strange lightness. As if my identity was slipping away. An individual's social existence is based upon the assumptions society has made about them. Society creates an image of the person based on their family, education, profession, friends and behaviour. Whenever the person is mentioned, people try to understand them through this image. Each individual exists in society through these images. And we destroyed those images. After that, there were no differences between professor, student, journalist, writer, Marathi or Bengali. We even gave up our names.

'Avinash, our assumptions based upon images are often far off the mark. What we believe to be true is most often based on the images that have been erected in our minds. When these images are destroyed, the vacuum that remains is like the weightlessness that exists in outer space. The social customs that bind humans is like the gravitational pull of the earth. When those norms are discarded, it is as if we are thrown into the realm of utmost freedom that exists in this universe. It is then that we come very close to the truth.'

'But Santosh, don't you think that a great constraint existed even in this state of utmost freedom? Didn't you discard the freedom to use language that you loved? The knowledge that you had struggled to gain for years and years? I feel that you lost a lot more than you gained, and remember I saw the final stage that you had reached at the end of twenty-five years. Can you call that a positive change?' I asked.

'It is indeed a positive change. Only we who have experienced the experiment will know it. But we had to submit before some harsh realities.'

'And what were those? Where did you go wrong?'

'I don't believe that we made any mistakes as such; there were only certain unavoidable incidents.

But in the re-creation of history, this was inevitable. Illnesses, changes in nature, destruction following bestial riots, the mental fragmentation that is part of great social change, we should have foreseen all that.'

'It was not unexpected,' Malini interrupted. 'The Professor had foreseen all this. Yet he insisted that we should face reality in a natural manner. Ours was not a controlled experiment carried out in a laboratory.'

'But didn't you fail to discern the element of love and goodness that is supposed to be a distinguishing feature of humans?'

'I don't think we failed. The truth is that these virtues only exist in the facade that man presents in society. The human animal's mental make-up is based on selfishness and pleasure. But he has the ability to conceal all this and pretends to be kind and loving. That is why all efforts from Vyasan to Marx to lead humans from deceit to purity have failed. Ideologies that failed to understand the element of evil and selfishness that exist in the human mind and assumed that economic equality will lead to a perfect society were doomed to fail. But we were able to understand that.'

The sun had set. Would Urmila have woken up? We slowly walked back to Michael's house. It seemed to me that Santosh and Malini were a bit startled every time they saw other people on the beach. How will they survive being back in the civilized world? When Urmila is fit to travel, we must go to Delhi. Professor Banerji must be waiting anxiously for us. Who knows – maybe there is something more to this experiment that the professor hasn't told me about.

'Santosh, you had told me about the huge spiders and poisonous lizards on the island. How did you manage to survive those? Did you discover any medicinal herbs?'

'Well, we didn't discover anything new per se. But when we squeezed the juice of certain green leaves, wc observed that some wounds healed quickly. Certain fruits had an intoxicating effect. But when the intoxication wore off, our bodies would be racked with pain. As there was no fire, we had to eat everything raw. We have even eaten raw fish. But we couldn't find an antidote to the poison of the lizards. We often used leeches to suck the poisoned blood. The island was full of leeches, both big and small.

It was only after I reached the island that I saw leeches at close quarters. Revolting creatures. They creep up your bodies so cleverly and stealthily that you become aware of them only when they bite you. I often wished for death when I sat in excruciating pain, waiting for a leech that was sucking blood from my feet to drop off. It was Rajesh who discovered a use for these leeches. Once Merlin became unconscious after being bitten by a lizard. Rajesh made a small leech suck the poisoned blood. We waited and watched. After about ten minutes the leech that had sucked the poisoned blood dropped dead and Merlin woke up. Sobbing she hugged Rajesh. As I said earlier, even though the experiment had laid down several rules, our old knowledge and the lives we had led before coming to the island continued to influence us.'

'What happened to both of them?'

'They died eventually. Not only them, apart from the three of us the rest of our group died at different points of the experiment. Not everyone died a natural death. Some were killed, some committed suicide, and some were accidental deaths. The Professor died of an illness … of malaria.'

Malini said, 'Santosh, it wasn't exactly like that. Death sought some of us out, others went searching for death. A gravely disappointed Rajesh sought death and committed suicide. He was never satisfied with anything. Finally, in the twentieth year of the experiment, he swam out into the sea and kept swimming. We believe that he is dead. There is no land for 700 kilometres around Alpha. There is no way he would have survived.'

8

Sacrifice

SANTOSH CONTINUED, 'FROM THE VERY FIRST DAY on the island everyone started to change. Once the outward garb of formal behaviour and dignity had been discarded, there were marked differences in our gestures and expressions. It was not as if we lost our identities immediately or saw each other as devoid of identities. For instance, the respect we had for the Professor distanced us from him.

'We were hesitant to approach him. It was perhaps our reluctance to see the renowned social scientist Upelendu Chatterjee as an ordinary man. Urmila had made one resolve before embarking on the experiment. Her first child must be the Professor's. Though the Professor preferred to watch everyone from a distance, eventually Urmila succeeded in getting what she wanted.

'On a slightly warm evening, she approached the Professor with an armful of wild fruits. She did not look like a docile student. Her eyes aglow with lust and a loving smile on her lips, she offered the fruits to him one by one. Her eyes were brimming with desire. She created a situation where he couldn't deny her, a state in which he had to respond in accordance with the rules that he himself had set. Unknowingly, he started stroking her lovely breasts, her navel and her buttocks. For him, it was a spiritual experience; a ritual that was performed with a regular rhythm. It was repeated on several days. It was like a *yagna* for him, with the chanting of mantras by a sanyasi and pure movements that continued throughout the different phases of the night and ended at dawn. Like the ritual offerings of a yagna, the Professor's semen poured into Urmila's vagina. For the others, sex was never elevated to such a spiritual experience.

'Only Urmila was able to fully experience the spirituality of that yagna. Malini was an intoxicating rhythm and Merlin Fernandez was a hurricane. They felt unmoved by the Professor's lovemaking as though it were an obscure Hindustani raga. Still, everyone approached him as if participating in a ritual. A small room inside the cave belonged to the Professor.

Nobody disturbed him there. As about twenty years separated us from him, it was convenient for the rest of us.

'One evening, maybe about three weeks after arriving on the island, the Professor and Urmila were strolling on the beach, when Pradeep approached them suddenly. He pushed the Professor away and rushed off, dragging Urmila with him. Though she tried to resist him, she was no match for his strength. The Professor stood aghast for a moment, unable to process what was happening in front of him. As he moved forward to stop Pradeep, something held him back. According to the rules of the experiment, no one belonged to anyone else. The stronger of the group vanquished the weaker individuals. No one needed to pay heed to another person's wishes. But didn't Urmila have her own desires? What right did Pradeep have to overpower her?

'Unable to arrive at an answer, the Professor sat on the beach. He could see Urmila being subdued by Pradeep's brute strength. The Professor suddenly thought of the words of an American girl he had met on his visit to the Pennsylvania University: "There is nothing like ultimate freedom. Our progress, contrary to what you may think, is not based on extreme social or economic freedom. It might be true that we were able to invest the energy we gained from breaking the ties and bonds of the family into developing science and technology. But the more important aspects are the basic differences in attitudes towards materialism and spirituality that exist in your country and mine. A society that declares material gains as transitory and privileges sacrifice over pleasure actually retards its progress. Untold freedom is enervating and makes the society idle and irresponsible."

'Was she right? Maybe. But a return is now impossible so let's go forward with optimism.'

9

Rajesh Menon – The History Teacher

'THOUGH THERE WERE THIRTEEN DISTINCT INDIVIDUALS on that island, there were certain factors which bound them together; the desire to be a part of this experiment, the guts to throw away their previous lives and so on. But many things separated them too. Rajesh Menon was quite different from all of them. We had noticed this during the journey on the boat. He once said that he had come just for the thrill, out of a deep curiosity to know what would happen. An adventurer on an adventure of a lifetime, he was a man who approached life headlong, expecting the unexpected. I really liked him,' Malini confessed.

A new character was entering the scene. The thirty-one-year-old history teacher Rajesh. I tried to remember Professor Banerji's biographical note about him. Born into an upper-class family, he was a researcher at Delhi University. He had a PhD for his work on old tombstones and the urns used to bury the dead. He was a bachelor. He wore brown-framed glasses, his hair was unruly, and he always had a cigarette dangling from his lips. He would get close to people rather swiftly, and just as easily distance himself. A chess aficionado, the only thing he wasn't interested in was teaching; like a butterfly that wished to soar into the open skies of freedom away from the dull, repetitive pages of history. He had once, along with a Brazilian called John Rozario, climbed halfway up the Kanchanjunga. During a visit to Madhya Pradesh to do research on the Gonds, he had been caught by the Naxalites and held captive for a month. For him, life was a continual search for novel experiences. It was on one such quest that he met Merlin Fernandez. Rajesh had gone to Koraput in Orissa on a study tour where Merlin had been posted as the sub-collector. Rajesh felt close to Merlin the moment they were introduced to each other. He pulled a few strings and was able to get Merlin transferred to Delhi. They were never separated after this. But Merlin's father did not approve of this relationship. It was when Rajesh realized that he was the target of the highly Westernized retired colonel's gun that he and Merlin decided to join the Professor's group.

'During the initial days on Alpha, they maintained a distance from the rest of us. Like a couple on their honeymoon, they behaved as if they were blissfully unaware of life around them.'

'Why did the Professor include two such people on his team? Weren't the members of the team selected after deep discussions and analysis?'

'It's true. But anyone who knew the essence of the experiment could adeptly hide his real intentions and participate in those discussions. Maybe they too did the same. Malini doesn't remember, but initially, Rajesh didn't like anyone else even looking at Merlin. Eventually, it was Malini who reframed their relationship.

'It was all pure madness. Even after a month on Alpha, they hadn't connected with anyone else. I dragged Rajesh into the cave one day. Till then he had never entered the caves. He was scared of darkness. Thirsting for light on dark nights, he would lie down on the sandy beach for the pleasure of starlight.

'Then, in accordance with the laws of the experiment, he too slowly changed his ways or perhaps the circumstances changed him. Initially, Merlin was dead against it. She hesitated to get close to us. Her mind was full of the fear her father had infused in her from childhood. The guilt that the Holy Book had filled her with controlled her actions. Merlin, who possessed the biggest and most beautiful breasts on the island, took some time to realize that sharing pleasure among friends was not a sin. The Professor and Hari succeeded in freeing her from the shackles of fear and helped her experience the intoxication of love. Finally, she became a mere puppet who obeyed all the rules of Alpha.

'Rajesh found it extremely difficult to see without his glasses. His eyes behaved strangely. He would see the same thing as two different objects; one real and the other an illusion. He would often eat the skin instead of the fruit or kiss his partner on the nose instead of on the lips. When he got off the boat, he had thrown away his glasses with great distress.'

'Did he live for twenty years seeing these illusory double images?'

'Maybe. We don't know if he was ever cured. But he always used to fumble when we communicated through gestures.'

'I forgot to ask you something. With this non-verbal communication system that all of you had devised, were you able to have detailed discussions or was it merely for basic communication?'

'It was not developed enough to have a deep and detailed discussion. We had intended to use it for urgent needs only. Most of the detailed discussions were conducted through meaningful silences. I had told you about the technique of using one's eyes for communication.'

'I find it impossible to comprehend. A discussion through glances? What else can eyes convey but passion or some basic emotions? Or were all your discussions merely an exchange of emotions?'

'Yes, we lived a life filled with emotions, unhindered by the complexities and debates of material life. Alpha did not have a place for ideological arguments. It allowed merely bestial fickleness and fights for possession. Humane behaviour had been plucked from us humans. It was in these circumstances that Merlin Fernandez committed suicide.'

10

Merlin Fernandez's Death

MERLIN BELONGED TO A WELL-TO-DO ANGLO-INDIAN family in Mangalore. Her grandfather Edwin Fernandez was a Scotsman. Even in the most adverse circumstances, their family never compromised with their dignity. She had completed her education in Bangalore and Mumbai. Merlin was top of her class when she finished her postgraduation in political science and was determined to succeed and be the best in everything she took up. It wasn't in her nature to yield to pressure or give up on her dreams. Her first posting as the sub-collector of Koraput came with several duties and responsibilities. Koraput was one of the most backward districts in Orissa. Food, health, education, housing – the district was lagging in all these areas. Starvation deaths and epidemics were commonplace. There were no hospitals anywhere except at the district headquarters and only four or five schools in the entire district. Within a rigid feudal system, progress was next to impossible. Merlin found it difficult to join the ranks of those officials who were duping the government by presenting them with false data. Every time she stepped out of her office, people stared at her as though she were a strange creature. The village folks were unfamiliar with the modern, urban clothes and make-up that Merlin wore. It was during this suffocating period that Rajesh Menon, the history teacher, reached Koraput. It was a strange meeting of two very different people; one who was suffering because she wasn't able to bring the benefits of development to the area and the other who was seeking the reasons as to why the area was underdeveloped.

'Merlin, do you really expect to change their ways?'

'Definitely. I am sure that I can slowly make them better humans.'

'You won't. You won't be able to even touch the deep roots of feudalism. Honestly, I didn't come here to study these people because I have any sort of affection for them. Do you know about the Rockefeller Scholarship? Quite a few dollars. I need to do something to get that. And then the money and fame will follow after I publish my findings in some international journal. That is all I need.'

Initially, Merlin didn't agree with Rajesh. She truly believed that she could bring about change. But over time, once she saw the manipulations of the landed classes and the biased decisions of the political leaders, she had to concede that Rajesh was right. That is how Merlin reached Delhi from Koraput, to the department of archaeology. As it was a largely ignored department, she had plenty of free time. She spent it going over the dead files that had recorded memories of the past. As no one was eager to push these files, most often the office would be empty. Only researchers of history like Rajesh or his friends frequented the place. It was during these days that Merlin became a voracious reader. She read everything, made copious notes and argued with Rajesh about many topics. By the time they had begun discussing the subject of anthropology, they were deeply in love. She became equally enthralled by both anthropology and Rajesh.

One day she asked him, 'Don't you think that the most wonderful thing in this world is the human being? What do we know of us who are strange and beyond analysis? We are filled with knowledge that has been around since prehistoric times. We have heard, seen and practised it and stored it up in millions of brain cells. How easily one's brain cells can distinguish between the lifestyle of the Neanderthal man and Einstein's theory of relativity, all of which is stored in the leaves of one's memory.'

Instead of replying to her question, he took her to Professor Upelendu Chatterjee one day.

'Professor, this is Merlin Fernandez, an IAS officer. Her favourite topic these days is anthropology. Even she doesn't know why she is fascinated by this subject. So if I don't introduce you to each other, it will be a disservice to both of you.'

Merlin and the Professor spoke for a long time, discussing various theories and nuances of anthropology over several days. Finally, the Professor asked her the same question that he had asked the others. 'Are you ready to participate in this experiment?' She saw light when she discussed various aspects of this experiment in great detail with Rajesh. An experiment for its own sake or experimenting with one's own life. She had no better way than this to escape Colonel Fernandez. She had great expectations from the freedom she would experience when they went back to the *beginning*. During the journey, Merlin and Rajesh talked a lot – about themselves, the world and everything that came to their minds. More than the end result, they were interested in the process of the experiment. It was an eagerness to live away from the hustle and bustle of urban life that was filled with deceit and hypocrisy. But their estimations of life on Alpha were to be proven wrong. They didn't imagine that a return to primaeval life would entail the slipping of the veneer of respectability and the respect for each other's freedom of choice. Merlin was unable to look dispassionately at the small insects that were trapped in the large spider webs. She wept in private. The Professor had warned them at thc outset not to disturb the ecosystem of Alpha and to live as a part of that system. So they lived without hurting the snakes and chameleons and lizards, without disturbing the spider webs, listening to the chirping of the yellow birds and cuckoos and they mated at night to the music of crickets. As part of the experiment, when the links of human bonding and love were broken, she too had to discard her humanity and live a completely different life.

When a more powerful male captured her from the other and mated with her, when she succumbed to their brute strength, she felt that the freedom she had been promised was a big lie. The guilt that was implanted by the Holy Book lay latent like a burning lump of coal in her subconscious mind. The flames from it eventually drove Merlin to suicide.

Just think … anyone in her situation would have done that. In the very first year on the island, Merlin gave birth to a handsome son who resembled Rajesh. If they had been living in the outside world, what would they have not given him? But on Alpha, he grew up ignorant of language and knowledge, playing in the dirt. One's biological children were not treated differently from the children born of anyone else in the group. They roamed around on the beach and ate everything they could find. Only during the breastfeeding period did the mothers keep their children with them. But the mothers would soon get pregnant again and their milk would dry up. The children grew up behaving like animals … it was unthinkable. Contravening the expectations of the experiment, the new generation did not show any signs of advanced mental abilities and development. But they were physically strong. Having grown up in a hostile environment, they had good health and immunity. Their lives were confined to hunting for food and the satiation of their feral sexuality. They lived fighting and squabbling for food and sex. They did not differentiate between their parents or siblings. Merlin wanted to tell her son that she was his mother. She tried several times but only met with failure. They couldn't understand each other at all.

Finally, one day her son ... not heeding to her cries and resistance ... It was beyond what she could bear. Though it wasn't against the rules of the experiment per se, it was enough to inflame the latent flames of guilt that lay in her subconscious mind. That night Merlin Fernandez committed suicide. Nobody except Rajesh shed tears. They had all become stoic enough to accept death and birth as inevitable. But Rajesh wept copiously. Later, like someone who had lost everything, he walked into the sea. His body never washed ashore. Could someone have rescued him? Or would he have become the prey of a shark or could he be on another island nearby... a Beta ... another culture. No one knows for sure.

The words Rajesh had inscribed on the rocks before walking into the sea stared sorrowfully at us.

'This was heaven ... human beings made it hell.'

11

Births and Deaths

'SOME DAYS AFTER WE REACHED THE ISLAND, WE LOST our sense of time. Nights gave way to days and merged into a blur. We couldn't keep track of the weeks and months. Summer, monsoon, spring and winter came one after the other. The small trees on Alpha sprouted and bloomed and withered away. For us, time became a complex puzzle. In the dark nights, under only the faint light of the stars, we found it difficult to distinguish shadows from human beings. We started forgetting our own names because no one called out for us anymore. What is in a name after all? They are just a means to recognize people in a society.'

'I'm afraid I cannot agree. Names are not merely means of recognition. If that had been the case, then we could have used numbers or geometric symbols instead of names. Everything has an organic existence. If we used another name instead of Upelendu Chatterjee, it wouldn't be right. When we utter that name his figure appears in our minds. It is not an image that merely resembles him physically, but his whole personality that we conjure in our minds.'

'Avinash, that is not because of the glory of the name, but because of the preconceived notions we have about the person. When we give up names, we can approach a person without any preconceived notions about them. Even after we had given up language completely, Hari used to recite poems, just rhythmic sounds without words. But we could easily discern the passion behind those words. On Alpha, unsullied humanity was predominant, not names or language. In truth, the island was a heaven of lovers.'

'Santosh, don't call it humanity. You can call it by some other name! After you abandoned everything that the human race has amassed over thousands of years and started living like animals, you in fact lost your humaneness. Emotions like love and anger are animalistic.'

'I did not mean that. A life devoid of the subterfuges of modern life and of honesty to one's own conscience does not require language or names.'

Malini came in wearing a light blue saree with her hair neatly combed. She looked like she was getting used to this lifestyle again and had recovered a little bit of her happiness. She was regaining her physical health too, but her face still looked haggard and dull and her voice still cracked when she spoke. She sat silently beside us, lost in thought. Was she thinking about Alpha, her children on the island or the friends and relationships she had lost there?

'Malini, you have been silent these past few days. What happened?'

'Avinash, I'm slowly trying to recollect my thoughts. But I feel like there are gaps in my memory. The incidents I remember are unconnected.'

'That's all I need. I will join the dots.'

'It must have been nearly a year after we had started afresh in Alpha. It had been around a week after I had given birth to my first child. My fair, curly-haired child would cry loudly. I was lying down in one of the caves breastfeeding my baby. Suddenly he started crying and shivering. A red rash spread all over his body. I didn't know what was wrong. No one else paid any attention to us. That was one of the rules. Leave everything to nature, only the lucky and the able should survive. One should never grieve over what is lost. I gathered him in my arms and went out. I couldn't understand what was ailing him. But I knew that he wasn't well. Though the rules of the experiment bound me, I couldn't tolerate it anymore. He was my son, wasn't he? His tiny face didn't resemble any of ours. I took my baby to Anjali. She was a doctor, a house surgeon from AIIMS. She had completed her basic medical education before getting involved in this experiment. And as per the rules of the experiment she had cast off her knowledge too. Yet I hoped fervently that she would be able to save my child.

'I saw her lying asleep under a tree, fatigued after sex or intoxicated by the wild fruits. She looked at me dispassionately and rolled over without saying a word. She had not become pregnant yet. When my baby's cries started irritating her, she gestured to me to throw the baby away. My heart ached for my child. Santosh too ignored us. The men on Alpha paid little attention to the women if we were going through a phase when they couldn't have sex with us. I gathered all the green leaves near me and squeezed the juice on my child's body. After a while, he stopped crying. One of the seven men on the island was his father. But fathers in Alpha felt no responsibility towards the children. Since they did not consider them as their own, they never felt any sorrow or pain for them. But women are different. The sperm of the male enters her body and after carrying the baby in her womb for nine months, the baby splits open her vagina and enters this world. So the child is literally her flesh and blood. I did not sleep the whole night but kept vigil beside my son. His eyes were revolving inside their sockets but slowly everything became normal. Three or four days later, he was alright.'

'Were you living isolated lives? Without helping one another? Even during childbirth?'

'We did help each other. But we did not use knowledge from our previous lives to overcome problems on Alpha. Giving birth is a natural biological process. No medical aid is really necessary. The forty-seven people on Alpha are living proof of this. So are the eleven who died of natural causes during childhood. Urmila helped me during my delivery. Though there were no hospitals, we did not experience much difficulty during childbirth. It became a natural process on the island after a while. But the main problem was the insensitivity and non-cooperation of the males. They would force us to have sex even when it was extremely difficult for us and would resort to force if we refused to comply with their wishes. But the deaths on the island were most painful. In those moments, we felt quite guilty about not using the knowledge that we had.'

'Were there instances when you deliberately chose not to use the knowledge that you had when you knew that it could have saved a life?'

'I can't say for sure. We had no other resources apart from the knowledge that we had acquired on Alpha. When the Professor contracted malaria, all of us wanted to save him. But we were helpless. We didn't know if there was a plant on the island that could be used as an antidote to malaria.'

Malini paused and gestured to Santosh. I didn't understand what she said. I hadn't decoded the meanings of their gestures. I hadn't said anything to provoke them. Then what was wrong? I had a strong suspicion that even while speaking to me they were communicating silently with each other. There was something that they were not telling me. As if they had decided to hide some things from me and were presenting only that part of the picture which they wanted me to see. I would see the other part of the picture only after Urmila started talking. How did a doctor, Anjali Sharma, join them? What role did the fair, slim, quiet Anjali Sharma from Varanasi play in this experiment?

12

Anjali's Story

ANJALI WAS BORN IN VARANASI, IN AN OLD HOUSE ON one of the bylanes that led to Manikarnika Ghat. Her father was a priest at the Vishwanath Temple. Anjali was his eldest daughter. She joined the All India Institute of Medical Science for her MBBS, after graduating from the Banaras Hindu University in zoology. She would go home once a month by the Kashi–Vishwanath Express.

Amidst the resounding chanting of mantras and Hindustani music, her father would tell her, 'You are a fool. Kashi is the nerve centre of this universe. The further you travel from Kashi the further you are moving away from God and truth. We can learn everything from Vishwanathan … whatever it may be, music, literature or science. The knowledge you glean in your classrooms in Delhi is not as great as this.' Anjali would listen in silence and sometimes smile. Her father always spoke in this manner. He was a man of strange ideas. A man who had submitted his life to the service of Vishwanathan with the firm conviction that there was nothing beyond this and whose life itself was a Ganges of love.

Santosh had once said to her, 'I've been to Kashi several times. It's such an unhygienic town. I couldn't see any of the glory you attribute to it. Your people make money out of half-burnt funeral pyres in Dashashwamedh and Manikarnika. Mantras, poojas and God are merely means of making money in Kashi.'

Anjali did not reply. These allegations were regularly raised against the priests of Kashi. Not everyone can experience the purity and the music of Kashi. Beneath the squalor and the greed, there was an abundance of purity and deep faith. It wasn't easy to convince outsiders that under the calm Ganges flowed the pure, indefinable love of Vishwanathan.

Anjali had two younger brothers who lived close to the temple and immersed themselves in its activities. She had earned a scholarship from the Central Government for her higher education. It was difficult for her community to accept her growth.

Anjali moved between her patients and medicines at AIIMS humming *Hamir Kalayani*, a raga she had learnt in her childhood. She was never lured by the deceitful veneer of Delhi. After studying the anatomy of the human body, even as she analyzed illnesses, she often asked unscientific questions such as: 'Why did God give illness to mankind? Why did he give us pain and sorrow along with happiness and comfort?' She was not able to find satisfactory answers to any of these questions. She dreamt of the faces of millions of micro bacteria that were readying themselves to attack man – amoebas, viruses, protozoa and many more as yet unclassified. Initially, she was scared but was soon filled with wonder at the thought that humans had the immunity to combat 99 per cent of them. During her third year of medicine, in the midst of a discussion, she asked her professor, 'Sir, you said that in certain circumstances most of the medicines fail to have an effect. Why is that so?'

'No particular reason. Our bodies sometimes behave in unfathomable ways. In favourable circumstances, when the body overcomes a disease, the medicines and the doctor get credit. But the same treatment can fail in unfavourable circumstances. No one quite knows why. But they don't lose their relevance just because they fail in certain circumstances. Luck is also a factor that makes medicine and treatment effective.'

Anjali did not argue any further. But the last sentence struck her deeply. During the course of her life, at several junctures, she rewrote that sentence. 'It is only when one is lucky that medicine and treatment work.'

She was working as a house surgeon when the Professor was admitted to the hospital because of high blood pressure. Anjali liked his eccentricities and her conversations with him. After three to four days when his blood pressure became normal, she said to him, 'You are a lucky man.'

The professor looked at her uncomprehendingly. He was a scientist who did not believe in fatalism. Stroking his grey beard he asked, 'Do you really think so?'

'Only when a person is lucky does treatment become effective.' This led to long hours of discussions and debates. She moved from allopathic medicine to anthropology, and it resulted in Anjali becoming the most interested participant in the Alpha experiment. She observed herself and others with the keenness of a researcher. When the others dropped the mask of respectability and adapted to a new life, she enthusiastically shared with them all the pleasures of a truly animal existence. She ate different fruits, had sex with different men and constantly sought novelty. She was the one who found the cave on the southernmost tip of the island. It wasn't really a cave, but more like a covered space with two rooms. A space where one could sleep without seeing the sky. It was so dark inside that you could only make out the silhouette of people in the dim light that seeped in through the small entrance. One of the small rooms was always kept reserved for the Professor. The difference in their ages and the feeling that they were merely pawns in the experiment, constrained them from behaving too casually with him. The Professor himself was besieged by doubts as to whether what he was doing was indeed right. He feared that the mad experiment he had envisaged would destroy twelve lives, apart from his own. It was Anjali with her enticing smiles and pleasant attitude towards life who freed the Professor from such morbid thoughts. His hopes rose when six children were born within three years on Alpha. He genuinely believed that in a period of twenty-five years the new generation would attain the level of knowledge that humankind had gained in thousands of years. In the beginning, he felt that the experiment was on the right path. Malini and Urmila's children learnt to walk rather early. But other developments were stunted due to the lack of proper care, nutrition and guidance. The children who learnt to walk did not start speaking or show any signs of mental development. The mothers on the other hand got pregnant again and readied themselves for the next childbirth. The children grew up rough and tough, eating what they could find, roaming all over the island and sleeping where they pleased.

Anjali often suppressed her maternal instincts, conforming to the rules of the experiment. She was distressed when everything she knew about the nourishment and well-being of children was deliberately ignored. She wept when they fell ill and when they died. She hated the experiment when she had to completely discard her medical knowledge even though she could have used it to prevent illness and death. Sometimes she gestured to the Professor, asking, 'Can't you allow me to save them from pain and death?' He only shook his head. On the day Anjali's daughter died of fever with her head resting in her mother's lap, her heart gave up and stopped beating and she bade goodbye to the island with her daughter. The vast sea gently gathered both bodies in its embrace.

13

Harikrishna Sarkar – The Poet

HARI DID NOT CONSIDER POEMS TO BE EITHER testimonials to revolutions or paeans of love; he saw them as rhythmic visions of truth that flowed from the depths of one's heart and soul. He wrote succinct verses that demanded the active participation of the reader. His poems would draw the readers close to him and together they would sojourn to a completely different plane. His poems were not only beautiful but also hypnotically thought-provoking.

Harikrishna Sarkar was a reporter for a regional daily in Delhi. He was always immersed in poetry and discussions. His poems became popular on university campuses and amongst the discontented youth in the city. Hari never spoke too much when he was with his friends. He would intently listen to others, and in the end, recite a poem that he had written earlier or composed on the spur of the moment. And his poems would convey everything that he had to say. He never spoke about his poems either. The poems would speak about Hari. He wrote sporadic reports for the newspaper that he worked for and received a few cheques now and then. Neither the job nor the remuneration had a definite format.

He used to be a heavy drinker. He was rather intoxicated when he met Malini at a party thrown by one of the top journalists in the country. She questioned him about the poem he had read out earlier. In response, he recited a series of fragmented poems. Enraged, she called him insane. Hari laughed and went on his way.

Much later, when he met her again in the long corridors of JNU, he handed her a poem scribbled inside a cigarette packet.

'Read it when you are alone and tear it up. This was written only for you.'

Inside her room in the hostel, she read the poem several times. Each time she read it, she fell into new realms of the meaning of life, new puzzles. She wanted to laugh and cry at the same time. For several days, everywhere she went she would look for

Hari. After months she met him at a crowded railway station in New Delhi and said, 'I've been looking for you for so many days! We have much to discuss.'

He walked silently with her. They sat opposite each other in an almost empty coffee house. 'Tell me everything ... let me listen.'

She did not know how to begin. When individuals think and act differently and when their activities fail to conform to the norms of society, they are labelled insane. Yet those are the people who carry society forward.

'If I tell you that it's a lovely poem, it would be empty praise, Hari. But do you honestly think I am beautiful enough to drive you mad?'

'You are definitely the beauty who has driven me mad. Your enticing eyes, your lips that hold the promise of lust, your beautiful breasts and your body drive me mad. That is why I said this poem is only for you.'

Malini, without paying any attention to his praise, asked seriously, 'But what is the point of this mad verse?'

'Malini, poems are not written with a utilitarian purpose in mind. For me, poetry is how I communicate my emotions. I'm not trying to make a point. By creating an impact in the mind of the reader I wish to be one with the reader and think together with him. Or her.'

He saw a glimmer in Malini's eyes. The glimmer of love. She gazed into his eyes and said, 'We will think together in a completely insane manner.'

They met at several places and would talk for hours. They travelled, thought and slept together. Hari dissolved every atom of her beauty in his madness. Hari Sarkar became an integral part of Malini's life.

During one of the many discussions before departing to Alpha, Hari expressed his disagreement about one aspect of their experiment to the Professor.

'I agree with everything you'rc saying. But why should we cast off language? How can language be an impediment to go back to the beginning?'

'My dear poet, language is the basis of humankind's development. There are nearly 7,000 languages in the world right now. Some have written scripts, others don't. It is language that preserves knowledge. Whether it is mathematics or science, knowledge is put to use through language. It is impossible to return to the beginning of time while retaining language.'

'But how can I give up language? I think, eat and even breathe language – the six to seven languages that I know. I find great pleasure in the rhythm and poetic beauty of language. How can I just give it up for twenty-five years?'

'I am not compelling you, Hari. Come with us only if you are a hundred per cent sure. But there's one thing to keep in mind, this is a rare opportunity for you to discover a language, one that is not among the six or seven that you know, a language unknown to mankind at the moment. A new language with new sounds and new words. Don't you want to find it?'

Hari couldn't keep away from a journey that sought novelty. 'Till now I have been using commonplace languages full of clichéd words, used by one and all. This is my chance to discover a personal language. To create original works in a new language.'

Aboard the boat to Alpha, Hari sat by himself and devised a system of sounds for this new language.

When he reached the island, he created a new language based on the sounds of the creatures that inhabited Alpha. A language that could be used by the yellow birds, the cuckoos and the humans alike. In this new language, he wrote poems about dawn and dusk, about the sea and the birds, about Urmila and Malini. Everyone listened attentively to his poems. In this raw and strange language with unfamiliar cadences, Hari sang aloud, and his poems reached the depths of their souls.

They realized that poetry is not just about words, but is a form of spiritual communication. It was as if someone was becoming closer to your heart. A few of them tried to learn these songs and sang to themselves when they were alone. On most evenings, Hari would lie on the sandy beaches and sing aloud almost as if it were a ritual. Some of them gathered around him and echoed his words.

But it's not as if Hari's new sound system helped him adapt to the new environment wholeheartedly. As the years went by they lost their ability to respond to art. Lust, anger and selfishness became their dominant passions. As his listeners decreased in number, Hari stopped reciting his poems. Ten years after coming to Alpha, Hari could hardly believe that he had ever been a poet. He became a man who was adept at fishing and was strong enough to overpower his adversaries. If sex had been an art form to him earlier, it slowly became a stunt to overpower his prey using vigour. Malini often wept. She couldn't bear to see Harikrishna Sarkar, the poet whom she had loved, behave like a wild and greedy animal. Such changes to one's core personality were taking place in everyone, albeit in different degrees. Only the Professor's basic nature remained unchanged, even with time. His was an elevated plane of mind which didn't easily give in to wild impulses.

14

Anwar Said's Murder

ANWAR SAID WAS BORN IN ALIGARH. HIS FATHER WAS proficient in Urdu and a professor at the Aligarh Muslim University. Anwar, even as a child, showed a preference for science over religion and would strongly disagree with anything that he did not believe in. Before he could complete his graduation, he was expelled from the university for his involvement in leftist politics. He later became the guiding light of the progressive youth of Aligarh. Anwar had not slept in his home after he turned nineteen. He was driven to awaken the youth of Kolkata about the travesty of religion with his secret pamphlets and circulars. During the Indo–Pak war, when revolutionary young men were being arrested in Aligarh, Anwar escaped to Delhi. After working in several places, he finally ended up as a domestic help at Upelendu Chatterjee's house. He did not get a chance to speak to the Professor initially. The Professor spoke very little even to his family members and did not pay any attention to his servant. One night as he sat in his library writing down some notes, he happened to notice Anwar reading in a small room next to the garage. Realizing that his servant was not an ordinary person, Upelendu Chatterjee called him to his room in the morning.

'Tell me the truth. Why are you here? Who are you?'

Anwar did not resist the probing questions. He confessed everything and how he had ended up there. The Professor asked him, 'Do you think that your way is right? Can we imitate the Chinese revolution that exhorted the villages to rise against the cities?'

'The circumstances here are different. But the fundamental aspects remain the same. We have many limitations. Time is also a factor. We moved from vaguely developed feudalism to immature capitalism. As both systems were not in their wholesome forms, the responses of the people were also different. The exploited are sometimes not even aware of their pathetic condition. In India, slaves find solace in their slavery and have earnest respect for their masters. We have created a society that is extremely fatalistic and does not value its own existence. How can we organize a revolution with them?'

'A revolution should not occur to satisfy anyone's personal desire. It should be the outcome of the desire of the populace. A revolution has no relevance if the populace doesn't desperately want it.'

'Inevitable changes in history did not occur because a couple of individuals or even a whole society desired it. Usually, beliefs and ideologies that spread like wildfire conquer history. Individuals can only be a part of history; they cannot change history according to their predilections. The present situation in India may not be conducive to a revolution. We are a half-literate population that is not responsive and has untold faith in God and fate. Because of these factors, the possibility of an open fight is rendered impossible. Yet we have hope. The hope that conducive circumstances will exist in the future.'

'Indeed, Anwar, you have the right to hope. But how desirable would this society wrought by revolution be? The power centre will shift from the feudal overlords and the capitalists to the party bosses. But will the strong stop exploiting the weak? Will you be able to keep the truth hidden if you take those who question the system to concentration camps? Do equality and freedom exist in any of the countries that have implemented this ideology?'

Anwar did not have an answer.

'Anwar, please don't misunderstand me. When I was your age, I too used to think as you do now. But as I studied more, read more, I understood that many concepts paraded in the name of socialism are false. Do you know what is happening in Russia and Hungary? They send dissenting intellectuals and writers to the labour camps in Siberia. A professor of literature is made to drive a tractor while an ordinary farmer who is related to the party secretary is nominated to be the vice-chancellor of a university. Where is equality in that system which does not respect an individual's intellect and hard work but moves only according to party decisions?'

'You are right. I understand. There is a great difference between dreams and reality. But what is the alternative? Flawed as it is, isn't this the best among existing ideologies?'

'There are other ways. I am constantly seeking other routes, other possibilities. I want to find the way to ultimate freedom by breaking all existing shackles. Are you ready to walk along that path?'

They discussed various aspects of the experiment. This happened three days before they were to set out for Alpha. Anwar Said became the last man to join the team.

From the first day on Alpha, Anwar felt inferior to the others. He felt that they did not consider him their equal because of his low social status and lack of formal education. When each of them found a mate, Anwar felt lonely and isolated. He felt that coming to Alpha had been a mistake. If this was ultimate freedom, it was dull. In the streets of Aligarh, crowds used to gather to listen to him. Even those who opposed his ideology respected him.

He wandered amidst the trees looking for food. Finally, after eating some fruits he fell asleep on a rock. Four or five days later he found Anjali. Like a butterfly flitting from flower to flower, she reached Anwar on the fifth day.

One day, Anwar who had fallen into a deep stupor after eating some intoxicating fruits had red ants swarming all over him. Aruna Kriplani saw him in this state by chance and rescued him; he had been unconscious for an entire night. Aruna removed the ants from his body and bathed him. His body had become swollen because of ant bites and took a week to return to normal. Aruna kissed his pain away. When his health became normal, Aruna belonged to Anwar and Anwar to Aruna. But they managed to hide their relationship from the others to maintain the pretence of obeying the rules of the experiment.

Five years after they reached Alpha, when they had lost every iota of humanity and become like animals, Hari killed Anwar Said. During a silly quarrel that developed into a flaming row, Hari smashed Anwar's head with a rock. In another world, Hari would have just forgiven him and moved on, but the ability to understand a different perspective and to forgive had been irrevocably lost.

Aruna ... she was responsible for everything. She often broke the rules of the experiment. She found freedom in breaking the rules. One day, Aruna decided to abandon her two children and the rest of the experiment and escape with Anwar. She was fed up with life on Alpha. Anwar also agreed to go with her as only Aruna had treated him as an equal. Shweta and Anjali had sex with him but only as part of the experiment. The men considered him lowly and distanced themselves from him. So Anwar put four to five logs together and made a boat. Then one day at the crack of dawn he set sail with Aruna. When the towering waves tossed the boat aside, they had no other option but to swim back ashore. Everyone hated them for trying to break the rules of the experiment. Anwar initially resisted but later begged pardon. Nobody forgave them, but Hari just couldn't control his anger. He smashed Anwar's head to pieces with a rock. Blood flowed on the sandy shores of Alpha for the first time that day. For days no one looked at one another. Aruna Kriplani was treated like a traitor. Wandering alone for the next five years, she died insane.

15

Aruna Kriplani

ARUNA KRIPLANI WAS AN ASSISTANT LIBRARIAN AT Jadavpur University. She lived with a distant relative near the library, which was far away from the bustling city life of Kolkata. She was treated like a paying guest in that house. Her aunt was only interested in the rent she paid them. Aruna's mother had passed away when she was a child. Her father worked as an accountant for a businessman in Surat.

Aruna had been educated in a convent school run by nuns. She was a voracious reader and had read Tagore, Bankim Chandra Chatterjee and most of the other prominent Bengali authors before she finished high school. Then she turned her attention to Western literature. She spent most of her time in the college library and felt a strange affinity for it. The library was like her second home. Luckily, she got a job there and her reading pivoted from literature to philosophy. More than stories and poems she was interested in reading about the problems of social life. Communism was spreading like wildfire in Jadavpur during those days. The new generation had lost hope in the democratic system of government. Everyone wanted fast and drastic change in governance and Aruna was their compatriot.

Three years after she got the job at the library, she married Kriplani, a lecturer of mathematics at a university. But they separated after three months of marriage. He couldn't accept Aruna's lifestyle or her politics. So once again she immersed herself in reading and thinking and working in her library.

Aruna's uncle and the Professor both hailed from a village near Kharagpur in Bengal. They used to be classmates. Upelendu was good at his studies during those years. After settling down in Delhi, he would visit his village occasionally. On one such visit, he met Aruna and took a liking to her. The way she spoke her mind and her boldness were quite unique. She started writing frequent letters to the Professor. The more she read, the more questions she had. When one doubt was resolved, another would rear its head. She was not content with the books she read, and dissatisfied with many of the Professor's replies. The world was full of such diverse people, speaking a multitude of languages, practising different religions. Even so, their anatomies and physiologies were the same. If only they had the desire to, they could live together peacefully. But the reality was quite different ... there were wars and riots and gross inequality. The strong and mighty used every possible means to exploit and suppress the weak. Dignity and love had deteriorated to mere formalities and selfishness reigned supreme. No existing religion or ideology has been able to explain the existence of depravity in humans. In order to establish righteousness, deceit and fraudulent practices are proclaimed to be the words of God. What is the ultimate truth? This question came up again and again in her letters to the Professor.

In one of his replies, the Professor wrote, 'Aruna, you read a lot. People have used their abilities and their knowledge to write these books. You don't really need to read books written by people whose thought processes are like yours or even inferior. All this will never reveal the ultimate truth. You have read more than what is necessary. Now empty your mind and close your eyes. What you find then, can be called God or a divine spirit – as you please.'

She did not write to the Professor for many days after that. She did not heed his advice either as she couldn't be without books. But she started reading the Bible and the Gita. She spent her days in the library pondering over matters of sin and morality. 'Please come to Delhi urgently. I want to discuss something important.' When the Professor rang her with great urgency in his voice, she took a week's leave and went to Delhi. The Professor spoke to her at length about the experiment he planned to carry out on Alpha. She was extremely interested right from the beginning. 'But when you talk about start all over again, what exactly do you mean? Can we deliberately discard knowledge and culture? And if we do so, won't it be merely a farce? How can we remove the deeply embedded elements of culture from our unconscious mind?'

'It is very difficult. There will be great mental pressure. What we consider right may be proven wrong. We may have to charge our mental make-up that differentiates the right from the wrong.'

'Are humans like elements in a chemistry lab? We may not be able to behave like we wish to or plan to. We may be able to implement certain decisions we have thrust upon ourselves for a short period of time, but will we be able to carry it on for twenty-five years?'

'We must. I need strong-minded people. I don't intend to curtail the natural emotions of human beings. On the contrary, I want to set them free. It is when human beings try to restrain themselves that they fail. I am asking you to disregard all restrictions. The mental pressures that you experience while living a life of respectability in society are much greater than when you live without any social constructs and restrictions.'

'I can't believe this.'

'That is because your mind has been trained a certain way since the day you were born. Not just you, people all over the world have been conditioned by such customs and lifestyles. You can't even imagine that we can live without these social shackles and taboos. It is a change from this state of mind that I am seeking.'

Aruna couldn't but accept this logic. Without even bothering to resign from her job, Aruna left for Alpha. When she set off on the journey she only took a copy of the Bible that the Mother in the convent had given her when she was in the fourth standard. She read and reread a single line, over and over again.

Blessed is he whose transgression is forgiven, whose sin is cured.

Upon reaching Alpha she left her Bible on the boat, and that is how she lost her last link with the written word.

She was bored during the initial days on the island. She whiled away her time looking at butterflies and chameleons and the struggle of the insects caught in spiders' webs. Then she began mating alternately with Pradeep and Christopher and gradually adapted to the new lifestyle. But she could never enjoy life on the island. Though she accepted the changes as integral aspects of the experiment, her mindset was still that of a serious-minded, bookish Bengali girl.

Having rescued Anwar from the red ants, she felt close to him. Suddenly, life seemed impossible without Anwar. Though she had sex with others, she thought of Anwar as her soulmate. When she realized that two children born to her did not display any of the expected mental development, she started hating the experiment. The anxiety about the end result of the experiment tormented her. She was beginning to think that this anarchic freedom was more dangerous than slavery, so she longed to escape. Anwar was more insistent on planning an escape. Finally, when their attempt ended in failure and she lost Anwar too, she roamed the island in utter dejection. Using twigs, she stubbornly wrote on the sands: 'Complete freedom is a myth.' When waves washed away the words written in one language, she would write these words again in another. Five years later, isolated from her surviving co-inhabitants and completely insane, she died in some corner of the island. She was thirty-eight years old.

16

Shweta Dasgupta

ALPHA WAS A SYMBOL OF TRUTH AND LOVE. THE SUN, moon and stars blessed the island by abundantly showering their light upon it. When multi-coloured butterflies flitted from flower to flower, the most beautiful girl on the island gazed at them in wonder.

Shweta Dasgupta, who had internalized the swift movements of Kathak and the enticing grace of Odissi, was researching various Indian dance forms with the help of a European fellowship. She believed that classical dance wasn't just a combination of gestures and a projection of emotions but reflections of culture. Shweta had toured all over India for her dance performances. She was interested in liberating dance forms from their formalistic rigour and presenting them in a unique style of her own.

For her, art wasn't meant to be confined to particular systems and repeated at every performance; rather, art was the intelligence and creative freedom to devise new systems of performance – this was what distinguished art from rituals.

Like tinkling anklets, Shweta's voice drew one's attention to the way she spoke rather than to what she was saying. Santosh would often attribute meanings she had not even intended to them and then argue with her about it. Shweta firmly believed that just as the progress of science was one of the indices of development, so was the growth of art. In music and dance evolving from the passionate rhythms of deep Africa to the delicate notes of Rabindrasangeet, and from the samba of Latin America to the lascivious Indian dances, we find the progress of cultures. In dance, the movements shift from fast to slow and the dancer depicts emotions using eyes and facial expressions. But Santosh found it difficult to concur with all this. When compared to scientific advancements, he felt that the progress of art was merely a shift from one scale to another. Shweta's art forms would never be comprehended by Santosh's scientific analysis.

Santosh brought Shweta to the Professor just the day before their journey to Alpha. Till then they had communicated only through letters or over the telephone. The Professor knew Shweta as Santosh's friend, a dancer who was a deep thinker. But after that first meeting itself, she was able to convince the Professor that she was not merely a dancer.

'I'm Shweta. I try to discover the meaning of life through the tinkling of anklets. This truth that you speak of, isn't it a myth? Very large when you look at it through one side of the microscope and extremely small from the opposite side?'

'That is because you are using a microscope to look at it. Only if you throw away all the mirrors will you be able to see the truth.'

'But haven't we always learnt to look through filters and lenses? We have reached a stage where we can't think about vision without the lens. It is as if we have stuck contact lenses in our eyes right from birth. For us, vision has become not a need, but an unavoidable desire.'

'Vision is in the eyes of the beholder; from the retina to the brain. There exists another myth called the mind. There are millions of cells inside our minds which persuade us to believe that the images falling on the retina of our eyes are real and convey the truth. We learn a lot about people, their actions and behaviour through our eyes. But often that vision is removed from truth and is illusory. The mother's breasts are a source of food for the baby but are an erogenous zone for the father. Humans cannot escape this paradox. Even if we avoid all lenses, the pupil of our eye acts like a mirror and converts truth into a mythical image and implants it on our retina.'

'The movements of a dancer always try to convey a clear meaning. The gestures that denote a deer and a lotus can manifest forests and the dawn. Similarly, different gestures gain different meanings from changing contexts and are used in more complex ways. This is a significant milestone in the progress of mankind. You must acknowledge progress in art, just like you acknowledge progress in science. If we abandon everything we have attained in the field of art and go back to the *beginning*, then all these will be merely incomprehensible sounds and gestures.'

'That is what should happen. We should be able to devise a new art form distinct from current meanings.

'From the moment you step on the island you should forget everything. Live like an ordinary person. Maybe I, who am not conversant with fine arts, will be the one to discover the essence of new art forms and you will uncover scientific truths.'

Shweta could not give up art. Though she tried to forget, the influence of dance was evident in her stance, the way she walked and even in her smallest gestures. She had small breasts and a tiny waist. Her diminutive nude figure provoked all men except the Professor. In her initial days on the island, she was forced to have sex with more than one man every day. As she was a highly sensuous woman, she was able to communicate easily without any language. Her destruction was her insatiable greed for the island's intoxicating wild fruits. Indulging in frequent sex and intoxication destroyed her health. As years passed, she forgot her art and only her insatiable appetite continued to thrive. She gave birth to three children. In her eleventh year on the island, when Shweta died a skeletal figure with drooping breasts, she only had her ten-year-old daughter beside her. The child did not know what had happened to her mother. She could not distinguish between death and sleep.

17

Pradeep Mehta's Paintings

PRADEEP BELONGED TO AN ORDINARY FAMILY IN BARODA. Though he worked as a freelance journalist, he was really an artist. From a young age, his paintings were declared to have given new dimensions to modern Indian art and were exhibited in international art galleries. The paintings in muted hues with a touch of impressionism bore a striking resemblance to the cave paintings of Ellora. But all of his paintings depicted the emptiness of modern life and challenged false codes of morality. He was once arrested for painting the national flag hoisted on the prime minister's penis in 6" x 4" size right in front of the parliament building in Delhi on Independence Day. Pradeep, who was Hari's friend, believed that India's progress was retarded due to regressive morality that curbed sexual freedom.

He met the Professor at an exhibition that showcased both Pradeep's art and Hari's poetry. To the Professor, Pradeep's paintings looked like the cave paintings of primitive humans. 'Why are you painting in a style that primitive men used?'

'The primitive man could think and act without deceit. Whatever we now see around us is untrue; false love, false sorrow, false happiness, everything is false. We cannot even believe our own eyes. That is why I started to think and paint like primitive men.'

'Can you really think like them?'

'Yes, I think so. That ability is my art.'

'Then we have a lot to discuss.' Pradeep and Hari spoke to the Professor for a long time and became keen participants of the experiment.

The first thing Pradeep did on the island was to look for plants that would yield colours. He painted incessantly on trees, leaves and caves using the green and red colours oozing from the stalks of plants. Though everyone else had discarded their knowledge and abilities, Pradeep carried his skill along with him. He argued that painting was not against the rules of the experiment. His style of painting in any case belonged to an ancient era. He was merely going back to it.

One day Pradeep saw tiny crabs in the sea. If you make scratches on your body with the front legs of a live crab, it leaves indelible marks resembling tattoos. Pradeep used the crabs to draw on Aruna and Shweta's bodies. Everyone else was too scared to try. He drew bunches of grapes around Shweta's breasts and a lotus beneath her navel. It took him ten days to complete a painting of Alpha on Aruna's bare back.

But gradually he lost interest in painting. He became engrossed in going fishing with Christopher and trying to capture Shweta for the night. He started to behave rudely even with the Professor. Once he pushed the Professor out of his small cave and started painting on its walls. The painting that took him months to complete was initially unfathomable to the others. It was a painting that portrayed all living creatures, from amoebas to human beings. He laughed at the wonderstruck Professor who stood gazing at it and left the cave never to return to it.

Pradeep hated children. He felt that childbirth and children were a hindrance to his happiness and pleasure. The children on Alpha feared him. Once he threw Shweta's one-month-old baby on the sand because he wanted to have sex with Shweta. The news of pregnancies infuriated him. He once brutally manhandled a pregnant Urmila which caused her to have a miscarriage.

Christopher remained Pradeep's companion till the end. They lived intoxicated by the wild fruits, eating raw fish and small birds. As time went by, their cruelties increased. When the Professor died, they behaved as if the control of the island had been passed on to them. They thought everyone should live in fear of them. When the new generation grew up, he felt attracted to the young girls. By the time these girls reached the age of fifteen, they would become pregnant.

Pradeep and Christopher forgot the fact that this was an experiment, and that this life was merely a part of that experiment. They reigned over Alpha until the twenty-fourth year on the island. That was when the new generation on Alpha banded together and turned against Pradeep and Christopher. One night they secretly attacked the cave. They killed most of the older generation with whatever sharp-edged stones they could find. They raped the older women. They killed Pradeep by making a crab bite his penis. Four men raped Urmila. But Malini was left unharmed. Everyone liked her; they even respected her.

They threw Pradeep, Christopher and Hari's bodies into the sea. Malini stayed in the cave taking care of Urmila and Santosh who were brutally wounded. Pradeep's blood had formed a pool beneath his massive painting.

18

The Professor's Death

IT WOULD RAIN OFTEN ON ALPHA. AS IT WAS SO CLOSE to the equator, the days were boiling hot, and it would inevitably pour in the evenings. This climate fostered the lush greenery on the island. The rains troubled the whole group as only the caves offered them some protection. Each of them had made a shelter of some sort using creepers and twigs for their personal use, but those temporary shelters could not withstand the torrential rains. Water seeped in even through the roofs of the caves when it rained heavily.

In the dark, the Professor sat under the falling raindrops thinking about the painful progress of his grand experiment. He had no hopes for the future. It was an empty existence. The progress was much slower than he had anticipated. He thought that the experiment was moving towards an absurd conclusion, one that he had not foreseen. Months and years were becoming insignificant. Like a baby who is just learning to stand up and walk, everything seemed sluggish.

He had great expectations from the new generation. His estimation that the already well-developed human brain would be able to comprehend quickly and analyze with ease had been proven to be hugely erroneous. Deprived of basic knowledge and life skills that are passed on informally from one generation to the next and the assortment of information that is acquired from family, friends and teachers, the human brain was compelled to perform at a far slower rate, like a computer that has lost its efficiency because of the lack of basic information input. When one person is made to gather knowledge all by themselves, that knowledge tends to be basic and rather scanty. Though there is active growth, it took place over a much longer period. It is doubtful whether mankind can progress at a greater speed than before. Is it that the greater intelligence thought to be possessed by the new generation was the result of information gained from the preceding generations? If we set that knowledge aside, then is the brain just a processor?

But enough time had not elapsed to arrive at such a conclusion. A child's brain attains the ability to analyze only at the age of twelve. Six more years will need to pass before the children on Alpha reach that age. But they aren't even showing the mental growth one expects from seven-year-olds. They merely roll in the mud crying for food and fall asleep after filling their stomachs. They can only produce grunts and muddled sounds. They do not even play properly. Gazing at the sun, moon, butterflies and dragonflies and slowly wandering all over the island, they live like three-year-olds. The older generation has lost every ounce of their humanity and become mere animals. The scientist, the poet and the dancer live like wild animals as if their intellect has been completely effaced by their base instincts.

There is no return. Everyone has lost everything. Family, jobs, social positions, even their health. If Professor Upelendu Chatterjee entered the JNU campus now, people would stare at him as if he were a ghost. The beautiful women who had come to Alpha would scare people with their saggy breasts and their scarecrow-like bodies. No, that is unthinkable. Hunger was the Professor's main problem. He was a vegetarian and so his diet was limited to wild fruits and roots. Practice had made his body strong enough to resist hunger.

Even though he saw his companions eating raw fish and the flesh of birds, he could never become carnivorous. He arrived at new conclusions about how long one could exist without food. He realized that one could go on for weeks without eating. He realized that hunger was more emotional than physiological. Man with his superior intellect was eating way more than he physiologically needed to and was thereby pushing his fellow beings into poverty. Rich people in more developed countries were pushing the weaker sections in less developed countries further into poverty. Man's selfishness and greed are the root causes of poverty and all the other ills the world faces. Food is only one of the factors that sustain life. There are other equally or even more important factors.

In the dim light, the Professor looked at his own body. It had changed a lot. It was grotesque. His neatly trimmed beard and clean nails were long gone. His skin was wrinkled as if he had aged quickly. A racking cough troubled him constantly. He worried whether he would die before the experiment was over and if he'd have to hand it over to someone else.

That fateful night, the Professor slept late. When he woke up he was burning with fever. It was as if it had come at night to take him away. The fever never left him. A week later, on a rainy evening, while the others stood around him, he closed his eyes forever. The others who had long lost sight of the aim of the experiment and had no other option, continued to live as they did.

19

Guru

THEY DID NOT GET BACK EVEN AFTER IT WAS QUITE dark. What had happened to them? This was the first time they had gone out since they'd come here. Have they returned before completing their story? That too, leaving behind Urmila, who is lying silently near me? I was trying to piece their stories together into a cohesive narrative. But what about the forty-seven people on Alpha, living like guinea pigs. Aren't people sometimes reduced to puppets even in the course of normal life? Aren't newly developed medicines and treatments first tried and tested in Third World countries like India? Is each generation fated to be trapped by people who have more power and skills of manipulation? Instead of sympathizing with them, perhaps one ought to consider this to be a law of nature. Even man's selfishness and his desire to conquer nature are part of the natural laws of the world.

They finally returned at about ten at night. I did not ask them anything – where they had been or what they had been doing. Seated on a chair on the balcony that night, Malini said, 'Avinash, we were wandering around the city. We saw so many people. We sat on the beach speaking about things lost in the suffocation of the last twenty-five years. Finally, we have come to a decision – to return to the island. After we finish telling you the story of our experiment, we will become irrelevant in this part of the world. We've remained alive only to tell you about it. But before returning we would like to see Dr Banerji; after all, the Professor had entrusted him with everything.'

'Let's go to him, of course, although unfortunately, he cannot speak. One side of his body is paralyzed. If we write down what we want to tell him he will be able to read, but he will not be able to reply.'

As if she had suddenly remembered something, Malini spoke, 'Avinash, the problems worsened when the new generation grew up. Within a period of fifteen years, the children had become quite sturdy. A hostile environment and their diet gave them extraordinary strength and immunity. They ate birds and small animals. Fish, frogs, crabs – they ate whatever they could find raw. When I saw them eating flesh oozing with blood, I feared that they would not hesitate to eat each other. But that hasn't happened till now. Some of their activities repulsed us, but the revulsion was also mixed with a sense of wonder. How cleverly they snatch things from one another. Nobody concedes anything. Yet they share with each other sometimes. They quickly learnt to kill birds by throwing stones at them and developed the skills to catch fish. The new generation treated us differently. They believed that we had some powers that they didn't. But they did not know how we had come by these powers. That must still be an unanswered question in their minds. Sometimes ships used to pass at a great distance from the island. They saw it as an inexplicable wonder. When the ships appeared, they would stare at them anxiously till they disappeared from view. They respected the sun and the moon and feared thunder and lightning. They did not grasp the repetitive nature of seasons or the possibility of agriculture. They ate what fruits they could find without gathering or storing them.

Basically, they live the very basic life of the ancient man. Though they made some weapons using sharp stones, they could not develop more weapons to hunt bigger animals. They were not able to make bows, arrows or nets.'

Santosh continued from where Malini had left off.

'Though the progress was barely noticeable, whatever they discovered they were able to use cleverly. They showed extraordinary expertise in throwing stones. You might find it difficult to believe this, but most of the children in the new generation have extremely good aim when throwing stones at birds. The great speed with which they can move their limbs and their natural responses are maybe the results of the greater development of their mental abilities as the Professor had believed. But the lack of basic information needed for activities retarded the possibility of faster and greater progress. Maybe their mental faculties did not receive the required raw material to reach their true potential.'

Avinash said, 'Santosh, we need to make some changes to the Professor's theory based on the experiences of the experiment. Though the development of the human brain is wonderful, its working is directly linked with the available information.'

'Yes. But the fundamental knowledge that is acquired should be transferred to the next generation through our genes. When animal instincts are thus transmitted, why aren't intellectual capabilities inherited?'

'That is because mankind's collective intellectual achievements are monumental. Only a very small part of the immense knowledge gained by society is stored in the brain of an individual. Most of us retain only relevant information about our chosen field of expertise and even that would be a tiny percentage of the existing knowledge in that particular field. Even an extremely intelligent geologist or a doctor would have assimilated only a small part of all existing knowledge. Knowledge is recorded and preserved in millions of books and computers to be used when needed. A man who learns to drive a car doesn't genetically pass on this ability to his progeny; he has to teach them. In the same way, education from a qualified teacher is an important aspect of growing up. This limitation of the human brain has been confirmed by this experiment. This is a problem for geneticists. Even if a highly intelligent person's cells are used to create a baby, knowledge needs to be imparted to the child as it grows up. The human brain might be a supercomputer that works quickly and as accurately in relation to the available data. So if you deliberately do not feed the computer of data or deprive it in a language that the computer understands, it will helplessly deteriorate just as the evolved modern-day humans will become like cave people.'

I found their theories acceptable. But the problem was the next phase of the experiment. We could try to give the forty-seven inhabitants of Alpha knowledge and culture bit by bit. We may be able to discover new dimensions of brain development. But would they cooperate? What good would it do to talk to these people who were suffering from disappointment and a great sense of loss that twenty-five years on the island had brought them?

'Malini, after Urmila regains consciousness, we must go to Dr Banerji. We will decide our future plans after that.'

20

Urmila

AT LAST, ON THE SEVENTH DAY AFTER LEAVING THE island, Urmila opened her eyes. She looked around anxiously at her strange surroundings. It was as if the light was frightening her. She blinked and sobbed for no reason. Though she tried to say something, only weird noises came out of her mouth. I couldn't make sense of the strange sounds she was making. But Malini could understand her. She switched off the lights and requested me to step out.

'She is scared of light. During the last year on Alpha, she had lived in the darkness of a cave. Light upsets her. She would close her eyes with her hands and start crying. It happened after the young generation's attack on Pradeep and Christopher. She was raped repeatedly. Boys who were her son's age had assaulted her brutally. She couldn't even protest. Let us leave her alone for a while. We will talk to her when she becomes normal.'

We did not speak that night. The next afternoon, when Malini brought Urmila to my room, she seemed normal. She stared at me as if I were a strange being. I said, 'I have a lot to learn from you, Urmila. No hurry though.'

After a while, she said in a low voice, 'I used to like Alpha a lot in the early days. I liked the plants, birds and the breeze. That was when I flitted around like a butterfly on the island. But with time, problems began. The ultimate freedom we thought we had gained deserted us slowly. We deliberately ignored our babies who were crying for our help. We did not even help them learn how to walk. Each one of us in pursuit of personal freedom paid no heed to the freedom of others. This slowly led to the deterioration of everyone's freedom, and the stronger males started controlling the females. Among the men, the physically stronger ones subjugated the weak and gained predominance in matters of food and sex. When lust turned into violence and repression, the era of love disappeared. I quickly started hating myself. I often thought of returning, but I could never do it.'

'We too felt the same. But there was a slight difference where Urmila was concerned. She never liked anyone interfering in her personal problems and freedom. She would react spontaneously if anyone tried to do so. As the others had lost their mental ability to accept these responses, it was Urmila who faced the most difficult problems.'

'Very often, personal freedom will need to be sacrificed for the sake of social freedom. I couldn't make such adjustments. I never liked Pradeep's domineering nature or Christopher's perverted sexual needs. I only felt close to the Professor and Santosh. When I had sex with the others, I felt I was lowering myself to the level of a whore.'

'I had wanted to ask you about this. Wouldn't uncontrolled sexuality deteriorate to prostitution?'

'No,' Malini responded. 'Prostitution is when you sell your body for money or material gains. We never considered such matters.'

'That's not entirely true. What about the sexuality of the woman who surrenders before authority or physical force to sustain her life and livelihood? As these are material concepts, it is in fact prostitution. A situation where a woman has to sell herself in the marketplace when the price is decided by the buyer and the price might be zero or lower.'

'I differ – prostitution isn't merely a business. It is cheating one's conscience. When you mate with a person whom you do not like but you have sex just to gain something, any activity of your body and mind with ulterior motives of profit is prostitution. But my preferences most often had no such aims. Living on Alpha, I liked to sing to myself and write short poems in Kannada and English on the sand. When the waves wiped my words away, I would write another word or draw a picture unseen by the others. I have always liked to break the rules in every game. I found great joy when I cheated while playing carrom or deceived my devoted boyfriend by sleeping with someone else. To be honest I got good marks in all my exams using shortcuts. Did you know that even before we left for Alpha and when the Professor was detailing the rules of the experiment, I was thinking of ways to break them? Just like we defeat the darkness of the night by using light.'

It felt that the story was becoming more layered and complex. To embark on an experiment that broke all existing systems of rules and then to secretly break the rules of that experiment itself. So you go back to where you began. Isn't it absurd? When one pieced everything together, the boundaries of reality and fiction kept getting blurred.

'With the Professor's death, I felt that I had lost everything. I couldn't respect or even consider anyone else my equal. Yet I was forced to copulate with Pradeep, Hari and Christopher. I feel like they wanted me because my body was more voluptuous than those of the others. And because they felt that they needed to destroy the arrogance they assumed I felt due to my closeness to the Professor. But I could never behave naturally with them. They knew that I hated them even though I succumbed to their brute force. So they hurt me and forced me to do things that revolted me. For the new generation who grew up seeing all this, I became a laboratory to experiment with their sexuality. I did not want to continue that absurd, hurtful existence for twenty-five years, in the vain hope of waiting for a stranger from the mainland. But there were no escape routes. By then everyone else had become so engrossed in the experiment that they forgot that this was, in fact, merely an experiment. Some began to believe that this was their life all along. They completely forgot the beauty of language and the light of ancient wisdom. Everyone behaved as though they had truly forgotten everything. The poet, the journalist and the scientist lived like savage men. I ardently desired to speak to someone openly. Maybe they too felt the same. But nobody dared to speak. The rules of the experiment controlled us like some unseen, unbreachable force.'

'Like Urmila, even I longed to talk to someone. But we were silenced by the thought that everyone else was obeying the unwritten rules of the experiment or that everyone else had completely lost touch with humane behaviour.'

'So was everyone the same? Did no one change after coming to Alpha? Was it all a huge misunderstanding, which wasn't cleared up as no one discussed these matters? It just goes on to prove that however hard we try, the characteristics of behaviour derived from culture never completely leave us.'

'Definitely – we were merely acting as if we had given up everything. In reality, no one had given up anything. Everyone was acutely aware of the fact that they were part of a huge experiment and thought about the fame it would bring them.'

'It's not exactly true as far as I'm concerned. More than the fame the experiment would bring, I wanted the unbridled sexual experiences. But most of the others desired fame. Even the Professor ultimately desired fame and international recognition,' said Malini.

This experiment on Alpha, which entailed giving up everything, was really to gain everything and attain new heights. The Professor desired to create an empirical foundation to establish that the inspiring progress of the Western world can be attributed to their lifestyle. He hoped to convince the Third World countries to accept that material reality is a crucial and predominant factor for human advancement. Renunciation was just a myth; everyone wanted to gain everything. Alpha was only a means to an end. But what about the by-products of this experiment: the new generation that had to live without knowing the meaning of this story?

They were denied not just fame and recognition but even a normal modern life. They are the unfortunates who gaze in wonder at the sun and the moon. They have been denied any knowledge and skills accumulated by their forefathers and have been forced to live like we did tens of thousands of years ago. Can the decision to deny these highly evolved human beings even basic knowledge ever be forgiven?

21

The Professor's Notes

PROFESSOR BANERJI LIVED IN A PEACEFUL OLD building in South Delhi. When we reached his place at ten in the morning, he was sleeping. His middle-aged servant was evidently displeased as she ushered us in. She said, 'He is not well at all; he shouldn't be disturbed.' I told her that I was his student and if she could just convey the message that I had returned from Alpha. We had to wait for nearly an hour before we were allowed inside his room. She let us meet him on the condition that we would not trouble him by talking to him for a long time.

Though partially paralyzed, the professor did not have any difficulty in recognizing us. He seemed healthier than before. Though he couldn't sit up straight, he could understand what we were trying to say. He was trying to speak to us. His lips moved, and I caught the word 'Upelendu'.

I shook my head. 'Sorry. He died fourteen years ago.'

Then I told him everything that I had seen and heard over the last few days. He listened to me patiently, as if he had been expecting to hear this saga.

'Malini,' he said. I knew that she was his former student. I called her. We spent the whole day with the professor. Malini gave long and detailed answers to his brief, almost monosyllabic, infrequent questions. Before we returned to our hotel room at night, he said to us:

'Come tomorrow morning. I have some notes written by Upelendu. I want to read those notes and piece them together with what we now knew about the experiment. Only then will we get a clear picture. Upelendu wasn't an ordinary anthropologist. He was a visionary who had very clear ideas and opinions about human progress and social justice.'

The professor's room was filled with the fragrance of medicinal oils as he had been undergoing extensive Ayurvedic treatment that had helped him recover a little bit of his health.

The next day he handed us Professor Upelendu's notes. They didn't seem to be in any apparent order. Not only that, they also seemed to be random and disconnected. They were just some papers in a file that he had handed over to Professor Banerji before leaving for Alpha. Malini started reading them one by one …

One

The cyclic occurrence of births and deaths has always fascinated me. Why does it happen to man when he is sixty or seventy, and to other organisms in due course? What is the force that controls these occurrences? Why is that man grows to be strong and healthy till the age of thirty, and then grow steadily weaker after fifty and then die? Why does growth and retardation or the process of growing old exist like a parabolic graph? How can one circumvent the inevitability of death that exists in life? How can we sustain the status quo once a human being has attained full growth? You might think these questions foolish. There may be people who consider this to be divine will. I aim to analyze observable facts and evidence. I always ask, 'Why cannot this be so?' One should not accept the verdict that 'it is so'. Death should not be inevitable. We should have the ability to control our death. I ask science the same question that Nachiketa asked Lord Yama. What is the difference between one and self? What is the difference between us and our bodies? Is there any physical action or process that can be detached from the intellect or the mind? So another question arises, where is the intellect situated in our body? Science tells us that it is in our numerous brain cells. Somehow everything seems vague to me.

Two

Wars are inevitable in the history of humankind. Man has climbed each step of progress through violence and suppression. Man has always developed new technologies to defeat his rivals. The science of war is the repression of the weak by the strong. If we had been peace-loving and decent, we wouldn't have achieved one-hundredth of the progress we now have. The ideology of progress has been learnt through the lessons of selfishness, deceit and fraud. Why is Hiroshima crying? So that many others may laugh.

Three

I think I am mad. It would be pathetic if an anthropology professor at JNU loses his sanity due to thinking and learning. I don't like to see the world as composed of many small countries. I am against cartography that draws lines dividing nations into states and districts. Who do the soldiers who guard the McMahon line in deep winter fire at? There shouldn't be countries and boundaries, authority and thrones. Everyone on earth should be able to live with freedom and love. Why did so much blood flow when India got freedom? When we move from the absurdity of boundaries to the absurdity of guarding them, millions of innocent lives are lost.

Four

I had a dream yesterday – aliens had landed on Earth. They were walking and talking. But their gait and conversation were unfamiliar to me. Just like people on Earth speak different languages, these aliens were speaking in a strange tongue and were moving with strange gestures. Their limbs couldn't be marked out distinctly as legs or arms. Why do we insist that the head be fixed on the top of the body? Can't it be fixed lower down or onto one side of the body? As I woke up from my dream, I felt as if a sharp nail had been driven into my forehead. Why are my thoughts so strange? As a sanyasi whom I'd met on the Gopalpur beach had once said, the most important part of the human body is the forehead. I think there is some truth in the belief that if you focus on a particular point and gather all your mental energy and fix it on that point you will experience inexplicable energy flowing through you.

Five

Today is the solar eclipse. Scientists from all over the world have been immersed in studying the eclipse with the help of their telescopes. There have been many eclipses before this. It is as absurd as the beginning of the earth. It is said that the rare cosmic rays that reach the surface of the earth during the eclipse affect the ecosystem. Does man's intellect gain anything during each eclipse? That assumption cannot be disregarded: The human brain gains strength or diversity with each eclipse.

Six

I do not like the idea of writing a will. I know that nothing we have earned is truly ours. They became our possessions due to selfishness or childish desires. I do not have the authority to decide how to divide these possessions. When the memory of the dead person fades from the minds of the living, that is when everything ends. I've not seen my grandfather. I don't know my grandfather's father's name. So many generations lived before them. There is no trace left of the fact that they had lived. When death is natural and ordinary, the writing of a will is irrelevant.

Seven

When was fire discovered? Anthropology will tell you that it was at a historical juncture in the Stone Age. That is the time man discovered the techniques to make fire. Fire has existed in various forms since the beginning of the universe. Our discoveries are not exactly new achievements; human beings merely saw pre-existing things anew. When one says that Columbus discovered America, it is as absurd as saying that the Red Indians were not humans.

Eight

Kanu had come to meet me yesterday, very secretly. The police were looking for him. He wanted a place where he could hide from the police. All routes of escape to China are temporarily closed. Kanu believes that it was not wrong to kill a few to bring about positive change in society. Those who are not useful to society should not be allowed to live. 'You can kill me immediately, according to the principles of the revolution of the masses. I am an anthropologist who is of no use to the sustenance of the progress of society. The farmer labouring in the fields or the miner deep inside the mines is far better than I am.' Kanu smiled without replying. I am not important enough to be killed by the revolutionaries. An apathetic, harmless teacher, even my department, the department of anthropology, is one of the most sidelined departments in the university.

… Malini stopped reading. There were two more papers marked separately. One was titled 'The History Chest' and the other 'Alpha: An Experiment of Truth'.

22

The History Chest

IT SEEMS AS IF THE PRIME MINISTER'S AUTOCRATIC nature had become more pronounced after the victory over Bangladesh. This is royal governance and not democracy. Sadly, the scientists and writers were supporting this too. They had great expectations. They spread tales that the country was on the verge of progress and that a strong power is needed to maintain control. How quickly the intellectuals succumb to the temptation of a few crumbs of positions and authority that are thrown at them. That woman is unashamedly praised so that they may become an academy chairman or an ambassador.

It was when she invited me home and spoke to me for an hour that I saw her true colours. They were the dictates of an autocrat cloaked beneath the demeanour of dignity.

'Indian culture is far ahead of other cultures. We have a great tradition in science, mathematics and literature. But we have never attempted to present our achievements before the world to gain recognition and acceptance. But those far inferior to us are able to earn affirmations and laurels as they market themselves successfully. We should put an end to this and be able to stand with our heads held high before the world. All attempts in this direction are heading towards success. Everything has been done to make sure that we make more progress than other countries in the fields of science and technology. But what happened in Harappa and Mohenjedaro should not be repeated. We are duty-bound to inform the coming generations of our achievements. When one reads the history of India a thousand years from now, they should know of our achievements. We should record history in a way that it will not be destroyed by natural disasters.' She wanted to entrust me with the duty of planting metallic tablets in parts of the capital city.

My name had been proposed along with two other historians. When she said that I was being given the unique chance of documenting history, I couldn't help but say, 'Madam, I'm not a historian. I am not well versed in documenting history. But I don't believe that one can bury the history of a society in metal tablets. It should be written in the hearts of the people. Even if Hitler and Chengiz Khan had documented their version of history in gold tablets, people would still have considered them cruel criminals.'

Her face reddened with anger; without saying anything more she got up and went inside. After that, I was put under the constant surveillance of the police.

Many people advised me to seek her pardon and obey her wishes – even my family and my colleagues. Her office called to inform me that my name was on the list of contenders for the Padma Bhushan and that I should meet her personally. As I had nothing more to say to her, I did not go. I heard that a prominent dignitary had expressed willingness to write her version of history.

When Malini finished reading, Professor Banerji laughed, 'She wanted to buy Upelendu. He was very conscious of his personal freedom and would not have fallen for that trick.'

'Was it the political situation that inspired this experiment?' asked Avinash.

'Definitely. He could not tolerate any constraints on his thoughts and action. It was during the period after this incident that we discussed Project Alpha and prepared our plans,' said Malini.

'But this happened much before Emergency was declared in India. Did the prime minister display autocratic tendencies even then?'

'Yes. She was a dictator from birth. She did not want to be merely mentioned in history, she wanted to recreate history on her own terms.'

'Was it right to leave the country in the name of an experiment instead of fighting this?'

'The Professor was quintessentially a scientist. He did not desire to don the guise of a social worker or a political diplomat. When one leaves a situation that is not conducive, it is not because the situation has been accepted but because one cannot exist in those circumstances.'

'But was this the only reason to begin this experiment?'

'No, it was merely a trigger. The real inspiration were the breakthroughs in the field of anthropology at the time. You can read about those in the next set of papers,' said Dr Banerji.

23

Alpha: An Experiment of Truth

BENJAMIN LEE WHORF'S STUDY ABOUT THE HOPI Indians of Arizona made me think about the connection between language and the world. Whorf believes that the progress and uniqueness of language mark the growth of a culture.

In his text *Language and Linguistics*, he wrote:

> The background linguistic system (in other words, grammar) of each language is not merely a reproducing instrument for voicing ideas but rather is itself the chapter of ideas ... We dissect nature along lines laid down by our native language.

The Hopi language doesn't follow any system like those found in Indo-European languages. It is a language that does not contain the concepts of time like yesterday, today and tomorrow; it is frozen in the present. Their language has no demarcations for days, months and years, and recognizes only three colours in the rainbow. Whorf collaborated with anthropologist Edward Sapir and developed the Sapir-Whorf hypothesis that prompted me to think in a very different direction. What will happen if we lose language? While the Hanunoo tribe in the Philippines have ninety-two different names for different types of rice, in English there is only one – rice. If we discard the word rice, won't it exist as a food item? In the same way, what if we abandon all knowledge? We will definitely not become primitive humans. The progress of evolution over millions of years has enabled the human brain to work better and quicker. All research and experiments in anthropology are confined to mere observations. Unlike in other branches of science, no one in the field of anthropology comes forward with a clear project for an experiment. Anthropology functions as a discipline that links history, life sciences and the study of fossils. It is in this context that an independent experiment becomes relevant.

Even in a study about the rising infant mortality rate in Alto do Cruzeiro, a small town in Brazil, conducted by Nancy Scheper-Hughes in 1965, the anthropologist directly intervenes at times. But if a natural result is to be obtained, we should never interfere with the experiment. It is here that I disagree with Richard Lee. In the study he conducted on the nomads of Kalahari, he could not become one of them and the intervention of the anthropologist adversely affected the experiment. Don't the Guarani Indians live in tandem with the forests without participating in the knowledge acquired by the outside world? I feel that if we pluck out all of our acquired knowledge and throw it away, within twenty-five years we will be able to regain all of it and will attain a lifestyle like that of the Guaranis. When I discussed Project Alpha with some friends in Chicago, they were amazed. They felt that life without any sort of knowledge would be tough. But I am positive. Yes. I believe Alpha is an experiment of truth.

After they had read the last of the notes, everyone fell silent. Professor Banerji had fallen asleep. Sometime later, we left his house.

When I woke up the next morning, I couldn't find the three of them.

'We are going back. Please don't come after us.' There was a note on the table, along with three poems that Harikrishna Sarkar had written to Malini.

24

Bharata Vaakyam

IN THE BEGINNING THERE WAS WATER; FROM THE water came microorganisms. In the millions of years that followed, the ecosystem became a complex life chain that contained plants, trees, birds, animals and human beings. As the nights welcomed days and the days welcomed nights, man grew different from other organisms. The wonderful abilities of his intellect made him capable of controlling the world. He used nature for himself and his selfish needs. Enslaving those that obeyed him and destroying those that rebelled against him, he became the quasi owner of the ecosystem.

Different languages and cultures sprung up in different parts of the Earth. Building forts and bulwarks, mankind progressed through war rather than peace. They penned glorious stories of bloodshed. This species grew on pride and deceit instead of balance and truth. The Earth that was one, was segregated by boundaries and boundary disputes, imperialism and anti-imperial struggles. Weapons of mass destruction and peace talks were all different stages of growth.

Many religions and ideologies came into being to make humans peace-loving and respectable. Christ, Buddha, Nabi and Gandhi advised them about the paths of love. Sri Krishna to Karl Marx taught them to use weapons to achieve righteousness and thereafter lead a life of equality. But the later generations of Dwaraka and the Soviet Union destroyed themselves by fighting amongst each another endlessly. Each person who tried to make man good failed. Man is fundamentally an evil animal, selfish and arrogant, and well-versed in lust and anger. Only for him is laughter a deceitful facade.

Postscript

Freedom

Freedom …
Becomes infinite and expansive
Like the sky for the eagle.
For the cannibals
Who hide with their poison-tipped arrows
I have to offer my body as food.
The cuckoo forgetting to sing
Croaks like a crow.
The song I yearned to sing for you
Becomes the cry of the brother who was
Shot down in Bengal.
My painting for you
On the canvas of my dreams
splattered with his blood

Becomes meaningless.
But I still have hope …
Tens of thousands of villages in India
Become a crowd of crows
Tearing the head of authority in Delhi.
The crows will soar high
With the new flag dipped in that blood.
Freedom like the sky for the eagle …
Like the stars for the night …
Like dreams for me.

Love

My friend, I don't know how to love you ...
Maybe I can pretend.
Praise the beauty of your
eyes and lips.
Using metaphors and similes compare
your body to the universe itself.
Create a palace of deceit
With painted lies.
I who wear the cap of arrogance
And the swaddling clothes of selfishness
Know not how to love you.
Pardon me.

Madness

I am mad.
Mad …
Insane insanity ...
Like the twilight that poisons the day,
Like the moth that flies towards the flames courting death …
From truth to lies,
From knowledge to ignorance,
To nothingness … infinite nothingness …
I am in that insane insanity.

Tropical Detective
A Hari Majestic Mystery

Zac O'Yeah is the author of popular comic thrillers *Hari – A Hero for Hire* (2015) and *Mr. Majestic!* (2013), apart from thirteen other books. He has been translated into French, German, Russian, Chinese, Kannada and other languages. He worked in the theatre and music business in Sweden until he retired early, at twenty-five, to come to India. His books range from detective fiction to history and travelogue. He has also translated Indian literature into Swedish. As a veteran travel writer, he is a frequent contributor to *National Geographic Traveller* magazine. He is also a columnist with *The Hindu BusinessLine* and an influential literary critic.

Check his updates on https://www.facebook.com/ZacOYeah

Other titles in the *Hari Majestic* series

Mr. Majestic! The Tout of Bengaluru

Hari – A Hero for Hire

Praise for *Tropical Detective*

'Fast-paced, humorous, and steeped in colloquialisms, *Tropical Detective* is a rollicking, fun ride with crime-busting hero, Hari Majestic. The reader is swept along on a journey from Bangalore to Gothenburg, Sweden, on the track of a stolen temple idol. Hari Majestic, immensely likeable, perennially in trouble, brings his understanding, affectionate gaze to everyone who crosses his path, even if they might wish him harm. Zac O'Yeah's crime fiction is entertaining and endearing, as is his protagonist'

Lavanya Sankaran

Praise for *Hari – A Hero for Hire*

'O'Yeah brings to this book all the larger-than-life pep and total unbelievability of a desi crime thriller. And puts a twist in it, every step of the way' *Sunday Standard*

'This is a book that doesn't take itself seriously – and succeeds, therefore, in pulling off a stunt Mr Majestic would be proud of: it's snazzy, jazzy, pizzazzy, all things irreverent' *New Indian Express*

'The machinations and trappings of the delightfully over-the-top Hari remind you of Kannada potboilers … it seems Indian crime fiction has finally dusted off the proverbial chip on its shoulder and arrived at a comfortable equanimity with its place in the canon. And that place is firmly desi' *Bangalore Mirror*

'Comic masterpiece … a brilliant comedy of manners … the book is a joy to read, because of O'Yeah's sparkling prose peppered with wit and dollops of observational humour' *Sakal Times*

‘Apart from Hari and his friends, Bengaluru is very much a character in the book, as full of attitude as all the others’ *Statesman*

Praise for *Mr Majestic!*

‘A novel set in Bangalore that’s not quite like anything done before in the English language. Gloriously, unabashedly Technicolor with full-on frontal lighting, over-the-top escapades and sheer joy seeping out of every frame’ *Outlook*

‘If you enjoy psychedelic writing, with lashings of humour and a satisfying whodunnit all rolled in one, yep, this could be the book for you’ *Postnoon*

‘It’s a narrative so filmi, you almost expect a song-and-dance sequence. A trip worth taking’ *Indian Express*

‘The real fun lies in discovering that *Mr. Majestic!* is an authentic Indian thriller, rather than a Western prototype shoehorned into an Indian setting. It is a masala crime caper, set to the rhythms – that word again – of Indian life, language and geographies’ *Hindu Literary Review*

‘Zac O’Yeah’s crime fiction is quirky, amusing and teeming with unforgettable characters. A deliciously waggish take on modern India with all its idiosyncrasies and complexities’ Tarquin Hall

Tropical Detective

A Hari Majestic Mystery

ZAC O'YEAH

PAN

First published 2017 by Pan
an imprint of Pan Macmillan Publishing India Private Limited
707, Kailash Building
26 K. G. Marg, New Delhi 110001
www.panmacmillan.co.in

Pan Macmillan, the Smithson, 6 Briset St, London EC1M 5NR, United Kingdom
Basingstoke and Oxford
Associated companies throughout the world
www.panmacmillan.com

ISBN 978-93-86215-24-6

3 5 7 9 8 6 4 2

Typeset by Manmohan Kumar
Printed and bound in India by Repro India Ltd

To my readers – read on!

Brothers, turn your faces to the south,
and come to me in the street of many noises,
which leads down to the muddy river.
    The reason is this.
    My own eyes have seen it.

The Moonstone by Wilkie Collins

Raju opened his eyes, looked about, and said, 'Velan, it's raining in the hills. I can feel it coming up under my feet, up my legs—' He sagged down.

The Guide by RK Narayan

1

The next few days can be emotionally challenging, but stay alert and be careful with electrical equipment.

'You cannot bask in the rays of yesterday's sun.' These were his wife's words from earlier that day. It wasn't the first time they had argued, but it was the only time since they had got married that she had directly challenged his stature as a hero. His horoscope had warned him that this could happen.

Her disconcerting pronouncement echoed inside his skull as he watched banana leaves with dregs of food blow away from the garbage heap outside the marriage hall and flutter past the two or three cinemas that hadn't yet been turned into shopping malls. The Bengaluru air had lost its usual scent and texture of lukewarm beer, and was turning chilly. It was going to rain. He'd probably drown. He thought of his cosy cot at home and his hot-blooded wife as he buttoned up his uniform jacket, which was too tight across his belly.

But what had she meant? For the last several months, he had paid the rent on time. He had a steady income and had been posted in front of one of the many ATMs that kept popping up along the street which used to have a reputation for being downmarket. The world was improving … and Hari Majestic was right at the centre of it!

Next to the ATM, a new bank was being built. Credit cards and a generally less cash-dependent society had replaced moneylenders and pawn-brokers, and easy-to-hire-and-fire people, like Hari, were in great demand. And you can't leave cash dispensing machines standing alone on CD Road; they'd get nicked in a jiffy.

He inched his plastic chair closer to the glass door. Not that it was going to help much when the downpour came. Theoretically, the floor of the air-conditioned ATM booth was large enough for a man to sleep on – cool in the summer, dry on rainy nights. However, after the closed-circuit camera had been installed, guards were discouraged from napping inside the booth – no matter if it rained – and if they did, their pay was slashed.

In both directions, the street stretched more or less empty save for stray dogs and a couple of other ATM watchmen, nodding off. He watched a bitch playing with two puppies. A few steps away a male dog, probably the father, kept an eye on them. Such a happy family. Why couldn't his family be like theirs?

A sense of duty forced Hari to stay awake. It wasn't just that there were grocery credit bills to clear at the Fair Price shop, but also that he really did see himself as a hero. And as if to reinforce his belief, there was a banner that the police had put up on the other side of the street: 'Alert Today, Alive Tomorrow.' So true. Occasionally, he tried to explain to his wife that he was a very important person who once used to have foreign clients. But she felt that his premarital lifestyle – as a habitual tout and conman – wasn't anything to gloat about.

If one looked at the bright side, as he preferred to do, twelve hours of sitting on a plastic chair and getting paid wasn't bad as jobs go. It was honest work. One didn't end up in jail for being honest. And if it was true that his career had hit rock-bottom, then there was only one way to go. Back up to the top. For he doubted it could get any worse.

A bolt of thunder flew from one horizon to the other. Right on cue the pre-monsoon rains exploded and Hari got up to stand on the steps in front of the ATM. The entrance was covered by an awning with the bank's back-lit logo on it, so he didn't get the full impact, merely the mud splashing up from the surface of the road. He combed his fluffy whiskers. Due to the increasing incidence of ATM heists, it had become mandatory that guards have big moustaches to scare off thieves. Not long ago a security guard at an ATM near Jayanagar Shopping Complex was attacked by miscreants who took his nightstick and beat him until he sustained severe injuries. His mistake: he didn't have a moustache.

But during rainy nights, the coconut oil Hari used to make his whiskers more pompous solidified it into a greasy lump which was cold and clammy against his upper lip, like two starved slugs nibbling on the snot trickling out of his nostrils.

The icy wetness seeped upwards from his rubber sandals and into the folds of his loincloth. He rescued a wedge of paan from his jacket pocket before it got soggy and chewed it. The tobacco and betel nut mixture kept him warm. He yawned. He checked his phone. It was well past midnight. Between 2 a.m. and 6 a.m., there were never any customers. As soon as the rain abated, he'd catch a short nap, he decided. If he napped outside the booth, the camera wouldn't capture it, and as long as he was only half asleep he could always claim to have worked part-time. Some of the other guards took the opportunity to roll down the shutters and close their ATMs, and do other work to augment their petty income. But as for Hari, he always did his best. Always.

At 9 a.m., when the daytime guard arrived, he'd go home and have a hot bath, change the oil in his moustache, eat breakfast and spend the rest of the day in his detective bureau waiting for clients, whiling away time by reviewing cold, unsolved cases. It wasn't easy to be a hero. His second-in-command, Triplex, had suggested that they get Hari's cyber expert Doc to hotwire the ATM and loot it, then pretend to investigate the theft and get paid by the bank. Simply double jackpot.

Hari didn't agree. To go to jail would be the last straw. His domineering mum was serving a seven-year sentence and, in the worst-case scenario, he'd be put in a family cell with her. His decision not to go along with the plan had created a rift between him and his freelancing staff: Triplex, Doc and Gaadi, who together perpetrated more petty crimes than they solved, broke traffic rules, got into fisticuffs in bars, and were frequently arrested for eve-teasing and nuisance-commitment.

It wasn't that he didn't get the larger picture. When it was loaded, the ATM held ₹15,00,000. More than what he'd make if he spent thirteen years guarding it. Looking at it that way, Hari felt that money and god were almost the same in this prosperous town that grew, according to what he had heard, at the rate of 600 square feet *per minute*. And here he was, armed with nothing but a bamboo nightstick and a moustache, within hearing distance of the particular rustle that crisp currency notes make and yet he himself had so little of it. Enough money and you were good, enough gods and you were also good. But here was the conundrum: no money meant that the gods were not likely to be on your side. Any god was going to be more interested in those who had the gold to provide nice things like gilded idols for temples. Hari turned his eyes upward and looked to the sky, as if trying to read his destiny from the rain drops.

The rain slowed to a trickle. He wiped the plastic chair dry and slumped down, popping another antacid pill. He hadn't seen a single vehicle pass in the last half hour.

He twirled his moustache, a gesture which comforted him, and tweeted: 'Holding the fort and protecting all you ☺ people's hard-earned cash.' He then wrapped his arms around himself for warmth, lowered his eye-lids to half-mast, put his brain on standby and prepared to review a masala movie version of his life. It was one of his standard dreams and it went like this: *Majestic is a hero.*

He knew that it was unlikely to get released theatrically, especially since the theatres around here, a neighbourhood which always had been the epicentre of Kannada cinema, were shutting down with alarming frequency. Some sixty-five of the city's 235 cinemas had been demolished in the last decade. Majestic Talkies, where Hari himself was virtually born, Kalpana, Sagar, Tribhuvan, Nartaki, where all Rajkumar films had premiered, and Sapna, which used to be popular for violent low-budget B-films – they were all gone and developers had taken over the plots.

The biopic of his heroic life had just come to the scene where he first kissed his wife-to-be when he became aware, through his 50 per cent slumber, that a lone rickshaw was rattling down CD Road. The two-stroke engine's tuk-tuk was reassuring in a city full of SUVs. The rickshaw stopped at the kerb nearby. The driver was going to sleep too, Hari thought.

That was when he heard rapid steps.

A foot thudded into his chest and reverberated rudely through the bones down to his paunch. Thrown off his chair, he toppled over and slammed into the waterlogged pavement with a mucky 'ka-zhoonck smashack!' Brain matter splattered all around ... or perhaps it was mud. Pain would most certainly be there, maybe cracks in the skull, too.

Opening his eyes, he saw, through tears of suffering, three towering men in dark clothes. Behind them was the auto-rickshaw. Balaclava masks covered their faces. According to the Do's and Don'ts posted inside the ATM booth, Rule #4 said: 'Don't wear a mask.' These thugs clearly hadn't read that one. Of course, Rule #1 said: 'Beware of thugs.'

This wasn't what he had expected of the night, but he was prepared to adjust. He analyzed the situation: if he got up and fought, and the camera captured his bravery, he'd get an increment or at least a citation. He might also get himself killed. Three against one gave him, what, 33 per cent odds for victory? Not too good. *Was this the divine test that he'd been waiting for?* He fumbled for his nightstick, but the big man stomped on his hand. It hurt.

'Boss, cool down,' he said to the big man. His ribs ached. 'No need to harm each other.'

Why couldn't people be reasonable? thought Hari as he saw the sandal approaching fast. He rolled over. The sandal touched his ear and then grazed the face, getting some nose and mouth that happened to be in the way. 'Dang!' He hit the pavement again. He twisted his body sideways, reeled around in the muck until the sandal lost touch with his body.

He got up halfway. But the big man was astonishingly fast and kicked Hari in the head, then in the gut and to complete the hat-trick he was about to stick his sandal up Hari's gastric system. Hari begged, 'No, not there ... I have indigestion already.'

A thinner man walked up to Hari. He made a slicing motion with two fingers across the throat. This was too much like a B-movie. He'd have to quickly rewrite the script if he wanted to stay alive.

'Okay, do what you must, but let's not become enemies by mistake,' suggested Hari, wondering whether to use the word 'please'. That word was uttered on CD Road only in extreme emergencies, usually before one got killed. The thin man held a finger to his lips, then he turned and sauntered across to the rickshaw.

Hari saw two of them lift a toolbox out of the vehicle and enter the ATM booth. The big one stayed with Hari, placing a sandal-clad foot on Hari's face. Hari took an executive decision. Other than hoping for the best, there was nothing to do but stay down and act scared.

'This is not going to be good for my career, boss.' The words were squeezed out from under the sandal's stiff sole that pressed down on his mouth, crumpling his moustache.

The two inside the booth pulled the metal shutter halfway down. Then the giant dragged Hari to where garbage had piled up in a corner of the construction site. Pits had been dug for the bank's foundation pillars and a vault. Was he going to get kicked to death now? A concrete mixer stood idle. Maybe they'd mix him into the concrete. He'd heard of such things.

A few days earlier, Hari had aerosol-sprayed one of his own mobile numbers on the plot's wall, and the words 'For Sale Contact', hoping to pull off a minor real estate scam. Now he lay under that 'For Sale' announcement and wondered who'd buy his services after this epic failure. His uncle had frequently pointed out how he tended to behave like a dog, with his tail between his legs, even though he wasn't a proper dog. But what was wrong with that? Hari liked dogs. He used to have a puppy that was half dog, half rat. They had been great friends until Underdog outgrew him and moved up the existential ladder. He had become a pet star of Kannada horror movies, where he often played a shaggy, rabid demon. Hari missed his merry companion at times like this.

Out of the corner of his eye, Hari saw the man tip up the plastic chair and plonk himself down on it. His uniform-like dark clothes, combined with the monkey cap that wouldn't be out of place on a watchman at this hour, ensured that no passer-by thought anything was amiss.

From his position, Hari wasn't able to make out what was going on inside the booth, but he guessed that they were disconnecting the machine in order to uproot it. That was how it was done. The free-standing money dispenser was bolted to the floor, nothing that stopped a determined thief for more than a few minutes. Unless somebody happened to be watching the closed-circuit camera feed with a finger on an alarm button, no one would know. All that would show up on the system was that the machine had gone offline and a repair crew would come whenever. Typically, during office hours.

There was a knock on the metal shutter and the massive man pushed the rickshaw soundlessly into position in front of the booth. He lifted off its black canvas hood in one swift move. It had already been unfastened. This operation was well planned, because the passenger seat was missing and the three carried out the cash dispenser, which now looked very small and unsafe, and stood it in the back of the vehicle. *There were hard ways and there were easy ways to make money*, thought Hari philosophically. At least it wasn't his money that was vanishing.

A tarpaulin was thrown over the ATM and the rickshaw's hood was put back in place. Then one of them came over, the thin B-filmy one, and he bent down to grab Hari's hand as if to shake it.

'No mention, boss. I prefer living to dying,' said Hari and sat up.

At that, the thin man put a pair of pliers around one of Hari's fingers, the nose-picking finger, and squeezed until the bone ached. He tilted his head as if to ask: *How does it feel?*

'It hurts,' said Hari and it struck him that there was something oddly familiar about this man. Who knows, maybe they both frequented the same cinemas and liked thriller comedies? One day, they might meet and have a laugh over this.

The thin man poked Hari in the chest.

'Yes, what about me?'

The man held up three fingers.

'You want to cut off so many? Wouldn't one be enough?'

He waved the fingers before Hari.

'Boss, I can count to three.'

Then he touched a finger to his wrist.

'Three o'clock?'

The man nodded and gave Hari a shove with the palm of his hand, pushing him back on the muddy ground.

'You want me to stay down until three o'clock? This is somewhat untoward, I'll lose my job for sure.'

The thin man gave the pliers another squeeze.

'Sooper. No problem, boss.' Hari winced and waggled his head sideways. 'All the very best and bye-bye.'

The robbers got into the front of the rickshaw. Two of them sat on either side of the driver, on a plank laid across the seat. As the rickshaw started with a roar and began to move its burden, Hari stretched his neck to catch a glimpse of the license plate. But the back of the vehicle had been covered with a poster in support of the ruling party. How clever, how meticulous.

Although he doubted that they'd come back to cut off his fingers, Hari pretended to black out. Sometimes watchmen were beaten to death, so he had been lucky. Yet he felt strangely low. He, who used to be a hero, had come to this. Sure enough, he had solved crimes – but the difficulty with heroism was that unless you performed daring deeds on a regular basis, you were out of the game. So, his wife was right in saying that yesterday's sun never shone on anybody.

2

> You must understand that what happens to you is part of an unfolding pattern – so avoid mixing personal and professional agendas.

He didn't get up at 3 a.m. There was nothing left to guard. At around 5 a.m., he started shivering from a muddy chill that had chewed its way into his bones and finally got up. Making it suitably theatrical, he held onto the trunk of a coconut tree. Some hundred yards down CD Road, the guard outside the next ATM was still asleep, wrapped in a blanket. A police car passed the traffic signal at the very end of the street on the way towards the railway station. Hari slammed his forehead against the coconut tree, again and again, until it occurred to him that a nut might fall and smash his skull.

But that was a minor problem. Right now, his job was in jeopardy. Sufficient bumps and bruising could save his neck.

He phoned Triplex. If the police pulled out call records, he'd clarify that he had simply dialled the Detective in Charge of Operations (DCO) at his own security company (and at his own expense) as a matter of procedure, to request backup – it was especially important to have somebody on his side when the cops showed up. However, Triplex didn't answer. Next, he tweeted, 'If you don't hear from me again in 24 hours, please start crowdfunding bail money.'

Then he made the call to the police control room. This sort of theft was pretty much a routine occurrence in a town with thousands of ATMs. When the yawning policeman picked up, Hari said, '*Swalpa* untoward mishap *agidey*.' He then uploaded what had transpired. A brief questioning followed. They'd do the needful.

After that, Hari contacted the bank's security division. If they had foresight there'd be a GPS tracking device inside the machine, but it was more likely that they had cut costs. Hiring a watchman was cheaper and he could always be made the scapegoat if something bad happened. He was told to stay put.

He crossed the street and relieved himself against a wall. All of a sudden, he was hit in the neck. *Had the robbers come back to cut off his fingers?*

A walking stick prodded him on the cheek. He turned to face an elderly gent clad in immaculate white shirt and polyester trousers. He thundered, 'Rascal, what is your purpose committing nuisance here? Can't you see this is not a urinal?'

Hari was about to say to his defence that the city had no more than 578 public toilets spread across an urban area of 800 square kilometres. And out of those, at any given time 29 per cent were out of order. Some of them existed only on paper due to absconding contractors. But then he noticed that the uncle was walking a monster of a dog. It growled. Hari was an expert on dog language and it was the kind of this-is-my-territory growl that meant it would gladly chew up his offending body parts, so he didn't argue. 'Sorry sir, shall pay the hundred rupees fine next time I meet a policeman.'

'You are a disgrace to your uniform. I shall have to report this.'

'Yes, sir.' Hari wiped his hands on his mud-spattered jacket and gave the uncle a visiting card with the detective bureau numbers (which were his mobile numbers). 'Please call in any complaint and disciplinary measures will be taken against me. If there is any other criminal case you need solved, please contact my boss.'

The uncle wasn't satisfied. 'You're dirty.'

'How do you mean?'

'Your uniform, it is dirty.'

'I hear you loud and clear, sir, and I'll have it dry-cleaned ASAP.'

'What are you saying, "ass up"? Using filthy language, too.'

'Sorry, I meant *as soon as possible*. A-S-A-P.'

'Speak properly or shut your mouth, rascal.'

Hari walked back to his post, tightening his loincloth. When he glanced back to check if the uncle had unleashed the monster after him, he saw it do 'number 1' against the same wall. To give it the benefit of the doubt, he supposed that the leaky dog suffered from some prostate disorder. It was a curiously unknown fact that although the city was home to no more than 173 registered pet dogs, over three lakh strays lived in its streets. *That's what,* Hari contemplated, *there's room for dogs in this world, but not for a struggling hero.*

The policemen arrived on an overloaded Cheetah motorcycle.

Hari knew the older one of the cops fairly well. Ropu had hairy earlobes and had worked at the K. G. Circle Police Station since time immemorial, and he used to be friends with Hari's uncle. Ropu was okay, never beat up suspects. The one who drove the Enfield was called Danger Ramboswamy: he was young, well-fed and looked like he didn't mind doling out whacks with his bamboo lathi to prove a point. The two policemen walked about on the crime scene, inspecting this and that, poking at things. Ropu observed, 'There's no ATM in the ATM.'

'It seems to have been stolen,' added Ramboswamy with an eye in Hari's direction.

As it turned out, the closed-circuit camera's lens had been covered with black tape – the kind that electricians used – and with that trick the system had been outsmarted, which meant that Hari was the only witness. The bigger question was whether anybody would believe him.

About half an hour later, a bank official got there to assess the damage. He was some kind of expert whom Hari hadn't met before in the course of his relations with the bank. He introduced himself politely as 'Solid Kuroopanna, fullest security level clearance'. But everything about him belied his veneer of politeness. He had small, cunning eyes and it was barely possible to make out the pupils. The whites had an unhealthy orange tint. There was a bright knife scar running from his ear to his mouth. He wore a synthetic off-white safari suit that had a concealed holster sewn into it, with a large-bored sidearm that jutted out conspicuously through the cloth. Kuroopanna studied the bolt holes in the floor, where the cash dispenser had stood, and said, 'If I may ask, what do you see as your duty?'

'To do my duty and you can quote me on that, sir.'

Kuroopanna glanced at Hari doubtfully. Hari saluted him.

'And do you feel that is what you have done?'

'More or less, sir.'

'How hard did you try to stop them from uprooting the ATM?'

'A little hard, sir. But they kicked me unconscious.' He moaned and pressed one palm to his bruised face.

'What you mean to say is, you were taking an eye-shut and were caught off guard?'

Hari thought it best to offer no comment.

'Don't be shy to admit it. It is understandable that you get sleepy at night.'

'It was dark also, sir.'

'You must be knowing something about this.'

'What would that be?'

'Since *you let* them rob *our* bank.' Not unexpectedly, Kuroopanna had a pet theory. After robberies, security guards sometimes got blamed, so Hari knew that by default he himself was going to be a primary suspect for the rest of his natural lifetime unless other potential perpetrators emerged out of the sewers. 'These men, were any of them familiar to you?'

The thin B-filmy man had something about him that rang a bell, as if he belonged in the CD Road area, but before Hari could frame an appropriate answer, the gent with the monster dog came past on his brisk morning walk.

Respectability oozed from him as compared to Hari, whose uniform was dirty, and he ranted, 'Constable, good you caught him!'

'Well, we haven't exactly ...,' said Ropu.

'He's the one who did it!'

'Did what?' asked Danger Ramboswamy.

'Yes, arrest the rascal.'

Hari sighed. This wasn't going well.

'For what purpose should he be arrested?' Ropu wanted to know.

'I saw him do it and to that I shall testify in court, even if his rascal chums try to silence me.'

'You saw him steal the ATM?' Kuroopanna interjected with a leading question.

The gent brandished his walking stick at Hari. 'No, the rascal committed nuisance in a public place.'

'What are you saying?' said Kuroopanna.

'That he took a piss,' clarified Ropu.

'Constable Ropu,' said Kuroopanna, 'it is best that this Hari Majestic character is taken into custody until the case is shut.'

'Chill-u, he's known to the boss. He's one of her informers.' Ropu spat out reddish paan juice on the pavement at the same time as he said the word *informers*. 'Let him go to the police station and make clarifications to clear his name.'

Kuroopanna suggested that Hari at least ought to take unpaid leave.

'Until when?' asked Hari.

'Until the investigation is over.'

'Sir, can I help with that?' said Hari.

'With what?'

'Solving this case. I'm a professional detective.' As Hari saw it, this might be a perfect opportunity to prove himself a hero.

'We'll call you.'

'Fine then, sir. Wish you speedy recovery of the ATM machine. All the very best, and bye-bye.'

Relieved, Hari thought that it could have ended on a worse note and in a best-case scenario he ought to survive this too. He walked to the police station around the corner, near K. G. Circle. Now he only had to play his cards right.

One random driver, busy violating a red light, attempted to mow him down at the zebra crossing. Hari jumped out of the way of the SUV and took shelter behind a big board erected in front of the police station: 'The Best Car Safety Device is a Rear-View Mirror with a Cop in It.' Indeed, it was a good omen that he hadn't been run over. First positive thing to happen in a long time.

He knew Sub-Inspector Pushpa well. As one of her long-standing collaborators, he had helped her crack many cases. Pushpa Aunty was the one who had certified him as a non-offender when he applied for the guard job in the first place. They pretended that none of them remembered that he, as a juvenile delinquent, had often been invited to the police station. But he was always acquitted. Back then his uncle had not yet lost his license to practise law and so Hari's rap-sheet was ambiguous.

She was a good cop too, and her moustache was enviably thicker than Hari's upper lip fluff. She was hard at work around the clock for she didn't believe that crime should pay (and ever since her husband had left her to become a cave-dwelling philosopher in the Himalayas, she didn't need to go home to cook). Her strong views intimidated Hari into trying to become a better human. Their special relationship was one of give and take, so he expected her to help him get off the hook this time too.

The metal detector at the entrance beeped lazily as Hari walked in. It was the steel rod in his right leg, which had once been broken in a ruckus involving antisocials. Everybody knew about his steel leg. Nobody frisked him. A few policemen napped on the rows of plastic chairs in the duty room. Antisocials did their antisocialism at night, commencing at around 11:30 p.m., after the bars shut. Technically speaking, that was when the police had to stay alert and remain so until the first back-alley dives raised their shutters at 8 a.m., but evidently that wasn't enough to stop ATMs from being stolen. Thanks to his lawyer uncle, Hari understood the judicial ecosystem – if one may call it that – that comprised law and crime. Crime was needed, as much as law was. No crime, and the police, advocates, judges, detectives, watchmen and sundry bank officials with full security clearances were going to be unemployed. An ATM heist was just another step in the obvious direction.

The duty room's walls were decorated with updated rowdy-sheets and snaps of noted offenders (the so-called history-sheeters) and their achievements during the past twelve months in the city: 2,727 cheating cases, 594 robberies, 212 murders out of which only 9 for gain, 35 cases of dacoity, 321 molestations, 63 rapes and 48 dowry deaths. The portrait of one notorious rowdy, Jai Kallanige, was encircled in red – his ominous alias was RIP alias Ripper Rowdy. Hari felt that the name sounded familiar and by a curious coincidence, his face (twisted hair, bloodshot eyes) resembled the driver of the SUV that had almost killed him in front of the police station. Hari made a mental note to keep an eye out for the SUV and collect tip-off money.

Pushpa was busy. Photographs were spread out on her desk. The report appeared to be a technical description of some kind of aluminium cylinder. Since when had she started taking interest in machinery?

'Good morning, Inspector-Aunty,' he greeted her. In his contacts with higher ups, whether gods or humans, Hari believed in starting on an upbeat note. So he stretched his smile until it covered the lower portion of his face like a wall-to-wall carpet as he enquired whether she had enjoyed her morning coffee already. 'Coffee *aayita*?'

'And you Hari, what about you – had your Chyawanprash? You must shape up, okay. Look at you, covered in shit, your face one big bruise. I'm sorry but I don't think you've remembered to take your Chyawanprash regularly.'

'I surely have. As a detective, one has to stay fit for fight.' He rolled his head, as if to claim that he ate healthy food supplements regularly. 'But sometimes things don't go according to plan.'

'So, what's that plan then, tell me?' She adjusted her peaked cap. 'I hear you got robbed?'

'Yes Aunty, but I'll fix it. No tension.' Then he gave his deposition again, anticipating the pertinent questions and describing kick by kick what happened, and for emphasis he showed her the bruises on his ribs and gut. He spread his hands wide, palms facing out, ready to be searched there and then – in case the sub-inspector had any suspicions that he may have pocketed the ATM.

The testimony was being typed up by Pushpa's secretary, Miss Ganakayantra. She was cute in her khaki sari, but Hari was a faithful husband and so he finished with a flourish, 'I sincerely do hope that this purely accidental happenstance will not irritate Aunty's bowel syndrome more than necessary.'

Ganakayantra did not take down that last line. That he wasn't handcuffed upon ending his monologue was undoubtedly auspicious, but then Pushpa asked, 'Did you forget to mention something?'

'What thing?'

'Ropu and Ramboswamy called and said that a witness stepped forward to cast doubts on your moral fibre.'

'He was some senile geriatric.'

'But his statement places you at the scene of the crime, acting in an antisocial manner. A prosecutor can use that against you.'

'I was hired to guard that ATM! Where else was I supposed to be? Aunty, am I in trouble?'

'What would you be charged with?' Pushpa asked. 'Pissing against a wall?'

Miss Ganakayantra blushed.

'For having lost that thing,' he said. 'It must have been full of cash.'

'Unless further evidence points in your direction, I doubt. But it is regrettable, this whole business, okay,' Pushpa added. Hari was sorry too and waggled his head. 'We have an estimate from the bank that the uprooted ATM contained over ten lakhs. It'll reflect badly on our crime statistics, nah.' She nodded sideways at the khaki-coloured wall.

'That is such a pity.'

'So how were they armed?'

'As in?'

'What weapons did they threaten you with?'

Hari made a pistol out of his hand, index and forefingers erect.

'A handgun?'

He moved the make-believe pistol to his throat and showed a slashing motion. 'No, scary move like this only. I took it that they might have a pistol or at least a machete.'

She stared at him 200 per cent hard. 'But you didn't actually see a weapon?'

'Not exactly, Inspector Aunty.'

'So they were fully unarmed?'

'Partly, at least. There were also three of them against me, a single hero. One of them carried a pair of pliers.'

'You're making this up?' She knitted her brow.

'No, Aunty. Now that you've jogged my memory, they must have used them to cut the ATM cables.' He wiggled the appropriate finger. 'Then they threatened to cut off this one.'

'Why?'

'Maybe because it is my nose picker?'

'They said that?'

'No, they didn't exactly say so. I never speak with criminals.'

'What else can you tell me about them?'

'One of them was big. Like a steamroller.'

'And the others?' She tugged at her earlobe, ostensibly in contemplation.

Hari wasn't sure if it meant that she smelled a rat, but he upped his ante. It was important to give the correct impression. He cranked up his smile a thousand watts and made motions that conveyed honesty, palms facing upward accompanied by a slow sideways headroll which made his skull rotate two or three times around. 'They wore masks. And didn't speak. Strange people, can't have been Indians.'

'What nonsense are you talking?'

'Must have been foreigners.'

'What makes you think that?'

'I saw their hands, remember?' Hari tried to act cool as cucumber raita. 'Looked like the foreign hand.'

'Weren't they wearing gloves?'

'Yes, Aunty.'

'Then what are you saying?'

'I think the gloves were not made in India.'

'How can you tell?'

'They were of cow hide. Also, they would have asked if I was married and how many children I have, and which school they go to in case I might be able to help them get their kids admitted into the same school. They were totally un-Indian and not very talkative.'

She cleared her throat as if to demonstrate how unimpressed she was. 'What about other identifying marks, like hairstyles?'

Hari recalled the murderous SUV driver from moments ago and debated with himself whether to lay out a smokescreen by picking him out from among the watch-out notices on the wall, but decided against it. He pretended to think. 'One of them may have had a lunatic fringe.'

Pushpa stared into the ceiling and appeared to pray, or at least Hari heard her utter the words 'oh god', and then she turned to her bulky computer. 'Okay, we'll analyze the surveillance videos. There's another issue. Minor, but we still must go over it, okay. The cash dispenser was disconnected at 2.13 a.m. but your call was logged at closer to 6 a.m. That's a four-hour delay. Any explanations or voluntary statements you wish to make?'

'I got dizzy from all the kicking.' He twiddled his moustaches. 'Hence, I was unconscious due to the *habeas corpus* beating and if I may say so, it is *suo moto* unfortunate that the bank doesn't have an automatic alarm for when ATMs go offline.'

His ex-lawyer uncle had taught him the correct legal words for each situation. Pushpa nevertheless regretted the situation Hari next found himself in: a caning by Constable Danger Ramboswamy in a back room was required to complete the interrogation. Hari knew the routine: hike up the loincloth and clench the buttocks tightly. It hurt, but he had been through worse. According to *Deccan Herald*, custodial death had become uncommon in the city off late so there was nothing to worry about. He was told to confess, but since he hadn't anything to confess to, Ramboswamy soon lost interest and stopped wasting energy on Hari.

After the formalities had been taken care of, Pushpa asked, 'You okay? Can't offer you any ice pack, we have no fridge. But how about coffee?' Her tone was friendlier now that Miss Ganakayantra wasn't recording the conversation.

'That'd be mighty nice, Aunty. The lathi charge was anyhow really very mild.' He smiled with all teeth showing. It did hurt when he smiled.

'I'm glad and let's hope this will not become a bad habit for you, okay.'

'Which one?'

'This one. So tell me.'

'What to tell, Inspector Aunty?'

'How is Diamond? Any good news?'

'We'd love to have a son, but can't afford. Supposing it turned out to be another daughter, you know, Aunty.'

As soon as the locality's coffeewallah, Coffee-Anand, plonked down steel tumblers with piping hot coffee before them and left to continue his rounds, she returned to the subject of the ATM. 'If you think you recognize any of them, you'd inform, okay?'

'I always do my duty to protect the laws of the land, Aunty, and will remain vigilant. What about CCTV images?'

'Just reviewed them. There's a few seconds of pictures from inside the booth. We see two masked men entering and immediately disabling the camera with black tape.'

'That is so mean of them. What's your official theory?'

'We're assuming that the thieves did this intentionally, so that the camera could not record the incident.' Scowling, Pushpa poured coffee from the tumbler into the saucer and back into the tumbler to raise froth.

'Oho, is that so?'

'In the available images they wear gloves, like you said. I don't think we'll get fingerprints.'

'So no leads?'

'There's a wide-angle camera outside a bar diagonally opposite and it captures the ATM from afar. Can't make out the registration plates of the rickshaw,' she said and fiddled with the mouse to her computer to rewind the security video clip, 'but the images bear out, ehrm, your version of events, okay.'

Hari nodded vigorously. Then she added, 'However, you seem to be napping when they attack you. And once you do wake up in the morning, it looks to me as if you're smashing your head against a coconut tree. Repeatedly.'

'Ayooh, I had eaten a hearty morsel. Missus uses a lot of oil in her cooking. Due to unfortunate circumstances, I got a bit woozy and stumbled into the tree. I'm sorry.'

'I'm sorry, too, that we shall be forced to book a case against you for violating the ATM security instructions issued by the Police Commissioner.'

'Right-u.' He had more or less anticipated that.

'There is also another circumstance.'

Hari felt the sweat build up under his scalp. 'Yes, Aunty?'

'Before they decamp, one of the suspects appears to bend down by your side and speak with you.'

'Is that so?' He feigned surprise.

'As I recall you said that you fainted, nah.' Her eyes narrowed as if she was X-raying Hari's brain.

But he'd been in the hot chair before. 'Maybe checking if I needed an ambulance?'

'Should I believe that? If it turns out you had anything whatsoever to do with these miscreants, maybe if you happened to meet them in a bar and plant stupid ideas …' She paused for effect.

'I stopped drinking after I got married.'

'If you're lying, your next seven years will be spent looking for your brain up your this one.'

'Which one?'

'That one.'

'Oho, I'm sure this one will not be in that one. I was in *de facto* coma at the time.' He stuck to his alibi, flimsy though it was.

'Well then.'

'I'll take your leave, Aunty.'

'One more thing before you go.'

'Yes, Aunty?'

'I expect that within twenty-four hours, you will surrender the certificate I had issued when you applied for the guard job.'

'Is that fully necessary?'

She was referring to a form with the round seal of the police station and the following text:

TO WHOMSOEVER IT MAY CONCERN. This is to Certify that Sh./~~Smt.~~ HARI MAJESTIC S/o, ~~D/o, W/o~~, Uncle

ONTAPPA KALLAPPA MENSINKAI alias 'OK Mamool' & ex-HEAD NURSE KOLAVERI alias 'Didi' who has reported that he/~~she~~ is residing at Puncherwallah Complex Chamber 101, CD Road (1st Floor), Bengaluru-560009 is not involved in any criminal offence as per the records of PS K. G. Circle in which area the above stated residence is located.

It was signed by her.

'It is a temporary measure, okay. Once the culprits are brought to book, you'll get it back. But at this stage, you cannot keep it with you as you are involved in a criminal offence.'

'Even if I'm only a victim? I'll never get another watchman job. And my wife will get so disappointed.'

'There are circumstances. If that certificate ends up in the hands of some editor at *Hottu-Hottu*, my next posting will be hunting Naxalites in Agumbe Rural District.'

'I'll think about it.' He'd make a colour xerox of the certificate before handing it in. Because losing it meant that his hero career was over. He changed the subject, 'According to Wikitravel, there are many rare insects in the Agumbe jungles.'

She stared at him for a beat or two. 'There is nothing to think about, okay. Hand it over or I'll have your name formally added to the rowdy-sheets.'

It irked that people like him were always considered guilty until proven otherwise. He'd heard that it was the other way around in foreign countries. One day he'd travel to such a country. Or so he hoped. 'When can I expect to get my good name cleared, Aunty?'

'We'll shall conduct further investigation into the matter and do the needful,' she dismissed him.

He salaamed her, impressed by how she managed to look into matters without leaving her desk. That was the difference between the police and gumshoes. He was doomed to walk these mean streets, on which he had grown up as an urchin and had made a living as a tout. He sauntered out past the poster that said: 'Prepare & Prevent, don't Repair & Repent.' So true, he thought and wondered whether to tweet something like: 'All is well that ends well if you ask me.' But it hadn't ended well; in fact, his troubles had barely begun.

3

You are keen on making up for time lost to lethargy and speak up to defend your laxity, but don't rock the boat.

The next problem: what was he going to say to his wife about having let an ATM get stolen? Losing a million of your employer's money was no small matter.

Best to postpone the inevitable until it became totally inevitable, so instead of going home for breakfast he took a left turn up CD Road. He passed an impressive beggar who had no arms, no legs, and, pretty amazingly, also no head. Hari did a double-take and gave the beggar a ₹5 coin in appreciation of his theatrical skills. A police-issued banner next to the headless beggar read, 'To Avoid "Hell-Met", Always Wear Helmet.'

Then he called Triplex again. Finally, there was an answer. 'What man?'

'You didn't pick up earlier.'

'I'm asleep.'

'Drink your coffee and get to office.'

'Why?'

'There's a mandatory staff meeting.'

'What does it mean?'

'Which?'

'Mandatory. It is a funny word.'

'It means that you should be there when you're not there. We have a detective bureau to run.'

'But I'm sleeping, man.'

'We've got work to do.'

'Majestic, don't start. I had a long night.'

'Doing what?'

'The usual … downloading hot item numbers.' Hari's best friend Triplex was a dreamer. His real name was Neel Yeenappa, but he was known as Triplex due to his fondness for triple-X movies. He'd been pirating ever since he was a toddler when his father concealed a video camera in his diaper and took him to those Ingmar Bergman movies that had Westerners showing their naked body parts. Currently, his grand vision was to create the thirteenth-most visited website on the Internet now that US federal prosecutors had closed down Megaupload.com, which had earlier held the position. At the time it was busted, the German-owned, Hong Kong-based filesharing website had accumulated assets worth $300,000,000 which made Triplex see his future in an entirely new light. But getting millions of video pirates to download from one's site wasn't an easy act to follow. Anyhow, Triplex was a believer who hoped for rain-free monsoons and to him it was unthinkable that global warming one day was going to turn Bengaluru's ten million inhabitants into mutton ghee roast. 'I've bought a 25TB hard disk and been thinking …'

'Thinking what?'

'I'm not as good as you in maths but don't you agree that a year's production of Indian cinema should fit on it and if I put it online under my brand Video King, I would have at least a billion takers in India, Russia, China, Birmingham and New Jersey, right? It's about having the correct focus, you often say. What's up with you, man?'

'Will tell you when you get to office. Better be there in five nanoseconds.' Hari knew that Triplex had a flexible concept of time, so if they agreed on five nanoseconds, then Triplex would be there in five hours.

'I don't understand. I must be dreaming,' said Triplex and disconnected the call.

Next, he called AC Gaadi, who was waiting for passengers to fleece at the Krantivira Sangoli Rayanna Railway Station's Pre-Paid Auto Stand, offering tourists an improved Pre-Paid rate, namely double meter. He was the toughie on the bureau's staff and loved to be in the middle of any crisis situation, so he was on his way before Hari hung up. Finally, Hari stepped into Doc's cybercafé, which was a few doors down from the detective bureau on the first floor of Puncherwallah Complex.

As everybody knew, CD Road used to be a somewhat disreputable street full of petty crooks, conmen, rowdies and bars, but in tune with the new economy it had gotten gentrified – only parts of the street were recognizable from Hari's childhood. Due to its proximity to the railway and main bus stations, CD Road was becoming prime property for hotels, restaurants and shopping complexes. One of the last old buildings, Puncherwallah Complex housed a news stall, a garage and pre-used vehicle dealer on the ground floor – which had recently become an 'Auto Spa' in keeping with the times – and upstairs there were a Kerala-style mess, an astrologer's ashram, the cybercafé and then the famous detective bureau, Diamond & Majestic Investigations Pvt Ltd.

Doc was the bureau's technical officer. He was a cheerful man, as if nothing bad ever happened. He wasn't a medical doctor, but wore a lab coat with five ballpoint pens in the front pocket as he tinkered with his rickety computers. He also had a magnifier lens attached to a band strapped around his head. He said, 'Hey Majestic, had breakfast? Movement's good?'

'No and no.'

Doc constantly dreamt of inventing the next big thing, some amazing software or at least an app that controlled bowel movements via Bluetooth. But the problem was that no matter what he thought of – like FaceTube or Youbook or PayApp – it always seemed as if somebody else had already invented something identical. Hari was the only one who took him seriously, because he believed in the value of having dreams.

'What happened?'

'I've been too caught up at the police station.'

'Doesn't sound nice.' Noticing that Hari's face was covered in nasty bruises, Doc took out a white metal cylinder from his desk drawer as if to cheer him up. 'Know what this is?'

He handed the cylinder to Hari who turned it over in his hands. It was heavy, maybe five kilos.

'An LPG cylinder for a micro-mini darshini?' Hari guessed.

'Try again.'

'A piece of junk?'

'It is the latest hoax.'

'Oho.' Hari felt foolish. He should have known.

'Your sub-inspector friend came to me to have it analyzed yesterday,' Doc said with obvious pride. 'Sending it to a forensics lab takes months. I opened it here on my very own desk and wrote her a report.'

'So, what is it?'

'She's retrieved a couple, so we can keep this one as a souvenir because I gave her the report for free. Someone is peddling these things claiming that they contain red mercury.'

What he meant was that this was another job done by Hari's staff that didn't bring in any cash. Hari recalled that Pushpa had been studying some technical documents when he stepped into the police station. 'And what's that supposed to be good for?'

'Not good, it's bad.'

'How bad?'

'They say it can be used to build an atomic bomb.'

Hari handed him back the cylinder.

'Don't take tension, Majestic.'

Doc had no clue about how much tension Hari was taking already.

'It turned out there's no radiation, it's a regular cylindrical block of aluminium worth about a grand.'

'So not a bomb, is that what you're saying?'

'What I'm saying is that antisocials are paying good money for these.'

'Why'd they do that?'

'The usual terrorists who want to blow up the social fabric of our society.'

'But you said it doesn't work?'

'That's the beauty of it. What a way to make a quick buck, no? Take scrap aluminium, sell it as make-believe bombs to terrorists who can't go to the police and complain. Perfect, no?'

Hari's skin prickled. He ought to have come up with this scam. That is to say, back in the days when he did scams. 'How does it work then if the thing itself doesn't work?'

'Works on the basis that terrorists are fools like anybody else and this sample is given so that they can have it lab-tested, but first they cough up a deposit, right, Majestic?'

'Correct, but why'd they part with any money at all?'

'Because if it was red mercury, it'd be expensive. So a couple of lakhs sounds cheap. And once the conman gets his money, he takes off – right? No need to wait for any negative lab reports.'

Hari felt really behind the times. His con years were truly over. 'And so the police haven't caught the conmen?'

'They're on the lookout, waiting for a tip-off. And that would be from us, perhaps? Seen such a cylinder before? I'm sure there'll be a reward if we catch them.'

'I'll do the needful.' Hari was familiar with police work: people like him risked their necks collecting information and in the best case, he got a cup of coffee, a samosa and fifty bucks. He didn't tell Doc that the detective bureau was about to shut down, but asked him to come for the staff meeting.

All the other customers at the cybercafé wore headsets and skyped with foreign girls or played Counter-Strike all day. Hari used it as his extended office, took five minutes of Internet credit, checked his emails – nothing except Viagra offers – and memorized the English word for the day from the online verbosity course he was taking: *claustrophobia*.

If he were to take a wild guess, he'd have supposed it to be a disease that Christians got, something rabidly contagious that Santa Claus was the carrier of and related to too much Christmas shopping. But it turned out to mean 'fear of being in a small space that seems difficult to get out of or an uncomfortable feeling that you do not have enough freedom', and although he knew that the Internet wasn't targeting him per se, it sounded too much like his horoscope for the day.

Logging off, he walked along the upper veranda to his office. It was a microscopic chamber that Hari had inherited from his uncle, with enough room for a desk, a shelf and a cot. One wall was covered with stacks of boxes containing armpit fans, further diminishing the available space. Above the director's seat – a foldable metal chair which Hari had the honour of occupying – hung a garlanded portrait of Uncle OK alias Mamool, real identity Ontappa Kallappa Mensinkai. Whenever there was trouble, Hari sought inspiration from his memory. Uncle had been indestructible.

Well, almost. Hari lit an incense stick and wedged it into the frame of the portrait. He wiped a tear from the corner of his eye. He couldn't remember having cried ever before. Then again, he had a selective memory.

As he counted his assets, he found that he owned one aluminium cylinder and many boxes full of worthless armpit fans. Life, if one were to take a macro-perspective, amounted to more loss than gain. The monies that he had earned as rewards for his earlier heroics had been invested by his late uncle in a scheme to manufacture miniature fans to strap under armpits. The idea was to put up stalls at sightseeing spots. But it turned out the fan blades got tangled up in the hairs of anybody who didn't shave their armpits. So when uncle died, Hari was left with two thousand armpit fans that nobody wanted and had to take up the guard job to pay off debts. When he looked at the stacks of boxes, it appeared as if they had multiplied. Now he had the right word for it: claustrophobia.

The difference between armpit fans and the fake radioactivity scam was how creative the latter was – selling crap that didn't require big investments. *How unbelievable*, he thought, *the innovative methods used these days to cheat people!* It was one of those glimpses of self-awareness that he hated. His desk was overlooked by framed pictures of gods, saints and film heroes, and as Hari sat down, he felt oppressed. These were illustrious people, the greatest of men – why couldn't he be one of them?

Hari smiled twice as much as normal to create a pleasant vibe when his colleagues loitered in. Getting pinkslipped was never fun, but now that he had lost his non-offender certificate, the question was how he was going to keep things together.

Of course, not all came. There was one missing person. For various reasons, the deputy director, Diamond Majestic alias 'Hari's better half', hadn't been summoned. After the previous day's argument, he knew that certain information was to be shared on a need-to-know basis.

The rest turned up to a man. Doc was as punctual as a robot. Gaadi too, turned up, and with his customary breakfast, two 650ml bottles of Knockout super-strong beer. As was his habit, Triplex came when he came to. He was a child of nature and therefore totally out of control. He preferred to sleep until afternoon unless there was a reason not to. Such as the end of the world, which it might well be worth taking a selfie before. In stark contrast to Hari's muddy uniform, he wore flashy silvery pants, white cowboy boots which managed to remain shockingly clean despite his daily (or nightly) roaming on CD Road, and a T-shirt which stated, in surprisingly correct English, 'If you have an opinion about me raise a hand.' He was a walking selfie and only his own image mattered to him.

As usual, Doc had an opinion and lectured the latecomer. 'Early bird catches the worm.'

It was probably some foreign phrase he had heard and tried to impress the others with.

'What man?'

'And eats it too.'

'Yuck. I'd rather stay in bed all day than eat maggots,' said Triplex.

'Doesn't matter if we're *on time or not*,' Hari broke in, 'because we're going to be *late*.' He used the English words for emphasis.

'As in dead?' said Doc.

'Something more or less exactly like that.'

'If that's the good news, then what is the bad news?' Triplex wanted to know.

'When are we supposed to die?' Gaadi asked.

None of them sounded surprised, more as if they were curious to know which of their or Hari's misdeeds had caught up with them. They exchanged looks full of meaning.

Hari knew that Triplex got easily bored since he had the attention span of a cockroach, so he made it graphic and narrated the saddest story ever told as he downloaded the infodumps behind the various bruises on his face and body. So that they'd accept it when they got fired for 'dereliction of duty' – he repeated the English phrase a few times. If they had been by his side when he needed them, the ATM may not have been stolen and hence this was largely their fault. His plan was for the speech to end with a reprimand. But true to character, Triplex yawned, prompting Hari to wrap up his endless tale of woes.

'... and that's how the tragedy ends and begins.'

'Why don't we offer to track down the ATM against a handsome cash reward? Say, one tenth of ten lakhs, you people are the brains here, how much will that make?' asked Triplex of Hari and Doc.

'One lakh,' said Hari.

'Not bad.'

'So we get twenty-five thousand per head and an additional couple of thousand in early bird discount if we find it today itself,' added Doc.

'Bonus, you mean,' corrected Hari. He scrutinized his colleagues, semi-reformed except for Gaadi who was unshakeable in his belief that a riot now and then did the city good by weeding out the weak links. Hari took care to remain diplomatic. 'We can always hope for the best, but we should be prepared for the worst.'

'Wishing will get you nowhere. We must prepare for war or die,' muttered Gaadi, and opened a beer to clear his thoughts. 'But swami, why should all of us get fired because one made a fool out of himself?' Acting the agent provocateur as usual, he then turned to Triplex. 'Besides, if they have fired us, what are the chances they'll hire us again?'

'Mistakes are proof that you are trying,' said Triplex. Like Hari, he believed in his heart of hearts that he too was born to be a hero.

'That's the spirit. You're an *optimist*, hence I'm happy for your sake,' said Hari.

'But I don't wear spectacles,' Triplex interrupted coquettishly.

'That's an *optician* you're thinking of. On the other hand, *optimist* means that you believe good things can happen to people like us and not only those living in Indiranagar or Koramangala,' said Hari who at every opportunity tried to teach his semi-incorrigible friends new wisdom. 'But that doesn't help.'

'What do you mean?'

Hari added a clarification, 'We're sunk.'

The three of them shrugged, grins were exchanged. To them this was no different from any other day. Triplex pushed down a hand in his pants and scratched himself. Gaadi burped. Doc adjusted the time on his wristwatch and, out of the blue, said, 'Happy birthday.'

'What-what?' said Hari.

'We've been concerned about you for a long time.'

'We are your friends, swami,' added Gaadi, offering Hari a bottle of Knockout. 'And we thought you needed a hand.'

'To do what?' said Hari, not quite 150 per cent on board, waving away the bottle. 'The reason I don't take alcohol is, as you know, due to the medical lack of a complete liver. Anyway, what's going on?'

'We're celebrating your birthday,' said Triplex.

'Boss, it's not today.'

'Doesn't matter,' Doc explained. 'You've been acting gloomy. So we decided we needed a cause to celebrate. Birthdays are fun days.'

'This is hardly the time to party,' said Hari. Although he appreciated their faithful friendship, he needed them to grasp the severity of the situation.

'Don't you want your gift?' said Triplex.

Hari felt touched by his second-in-command's words. He had never received a birthday gift before. 'What gift?'

Triplex pointed at the stacked-up boxes with armpit fans.

Hari stared at Gaadi and Doc. 'Is he joking?'

They too pointed in the same direction.

Hari double-checked and it did seem that the pile of boxes had grown. *Had they got him more fans as a birthday gift?* Hari got up and removed some boxes, until he saw something hidden behind them.

Then a light bulb started flashing inside his skull. First only 30 watts, then it was 100 watts and his eyes felt hot and dry from the heat. It was an ATM machine. For a moment, he doubted his own senses. Then he became aware of the merriment behind his back. His three best friends were chanting, in English, *'For he's a bloody good fellow …'*

It was as if two IEDs had been implanted in his armpits, exploding roughly at the same time and blowing the mushroom clouds upwards. What he saw was undoubtedly the same cash dispenser that had been stolen last night on his watch. He slapped himself on both cheeks. He made calculations. A couple of weeks back Triplex had spoken randomly about robbing the ATM, or so Hari had thought, dismissing the plan. The plot thickened like tomato soup with too much corn flour and too many Andhra chillies, but no croutons.

'So a very merry birthday to you,' said Doc. 'You can stop complaining about not having money to pay us salaries and you can afford to have as many kids as your wife wants to.'

Hari glared at Doc. His arguments were absolutely rational. But the outcome was totally crazy.

'You've become fully insane!' He guessed what his wife was going to think. Above all, he knew for sure that Sub-Inspector Pushpa would take him into the backroom of the police station and make him dig his brain out via colonoscopy.

'One doubt, Majestic: why are you not happy?' said Doc.

'You all should have been thinking before you did anything idiotic,' Hari shot back. 'The cops are going to stick my head into my bum.'

'We were basically thinking,' said Triplex matter-of-factly, 'that the bank treats you like a slave, but doesn't pay you enough. We simply helped you get even.'

'I can't believe it!'

'Don't you see, Majestic, this is what you deserve,' Doc added.

'You are madmen.'

Despite his academic style, Doc had problems when people called him mad because his native place was the village of Moira in Goa, known for its extra big bananas and for its eccentric inhabitants frequently going bananas. He appeared embarrassed, and somewhat distanced himself from the crime. 'But what has Triplex done wrong this time? He planned this for you and we're all trying to help out.'

Laughing, Triplex shaped his hand into a pistol and waved it at Hari. 'And you, hero number one, you looked so scared when you were on the ground.'

'No, I was acting.' Hari turned to Gaadi. 'And why'd you have to kick me in the face during the heist?'

AC Gaadi's features hardened and he gave Hari a penetrating look as if one of them had turned into an idiot. 'I too was only acting.'

'But so hard!'

'Beg your sorry, swami,' said Gaadi, who was busy lighting a bidi. Out of health concerns, he limited his smoking. Rule of thumb was to have a smoke after every beer. That's why he started the day with a few bottles.

Triplex patiently explained, 'It had to look real or you'd have gotten arrested. And that would have been bad, no? So I told Gaadi to do it properly.'

'With a dirty chappal … in the face!'

'Yeah, all right swami, you need to toughen up or I'll kick you again right now if you don't start talking in plain Kannada. You always complain you don't have cash and so now it is time to stop whining. I don't want to make it personal but you owe me three years' salary and I have about seventy-five thousand pending parking tickets to pay.'

'Don't exaggerate, the police didn't issue more than 74,233 traffic fines during the last one year,' said Hari, who knew his facts.

'You're calling me a liar? Want me to kick butt? My foot loves butt.' AC Gaadi started stretching his kicking foot.

Hari tried to tear out his hair but his fingers slipped in the coconut oil. 'We're detectives. We don't rob ATMs. I'll cut your salary for that.'

'As if that will make a difference to me,' said Gaadi, his leg already pedalling the air between them.

To avoid having his friends unfriend him, Hari tested another tactic. 'You, Triplex, have been wanting to steal that ATM ever since I joined bank security. Doc, the technical modus operandi has your fingerprints over it. I bet the ATM machine has left DNA traces in the back of your rickshaw, AC. The evidence is there. Do you want to go to jail for the rest of your lives? It's up to you.'

There were a few seconds of unconventional silence in the office.

'What are you saying?' said Triplex.

'Shall I repeat?'

'No need, nobody needs to find out you took it.'

'Me? *I took it?*'

'Yeah, look, it's right here in your office, isn't it? Or are you blaming me? It hasn't even got my fingerprints on it.'

Hari felt defeated. 'No bank will ever hire me to watch their ATM now.'

All three of them regarded him as if he were the stupidest existential form on earth.

'But don't you see,' insisted Triplex, 'that is just it! You don't need a crappy job now that you have your own ATM. Swipe your card to take out cash whenever you have to pay us salaries.'

'I don't have any card or bank account.'

Gaadi quipped, 'Try dynamite.'

'Or pretend that you found it and sell it back to the bank,' Doc added.

Deep within, he was proud of his staff. They weren't fully incompetent. He too had felt that the beating was somewhat gentle and that's why he had smashed his head against the coconut tree, to get impressive bruises. However, even then it wasn't legally and morally correct and he seriously doubted that they'd get away with it. Aloud he said, 'Thank you all for remembering my non-birthday but, however, I think you have to put it back where you found it.'

'It's not that easy, Majestic.'

'Why not?'

'First of all, we haven't done anything *wrong*. At least I just disconnected it because I was ordered to,' said Doc, and looked around at the other two.

Hari walked to the doorway; he needed to breathe some fresh exhaust fumes.

Doc sounded doubtful as he continued, 'Couldn't vouch for those people.'

'What do you mean?' growled Gaadi. Merry after his double-pints, he was rooting for a riot.

Doc wagged a finger at him, 'Who thought up this stupid plan? Not I! Who was the first to agree with it? Not me … I did what I did because you people promised me a quarter of the loot so that I can upgrade my computers.'

Nothing more was needed in CD Road. They had been friends for years, but a few careless words tore apart everything in a matter of seconds. Gaadi lost it. His verbal skills weren't great so he instead kickboxed Doc in full Far East style (learnt from watching Hong Kong cinema on pirated DVDs and then some do-it-yourself trial and error) so that Doc reeled out through the open door. Hari had to jump out of the way in order to avoid becoming collateral damage.

It was a case of software against hardware, and the computer geek was no match for the rickshaw driver, with Gaadi's foot pushing him from behind.

Then again, Hari knew from recent experience how painful it was to get kicked by Gaadi and he sympathized with the weakling. But Doc deserved what he got, for without his technical expertise the ATM would have stayed in its place and none of this could have happened in the first place. He analyzed each kick from up close as Gaadi stayed with Doc, *whammy*, triple-*whammy*, kickboxing like a 200-pound ballerina as Doc staggered against the veranda railing. The kicking, however, had a bad side effect.

'Don't do it, boss!' shouted Hari, but too late as he saw Doc topple over the railing.

One moment he was there, then only his feet were visible, struggling to hook their toenails onto the railing, and finally they too were gone.

'Wow!' said Triplex, who always felt Doc was pedantic and needed to be taught a lesson. 'That's what I'm talking about!'

'Sorry Doc, but next time you'll think twice!' shouted Gaadi, thumping his fists on his broad chest, letting off a massive drum roll.

Anyway, it was a one-storey fall, survivable. From the veranda, Hari peeked down into the street and saw that Doc had landed on a juice cart, crushing a mountain of oranges and saving the juicer a lot of work. Excellent, maybe they could all get free juice. Then he happened to glance across the street where onlookers were rapidly forming a crowd.

His eyes zoomed in and among them he made out the bank security officer Solid Kuroopanna dressed in the safari suit with the built-in shoulder holster. Kuroopanna's head started tilting upwards, towards Hari's office. Hari ducked away in less than a nanosecond. *This is bad*, he thought as he crawled back inside.

Gaadi came after him into the office and shot around hostile eyeballs as if he had two sawn-off shotguns implanted into the eye sockets, triggered by the dysfunctional anger management centre in his hypothalamus. He put down a heavy foot on Hari's back.

Hari stopped crawling. This was the end.

'What is going on here?' said Diamond. The way it must have seemed to her, seconds later as she walked into to office, was probably not so good.

Hari was begging Gaadi not to kick him again. 'You are destroying my career, and my reputation, and my marriage will turn into buttermilk.'

'Buttermilk?' said Diamond, giving Gaadi a tight slap, like she'd just downed her morning glucose. The she turned to look down at Hari on the floor. 'Are you hurt, my dear?'

'Eh, not much,' he said. As usual, Hari fell in love again – if he wasn't already married to Diamond and currently under Gaadi's foot, he'd be kneeling and proposing. When they first met, Hari spotted in her the perfect co-star for his private biopic. Diamond could have been an actress, if it wasn't for her chipped front tooth. Scenes that demanded romantic smiles were out of the question.

'Will you kindly step off my husband's back, please,' she said to Gaadi.

Gaadi wasn't quite sure what to do. Usually he'd have kicked the guts out of any person lying down, but now he suddenly lost momentum. He said to Hari, 'Are you going to hurt my sentiments?'

'No such plan,' said Hari.

'Okay, mind it, swami.'

He took his foot off Hari's spine and Hari crawled up forcing his lips into the widest grin possible without cutting off blood supply to his brain. He didn't want to seem like a sissy in front of the guys and ask Diamond for a comforting hug. Such things were not done in public even if he wanted her to blow coolly on his bruises.

'You people have some explaining to do,' she said as she studied the three of them.

Hari said, 'I'm not sure I know what you're talking about, honey. Had your coffee?'

4

> Being the master of your own future is more important nowadays than it once was – and if you have the slightest chance to put a loved one's mind at rest you must.

The deputy director indicated that she had some pressing matters that needed clarifications.

'My dear, why didn't you show up for breakfast at home?'

'Well, you see …'

'Your uniform is dirty, you can't walk around like this only.'

'No, I wasn't meaning to …'

'And why was Doc lying face down on a fruit-seller's cart in the street? I had to give him first aid.'

Hari mumbled, 'Honey, I hope it wasn't mouth-to-mouth.'

She had worked as a nurse before she became Mrs Majestic, but he had persuaded her to quit as he worried that she'd have to revive male patients. Apart from being the owner of a sharp mind, she was extraordinarily good-looking. She used a minimum of make-up: lip balm in a matte shade, a single line of under-eye kohl, light nail polish. She smelt faintly of jasmine and rosewater and, well, coconut. Her hair was oiled with the purest Parachute brand coconut oil and braided in a messy style – making it appear as if half of her brain had somehow penetrated out through the left ear. The hair was tied up in a funky bandana. She wore tight jeans and a baggy chequered shirt, feminine in a tough way.

'And what's this, my dear, an unauthorized staff meeting?'

'It's been a busy night, so we had a debriefing,' he said.

'Which resulted in Doc being found almost dead downstairs?'

'A sort of crisis management workshop, you could say, to build up competence and handle future challenges.'

He deflected doubts with tiny white lies so as to spare her feelings. A strategic thinker, he decided to let Diamond deal with the total fallout among the staff. It might smoothen things out. Secondly, he wanted to put the previous day's argument behind and the best way of doing so was to let her decide everything. Thirdly, as an ex-nurse, she was used to lunacy. So the buck stopped somewhere within her reach. He did a quick pre-mortem of his staff. They were the ones to blame for everything. Gaadi gave a beery but meek burp. Triplex gazed down at his lower body, maybe thinking of giving himself a blow job.

'As deputy director, I am to be informed before you do any such thing.'

'What thing?'

'Don't ... never mind.' She walked around the tiny office, inspecting this and that, occasionally frowning.

'But honey, a full report would have been on your desk within thirty nanoseconds if you had the patience to wait.'

'Don't you get it that I get worried when you don't come home? I cooked appams and egg roast. So I called Pushpa madam, she said …'

'She is too gossipy,' said Hari, making a conscious effort not to glance in the direction of the stolen cash dispenser which, fortunately, was pretty well concealed behind the fan boxes.

But she caught the slight movement of his eye.

'Have you bought more useless armpit fans?' She stopped at the mountainous stack, kicking one of the bottommost boxes somewhat dismissively. 'There's like twice as many.'

'It must be an optical illusion, but I can assure you there's good money in there,' he said.

She sniffed the air.

'Is this the office of a professional detective bureau or …' her attention was grabbed by the empty beer bottle that Gaadi had chucked under the office cot '… or a bar where you people fight?'

Hari shrunk a bit. Either that or his sandal-size had suddenly doubled.

'There's nothing unprofessional going on here, honey.'

'The impression I get is that you people nearly killed your friend Doc.' She turned to Triplex. 'And you, dirty boy, wipe that leer off your face or I'm going to throw you out of here faster than you know what hit you.'

Diamond had never taken to Triplex, mainly because of his unhealthy interest in everything immoral. But he was no veg puff. He stood up and in his cowboy boots he was almost as tall as Diamond, who hailed from Tellicherry in Kerala, a town known for its sportswomen and circus acrobats. Triplex himself was born in Herohalli, on the outskirts of Bengaluru, and that kind of place name saddled him with certain obligations.

'Who are you calling dirty,' he said and lowered his voice before adding in English, '*bitch*?'

There was silence. Hari was beginning to feel like pork vindaloo with spicy vinegar sweating out through his pores. Despite whatever quarrels they had, Hari knew that Triplex said what he said out of solidarity: mates stood up for mates, and the best man was always one step behind the groom. But he wished that Triplex had taken the English classes seriously and learnt more than just the cuss words. Finally, he felt that he had to break the silence.

'Don't be naughty,' he admonished Triplex.

Diamond drew an ominous breath and the combustible situation exploded like a Bollywood scene scripted by pyrotechnists. Her voice went up by one octave. 'Did you just call me something?'

'Call you?' said Triplex and looked around the room for support, grinning. 'I don't take down numbers from toilet walls.'

Gaadi leered back. Hari didn't dare to. Doc, who seemed to have pulped a good many kilos of oranges, was busy stewing in his juices by the doorway. Hari was aware that his bachelor friends had felt betrayed by his marriage and ever since then there'd been a Cold War of sorts between them and his wife, but now it was heating up too fast. In order to defuse the remark, Hari said, 'I think Triplex meant that we must have a nice picnic on the *beach*? The next semi-deluxe bus for Mangaluru is leaving at noon.'

As a former tout, he knew the private bus timetables by heart.

She harrumphed. 'Don't give me that sorry dog-face.' *Ouch*, that hurt. But he took it like a man. Diamond challenged Triplex. 'Can you repeat that last word again?'

'Toilet wall?'

'Honey,' interjected Hari, 'I think we'll miss the bus if we don't ...'

'No, my dear, let's hear what this dirty boy has to say.'

Triplex chuckled.

'I know you're a retard, but say it again. If you dare!'

Triplex's eyes turned a dangerous hue of purple. 'Are you sure you want it?'

Hari understood that Triplex didn't wish to offend Diamond on purpose. But sometimes gentlemen had to do what they had to do.

'Yes,' she said.

Triplex rose to the bait. 'Stop being a *bitch*, bitch.'

'If you consider it correctly, then it is logical,' added Doc, who hovered by the doorway, not daring to enter the office again. 'If according to yourself, he, meaning your husband, is dog-like, which we can all agree upon, then you must be his bitch. By the way, the juice-wallah wants reimbursement for fifty kilos of wasted oranges. I told him to invoice the company.'

Doc must've got a concussion because his logic was like uncooked mutton brain.

'He should pay us since you helped him pulp those oranges,' said Hari who was desperate to change the subject.

Diamond was a take-charge woman. 'Hand in your company business cards and leave these premises.'

'What did I do?' said Doc.

'Which part was unclear? Do as I say.'

'What about me, sister?' said Gaadi.

'You too.'

'Why?'

'Because look at yourself – that's why!' she said raising her voice by twelve octaves this time.

Hari inferred that she was somewhat upset and therefore overreacting. Things would be fine later. Diamond had never had much sympathy for rickshaw drivers. People loved heaping abuse on these hardcore motorists, not realizing that the city's infrastructure collapsed the moment the 151,000 rickshaws that plugged the gap between mass and private transportation went off the streets.

Gaadi was bamboozled, as if she was a foreign television programme without subtitles. Although a bachelor, he had great body personality – potbellied like a proper son-in-law, always a half-full beer in one hand and a smouldering bidi in the other, semi-catatonic stare and hair that was henna red, his uniform stained by oily non-veg korma. In other words, the classic man. He burped more aggressively this time. 'You're making a mistake, sister.'

'Let it be my mistake if I keep him and throw you out. You're all bad influences on my husband. See what you've done to him.' She aimed an accusatory finger at Hari. She echoed her late uncle-in-law's way of speaking.

'So what if we weren't able to make a man out of him?' Gaadi retorted.

'I tell you I've been doing what I can to manage this company and turn it into an expert security outfit, and what do you people do? You lose ten lakhs that you were supposed to guard!'

'That's not quite …'

But Hari could barely start on the explanation before Gaadi was shouting at Diamond.

'We didn't lose anything, sister.' Gaadi shook his Knockout at Hari. 'He's the one you should fire for losing that thing.'

That was uncalled for, thought Hari.

'Like he rightly put it, it was your husband who was unguarding it,' added Doc who lurched in and out through the door. He feared another lesson in kickboxing. 'Not us.'

All of a sudden, it was as if everything was his fault, when in reality his colleagues had perpetrated the heist. Stunned, Hari mulled over what was worse: saying goodbye and all the very best to his three mates or ruining the family peace. Very hard choice. Hari, who was totally blameless, reasoned with Diamond. 'Honey, let's go home and have egg roast, I'm starving. It's been a hard night's morning.'

'My dear, have I ever told you how *exasperating* you can be?'

She was apparently not happy about the state of affairs. Then again, Hari knew that his friends were a mad bunch who could drive any woman nuts.

'I think you mentioned it once,' he said diplomatically, though he didn't let on that he hadn't dared to google the word. He added, 'But I'm planning self-improvements, honey.'

'That'll be the day when I believe in God.'

'No, it'll happen much sooner than that,' he assured her, knowing that she shared the same rationalist background that many educated people from Kerala did. 'But …'

'*No buts!* Regarding this crisis with the stolen ATM, I expect you to have it cleared up by Monday morning, my dear.' She took a deep breath. She then addressed the rest of the staff, 'Until further notice, none of you may undertake any work on behalf of this firm. And stay away from my husband. You hear?'

'Ya, we're not deaf like you,' said Triplex and walked out with a miniature fan in his hand, aiming it at his nose as if something was stinking in the office, his white cowboy boots clicking against the unpainted concrete floor. 'You stay away from me too, bitch.'

'But how do we run this company without staff?' Hari said softly after his colleagues had vacated the premises, in the puppy tone he used whenever she was irritated.

She kissed him on the top of his greasy, thinning hair.

'I'm sorry I lost my temper there.' Tenderness in her tone, as if he were welcome back in from the cold. 'I'm glad you did try to stop the thieves, even if you failed in the end. Maybe you should go see a doctor? You're pretty badly bruised, as if a coconut dropped on your head.'

She didn't know how right she was.

'I can't afford to be sick, honey.' Though if he broke into the cash dispenser, he could take a month off and get himself admitted to the Jindal Nature Cure Institute and rid himself of all that ailed him. It was what any sane person would do in his place, but for some reason he felt it his duty to protect that money even if it was already stolen. And that included protecting it against himself.

She looked around the crummy office.

'Now that those dirty fellows are gone, we should clean the rest of this dump out. Junk that trash.' She indicated the fan boxes and the shelf with Hari's self-help books and his uncle's Old Monk empties.

'Many things here are the only memories I have of my uncle. Value is not only in cash but remembrance too.'

She smiled cutely at him. She had been fond of his uncle, who was a well-educated man, a litterateur and a lawyer, if a dipsomaniac – like many intellectuals were. 'I don't know how to put this. Brace yourself.'

'I'm ready for anything, honey. Anything you say.'

'Really, anything?'

'Yes.'

'You're suspended.'

'I know, the uncle from the bank already told me so.'

'No, I mean you're suspended from our detective agency.'

'Why, honey?'

It was the second time in one day that he was being suspended and it was getting to be a bit of an irritant.

'Don't take it personally, my dear. It is a practical matter. Pushpa madam said you were asleep when the heist took place and after the thieves left you stayed asleep for another three hours before reporting the crime. What conclusion do we draw?'

'Your guess is as good as mine.' Hari worried that he was headed for the doghouse. In a sense, he'd probably feel more at home in a doghouse.

'Pushpa suggested that an internal affairs enquiry must be conducted. It is a formality, but it has to be done.'

'But there is no evidence of wrongdoing.'

'No evidence doesn't mean no wrongdoing. And now, my dear husband,' she went on, 'you'll go and buy a chicken. Skin out.'

'That's a sooper idea. But I have no money, honey.'

'Surely you can "fix" that, hero,' she said teasingly.

It wasn't a coincidence that she had been named Diamond; she was as hard as one. But if he got her a broiler, chances were there'd be a romantic evening – and the timing was perfect, because he wouldn't have to go to work.

After Diamond went to the parlour to have her legs waxed, which strongly suggested that there was potential love in the air, he made a desperate attempt to patch up with his colleagues, texting them inane non-veg SMS jokes. When push came to shove, he needed them more than they needed him. Nobody responded to his social networking attempts. He felt totally unfriended. Getting a grip on himself, he unfolded a sheet of foolscap on the desk. He wrote: 'Top Secret Classified Report. Not to be taken out of this office.' This was to be the true, uncensored version. In his mind, he went back to what happened during the heist as he made mental notes for the internal affairs' report. But there was nothing that he was able to write down without making things worse. He put the blank report in a desk drawer. What he needed was cash.

He went down to the railway station to do some touting, although it, in theory, was illegal. Any person caught acting as a guide without a licence from the competent authority was liable to a fine of up to ₹2,000 and imprisonment of fifteen days. But he needed to feed his family.

He got lucky. He didn't get arrested. He found cheap rooms for a gang of backpackers from Denmark who also wanted to score bhang cookies, and made enough to go to Taison's Chick-Hen Mart, the butcher who specialized in extra tough hens at ₹99 per kilo. As Taison killed and skinned it, Hari waited outside the booth and glimpsed Solid Kuroopanna ambling down the pavement. Kuroopanna stopped to buy a tumbler of coffee, but his orange eyes were nailed on Hari. Taisonappa himself – who owned the butchery – was in a chatty mood and told Hari that he had opened a home-stay right on top of the shop. He called it Coorg View even though it was 280 km from Coorg, his native place. He wanted Hari to divert tourists bound for the picturesque hill station, in case he met any at the railway station. Hari promised to do his best.

He carried the dead hen up the stairs in a somewhat crumbling block of apartments called Cyber Villas overlooking the open sewer in Main Drain Semi-Slum. There were piles of shoes on the landing outside the door of their 1BHK. Diamond had a decent collection of embroidered mojaris and ethnic juttis, flashy pumps and slingbacks, and a pair of leather kolhapuris. He kicked off his rubber slippers and entered the dwelling.

The walls in the hall were chutney green, the floor dosa-yellow with darker patches. Diamond had decorated with handicrafts from Kerala and educational posters. As the flat wasn't Vaastu compliant, but had a door facing in an unlucky direction, their rent was affordable. In order to nullify bad karma, he had bought a 'Vaastu goldfish' from Pandit Pundit to keep in a jar by the door. Hari always worried that Diamond, in a rationalist fit, was going to fry it in coconut oil, but the fish still stared dumbly at him, unaware of how deadly life was.

'Papa!' Shrieks of joy greeted him right inside the door.

'What is my girlfriend up to? Had coffee?' he bent down to give her a hug.

'Papa me too!'

They were twins and knew how to walk, run and act by and large human. Their English vocabulary consisted of the words 'papa' and 'mama' plus some guttural make-believe lingo. The firstborn's name was Ondu and her sister, who was younger by minutes, was Eradu. Ever since their birth, he'd been away from home working day and night to make ends meet. Yet, remarkably enough they recognized him as their father.

Hari spoke to both daughters. 'Had your tiffin? Had fun?'

He found Diamond deep-frying bread pakoras and handed over the hen. The homely kitchen had a single-burner gas stove, a half-sized fridge, a clay drinking water jar and a table for two plus two. All in all, the 1BHK was perhaps too cosy for a joint family, but big enough for a couple with two toddling daughters. As she cooked dinner, on the first day in a long time when he didn't have to go to guard the ATM booth, he discovered that it was surprisingly difficult to have a conversation. There was too much troubling him.

She noticed it and hugged him tenderly. 'Hari, Hari … You may not be the hero you once were, but as long as you don't start drinking again, our next daughter is going to be proud of you too. If it is a girl again.'

It was as if two fans had revved up in his armpits and torn off the hair. 'You are?'

'I am.'

'That's …'

'What?'

Despite having fathered two daughters, he eagerly anticipated getting the son every hero needed to take on the mantle, to carry on the 'Majestic' lineage. That'd be the silver lining on what otherwise looked like a black cloud hovering over him. Hari's family also included a bossy mum who had resurfaced after decades. Now and then he visited her in Parappana Agrahara Jail. Her days started at 3 a.m. with vegetable peeling. The morning meal involved bathtub-sized cauldrons of upma, a gluey preparation of semolina and veggies. Once she was released and moved in with Hari and Diamond, if she followed the same recipe, it'd result in 5,000 portions. As per his calculation, that amount of upma would take him thirteen years to eat – an eternity's worth of prison food. His only hope was that she'd stay put in jail – and why shouldn't she? Currently she was earning better there than before she was put in jail. The prison canteen was a black-market hotspot: she sold single cigarettes for ₹50, liquor at ₹300 to ₹3,000 depending on brand, smuggled SIM cards cost ₹1,000; mobile phone rental was ₹1,00,000 per month and a personalized diet of non-veg including seafood (but no trace of the dreaded upma) cost ₹2,00,000 per month, inclusive of an unlimited supply of liquor and cigarettes. Cocaine and opium was costlier and generally sold concealed in tender coconuts, papayas and water melons. She didn't share any of her income with Hari, so there was no scope to rent a bigger apartment.

He tentatively named his son-to-come Raju in honour of a superstar who had begun his career in the 1960s on the BMTC line 10A. Hari's uncle often travelled by that bus to City Market and he had never tired of telling how Rajinikanth, before joining the movies, handed out the bus tickets as if they were tickets to the upper balcony in a cinema hall. The hypothetical son's nickname would be '10A'. Hari helped himself to a spoonful of Chyawanprash and rinsed it down with a tumbler of lukewarm water from the clay jar on the kitchen counter.

'Why so quiet?' she asked. 'I thought you'd be happy.'

'I am, honey, it's just that …'

She glanced back quizzically while pulling out the hen's intestines.

'Things weigh on my mind,' he said.

She waited, but when he said nothing more, she said, 'Remember how we used to speak so much when we got married?'

'I wish I could go back to those days.'

'Open yourself up to me.' Was she speaking to him or the disembowelled hen? He wasn't sure because her hand was groping around inside the latter.

'Honey, I assure you one crore per cent that *I've* done nothing wrong.'

'I'm sorry that you had to face suspension, but you must understand my position as deputy director and the responsibilities that come with it. And I had no choice but to show those thugs who the boss is.'

Now she was definitely speaking to him.

'It's not that. I must be in a state of post-traumatic shock. I got suspended twice in a day and now our family is going to grow by twenty-five per cent which means that I must earn twenty-five per cent more.' Deep within, Hari Majestic worried that he may not ever live up to his surname again. Not that it was his real name. He was named after a movie theatre, Majestic Talkies, where his mother had dumped him as a newborn baby and from where he had been adopted by the cleaning lady. Everything had been complicated since the beginning.

'Life is not about money alone. Life is full of stimulating challenges that we must overcome,' Diamond said as if reading his mind. 'You'll find a new guard job tomorrow.'

'I don't have the needful police certificate.'

'Come on, you're the one who always says one should look at things from the brightest side. As long as you're without a job you'll get to spend more time with the kids. And once you find that lost cash dispenser, Pushpa will give you back your certificate and you can apply for jobs again.'

He was glad that yesterday's argument was fading into the past. After dinner there was a chance that he and she might cuddle on the cot. For a moment, he was almost about to tell her that he already had taken possession of the cash dispenser, but then he decided that it was better to bring the truth out little by little in digestible chunks. He mustered up a smile. 'Honey, Triplex has a plan ...'

The mention of that name didn't please her. 'I don't trust him. He's a bad character.'

'He's a character all right.' Hari hesitated, but then he had to ask because it bothered him so much, 'Why did you have to speak like that in front of my friends?'

'Because I had to.'

'But why?'

'Because they are my employees.' She was rubbing the unfortunate hen with more red chilli powder and too much salt, as if it were a stand-in for Hari's friends. 'I must show them who wears the boots and who wears the chappals.'

'They're still *my* friends.' Though he wasn't too sure about that. 'Besides, Triplex wears boots.'

She stared at him for five to six seconds. 'If I'm not in charge, there's no knowing what all they will do, half-criminals that they are. Has it occurred to you that any one of them surely is capable of robbing an ATM?'

'No, they'd never do anything so stupid.'

'Maybe not,' she said, 'but when it comes to that Triplex, nothing would surprise me.'

'He is full of surprises.'

'I don't want to hear you defend that boy.' She shovelled a fistful of green chillies into the rump of the hen. She wasn't facing him while she gave him a dressing down, talking in a monotone, as she dunked the hen in pepper and turmeric, telling it to up its act or face the music. 'You're a blind man being led by a blind, deaf, dumb and idiotic loser, my dear, if you go on trusting that dirty boy.'

He defused the situation as best he could. 'How about I take you out to a nice Kerala-style canteen and we eat a romantic mackerel fried in coconut oil like we used to? And forget about this whole incident? Let the boys come back to work tomorrow.'

'I am serious and you're mocking me?' Diamond heaved a deep breath. 'Are you trying to give me a nervous breakdown?'

'Absolutely not. I'll go and have a fresh horoscope drawn up. And another for Triplex. I'm sure things will get better after that.'

'The sun is not rotating around you.'

'Oho? The sun isn't rotating, is it so?' he said, because he didn't understand what she was getting at. Although he had no clue as to how it happened, they were repeating the quarrel from last night.

'It is a simple astronomical truth.'

Hari twiddled his moustache. 'Astrology would beg to differ.'

'Your horoscope is a load of lies and that astrologer of yours is a conman.'

'Don't say that, honey,' pleaded Hari.

His horoscope seemed to be the last thing on earth that was on his side. Why did they have to argue so much over it? He wanted to highlight the virtues he displayed on a daily basis – hadn't he brought home a plump hen? But the hen hadn't saved the day. Maybe it was the pressure of raising two daughters with no money, and a third kid on the way, but Hari knew how the rest of it was going to go down. The twins got the leg pieces and the wings, and Hari was typically left with the meatless neck to use as he saw fit.

'Know what I'm thinking? Of course you don't,' she said.

He decided to back off, but she followed him from the kitchen and to the bedroom, brandishing the hen at him. He changed from his uniform shirt and loincloth into stonewashed jeans and a neon nylon tee promoting the new Rajinikanth starrer.

'Well, don't you have *anything* to say, my dear?' she said, the hapless hen dangling from her left hand.

He shook his head and walked to the door, where he wore his rubber slippers again. He didn't want to fight. He loved her too much.

'Are you going somewhere?'

He nodded. Life had never been excessively simple, not since that day when he was born by mistake. There was only one thing that made sense.

'You've given me a deadline until Monday to set everything straight so I should get started. If I fail, you might be happier without me, honey.'

She seemed unable to make up her mind on that count, but Hari knew it was best not to give people alternatives or they dithered eternally.

'You're leaving me?'

'No honey, I'll come back when this thing has been sorted out.'

She followed him out the door and continued harshly, 'Even if you miss dinner,' how did she know he wanted to avoid that neck? '... I expect you to do the dishes.'

He knew that the word 'else' was coming and so was going down the steps by the time it echoed after him.

'Or else!'

There was that late afternoon lull on CD Road when people had eaten their tiffin and waited for the evening snack hour to commence at their favourite roadside stalls. Though he hadn't had lunch *or* breakfast, he had no appetite. He walked past other banks' unrobbed ATMs and saw that some were being recharged with cash. Money, that was what everyone believed in. He glanced over his shoulder and saw the burning eyes of Kuroopanna shine in midst of the crowds, like two searchlights. Kuroopanna was not a particularly discreet spy.

The cash dispenser was too heavy to carry out of the office without help and anyway there were too many witnesses in the daytime. It had to happen later. Wait until Kuroopanna stopped following him and then dump the machine somewhere not too far from the ATM booth after having emptied some of the cash to make it look like a failed robbery. He had lots of stuff to figure out. Meanwhile, he decided to go watch *OM*. It had been running off and on for twenty years and he had seen it a hundred times. He worshipped the songs, especially 'Coma, Coma Prema'. Bananas flew through the air and Ambassador cars burned as gangsters showed how to make love. The movie had semi-brilliant acting with actual rowdies playing themselves and Hari's uncle had a walk-on part in the Sarovar Pub fight scene – even that pub, once the hotspot of Lavelle Road, had been bulldozed. Hari felt nostalgic. The world around him was collapsing, but at least *OM* had been re-released in a fresh digitally restored copy.

He looked forward to glimpsing his uncle in it. It was bound to make him upbeat and give him useful ideas.

5

Explore different avenues so that you're sufficiently grounded to meet long term goals with speed and precision.

He bought a ticket at the counter rather than from the counterfeiter. Fakes were cheaper, but he was a responsible householder. The hall was near empty and yet somebody else had occupied Hari's favourite seat – using a duplicate ticket.

It was a special seat and Hari always asked for it because he had practically been born under the same number – row B, seat number 16 – but in a different theatre. It happened to be the best seat in the hall: biggest picture, vivid colours, loudest sound. Most people didn't know that cinemas were calibrated with focus on a particular seat. Obviously, it would have been an architectural impossibility to build a cinema where all seats were equal, so there had to be a 'maharaja throne', and Hari had mathematically established that it was the one he was born under. He had kept the algorithm a secret and only told Triplex, so that there would be no competition over that seat. Yet, it was taken.

Again, he wouldn't have bothered, because he got almost as good an experience from the next seat. But what irked him was that the teenager in the maharaja seat had rigged up a video camera. Hari understood what was going on.

As these old theatres weren't equipped with audio jacks for semi-deafs, he wasn't doing a 'telesync' but rather a plain 'cam' which was piracy terminology for a straightforward theatre rip. He relied on the inbuilt microphone to capture sound. With regard to Indian films that was tricky, because thrills were often mixed with romance and comedy, and buyers later complained of audible laughter, coughing, paan-spitting, tongue-scraping and loud sobs muddling the audio track.

Ripping the film in a near-empty hall was smart. But there was an unspoken law that the local Sandalwood films should never be pirated. Only outside films like Bollywood, Kollywood, Mollywood, Tollywood and Hollywood were free prey. And even if by mistake one happened to pirate a Kannada movie, one must never do it to Real-Star Upendra. If *OM* didn't generate revenue, then how was Upendra going to make more blockbusters?

Hari advised the pirate, 'Ayooh, you simply cannot do that, boss.'

The pirate replied tersely. 'Listen old fart, I'm trying to record this so that Triplex the Video King can upload it tomorrow, and if you can't be quiet I'll tear your moustache off and stuff it down your throat.'

He flicked a knife out, ready to implement the threat. With a 'bye-bye and all the very best,' Hari walked several rows up. The world had changed. Not necessarily for the better. Then, like a slow-release headache pill malfunction, a painful thought popped up. Obviously, this young man who lacked a sense of history had no clue that Hari was Mr Majestic, way above Triplex the Video King. Hari felt alienated. This was not his world any longer. It was the late 2010s, an era where oldies born in the 1980s didn't belong.

Video King? In the good old days when Triplex and he pirated films, they had done it in a morally responsible way. But this ... He experienced a repeat of the same outrage he had felt during the robbery last night: there had been no need to kick the hell out of him. Triplex could have told him he was taking the ATM and he'd have requested him not to but ultimately let them carry on since he was outnumbered.

Earlier he'd always watch movies with Triplex. Films were more fun if you had somebody to chat with, comment on scenes, mouth lines, repeat jokes, share snacks and throw coins at the best stars. But now, he found it hard to get absorbed by the film. His troubled thoughts returned to his various failures and then on to Diamond, his big love and the mother of his daughters. The morning's depression returned with double force. So when the intermission came, he walked out.

Once he had had the biggest smile in town. Now his face was like an overcast day. Life had been cheap and fun when he was young. Recently, he had been diagnosed with high blood pressure. Not record high, but enough to cause worry. But it wasn't just the BP. His stomach was giving him a lot of shit. His liver was in bad shape. The environment was increasingly toxic and when he blew his nose there were two black dots, each about one-inch wide, in his hankie. Then there was that thinning of the hair – right where a bald spot might be expected to appear. He used to have hair as wild as the jungles. Maybe if he visited a bar he'd see a nicer-looking face in the mirror? According to statistics he had computed, his looks always improved by 33 per cent whenever he stepped into a bar.

The bar around the corner used to be called Deluxe, but instead of renovating, the owner had invested in a new board and upgraded the name to Finest Kwality Bar – which made sense, it was cheaper than hiring carpenters. But having hired the cheapest possible board maker, within a few months the first letter, 'F', and two others had fallen off so that it now, slightly unfortunately, read 'ine Kwality Bar'. The interiors, however, were pure 1990s' vintage and that's why Hari felt at home there: it was where he had grown up as an underage drinker. Wooden tables, cane chairs. No Formica or plastic like the lower end bars of today.

It lay opposite his office and ever since their teens, he and Triplex had spent afternoons and evenings there, sometimes mornings too, analysing life's ups and downs. Many problems had been solved over a few bottles. It was sheer reflex to go there – men of all generations did so when they didn't have better ideas.

The barkeep's nickname was Peggy, a morose gent who puzzlingly enough also happened to be the convener of the CD Road laughing club. He was busy doing puja to Lord Venkateshwara whose laminated portrait adorned the wall behind the bar. Distorted bhajans busted the speakers. Peggy was deeply religious, like most bar-keepers in CD Road, and only took payment from the right hand. If you tried to pay him with the left, he threw you out. But as much as Hari proffered his money, he had to wait for his beverage. His credit wasn't as good as god's.

Peggy moved the incense sticks in circles before the idol, then dipped them into the cashbox setting a few banknotes on fire.

Only after that did Hari get his Thums Up. In the early days after he stopped drinking, he often felt stoned when he met people who didn't have two heads. Nowadays, with a clearer focus and better night-time vision, he simply savoured the fumes from the surrounding tables and memories of happier times. As a rule, the cola contained enough sugar and caffeine to perk him up. But tonight, it didn't help.

Hari stared at the tabletop. Somebody had carved words into it. It was as if the table was talking to him. 'I'm drinker. You one? I want like-minded friendship.' There was a mobile number. He decided not to call just because some loser had been occupying the same chair. At the adjacent table, a tout was at work. New generation, born with a Bluetooth gizmo attached to his ear. On his laptop, he filled in online forms for a fellow who spoke in a rural dialect and knew no English. The tout assured him that he'd get his dreams fulfilled. The rustic would pay a bomb for a visa to whichever country he wanted to migrate to. There he'd realize that he had no chance unless he knew how to fill in his forms himself and in good English.

That was when the bad call came, the one he'd anticipated.

They were working late. Not surprising, since they had been robbed that morning. The bank wished to terminate their contract due to 'obvious reasons', a junior manager informed him, and possibly 'sue for damages'.

'But sir, I swear I had nothing to do with the heist,' said Hari.

This statement was followed by mutual silence. The job-seeker was quarrelling in the background with the tout about the advance he was expected to pay. Hari cupped his hand over the phone, 'I'm too super-busy, Kitnewallah sir. Right now,

I am preventing a street fight. Can you hear the shouting in the background? One VIP possibly dead. But we may resurrect him, god willing. We have nurses on the payroll.'

'Mister Majestic,' said Junior Manager Kitnewallah who didn't fall for cheap tricks, 'I'm sure you work hard or our bank wouldn't have hired you, but …'

'Yes, you selected the right man.'

'Don't put words in my mouth.'

'Then what is the problem? Surely you can give us another chance, sir.'

'*Mister* Majestic, your job with us was to see to it that this wouldn't happen. *Now the shit has hit the fan*.' Kitnewallah threw in an English expression.

Hari was uncertain of its meaning. 'Whose shit, sir?'

'Yours.'

'And whose fan?'

'Yours too.'

'Since you're interested in fans, would your bank like to invest in a consignment of armpit fans?'

'No.'

'Why not?'

'Because you are terminated.' The manager made a great hullabaloo about the Indian Penal Code Sections under which they considered filing cases against Diamond & Majestic Investigations Pvt Ltd: 406, 420, 465, 468 and 471. Technically, Hari didn't need him to say more – having been brought up by an advocate, he knew the accusations were criminal breach of trust, cheating, forgery, forgery for the purpose of cheating and using as genuine a forged document. 'Mister Majestic, it turns out you withheld vital information from us.'

'Says which liar?'

'Are you calling me a liar?'

This wasn't going well.

'No, but somebody may have lied to you.'

'Hardly the security consultants that we've hired. They are professionals. Your police clearance certificate has been retracted and there is suspicion about how it came to be issued in the first place, considering your background. Furthermore, your company was registered in your wife's name, but it turns out several operatives at the agency have featured on the rowdy-sheets.'

'How can you say a thing like that?' He felt badly let down. 'You must allow us to do it again, please sir, and next time no untoward incidents will happen.'

Kitnewallah wasn't listening. 'I'm saying it for the last time, *Mister Majestic*. As per contract, we may terminate without disclosing a reason. We expect you to fully cooperate with the investigation into the matter or you shall face legal consequences as mentioned. Why am I even wasting my time speaking to you?'

Hari heard the phone go dead. He laid it down on the table. Whenever it rang, it heralded misery. Reality was a formidable enemy to be up against, different from the romcom thrillers where a Happy End was guaranteed.

It was nearing 11:29 p.m. The bar was closing in 60 seconds and he should have been going home, but he was ready to order an alcoholic drink to flog his liver with – or whatever shreds remained of it. He needed to kill brain cells too. Any cells that thought of him as a failure had to die. So, he decided on a fresh lime soda, sweet and salt, with gin and a green chilli on the side. He hadn't had a drink since his marriage. It was high time to start again. But right then his phone went ballistic.

'Hello sir, Naanu Gotillamma here, special correspondent for *Hottu-Hottu* breaking news service.'

'Yes?'

She sounded gorgeous. 'Are you possibly the head of Diamond Majestic Investigations Private Limited?'

'It depends. And the company's name is Diamond *and* Majestic.'

'Can I take your interview?'

Hari sensed that this might be good promotion for his firm. 'When?'

'Like right now or immediately as per your convenience.'

'Well, you must be knowing that I am a full-time hero and quite busy at that. But what do you want from me?'

'An anonymous whistleblower gave me this number. ATM heist, early this morning – sounds familiar? One of your employees was supposed to guard the ATM but he fell asleep, leading to the theft of one million rupees. We're doing a story about financial security or lack thereof in the new digital economy. Have you done anything to punish the employee in question?'

'How do you mean?'

'Has the thought occurred to you that it might have been an insider job?'

'It was not!'

'How can you be so sure?'

Hari understood that he was becoming the face of incompetence, exactly as Diamond had predicted. 'Ma'am, I'm not at liberty to comment. We have a confidentiality clause in our contracts. But the security guard will be dealt with and there'll be an investigation.'

'Well, I've been reliably informed that your contract's been terminated, so there is no need for confidentiality. Here's a helpful hint. I suggest we meet and you talk, that way you can tell the world your version.'

'And what if I don't?' His throat felt parched, he needed that drink badly.

'Then I'll write that you are absconding and people make their conclusions freely.' She laughed a superior laugh. 'So, what say you? Where are you at this moment? I can be there in twenty.'

'In my office, reviewing the matter as we speak.' He could see Puncherwallah Complex from the bar so he wasn't lying too much – he'd oil his moustache and glorify his own struggle. Maybe his bad fortunes were ending?

Now was the right time to drink. But it was past closing time and Peggy was busy washing down the interiors with disinfectant to remove the wickedness of the day. Hari had no option but to face his destiny sober. He was glad he had changed from the guard's uniform to a flashier outfit and tugged the neon nylon tee down over his paunch. The poster by the exit read: 'Accidents Don't Happen, They Are Caused', and then he passed some exhibitionist who stood outside the bar and spoke random nonsense to his genitals.

For once the office slogan, 'Open 24x7', proved correct, he thought as he unlocked the padlock, switched on the lights and sat down behind his desk. He'd barely had time to comb his moustache when he heard a car revving in the street, then stopping. Doors slammed. *Had the reporter already arrived?*

Suddenly there was a power cut and the office turned dark. The veranda in front was lit up by the full moon. How romantic. Minutes later, he heard steps coming closer. They weren't femininely coy or coyly feminine.

The doorway blacked out. It didn't look like any hot chick to him. More like two men. 'We came to see the person in charge.'

'In charge of what?' said Hari and pretended to be busy reshaping a paperclip.

'Who takes responsibility here, please?'

'For what?'

'Can you just answer my question?'

'It depends.'

The lights flickered. Then they came back on. It hadn't been a full power cut, just a power cutlet. The two looked seriously tough. One of them was a familiar face: a red knife scar, orange eyes, gun stitched into his safari suit.

'I think you can guess what this is about.' Kuroopanna's tiny eyes slid around the office, surveying the accumulated rubbish and armpit fan boxes, and then he stared at Hari. 'We've met before, haven't we?'

'I can't remember. I meet a lot of people.'

'Hari? Aren't you Hari Majestic? I thought you were just a watchman, but it turns out you're a big shot detective with – what shall I call it – a shady past. I believe you spoke to one of the bank's junior managers, Shree Kitnewallah, earlier tonight. He may have told you to cooperate.'

Hari nodded at the other man, who wore shades and was puffing quietly on a menthol cigarette. 'Would both of you like to show me ID proof?'

'You know who I am.' Solid Kuroopanna sat down at the desk. 'Hope you don't mind if I take a moment of your precious time.'

'I have an interview,' said Hari. 'Following which I must go home for dinner and wash the dishes.'

'This will not take long.'

Hari waggled his head vaguely because when people said something would be quick they meant the opposite. 'I understand your bank's security is not working well. If you're looking for openings, I can set up an appointment for tomorrow. We have a staff shortage.'

'You're a slippery fish, Majestic.'

'Thank you for the compliment. I'll request the deputy director to attend since you wish to meet my superior, so please come back first thing tomorrow,' he said in order to stall, stopped to think and then added, 'You never know, but she might be in the mood to hire incompetent people.'

Kuroopanna picked some dirt from under his finger nails and then wiped it off on the edge of Hari's desk. 'There are things that can wait and things that cannot.'

The backup man with the cooling glasses wasn't very talkative, but started unwrapping a long parcel of newsprint. Hari saw that it contained a strip of metal fashioned out of broken car chassis, sharpened along both edges. Known as a 'long' it was useful for silent assassinations.

The unexpectedly polite, soft-spoken Kuroopanna may have been a poet in a previous lifetime. The silent one by the doorway was more difficult to put a finger on. Count Dracula? He looked bloody deranged the way he chain-smoked menthol cigarettes. Codename: Mental Menthol.

'And what is it that is so urgent … sir?'

'Know what, Majestic? You don't have to worry unduly. We're conducting an investigation and we request your help. That's why we came to find out who is *really* in charge here.'

'I'm only … working here … temporarily.' Hari played for time as he continued with a quick risk assessment. They didn't look like they'd be easily fobbed off. He eyed the long – maybe they'd chop off his head and leave the rest of his body for his family? Then he thought for a nanosecond. *Was he being headhunted? Was that good or bad?* 'But okay, I'll make time for you, sir. I have a few minutes until my next appointment. I am famous hereabouts. How can I be of assistance?'

'Mobile.'

'What mobile?'

'Your mobile.' Kuroopanna held out a hand. 'Don't make me repeat myself, Majestic. Show him what we mean, Kelasamadi.'

Mental Menthol, a.k.a. Kelasamadi, had finished unwrapping his makeshift sword and swung it at the bookshelf, where Hari kept his precious collection of self-help literature. It cut right through the pirated favourites like *Who Moved My Mixed-Veg Pickle?* and *The Monk Who Sold His Skunk*. It was possible that Mental wasn't into books: his expression behind the cooling glasses was unknowable.

'Be careful with that, sir!'

'Mobile, *please*,' Kuroopanna repeated.

Hari handed one of them over. No need to tell them that he always carried two. One in the front pocket, one in the back. Front office and back office, respectively.

'Thank you for your cooperation.' Kuroopanna tossed it to his silent partner, who batted it with the sword, chopping the

Nokia in two. It dropped to the floor and he stomped on it until the plastic was pulverized.

Hari said, 'No mention.'

'Let's go then,' Kuroopanna said in his soft voice. 'Yes?'

'I should really wait for that journalist. It's kind of important to set the record straight.'

'Don't waste your time on her.'

'How do you know she's a woman?'

'There isn't any journalist coming.'

'But the madam sounded like a journalist on the phone.' He waved a hand at the shattered mobile.

'She is, but she's also my setup and I got her to make the call.'

'Why?'

'To make sure. I had to figure out whether you're just a lowly watchman or if you are the well-known detective. To avoid any mix-ups. And to establish that you're responsible for this ...' He took a look around the crummy office, 'this dump.'

'I'd wish to speak to madam herself and clarify, sir.'

'Don't bother; she's going to write whatever she wants to anyway.'

Hari so wished that his uncle had been around to defend him, but the silent associate chopped up a few more books and Hari made up his mind before Mental Menthol decided to give him a close shave with the home-cut sword. His options were limited to either revealing that the cash dispenser was hidden in the office and by that admitting that he was the culprit *or*, if the bank management wanted his help so much, he'd pretend to go along with them until such a time when he could 'find' the machine someplace other than in his own office. Even if it was unconventional to take on cases in this manner, especially if you yourself were both victim and culprit, business was business.

'Okay, sir, I'm ready to go,' he said.

Mental Menthol picked up the sheet of newsprint from the floor and wrapped the long again. It was an illegal weapon, so it couldn't be carried openly in public. Hari was happy to notice that he was a law-abiding citizen.

At that hour, CD Road was empty. In front of Puncherwallah Complex, a red Premier Padmini four-door sedan was parked next to the traffic police banner that read: 'Anyone Driving Slower than You is an Idiot and Anyone Going Faster is a Maniac.' The Padmini was the first Indian-built car that came with tinted windows, so it became an instant hit with the underworld bosses in the 1980s. It had a four-cylinder diesel engine and its top speed, close to 140kmph, was way more than roads could handle in those days. Hari always dreamt of owning one when he stood at red lights and peddled pirated video-CDs to car owners. But the manufacturing ended in 2000 due to the imported cars that flooded the market, when anybody could walk into a showroom and leave with a Porsche.

'Ah! A veteran car. Very nice,' said Hari by way of small talk. No need to make enemies. So far, they had been well-behaved and courteous, and had only damaged a few books and a phone. 'To drive at night, I mean. Less traffic jams, so we'll reach faster. Wherever it is that we're going. Sir, by the way, what's our destination? I am a little busy.'

No answer. Mental Menthol whispered hoarsely, 'Shall we put him in the dickie as usual?' It sounded as if he smoked too much.

'No please, not the dickie, Kelasamadi sir,' said Hari. But he saw to his relief that the bonnet wasn't riddled with bullet holes. That was good. He used the latest English addition to his vocabulary, 'I suffer from *claustrophobia.*'

'Is it contagious?' asked Mental Menthol.

'No,' said Kuroopanna. 'I think it is like homosexuality.'

'You're mixing it up with homophobia. Claustrophobia is a legitimate mental illness,' Hari clarified. 'If you lock me in there, I might panic and die, and then I won't be of much use to you, sir.'

Before he had time to speak again, Mental Menthol grabbed him by the neck and pushed him head first into the cramped dickie. Hari was made to lie on top of a jack and some other tools. He got the feeling that blood and involuntary bowel movements had been washed off the rubber matting all too frequently.

A sad thought struck him. He used to change his underwear daily, because he thought it was important to die in clean drawers. But as he grew older, he stopped when he figured that it doesn't really matter what you wear when you die – the undertaker will anyway change your clothes into something finer than what you ever wore when alive. But even then, he wished that he had worn freshly laundered underpants.

6

> You meet people from all walks of life, but never mind how good your good self thinks you are, you must handle those whose sentiments easily get hurt with level-headedness.

If life was bad it could always get worse, was what the stars often suggested. But despite the odds being stacked against him like a ton of rotten mackerel, as the car started moving, Hari did his best to look at the bright side of things. It was hard, because it was very dark in the dickie. He'd been in trouble before, but had always survived, so why should this be any different?

He had to be smart. If he used his backup mobile to call Triplex or Gaadi, his ace trouble-shooters, they'd be unlikely to take the call after what had happened. Instead, he tweeted that he had been kidnapped, 'Mayday, Mayday, SOS!' That should bring the world to his rescue. A minor problem was that he had no Twitter followers outside his closest circuit.

He felt claustrophobic – but reminded himself to stay cool. It was time to ask himself a few pertinent questions. If they wished to kill him, they could have done the needful there and then. So, that wasn't Plan A. Was he going to meet the bank managers? Well, he'd listen to what the bankers had to say, agree to everything and think up a suitable excuse, subterfuge or survival strategy.

There had to be a way out, a Plan B. For a second, he contemplated kicking open the dickie. It was an old car, the lock must be rusty. Might there be some implements he could use to break it open? He switched on his phone torch and inspected the tool collection. A spanner, no good. The jack? Perhaps. But he hadn't got enough time to go through with it, because the drive ended abruptly. It was as if they ran into something; the car jumped and Hari was thrown around in the dickie. The drive had only lasted some minutes – though in the dark it was hard to tell. Might as well start preparing that defence speech.

'So, did I ever tell you this incredible story of how I found out that I suffer from claustrophobia?' he said when they opened the dickie and stared down at him.

No answer.

'You *are* working for the bank, right?' he asked, grasping that they could well be after the heist loot for themselves.

Kuroopanna smiled distantly. 'Get out.'

Hari had to put in more effort to break the ice. He saw his own nervous mirror image in Mental Menthol's sunglasses. He couldn't make up his mind about whether it was safer to stay in the dickie or go with them. He had learnt the word 'agoraphobia' a few weeks earlier from his online verbosity course. 'The claustrophobia is connected to my *agoraphobia.* It means I also have a fear of public places. So, I'm at both ends at the same time. If I step out of this dickie, I must immediately go back in. When inside, I get restless and run for the door. People consider me versatile.'

'Enough bullshit, my friend.' Solid Kuroopanna boxed Hari's ears and slapped him on the face.

It took Hari by surprise. He'd been polite until then. He didn't act like a bank employee. Or was he getting irritated?

'Can we go home to my comfort zone now, please?'

'We have some work to do … you and I.'

'Oh, sooper, I love teamwork,' said Hari, relieved. He sat up in the dickie, wondering where they had brought him.

The car had stopped on the shoulder of a road, two wheels up on the pavement, and a dark construction site was visible in the gloomy streetlight. There he read the words 'For Sale Contact' followed by his own mobile number. Then he knew all too well. Furthermore, the car's light beams shone on a board according to which a branch of the private bank that Hari had been working for and a commercial complex was going to come up there. A mall, a food court and a multiplex, too.

He had been driven back to the crime scene.

Maybe they were going to stage a reconstruction of the previous night's events?

Or maybe not … Kuroopanna picked a cricket bat from the back seat of the car. Slapping the bat against his bare hand, he indicated that Hari should climb out of the dickie. This time Hari cooperated. They would hopefully let him go if he obeyed. Mental Menthol got into the driver's seat, made a tight turn and backed the car through an opening in a temporary fence of corrugated metal sheets onto a grassy wasteland shielded off from view. Kuroopanna gave Hari a shove and they walked in the car's tracks.

Mental manoeuvred the vehicle so that its headlights shone down a muddy pit at the centre of the construction site. There wasn't one civilized individual in sight.

'Construction site at night? How romantic,' said Hari. He didn't like the silence. 'What are we doing here?'

'Let me ask the questions.'

'You know, we're colleagues,' said Hari to be chatty. 'It means that we're on the same side.'

Mental Menthol got out of the car with the long. Its sharpened edge glimmered. He walked to Hari's other side.

'Save your breath,' said Kuroopanna and knocked the cricket bat into Hari's midriff approximately where his liver used to be. It sank in deep. It was as if there was a cavity under the skin. It was probably more psychological than real, but it hurt.

A crumpled newspaper page fluttered in the low beams of the Padmini's headlights, down into the foundation pits. He had heard that in America there was a tradition of underworld burials, where bodies were dumped in the pits in construction sites, after which cement was poured on top. Shopping malls then came up over them, making it unlikely that the corpses would be found unless the mall was torn down first which meant having to relocate hundreds of shops. How smart they were, the Americans.

If Kuroopanna thought that he knew where the money was, surely, he wasn't going to kill Hari?

Or should he make a run for it before it was too late? He vacillated, tried to determine the best plan. At that instant. Googly.

Thud. Kuroopanna had mistaken his skull for a cricket ball.

He heard the wooden echo inside his cranium nanoseconds before he stumbled to his knees. These things happen.

A blackout.

He heard a childish voice: 'Papa, why are you crying?'

He opened his eyes and saw his oldest daughter Ondu's face. *Was he delusional?* She was speaking complete sentences. She touched his arm. No, it wasn't a hallucination.

'I'm not crying,' he said and studied his surroundings. Everything appeared too normal. He was lying on the spare sleeping mat on the living room floor instead of on the cot. Judging by the light seeping in through the chick screens, it was morning. He made out the 'Good Habits' poster Diamond had taped up on the wall. It extolled virtues: Early to Rise. Daily Bath. Help Others. Take Part in Social Activities.

No enforcers. *How had he ended up at home?* Last he remembered, he was near death.

'You were,' Ondu insisted, the way a toddler who refused to obey her parents did.

Her twin sister Eradu was also awake.

'Papa, were you having a sad dream?' Eradu asked.

Ondu and Eradu were like the moon and the sun. Something or the other had happened in the womb, because a pair of twins had never been so unlike each other. Or maybe they were born with half a brain each: one was pure emotion, the other sheer logic. One was tall and thin; the other was like a ball.

Eradu always picked up on Hari's moods. Her marginally older sister Ondu told Hari, 'Behave like a grownup.'

He lied to his daughters. 'Not to worry. This moisture is just pre-monsoon sweat.' He wiped his face with his sleeping towel which, when folded, served as a cushion. 'Go do your homework. See what it says on the poster: good habits mean reading and studying.'

'I don't know how to read yet,' said Ondu who had inherited her father's quick mind.

'Then go teach yourself,' he said, because he was a self-made man and wished the same for his offspring. He tightened his loincloth. *So all had been a dream?* He hated nightmares. While he patted his oldest daughter's curls, he continued analysing the scene. He was a detective and therefore he knew that if things were normal, he wouldn't be waking up at home. He'd be sitting outside an ATM booth.

So he was still in the nightmare. Not good. This wasn't any run-off-the-mill horror story. It meant one out of two possible things. Either it was a symptom of post-traumatic shock, telling him that he was about to come and go, as in, come apart and go insane.

Or it was his subconscious getting him ready for the inevitable, that which his consciousness was wilfully ignoring: he'd succumbed and robbed the ATM with Triplex. The dream prepared him for the consequences. Should he visit Sri Pandit Pundit and ask the astrologer for alternative interpretations?

Something hit his face. His eyes snapped open. Pain flashed, thoughts ached. He'd been hit from behind. A cricket bat was tapping at his cheek. *Not again.* He placed his palms on the ground, the dirt gritted against his fingers, and got up on all fours.

In the distance, he heard the rustle of nocturnal animals, bandicoots. He felt giddy. The night was like overcooked prawns in a seedy bar: too spicy, oil-fried to death and seriously bad for health. He wanted to throw up, but hadn't eaten since the previous evening's supper twenty-four hours ago.

So, no puking.

And at least he hadn't been buried alive.

Not yet.

That was on the plus side. Hari briefly thought about whether to gherao the bank, but if he gheraoed alone it would hardly lead to anything. The only professional rioter he knew was AC Gaadi, whom his wife had fired. Better be constructive. Instead he'd take the civilized route, file a complaint against the bank – it was their fault, they should never have hired him in the first place. ATMs were routinely stolen; being the guard of one was akin to playing Russian roulette. But then.

Then, then, then ... The unfinished thought kept ringing in his ears as Mental placed the sharp blade of the long against the back of his neck. Hari felt it tickle the fine hairs at the nape. It was very much execution style. They intended to kill him, big surprise. Kuroopanna stepped around to face Hari.

'Don't move now or Kelasamadi might accidentally chop off your head,' said Kuroopanna.

He placed the tip of the cricket bat against Hari's nose. Hari made quick calculations. He'd studied plenty of human anatomy on the Net. If he batted upwards, it'd drive Hari's nasal bone into his cerebrum, resulting in brain death. *Don't think bad thoughts. Brain death leads to painlessness.* He peeked back at the street and the car. Its lights shone into his eyes. Where were the bank managers whom he expected to plead his case before?

He suddenly knew with certainty that he wasn't going to see his daughters again. Or his wife. He loved them so much. His last conversation with Diamond was flowing like honeydew in his ears. What were her words again – 'come home tonight and do the dishes. Or else …' Oh, there was nothing that he'd rather do than wash the kadai that was sticky with coconut oil and the tawa greasy from frying parathas.

'How was your experience?' said Kuroopanna in his kindest voice.

'What do you mean?'

'How would you rate the services of our bank?'

'Like which services?'

'Anything you want to say about the services you performed last night?'

Hari forced himself to focus, he had probably only suffered light brain damage so far. 'Me?'

'Tell us, and we shall get this over with quickly.'

'Sooper, what do you want?'

'Money,' whispered Mental Menthol in his sweetly cigarette smoky voice.

Such a typical Bengaluru concern. With brain cogs whirling fast like the blades of a grinder, Hari said, 'That's what makes the city go round.'

'Stop your wisecracking. *Where* is the money?' elaborated Kuroopanna. 'If, as *you* say, we're on the same side and *you* help us find it, there'll be a finder's fee.'

Hari recognized what was happening. It was the good cop, bad cop routine.

'I hear you loud and clear, but I'm confused. Exactly what money are we talking about? I have twenty-five rupees in my pocket.' He spoke too much, nervously, but couldn't hold back with the two weapons tickling his skin. The cricket bat was currently tapping his throat as if preparing to tee off. A smash there would drive his neck into the makeshift sword and slice it.

'That's not the kind of money we're talking about,' Kuroopanna tut-tutted. 'Let me put it this way, Majestic: there's a teller machine missing and you will please tell us where it is.'

'Frisk me if you wish.'

So far, they hadn't and it was fairly evident that he had no cash dispenser on him. All he had was his second Nokia in his back pocket and a miniature spray paint can in a front pocket – for painting his contact numbers on the perimeter walls of vacant plots in the hope of making a quick buck.

'Majestic, we know that you won't be carrying the money on you.'

'You are so correct, sir.'

'So take us to it. Once we get it back, you'll go free and everything will return to normal.'

'Oho, is it so?' The long sword cut against his skin and he swallowed a glob of dry, stringy saliva. It tasted of burnt plastic. Was that the flavour of his intestines?

'Shall I behead him?' Mental asked.

'Hold on, Kelasamadi sir,' said Hari.

'He's getting tired of you,' said Kuroopanna.

'But what if I tell you the truth?' said Hari.

'Yes, kindly tell us where you stashed the cash.'

'That may seem like a plan, but only if I had it stashed.' He held his breath. If he gave them the ATM, they might decide to kill him anyway and steal it for themselves. He had to improve his bargaining position first. He could get Gaadi to shift the ATM and then pretend to crack the case, maybe call some journalists to cover the events to make sure that everything was on record.

'You are a smooth talker, aren't you? Let's see what we can do about that.'

A kick in the butt from Mental, who stood behind, sent Hari sprawling. It winded him.

'Do you want to die?' said Mental, getting the toes in hard a couple of times in Hari's ribs, but soon getting out of breath like a habitual smoker. Nevertheless, he wore business-like pointy leather shoes. Brand new, so the leather hadn't softened yet. These kicks hurt more than when one was kicked with a rubber sandal. He didn't fight back; being human had by no means been easy anyway, so he shut his eyes and prepared for the next reincarnation.

'He can't die until I say so, Kelasamadi,' said Kuroopanna.

Hari hoped so too. Mental gave him one last kick. Hari's non-violent strategy had worked. Perhaps they'd leave him there in a bloody heap, then he could drag himself home and wash the dishes.

'You all right?' said Kuroopanna.

'Uh, so-so, but thanks for asking,' said Hari.

'Thank you for not fighting back. We appreciate your cooperation.'

'No mention, I simply don't like to make enemies.'

'Then tell me where the ten lakhs forty-three thousand and eight hundred rupees is.'

That was a precise figure, Hari's mathematical mind observed. On the other hand, if the bank gave a 10 per cent finder's fee, it would mean ₹1,04,380 in somebody's pocket.

'Oho, was it that much?' he said. 'Big reward, huh?'

'Listen, here's the deal. And I'll sugar-coat the pill,' said Kuroopanna. 'Spill the beans, you survive and get a cut of the reward.'

'How big?'

'We'll give you ten thousand. Reasonable?'

'I'll try my best to look for the money and call you as soon as I find it.'

'Glad to hear, but whether you're going to confess or not, it is time for you to open your mouth wide,' said Kuroopanna.

'Why?' said Hari.

The moment he opened it to ask the question, Kuroopanna shoved the bat in Hari's mouth, the teeth crunched and then the bat got stuck at his Adam's apple. As Kuroopanna pumped it in and out, he went on speaking, 'You don't, you die. But don't take this personally. If we kill you, it's only business and in our kind of business there will always be collateral damage.'

Finally, after what seemed like a short eternity, Kuroopanna pulled out the bat.

Gums bleeding, as his brain went through options, Hari said, 'But why should I tell you if I find the money? You might take it and kill me anyway.'

'We will kill you painlessly,' said Mental Menthol, who seemed about to go loose cannon on Hari.

Hari thought feverishly. 'And otherwise?'

'If you wish, we kill you painfully.' Kuroopanna slammed the bat into Hari's mouth again.

Mental Menthol bent down to pick up a piece of rope from the construction garbage on the ground. It was long and thick enough to strangle somebody with.

Kuroopanna added, 'Show him how this is going to work, Kelasamadi.'

Mental dug out a pack of cigarettes and sat himself down on Hari's back. Hari's face pressed into the muddy ground and with the bat in his mouth he was barely able to breathe. What made this position particularly uncomfortable was the small can of spray paint in his front pocket, which pressed into his groin. Then Mental bent Hari's legs up at the knees and tied the feet together with the rope.

Once his feet were secured, he heard a match being struck and then there was cigarette smoke – menthol.

'Are you with us or against us?' Kuroopanna asked and pulled out the cricket bat.

Hari could finally breathe easier. He knew that whether he told them what they wanted to know, or not, something bad was going to happen, so he said, 'As you like.'

'Then suck on this,' Kuroopanna said and rammed the bat back in.

'Hold still,' Mental added as he removed Hari's rubber sandals.

'Uhun-ghuguni,' Hari gagged.

Instantly, he felt something strangely warm against his soles. At first it wasn't painful, merely unpleasant, a tingling. As the heat grew, he knew what it was. Mental was burning him with the cigarette. Luckily his feet were used to hardships – he had walked on cracked pavements ever since he was a peddling toddler. But soon he smelt burnt meat. Inch by inch his feet were being grilled. At that moment, he deeply sympathized with the millions of tandoori kebabs that were gobbled up every year.

After each puff, Mental wiped off hot ash on one of Hari's toes, allowing the cigarette to smoulder against the skin until it was time for the next drag. It had never struck Hari before exactly how unhealthy passive smoking could be.

'Tell us,' Kuroopanna repeated and bent down before Hari's face, prodding with the tip of the bat between Hari's lips, wedging it in and pulling it out. 'Did … you … swallow the ATM?'

Mental extinguished his first cigarette by grinding it into the soft skin on the ankle. Hari sobbed. The bat pressed against his teeth. He'd probably have to get dentures. But luckily it was too big to slide all the way down his throat to the rectum. No amount of antacid would take care of that.

'Think harder.'

He gagged again. 'Uh-uh.'

'Trying to say something?' Kuroopanna pulled the bat out.

'I thought I should tell you that you're liable to be charged under Sections 294-b for using filthy language, 324 for voluntarily causing grievous hurt by dangerous weapon, 341 for wrongful restraint, 342 for wrongful confinement, 366 for abduction, 504 for intentional insult, and 506-ii for criminal intimidation by threatening with dire consequences if this goes on for much longer.'

'Are you threatening us?'

'I'm cautioning you. If you want to be threatened, then I can fix that too ...'

He couldn't finish the sentence before the bat got stuck deep in his throat again. This time it did feel like it hit the rectum from within.

Mental lit another menthol. Had he brought a pack of ten or twenty?

7

You're involved in something that requires you to take more risks than is good for you – and may need help to comprehend the situation.

Taking a macro perspective, he was no more than thirty-three years old and according to his own reckoning too young to get crucified. But his feet were on fire, one spot after another being cooked with red-hot ashes. The cricket bat poked into his tonsils. His wife would be so angry if he died. No, he had to go home and wash the dishes.

He signalled surrender by using a trembling finger.

The bat plopped out of his mouth.

'You're ready?'

'Yes sir, that was scary,' said Hari. He coughed out slime. 'You almost made me feel like a kebab – and minced my tongue, so how would I have been spilling any beans then? Did you think of that?'

'I figured you'd be smart enough to talk before it got that bad,' said Kuroopanna courteously.

'Yes sir, I have IQ. May I turn around? I can't speak lying face down.' He calculated 58–42 odds against Plan C being successful, and 79–21 against his own survival. Fair enough. Anybody who wanted to win had to gamble.

'Sounds to me like you're speaking.'

'But I have the secret treasure map in my pocket …'

'No kidding.'

'Honestly, I'm not making it up. It shows where the money is buried.'

'Bullshit.'

'If you don't trust me, just check the map. It's real.'

Mental Menthol rose up on his knees, legs spread on either side of Hari, preventing him from moving more than necessary – giving him just enough leeway to roll over on his back. Mental had a fresh cigarette in the corner of his mouth and was about to light it. He looked like he wanted to use Hari's mouth as an ashtray.

Hari looked up at Mental, who was digging for a matchbox. He asked, 'May I take out the map?'

'Sure you can,' Kuroopanna replied in that annoyingly friendly tone. 'If you had told us about it earlier, our friendship wouldn't have had to sour. I hope you understand we're doing what we're paid to.'

'And I hope you got well paid.'

'I'm positive that you'd have done the same.'

'Next time I'm in your situation, I'll definitely follow the good example you have set,' said Hari and pulled the small can of spray paint out. He counted on it being too dark for them to see what he was up to and besides, Mental was wearing his sunglasses. 'Zero per cent hard feelings.'

'I'm glad,' said Kuroopanna.

Hari waited a beat, until Mental put a match to his menthol cigarette.

He inhaled. The flame grew.

There was no time to shake the can. Hari pressed the button and black paint shot out onto Mental's face. On coming into contact with the match and cigarette, the jet of combustible gas exploded into a ray of fire, turning the can into a flamethrower.

Mental screamed. He threw himself off Hari, aided by the knee that Hari rammed into his crotch. The human ball of flames was a spectacular sight, like a flambéed frog jumping about in the night outside a French restaurant in Pondicherry.

Hari acted fast. The paint can could blow up in his hand any second. He aimed the improvised weapon of mass destruction against Kuroopanna and his polyester pants caught fire. Safari suits weren't fireproof. 'Whoosh!' and he was ablaze. The material burned with an infernal heat, tonsuring a man's scrotum in a jiffy.

Hari threw the can. It exploded in the air.

Drops of black paint rained over them.

Kuroopanna wailed like a mammal in heat. He struggled to pull off his pants. While Kuroopanna was busy, Hari grabbed the sharp long sword and sawed off the rope that had been tied around his ankles, picked up his rubber sandals and shouted, 'Bye-bye and all the very best!'

Then he took off. Hurrying away from the construction site, past the looted ATM booth, he rounded a banner that said, 'Drive Like Hell & You Will Get There' and ran like hell down CD Road.

Things had almost gotten out of hand for a moment. But he had taken care of the situation and was alive as usual. He slowed down. The screams grew fainter. Either the two were going to survive or not. If it was the latter, he'd apologize later – in the next life.

Right there and then, he had more pressing concerns. He needed a disinfectant footbath and then soothing coconut oil for his blistered toes. But no pharmacies were open. This late everything was quiet except for the stray dogs that barked at every turn of the road and the distant wails from the construction site. Mental Menthol a.k.a. Kelasamadi would want to see a plastic surgeon urgently and Solid Kuroopanna might consider a bollock transplant. After some hundred yards, Hari slowed down to a limp. He wasn't going to be able to carry on for much longer. A sedentary lifestyle as a watchman didn't promote fitness. The burnt skin was coming off his feet.

But his mind was making calculations. The office wasn't a safe hiding place. Home didn't seem like the right option either. Kuroopanna probably knew where he lived. He didn't want to put Diamond and the kids at risk. It'd be a great Plan D to get out of town and perhaps travel to Bhutan. *But how?* He had little money … unless he emptied the stolen ATM.

Enforcers, that was what they turned out to be. Not bank security officials, but plain and simple bounty hunters, and why was it that Hari wasn't too surprised?

He turned towards the bus station. There'd be people round the clock. Safer. As he reached the platforms, he stretched out on a bench. He needed to rest his feet. The burn wounds wept where the cigarette torture had lacerated the skin. As he analyzed the situation, he felt utterly alone in this fix. It was the loneliness of a waterless tap in the Thar Desert. The helplessness of piled up garbage on the roadside during a three-week strike. His adoptive uncle was dead. His biological mother was serving seven years in jail. His friends and he had traded their don't-call-me's, I'll-call-you's. There was a great lack of testosterone in his marital life.

He cried himself to sleep.

There were lots of tears. He was drowning in them. A bus conductor was pouring a bucket of cold water over him. A police constable prodded him with his bamboo lathi. It was the same constable who had come with Ropu Uncle to investigate the crime scene and then interrogated him at the police station, Danger Ramboswamy. The game was over, it seemed.

'You can't sleep here.'

'Where am I?' said Hari and looked around.

He wasn't in jail yet, but lying on a bench at the city bus station.

'Drunk, huh?' This Ramboswamy was one cop who was deducing a lot.

'Drunkenness is not allowed in the bus stand,' the conductor added.

Hari faced the constable. 'Sorry boss, had a rough night. Had your coffee? I'll take your leave now.'

'Wait a minute, not so fast.' Constable Ramboswamy was youngish, with a moustache that curled up at the ends, dressed in khaki and an open-face half-helmet of the army type, popular among motorcyclists in Bengaluru. No visor, no goggles.

Hari used to wear a second-hand military helmet when he rode a motorcycle, before he had to pawn it and buy a third-hand scooter. The police bike stood by the curb pot-potting to itself in its subdued macho manner. Hari loved the sound of a well-maintained Enfield engine.

The constable eyed him back. 'What happened?'

'Nothing.'

'Got beaten up?' He sounded suspicious.

'No, it was an accident.' Certain people might get angry if he made allegations to the effect that the bank had sent contract killers to torture him. A court case might be slapped. A skilful lawyer would argue that the enforcers had the right to do what they did and that he was wrong in resisting it.

'Aren't you the loser whose ATM got uprooted the night before last?'

'It is possible,' mumbled Hari and ground the heels of his hands into his blurry eyes. 'It is very tiring to lose ATMs, so I had to take a nap.'

'Lost your job, what?'

'Life is hard, boss.' Hari scratched his dandruff.

'What kind of accident?'

A lonesome red heart-shaped Styrofoam cut-out with the words 'Newly Wedded' painted on it with bright golden letters was blown across the asphalt by a dusty wind. The month of May was peak wedding season, with many auspicious dates. The heart must have fallen off a passing car: cars were standard wedding gifts within the liberalized economy. Hari watched it flutter about ghostlike, a lost soul like himself. It gave him an idea. 'Stag party yesterday at the Press Club in Cubbon Park got out of hand. Boss, where am I?'

'Don't know where you are?' The cop found that hilarious, but people whose friends were members of the Press Club were treated with a degree of respect, so he stopped jabbing Hari with the bamboo stick. 'You're at the city bus stand.'

'Last I remember, I was going for a wedding,' improvised Hari.

'Whose would that be?'

'My own.'

'Heartiest congratulations.'

'Uh. Did you happen to see a red Padmini nearby?'

'No, why's that?'

'It was a dowry gift from the editor at *Deccan Herald.*' He indicated the Styrofoam heart on the ground. 'Must have gotten jacked. Uh, what time is it?'

'Close to seven-thirty.'

'My bad luck will continue forever!' Hari slapped himself on the forehead. 'My friends are such jokers to leave me here without a vehicle. The muhurat is at 7:36 a.m. and I'm going to miss it totally.'

'Sounds fully inauspicious.' It was well-known that the perfect timing averted problems. A proper muhurat easily made the Mumbai Sensex surge over 201 points. 'But don't worry, it should be fine if you're a few minutes late. You might face minor marital discord only.'

'You don't know my wife.'

'I thought you weren't married.'

'My wife-to-be ... will never forgive me if I miss our arranged marriage, especially after losing that ATM,' said Hari.

The constable's attitude changed. 'Where's it that you need to be?'

'CD Road, Puncherwallah Complex, the venerable Sri Pundit's chambers.'

'Brother, you still have six minutes, I'll give you a drop.'

Feeling emboldened by the upgrade from crook to brother, Hari said, 'Sooper. Can you put the siren on?' The enforcers wouldn't dare to attack a police motorcycle.

'No,' said Constable Ramboswamy.

Nevertheless, it was good to ride pillion on an Enfield – *the road to salvation always leads in unexpected directions*, he idly thought as they cruised through the traffic that was getting denser. Pundit, the astrologer, would have to pull off a miracle to get everything back on track. However, Hari trusted astrologers because theirs was a rational science based on the motions of solid stuff: planets, stars, comets, astronauts, satellites, ISRO and NASA. Nothing flimsy about it, pure mathematics. And apart from the stellar advice Pundit-ji offered and without which Hari never undertook anything that mattered, he was also a low-budget psychoanalyst.

'Something is wrong, guru.'

'What?'

'Everything.'

'How come?'

'Your horoscope usually promises me a better future, but I think it may have turned me into a permanent loser.'

Hari sat in the visitor's chair in the global headquarters of the Venerable Pandit Pundit Dotcom Forecast Consultations & Astro Research Institute, which shared the first floor of Puncherwallah Complex with Hari's own detective bureau, Doc's cybercafé and a non-vegetarian canteen, Friendly Mess, run by the affable Suleiman. The wall was covered with posters for medical camps that Pandit Pundit regularly conducted – *'All type disease cure with fresh herbal stuffed fish medicine sexual weakness unhappy married life lack of stamina semen back pain joint pain stomach gas trouble sugar asthma allergy job issues visa application etc contact once to get rid of problems forever live healthy with natural therapy trusted by billions.'* With the advent of DTP, his posters had become free of spelling errors, but no software could stop Pundit from committing grammatical atrocities.

Hari explained his problems with the stolen ATM (except he didn't say it was in his office next-door) and showed Pundit, who was dressed in white and wore a Mysuru style turban, the cigarette burns on his feet – they had formed scabs and didn't look too disgusting.

'Please don't think too much about it,' the wise man said and adopted that otherworldly, transcendental, esoteric tone that used to offer Hari much succour, but which suddenly began to bother him.

'Hari is a loser,' added Pundit's cheeky parrot, showing off its snooty English-speaking acumen from its cage by the window. Hari decided there and then that at the first opportunity he'd sell it to some Chettinad restaurateur as pigeon roast.

'I can't stop brooding.'

'But you must: it uses up brain tissue and makes it shrink.'

'Oho, is it so?'

The eternal truth that Pundit always taught was that ordinary people should avoid thinking and instead leave it to the experts – such as himself. *But wasn't all defeated*, wondered Hari, *the moment one understood that one wasn't supposed to think? Because once one knew, one already crossed the line and understood too much, by when one was hopelessly lost.*

'See, I knew you wouldn't understand,' said Pundit and reverted to his archaic charts.

After forty-five seconds, Hari got restless. His wife always went on about astrology being a superstition, something that Hari refused to accept. But aloud he said: 'Meaning?'

'It could get worse. You agree, isn't it?'

Judging from recent experiences, it did seem to be true. So, for the sake of argument, he nodded. 'I hear you.'

'So until it gets worse, don't think about it.'

'It just got worse.'

Pundit browsed mystical computer printouts of ancient documents. 'Is it to do with your wife? In that case, I have something interesting to read out to you.'

'What?' Hari said cautiously.

'She's a churchgoer, right?'

'Correct-u, but she combines it with Sufism, rationalism and atheism.' Diamond's father was a Christian, her mother a Muslim, so to please both her parents she took the children to the Rice Memorial Church in Avenue Road on Sunday mornings, on Thursdays she wore a headscarf and visited a Sufi shrine, and the rest of the week she devoted to forensic science and acted rationally like a person born in Kerala ought to.

'Tricky case, then. However, in their sacred scripture, which I recently downloaded to scrutinize, it says, and I am quoting: "Rather dwell with a lion and a dragon, than keep house with a wicked woman. The wickedness of a woman changes her face and darkens her countenance like sackcloth." Picture that next time you see her.'

'I'm picturing.'

'Myself I'm unmarried due to my spiritual pursuits, so I have no issue with women, but for you this Biblical wisdom is relevant: "As the climbing up a sandy way is to the feet of the aged, so is a wife full of words to a quiet man. A woman is full of anger, impudence, and much reproach." Do you recognize yourself? Or your wife?'

'Partly.'

'Here comes the suggested solution: "Cut her off from thy flesh, give her a bill of divorce and let her go." Does that answer your problem?' said Pundit, making esoteric sounds by clicking his tongue according to a mysterious rhythm, satisfied with the eloquence of his own sermon.

'But I love my wife, guru-ji,' said Hari. 'Isn't there another option?'

'Hari is a loser,' said the parrot.

'Then I know what must be done.' Pundit paid no attention to his rude pet (when it suited him, he pretended not to know the English language) and pressed his hands together, palm to palm.

'You do?' said Hari eagerly.

'See, what has happened is that you have become depressed. It can be triggered by multiple causes.'

'What cause is it then?'

'For example, loss of money, trouble with colleagues, discord at home, making fresh enemies – so many causes are there. Recognize any such cause?'

'It is possible.'

'Then you must go on pilgrimage.'

'Pilgrimage?' It had never occurred to Hari. But all things considered, his guru might be onto something. Besides, he had to urgently get out of town before more enforcers came after him. 'Where? To Benares or Jerusalem or Bhutan?'

'Go and see the Ninth Avatar in the ancient Halegudehalli temple.'

'Ninth Avatar?'

'The correct doctrine is given in the *Bhagavad-Gita* when Lord Krishna tells Arjuna: "Whenever there is a decline of righteousness and rise of unrighteousness then I send forth myself. For the protection of the good, for the destruction of the wicked and for the establishment of righteousness, I come into being from age to age." It's all online.'

'But guru, how will it help me?'

'Which one?'

'That one: the ninth one.'

'The Ninth Avatar is the latest, very up to date. The tenth hasn't come yet and when he comes, the world will end – which will take care of problems. Until then, I have heard that this particular darshan cures any modern psychiatric illnesses, in addition to which it is said that such an experience has a tonic-like effect on marriage. My prophecy has been uttered. Please pay a voluntary donation to my parrot.'

Interestingly enough, Pundit never touched money himself. He believed that everything in this world, including money, was soiled by the deeds of those whose hands it passed through, so the deviant parrot handled his bookkeeping and filed his tax returns – his returns were always the same every year anyway since he declared zero income, because it was the parrot who took in the money and animals didn't pay tax in India. Not yet. Pundit was also against newspaper horoscopes for free, because he felt that people should pay for their future or be without one.

'Guru, I hear you. But, where is it?'

'In its cage, by the door.'

'But this temple you mentioned?'

'Ah, the temple. It used to be popular in the 1970s, before there were Internet darshan options, it was where the who's who went. Movie stars before launching a film. Leaders before taking the lead. Near Srirangapatnam, if I remember correctly. You go there and enquire.'

Srirangapatnam. That was one hundred kilometres away. A safe distance. He must go. He dug in his pocket. He came up with a fistful of coins. The parrot nodded at the pile of cash at its feet, and said, 'Hari is a loser.'

A small idea struck Hari: 'Guru, to help me go on pilgrimage, I'm sure you won't mind if I borrow money for petrol from your tandoori parrot? I'll swing by tomorrow first thing and pay back with a 700 per cent interest.'

The parrot was gaping, wordlessly.

8

Take a break, forget painful memories of the past; it may improve your karma.

Plan E was to go to the nearest pharmacy and get ointment for the burns on his feet and then immediately skip town. But standing for a moment on the veranda, brooding, he happened to glance down and spot a red Premier Padmini coming to a halt right across the street.

A different car? Fat chance. Padminis were increasingly rare in modern traffic and it was a red one at that – the colour of blood. Kelasamadi, alias Mental Menthol, was alone at the wheel. His face had uneven black paint stains. He didn't look friendly. There could be a sharpshooter lurking in the dickie. Hari ducked behind the railing.

The enforcer got out of the car. His hair had burnt up partially, his moustache was a line of ashes, his face had blisters, and his eyes looked like hardboiled eggs that had been ghee roasted, with onions for eyebrows. No doubt he'd make Hari cough up

₹10,43,800 plus enough to cover his hospitalization and whatever new garments he had to buy for himself – and by the looks of it, the black T-shirt with the Superman logo on the chest alone was going to cost Hari ₹250 or so. Money he didn't have.

He had to get out of there fast. The office complex was a suicide trap in case Mental Menthol came upstairs. What Hari had borrowed from Pundit's parrot amounted to ₹600 and that wouldn't go far. Only as far as Srirangapatnam and only if he made it to his scooter alive – it stood parked in the dead-end alley behind the Puncherwallah Complex which had no emergency exit. There was only one way in or out and that was the street entrance facing Mental Menthol.

Hari peeked through the holes in the latticed screen of the veranda railing. Mental went to the Sandalwood Darshini and bought a coffee or tea – Hari couldn't smell the difference from that distance – and capsicum bhajjis. No doubt that morning snack too was going to end up on Hari's tab.

Mental positioned himself at one of the pavement-side steel-topped tables, laid out his mobile and something parcelled in newsprint – roughly the size of a long – on it. From there, he could keep a close watch on the facade of the entire Puncherwallah Complex including the door to Hari's office.

Since it was morning, he might assume that Hari hadn't arrived yet. He went to work on his breakfast. Hari wondered whether it was worth the risk to sneak out through the main entrance while he ate. But that very second, Mental turned to check as if he had telepathically phone-tapped Hari's mind.

Instead, Hari crawled across to the staircase. Still hunching down, he climbed upstairs to the roof. Puncherwallah Complex was an old-fashioned two-storey building. Its roof was flat and surrounded by a low parapet, but as long as he kept his distance from the front part he was out of sight.

Having anticipated this happening to him – he had once been forced to jump off a third-storey roof – and knowing that bad things had an innate tendency to repeat themselves thrice, Hari had hidden a rope behind the water tanks. But had it rotted over the last few monsoons? Too many ifs and buts as usual.

He tied it to a water pipe and tested the knot by pulling hard. Should hold his weight. Despite putting on five kilograms since he had got married, he wasn't fat. Okay, maybe somewhat paunchy.

In the dead-end behind the building, the garage owner, Puncherwallah, stored car parts. Stacked along the walls were bumpers and wheel rims, carburettors and mufflers, rustycrankshafts, dented bonnets and worn tires. Hari calculated the risks. If he fell on some sharp car part he might get a little bit impaled. But he wasn't scared of high drops; he was more terrified of low feelings.

He chucked his rubber sandals down. They landed near his scooter. He swung a leg over the parapet and searched for a foothold. There was none. *Focus*, he ordered himself. *Once good karma gains momentum it can go a long way.* He held on to the rope with both hands. Then he lay on his stomach on the parapet and lifted the other foot over. With both legs dangling over empty space, he slowly slid his body backwards.

He coiled some rope around one hand. Why hadn't he invested in a rope-ladder? Why was he so stingy when it came to matters of life and death? Again, he felt the panic grow. He lowered himself down, letting go of the rope an inch at a time, but there was no foothold anywhere. Then suddenly his toes touched the upper side of a window frame. The window was open. He used its steel bars to climb down. Eventually, he reached the ledge and balanced on it.

Perched there, he rested his arms. It was the kitchen window of Suleiman's mess, its bars furry with dust and crud. The kitchen was empty save for a somewhat dead goat that stared straight at Hari, as if lecturing him about mortality and reincarnation.

Locking eyes with the goat, he was reminded of the fact that Suleiman would be cooking his famous VIP biriyani for lunch and he hadn't eaten for ages. Maybe that's why he felt weak and his nerves were all over the place?

He grabbed the lowest window bar with one hand, slippery from the kitchen's oily fumes, and kept the rope coiled around the other. It cut into his wrist, but he needed to keep going for a few more metres to reach the ground. Holding on to the window bars, he fumbled with his feet and toes – but there was nothing to support himself on. The wall was bare. The point of no return was way up there. He craned his neck to look back at the roof. He couldn't possibly climb up again.

The only way was down. In hindsight, he knew that a portion of wall that had several open windows and more outside plumbing would have been an ideal escape route. Here, his arms were stretched taut, his feet trod thin air, and he had nowhere to go. He felt about desperately with his bare feet as he stretched his arms another quarter of an inch and finally his toes touched glass. With his toenails erect, he sensed the upper part of a windowpane – this window was shut.

His arms were beginning to tire. Blood circulation was gone in the hand that the rope was twisted around. The other still held on to the kitchen window's greasy bottom bar, but he was slowly losing his grip.

Using his toes, he knocked on the glass pane, but nobody opened the window. Considering its position, it might be the window to the toilet at the back of Puncherwallah's garage. He kicked harder. If the crew was stripping a stolen car for spares and cutting its chassis up into longs, they wouldn't hear a thing.

Hari had no option but to carry on and so finally let go of the kitchen window's bar. He straightaway lost his balance and hung from one arm. The rope was strangling his hand, almost amputating it. At any moment, the arm might tear at the armpit.

I'm stupid and deserve what I get, he thought in a tragic moment of self-realization. Then there was a jerk in the rope. He plummeted ten inches. A sudden rain drenched him. The water pipe?

It broke. He fell.

His past deeds flashed before his third eye, then he crashed on top of the stacks of tires that were waiting to be retreaded and vulcanized in order to be sold off as 'semi-new'. It wasn't more than a few feet and the touchdown was soft.

The stray dogs that lived in the back alley, most of them mangled by drunk drivers and who guarded his scooter, gathered around and licked his face, happy to see him. One of them even brought him his rubber slippers. He was touched. They wagged their tails. He petted them and promised to bring them tiffin. They loved parathas.

He kicked life into the scooter. He had to kick it many times, because it too seemed to be the victim of some kind of near-death experience. He wished it was an Enfield, then he'd have ruled the streets.

Finally, he zipped out of the alley in the opposite direction from where Mental Menthol had positioned himself and drove towards the R. K. Narayan Circle Petrol Bunk. CD Road was a one-way street, which meant that Mental, if he spotted Hari's takeoff, had to drive past the banner stating 'Everything Bad Comes Your Way, if You Drive in the Wrong Lane,' against the oncoming traffic. A scooter easily surfed upriver between the ferocious buses and trucks, but if Mental wanted to play it safe he would have to drive around the block first and follow on a parallel street.

After using some of the holy parrot's sacred money to tank up at the Petrol Bunk, he didn't stop again. At the next corner, he swerved towards the bypass to the south of the bus stand and the Namma Metro semi-construction site, taking a turn into Dr T. C. M. Royan Road, which brought him to the City Market, where he did a U-turn up the Balagangadharanathamahaswamiji flyover that sent traffic out onto the Mysuru Road. That early, the traffic jams hadn't yet started so he kept going at a first-rate speed along the highway through Chamarajpete. At the NICE Ring Road, vehicles lined up at white tollgates and glass booths, the motorway ramps like tentacles of a giant octopus reaching down to grab cars. After the toll plaza, he continued down along Mysuru Road. There was a certain safety in being on the Mysuru Road. Mysuru was a royal city of culture and civilization.

Soon he was out of Bengaluru proper, but still the landscape that flanked the highway was crammed with housing colonies, industrial estates – the city just didn't want to end. He already missed it, the most incredible city on earth, and wondered when he might be returning. Maybe never?

He kept driving through Ramanagram and Mandya towards the Cauvery River basin. En route he saw barely two traffic accidents and not more than one of them fatal. Considering how this road was the most accident-prone stretch in south India, it was auspicious.

Two hours later, with the wind whistling in his wispy moustache, he cruised across the long bridge to the island of Srirangapatnam, a place of historical importance. Once on the island, with the river crocodiles between him and his problems, he let the Bajaj scooty roll to a halt outside the first food joint he spotted. It had been ages since he had eaten and so, before he went deeper into the hinterland where there might not be a single canteen, he ought to grab a bite.

Al-Kabab Chainees Café stood next to the Fully Hijab Burkha Exclusive Matching Centre. The names told him that it was going to be a non-vegetarian lunch. It worried him. He remembered the empty stare of the dead goat through Suleiman's kitchen window. He was trying to become a full-time vegetarian on account of the guidance his astrologer provided for how to improve his rebirth options. Yet, he acknowledged that bad habits were hard to shake off.

The menu was painted in red on the green wall. A biriyani was ₹50 and oil-fry kebabs ₹25, a steal compared to Bengaluru rates – even Suleiman charged more at his mess in Puncherwallah Complex. Then he saw that there was a veggie biriyani on offer, too. It was best for karma.

Sitting down, he whipped out his phone, added the restaurant to TripAdvisor ('cheapest & bestest'), downloaded Wikitravel's take on the area, edited in a good review of the restaurant based on its rates, and then threw in his own mobile number in case people needed tour guidance. He memorized catchy phrases that could come in handy in case he had an opportunity for some unlicensed touting. He noticed that there were several missed calls. Diamond must be worried. Actually, he ought to let her know that some torpedoes might smash a sledgehammer into their door, but he allowed himself to get distracted when two foreign tourists walked in as if on cue. Suddenly his poor luck had turned and it was the time to prove that he was the king of touts.

They were two young hippies who had missed the 1960s by many decades. They put their motorcycle helmets down on a table and studied the kebab-heavy menu on the wall. Hari overheard them ask for boiled potatoes – the one dish that was not on the menu. The waiters got confused and discussed the matter between themselves. The tourists would like carrot and cauliflower too.

'Veg biriyani!' The waiters agreed, once they understood.

'But no spizes, ze plain boil vegetable,' the male specimen clarified. 'And ze big plate, we want ze double porzion.'

Their accents sounded French. The waiters offered to cook two portions of mix-veggie biriyani without the rice and spice – if they so wished – but with aloo, gajjar, mutter, gobi and whatever else was in the larder.

'Ow much?' said the Frenchman.

A waiter referred to the menu: 'Fifty per plate, sir, so hundred if you want a double portion.'

The Frenchman, scary with his dreadlocks, gaudy pyjama bottoms and yin-yang-tattooed eyelids, threw a tantrum. 'But zat's too much!'

His companion was a girl, a blonde with more tattoos, of motorcycles, dragons and paté de foie gras: they debated in their own language, groaned exaggeratedly and made gestures towards their heads.

'Zis is a rip-ov, oui can't pay for ze spice and rice zat oui do not eat.' At that, the two staged a dramatic walkout. The waiters remained confused – they had tried to understand what the crazy white people wanted and when they accommodated the French culinary requirements, this was the outcome.

Hari knew tourists like he knew his own ear wax, but these rural restaurateurs didn't. He called out in his most educated English: 'Sorry sir and madam, I hope it is not a bother if I disturb, but is there a problem, yes no?'

Finding a willing listener, the male tourist ranted about how hard it was to be a tourist in India. Hari nodded in sympathy although two plates of boiled vegetables for ₹100 was definitely cheaper than if you shopped at Hopcoms and bought a pressure cooker and cooked it yourself. 'Before I take you on my award-winning guided tour of Srirangapatnam, maybe you should try the Chinese vegetarian menu?'

'Zey have Zinese food in India?'

'Tipu Sultan, the erstwhile ruler of this island, imported rocket technology from China to use against the Englishmen. There is one particular dish that has been perfected here since those days, gobi manchurian, and if you enjoy cauliflower it is tasty because it is cooked with tasting-powder.' Tasting-powder was the local name for MSG, without which food was hardly worth eating.

In his educationist mood, Hari had overloaded their brains with mind-bending data, because they agreed to give gobi manchurian a shot.

While waiting for the grub, he entertained them with nuggets from Wikitravel about the year 1799 and the death of Tipu, the last sultan, and the theft of his legendary sword by looting British soldiers. The Siege of Srirangapatnam ended the long-drawn Mysuru wars.

This was going well. They were connecting. The tourists got their plateful of the bright orange cauliflower dish.

'It iz like zicken,' said the male.

Hari waggled his head, 'Indian cooking art. Not even in China will you get such good Chinese food items. *Bon appétit.*'

The woman spoke rapidly in French. The man faced Hari again: 'Oui wanted vegetable. Vou lied to us, zis zicken.'

'I'm promising you it is nothing but deep-fried cauliflower in chilli ketchup sauce. Tasting-powder makes it taste of meat, but it is only in your mind – it is one thousand per cent vegetarian.'

'Oui're not paying for zis ... fake zicken. Oui don't want it.'

Hari said, 'There is a famous temple nearby, the Halegude where you get cured from mental problems. Want to come along?'

'Oui zon't haf mental problem! Vou haff!'

Hari wondered if he'd be able to survive if he ever went to a foreign country, if the natural attitude was to question every food item on one's plate. But probably things were done differently in foreign countries.

After the French left in a huff, he took directions from the grey-bearded man who sat behind the cash counter. His name was Zakaria and he had run the Al-Kabab Chainees Café since he was a teenager. It had started as a roadside stall selling boiled eggs and sliced and spiced cucumbers to pilgrims, tourists and motorists. Yes, he knew Halegudehalli village. He told Hari of the tales surrounding the temple – though he himself was a Muslim, he used to go for the annual fair in his childhood. In those days, fakirs slept on beds of nails. Yogis knotted their legs around their necks. Potions were sold. Then rationalism became popular in the 1970s; miracles ended at Halegude temple after it was proved that one particular guru, TDK Baba, had stuffed sweetmeats inside his pyjamas to make them appear magically at his feet when he danced the bharatanatyam. People stopped coming.

The turn-off wasn't signposted, for Halegude had fallen off the map long ago, though lately it had gained in popularity again. Just a couple of days ago two businessmen from Bengaluru had asked for directions. And now Hari was on his way there. So maybe miracles were happening again.

The landscape was beautiful – a patchwork of yellow and green paddy fields with toddy palms near isolated farmsteads. He negotiated the potholes with care. Muddy water from a pre-monsoon shower had stagnated in them, concealing them. The size of the potholes in Bengaluru were big, the most devious of which could swallow a scooter or even half a camel. But these were larger than the *Lord of the Rings.* He hoped that as long as he didn't trouble them, the potholes wouldn't trouble him.

Soon he saw the temple's soaring gopuram. It was surrounded by a village that was named after it as Halegudehalli. The cluster of huts was centred around the sanctuary that stood on an outcrop of gneiss, at an elevation that signalled sacredness.

He drove into the village square. When he offed the scooty, he noticed how quiet it was. It was the time for post-lunch naps. It was well into the afternoon and the heat was heavy. Nearby was a market street, which also was the only street in the village. Off it lay narrow winding residential alleys lined with mud huts. Most of the shops had downed their shutters.

Hari had been informed at Al-Kabab Chainees Café that there was one lodging option, a choultry for the convenience of pilgrims. You paid as you liked. At that rate, he could stay as long as he needed.

One kiosk had bunches of bananas and refreshments of the local Poopy soda brand. He picked this shop because it was the only one which was vaguely crowded. As a Bengaluru boy, he was unused to situations where there were less than a million people around at the same time.

Five men sat gossiping in front. One of them appeared not to be fully sober because he kept toppling over backwards. The strangest thing was that when Hari walked up, they fell silent and the drunk stopped dropping off the bench. They didn't even enquire about his native place. Perhaps they got intimidated by his fancy stonewashed jeans, neon T-shirt, blue and white bathroom slippers?

Hari asked for a jeera masala soda to help him digest the lunch. He'd forgotten to bring his antacids. The beverage was lukewarm.

He downed it. None of them spoke. All he heard was a chorus of voices from inside the next-door hut called Brilliantly Radiating Tutorials where a class of Spoken English was on: '*What does your elephant eat? ... It eats vegetables and chapatti ... Does it drink tea through its trunk? ... It does not drink tea but drinks coffee ...*' Hari, who loved coffee, liked what he heard.

He checked his mobile. He must really call Diamond and let her know his whereabouts. If he explained properly, she might understand why he hadn't come home to do the dishes. He checked the phone. No signal. He'd do damage control later. For the time being, he had to carry on and so he said to nobody in particular, 'There ain't no bar.'

The shopkeeper replied, 'We have no bars in our village. It is a sacred town.'

The drunk nodded vigorously and fell off the bench again. Before Hari could ask for directions and make them more tongue-tied, he spotted the choultry opposite the steps leading up to the temple. Its year of construction, carved into the plaster over its entrance, was 1906. Heritage hotel, he thought and slipped his Poopy bottle into the crate with empties.

A clerk slept in the office. Hari woke him up. Dressed in a clean dhoti, the clerk yawned and rubbed his eyes, looked at Hari and muttered, 'You're not the one.'

'Sorry boss?'

'Nothing, I thought I was dreaming.'

'Well, I'm not a dream,' said Hari.

He was made to register in a ledger. They didn't have many guests. Above his entry were the only other visitors that same month, almost certainly the two that old Zakaria at the Al-Kabab had referred to – who had arrived last Friday evening.

Illegible scrawls, too, he observed as he tried to make out their names, R.*scrawl.* I.*scrawl.* P.*scrawl* and D.*scrawl.* A.*scrawl.* They wrote their native place and purpose of visit as 'foreign, tourist', but the roadside restaurateur had said the two businessmen came from Bengaluru. How odd. The first one's initials – 'RIP' – struck Hari as inauspicious in English, though probably his name was completely normal if one could just read the handwriting. They had donated ₹10 each, according to the ledger, and Hari followed the example they had set.

Hari had the choultry to himself. The sleeping arrangement consisted of one dormitory with straw mats on the floor. There was a toilet-cum-bathroom in a shed at the back. The comforts were sufficient. When he got hungry, he'd drive to the main road and have that hearty biriyani at Al-Kabab.

No locks on the doors. This wasn't Bengaluru, there weren't bad people around. It was calm and peaceful. He'd start a new life as the village hero. If they needed one. Until a few days ago, he'd been feeling burnt out like a second-hand tandoor from Patiala, but now he took selfies and tweeted, 'I'm in paradise.' But there was still no signal.

9

Kindly draw up blueprints for the rest of your life, because an unknown factor is introduced in your horoscope and it can be either too good or very bad.

The temple stood in its own walled compound.

He climbed up a flight of rock-cut steps to the gate which was topped by a tower with painted figures on it. The temple elephant looked positively antique where it stood in the shade of the gate, next to a pile of sacred coconuts. It blessed Hari with a light tap of its trunk on his balding pate. He offered it a coin in return and entered the courtyard. He left his slippers outside.

Like all temples in the south, this was built on a stone plinth. The main structure had no tower, it was squat and flattish. Its plain facade was some ten metres wide. The nine black pillars holding up the roof, and their brackets, displayed carvings of celestial beings. After inhaling the sacred atmosphere, he continued into the dark sanctum. Compared to the heat outside, the air was cool. There were no electric lights. In addition to what seeped in through the window grilles, the interiors were sparsely decorated with abstract curlicues lit up by spluttering oil lamps. It was a dignified space.

He enjoyed the stillness. The priests must be taking their lunch siestas and would return at whatever hour the puja was. It was nice of them to keep the premises open for people who came to seek blessings during off-hours. It was that same unguarded, unworried attitude that he'd encountered at the choultry.

He circumambulated the central sanctum in which an idol of the presiding deity held up a trident. Nataraja, the dancing one, the hero god. After having taken the darshan he sat down on the stone steps out in front. *Where was the Ninth Avatar?* Looking around the courtyard, he discovered auxiliary shrines built into its wall.

He had to tiptoe across to the colonnaded passageway as the hot flagstones burnt the already charred soles of his feet. Convinced that he was going to find the correct avatar in the ninth shrine, he started at the beginning and moved clockwise, taking the darshan of each avatar. There was the fish, the tortoise, and the boar. Finally, he reached the ninth.

Its doors were locked with a thick iron chain and a big brass padlock. He proceeded to the tenth – the future avatar, who technically speaking wasn't supposed to be there yet. But he was. The ultimate incarnation was going to come from the sky upon a white horse and wreak destruction upon those who collected too much bad karma. Better placate it, so he did.

Only the ninth was unavailable. Oddly enough, all shrines afforded him glimpses of their avatars, except the one he had come for. He backtracked to the shrine of the Ninth Avatar, who didn't respond when he knocked hesitantly on the ancient double doors. But he hoped that the Avatar would listen if he spoke a few pleading words. 'Hello boss? Had your coffee? Sorry to disturb, but I've come from far away to see you regarding a matter of life and death.'

No reply. Nothing to do but wait, he thought as the greasy lunch did cartwheels in his bowels. He lay down on the cool stone slabs in the shadow of the colonnade. After all, he hadn't slept much for several nights. It was quiet and calm here. Soon he was snoring.

Something poked his nose and it wasn't his own forefinger. He woke up and saw three sharp spearheads inches from his eyes. The village drunkard, whom he recognized from outside the refreshment kiosk, had trouble fitting the trident in since Hari had only two nostrils.

'What are you doing?' A perfectly justified question.

'You're a tourist?' said the villager, probably looking forward to an afternoon row.

'Uh-uh.' He had read in the newspapers about city dwellers being mistaken for cattle thieves, tied to poles and whipped all night before they were handed over to the police. He didn't exactly want that. 'Kindly hand me over to the police.'

'I am the police. You're not so brave now, are you?'

'No-no, I'm the least brave tourist you'll ever meet,' said Hari and understood why the village didn't attract tourists.

He also saw his mistaken optimism regarding the goodness of the hinterland paradise. In the city, he knew what threats he faced: deceitful friends, violent enforcers, irritable wife, etc. Speaking of which, his phone started ringing. He checked the screen. Miracle of miracles – there was coverage. Perhaps because the temple was at an elevation.

It was Diamond. 'I've got to take this call.'

'Touch it and it'll be the last thing you do.'

The trident was jabbing at his face. After some time, the phone stopped ringing. He prepared to die without saying goodbye and all the very best to his beloved wife when an authoritative voice came from someplace behind. 'What's going on?'

'That's the question I'm asking myself,' said Hari. With two of the three prongs of the trident jammed into his nostrils, he was unable to turn sufficiently to take in the sight of the newcomer.

'Good you came, baba, I was about to come get you.'

The new arrival questioned the villager, 'What are you doing to that poor pilgrim?'

'See for yourself: I caught the thief.'

'What was he stealing?'

'Nothing yet.'

'So what do you mean to say?'

'He's planning to. Like the ones who took the million-year-old god.'

There was an obvious communication gap between the rural and the urban. A misunderstanding that had to be corrected before Hari found himself before a kangaroo court, being lynched. So, he adapted a polite, if nasal, tone: 'Sir, kindly remove that trishul from my nose and I'll explain everything.'

'Don't try to trick me!'

'Put down your weapon, Smaranashakti Kaledukondiruvavanu! Why don't we hear what our guest has to say?' reasoned the baba. 'As I often say, dialogue is preferable to disagreement.'

'I fully agree,' said Hari.

The villager pulled out the trident from Hari's nose, but eyed him with distrust. Hari heaved a breath of relief and sat up.

The baba had green glass beads studding his ears, his bare upper torso bore streaks of sacred ash and around his neck were layers of rudraksha necklaces. Indeed, he looked like he might be the priest of the temple.

Hari argued: 'Honestly I haven't stolen anything. I came to seek blessings, oh Noble One.' But he didn't go into the reason he wished to see the Ninth Avatar: that he was under suspicion of having looted an ATM. That information was to be shared on a need-to-know basis.

'That's what he'd say if he was a dacoit, isn't it?' gloated the villager and swung the trident in Hari's direction. 'Remember those loud-mouthed tourists who had come to get blessings for an import-export venture last week? After that the troubles happened.'

'Let me handle this, Smaranashakti. You go and take your afternoon nap like you do every day,' said the baba. 'I shall let you know if I need you.'

The villager was shooed away, but Hari remained tense as there was no way of knowing if the self-appointed vigilante would muster up a posse of rural rowdies. The baba sensed his inner turmoil and said, in his cultured voice, 'Please don't mind. The mood is dire these days.'

'Oho, is it so?'

'Pray tell what transpired.' He indicated that they sit down on two cut-stone blocks that lined the edge of the colonnaded passage.

'My good self was taking rest after a long journey and woke up with this thing in my nose, oh Great Master.'

'Excuse my friend's aggressiveness. Smaranashakti is the village constable; very dedicated to his job, he tries to nab criminals before they commit crimes.' The baba smiled. A learned man, one could tell from his Sanskritized Kannada, his thick spectacles, his hairy ears, his starched and ironed dhoti.

'Tondare illa,' said Hari, who was used to mishaps. He indicated the wooden doors to the ninth shrine. 'I was simply waiting for this to open up. Now that you've arrived, Lord of the Universe, I can take my darshan and go.'

'You've heard of our special idol?'

'Of course, that's why I came all the way from Bengaluru.'

'I see,' said the baba and took out a bunch of keys. He got the old lock open with some difficulty. 'We never used to keep this door closed.'

'Why not?'

'It's been fine for a thousand years, but now, the constable has ordered that we must lock up the shrine.'

The doors opened with a creak. The chamber was small, smelt of ashes and earth, and there was a pedestal in its centre. Empty. *What was this?* Had the deity gone missing from a locked room? Which meant that his way to salvation had led to a dead end. The pedestal wasn't completely empty though. A page from a guidebook – Hari recognized the *Lonely Planet* from the typography and page layout – was taped to its front. 'What is this, a joke?'

'If it is a joke, the joke's on us. The Avatar left.'

'Ayooh? Decamped just like that only?'

'We think stolen, by outsiders. Two tourists came and wanted to get their business blessed.' Baba explained that the ransackers left the guidebook page behind, which Hari, on closer scrutiny, determined to be from a pirated edition.

Since it gave a description of the lost sculpture and displayed a sketch of it, the villagers had taped it to the pedestal to have something to show. Hari read through what was printed on the page: '*To ensure that your travels are happy, visit the Halegude temple (Halegudehalli bazaar, 6am-1pm & 4-9pm) 5km from Srirangapatnam where a small but rare bronze sculpture of the Ninth Avatar is supposed to ensure mental health, safe passage, marital bliss and decent job offers, and cure liver cancer. Its face is finely drawn and eyes inlaid with yellow diamonds. The village has no facilities so carry provisions. Open daily; free entry.*'

Yellow diamonds. So the statue had to be valuable, Hari surmised, and he also caught the subtext in the baba's statement: two alleged tourists had been singled out as the perpetrators. Aloud he said, 'Oho. Why do you not suspect insiders?'

'That guidebook is written in English. Nobody here in the village knows much English – except for myself and some of the children I teach in the afternoons.'

Hari remembered the chorus of voices that he had heard from the tutorial centre next to the kiosk. Which could mean that the culprit was either the village saint or one of the children he taught; it was a definitive possibility.

'Why lock the cage if the bird has flown?'

'So that no evidence vanishes.'

'Why not instead lock it before it flies ... I mean, before it is stolen?' said Hari, taking a backstabbing dig at the bellicose constable.

'We didn't do it before for the convenience of devotees who'd come at odd hours and may have walked far, and besides it isn't a good practice to keep gods imprisoned. They don't like it. Even gods need freedom. What to do?' The baba sounded wistful. 'There'll be less pilgrims now that we don't have the Avatar.'

'I'm too sorry to hear that, oh Heavenly Gem. And I suppose you can't surf to Flipkart and buy a replacement.'

'It's not the same thing.'

'Nice to have met you. I'll take your leave now and wish you all the best.' He stretched out a hand to shake, English ishtyle. 'Myself Hari.'

'Professor Raju, at your service. It was a pleasure to see a young pilgrim and I am truly sorry that you didn't get darshan of the avatar.'

'Raju?' echoed Hari. *What a coincidence!* That was the name he was going to give his son when he was born and if his son became a professor then life would be picture perfect. He already liked this baba. Was there a deeper meaning to this chance encounter?

'Would you like coffee before you go back? You look like you need some.'

Hari now liked him even more. A boy was entering the temple courtyard with a kettle and a portable kerosene stove. He boiled milk that he mixed with a fully black decoction out of a steel filter in two chipped porcelain cups. It was a very tasty blend of chicory and sugar. The baba offered Hari a banana as a snack, it had the sweetest taste – like bananas only from the Mysuru area did.

'So, what are you going to do about the idol?'

'I may as well chuck up my job and become a civilian again. I wasn't always a baba, you know. I used to teach at a college. I was an associate professor of history,' he spoke ruefully.

'And then you changed your mind?' said Hari, becoming more and more intrigued with this prophet. Till recently, astrology had been a religion to him, until he started having minor doubts. His astrologer had advised him to seek darshan of the Ninth Avatar to set things right, but the Avatar had vamoosed – if Pundit foretold the future, shouldn't he have seen that coming? 'How come you chucked up a good job, oh Thinker of the Loftiest Thoughts?'

'I didn't resign, I died.'

'I'm sorry if I asked an insensitive question,' Hari apologized. 'I understand that if one is dead, one wouldn't want to talk loudly about it.'

'No-no, I don't mind,' the baba said and took a sip of coffee. 'I don't get many opportunities to chat. People hereabouts are superstitious and I don't want them to start treating me like some resurrected saint. I'm a teacher. You seem educated.'

'I went to school,' said Hari but omitted to mention that he was expelled at thirteen and was quite superstitious when it came to that. 'But you appear so alive. You even drink coffee, how come?'

'This was years ago. I had gone for my customary morning walk near Manasa Gangothri, where I taught, but due to the laces of my sneakers coming untied, I stumbled into the Kukarahalli Tank. It was a stupid mishap, but it was what I needed. In those days, I was pompous and full of myself.'

'Oho? Then what?'

'I couldn't pull myself up, so I drowned.'

'Oho. Even I don't know how to swim, so I'd have done the same thing probably. That must have been painful.'

'Actually, I don't remember a thing until I woke up in hospital. They said I was brought in clinically dead, but then an old swami known as TDK Baba had come to visit the emergency room for some purpose. He used to be famous for his miracles but then he stopped performing them, because the constitution favours rationalism. Anyway, he placed these rudraksha beads around my neck.' He indicated the rosaries with the large, dark, thorny beads. 'He chanted the Aum and in the middle of it I was alive again. I've never taken these beads off, not since that day.'

'That is an extraordinary story, oh Custodian of Philosophy.'

'Isn't it? Hardly believe it myself.' He pinched his own arm to show how amazed he was about it. 'Afterwards, when I wished to thank him, TDK Baba told me I was needed at this temple – they lacked one Brahmin, ideally somebody who knows history and can value it.'

A moment of silence passed before Hari realized what a great feat TDK Baba had pulled off. 'And you happened to be a professor of history!'

The baba restarted, 'No, associate professor. But you know there are many legends surrounding this temple. They fascinate me and maybe it is my purpose to write them down. For example, nobody can tell how old the Avatar is, it is likely to be older than this temple itself. People believe it to be millions of years old.'

'Wah!'

'But as a historian, I'd peg it at one and a half millennia. It's typical of Gupta era craftsmanship. This temple's construction dates from around the eleventh century.'

'Do you mean to say that the Ninth Avatar came first and the temple followed?'

'Rather the other way around. It is said that the Avatar sought sanctuary here when there was turmoil in the north about a thousand years ago. Being a sacred Avatar, three monks rescued it and carried it between the holy cities, guided by gods in their dreams.'

'Is it so?'

'Yes, I heard it from TDK Baba, who was the last in that lineage of protectors. They wore disguises and pretended to be beggars. Eventually, after one hundred years of wandering they or, more likely, their disciples installed the Avatar here as an ambassador to the court of Nataraja. This temple was brand new then, totally state-of-the-art. The gods commanded the old monks that the Avatar must be watched over by them in eight-hour shifts, night and day, until the end of the world.'

'Oho, so does it mean that the end of the world is coming?' If Hari told Triplex about this, he'd perhaps bury the hatchet and want to come and snap a selfie for his Facebook page.

'It may be an omen. The original custodians predicted disaster to any ungodly person who laid hands on the Avatar. It is my conviction too that crime brings its own fatality with it. He who took our deity will regret it. For whomever it is with, it'll be a curse. That is spelled out with golden letters on the back wall where you can see it written.'

The thieves had missed the warning in the ancient script. Hari felt a little sorry for them. The wrath of gods was not like some ordinary street squabble.

'For many generations the monks watched over the Avatar. Whenever one of them died the other two elected a new successor. Tipu, who was once the sultan, also ruled over this village and he made a grant to keep things spic and span. Then outsiders killed him in 1799. In the looting that followed, the soldiers loaded their carts with the gold and jewels, but luckily they didn't concern themselves with antiques.'

'Speaking of which, you need to improve your security. Because I've heard that history always repeats itself,' said Hari.

There were no closed-circuit cameras or burglar alarms that he could see in the temple. Perhaps because the village had no electricity. A modern security system would be costly, since they'd first have to buy a generator.

'Maybe so,' the baba continued with sorrow in his voice. 'But you must have seen how the Srirangapatnam fort is in ruins and Tipu Sultan's armoury is used by bad-character elements for antisocial purposes despite it being a protected monument. It is covered in graffiti, empty bottles, cigarette butts. If that is the case with a historical monument, then how do you expect us to protect ourselves?'

'Send out mass emails seeking donations to buy a CCTV system and somebody is bound to respond,' said Hari, who knew an awful lot about spamming.

'Isn't that like scamming?'

'Then crowdfund an app that generates revenue, oh Tastiest Lotus Stem Curry?'

The baba, being a former history professor, lived in the past and didn't seem to understand what Hari was saying.

'We got the temple listed in *Lonely Planet*, but what good did that do? It helped the thieves find us,' he said, fingering the guidebook page. 'We were rather hoping that foreigners would donate towards the upkeep, but they take a look and leave without paying. This morning a French couple came, complained that there were no erotic sculptures and when I told them to experience the blissful sacredness in the air, they said they were going to write to *Lonely Planet* and tell them to remove the listing.'

'Why don't you charge an entrance fee? They value it more if they pay through their noses, foreigners are like that only.'

'This is god's home and it is open to all even if you have no credit card. That's the way the gods like it. You gift what you wish, according to your heart.' After a brief pause, the baba added, 'Nowadays youths don't want to become monks, they want to go to Bengaluru rather than renounce the material world. That's the way it is.'

'But at least you're here.' Hari was beginning to see what a responsibility the baba carried on his shoulders.

'I am the last one. Being a lone guardian, I have to sleep some time. That's why the idol was lost. I'm shame-faced.'

Hari sympathized with the baba's conundrum. He too had been asleep when he ought to have been guarding the ATM. Then it was as if a neon light started flickering in his hair and something buzzed around his ears. First, he thought he was being attacked by a swarm of fireflies, but then he realized he was getting a bright idea.

10

It is difficult to think of a more messed up time in your life but the sages of old used to talk of emptying the mind of stupidity. However, yours currently seems to be so cluttered with it that it's hard to know what advice to offer you.

His phone began to ring again. Diamond. But he didn't pick up – Plan F was hatching and he couldn't interrupt his train of thought. This was what he had come here for and the gods had, via dreams and nightmares, directed his steps. Being the right man in the right place and at the right time was something that happened to a select few.

He cleared his throat pompously. 'Oh Holy Ghost, by a lucky chance I am a full-time detective and whoever perpetrated this vandalism can be booked under Penal Code section 295 for damaging a place of worship with intent to insult the religion; section 380 for idol theft in a building of worship, 411 for possession of stolen property and 457 sub clause 2 for housebreaking in temple. So here is what we'll do, you and the other villagers hang tight and avoid stuffing trishuls up the noses of innocent pilgrims, while I bring back the correct Avatar. No need to get depressed.'

The baba sipped on his chicory beverage which must have turned into cold coffee and nodded sagely. 'Thank you, but we have no money to pay for your valuable services.'

Hari wasn't about to give up that easily. He was currently unemployed and a case was a case, money or not. Besides, if the theft of the Avatar heralded the end of the world, it was his duty to stop that from happening. 'No worries, our firm undertakes work on a *pro bono* basis when there is a *suo moto* cause.'

'Really?'

'It means that I'll foot the cost from a discretionary budget,' said Hari who was getting carried away by a strong emotion – after all the baba had rescued him from having a non-existent third nostril pierced with a trident, so he'd like to return the favour.

'I understand Latin. But how will you go about it?'

'The suspects signed the choultry guestbook, so I'll take their names from there.' From the pedestal, Hari tore off the page with the sketch of the statue and pocketed it, and then he asked the baba to describe the two export-import tourists.

The baba had chatted with them like he did with all pilgrims. One of them had stunning red eyes, red shoes, a Mohawk hairdo and a Chaplin moustache; the other looked even more crooked with a forked tongue and piercings in his eyebrows, nose, lips, fingers, toes and every other visible body part, and tattoos of skulls and crossbones. A bit weird to be businessmen, but then again foreigners always looked weird. 'But how will the guestbook entry help you find them? Their names are barely legible and they gave no addresses. The police already checked.'

'That may be true, but I think I'll find them in Bengaluru.'

'They spoke English.'

'Some deviant people in the city do that.'

'And they claimed to be NRIs.'

'Many pretend to be, just go to a mall and have a look, you shall find too many.'

'A mall? They can be anywhere in the world, even in America.'

'They could, but they aren't.'

'What do you mean?'

'Old Zakaria, who runs an eatery by the main road, spoke with them in Kannada and he said it didn't sound like any refined Mysuru dialect, but more as if they were dirty fellows from Bengaluru. So, I'll find them and retrieve the selfsame statue. It will not be complicated.'

'My god!' The baba seemed impressed.

Hari started to feel upbeat: from zero to hero. And if a drowned man recuperated thanks to the temple's boons, Hari had no reason to worry. 'Bye-bye, oh King of Kong, and all the very best. I will not sleep until the idol is back where it belongs.' He codenamed the mission that he was about to undertake 'Operation Idol'.

A few hours later, Hari drove down CD Road and scanned the cross streets for a red Premier Padmini. It had been lurking in the vicinity that morning, but now it wasn't. Then he risked a visit to Puncherwallah Complex and Doc's cybercafé – he figured that the torpedoes wouldn't search for him in the booths there. To act irrationally was sometimes strategically best, thought Hari.

Besides, Doc was still friendly and let him use the Internet on credit, which was crucial – since he had neither much money nor many friends. Doc was angrier with Gaadi, in fact. Due to his fall, he had to buy a cervical collar from the pharmacy and it had cost him ₹500. After he stopped complaining about Gaadi kicking him off the first-floor veranda, he mentioned: 'Diamond has been calling.'

'Oho, regarding what?'

'She wants you to come home.'

Hari smiled. 'It's nice to be welcomed to one's own home.'

'She didn't sound happy.'

'Is that so?' When he checked his phone, it showed some eighty missed calls from Diamond. He thought he should wait until he figured out a strategy to deal with her worries. He was determined to return as a hero.

'You should ...'

'I'll call her in five minutes as soon as I've fixed a few things,' he said. But he spent an hour doing background research on the temple.

Everything checked out. Newspapers reported the theft in its bare-bones version:

'The Halegude Temple in Srirangapatnam Municipality limits was burgled and valuables were looted. The incident came to light Saturday morning when the priest found a shrine ransacked. Allegedly, one idol was stolen. The donation box was also pilfered by the selfsame mischief mongers. The Srirangapatnam Police constable Smaranashakti Kaledukondiruvavanu rushed to the spot

and registered a case. The hereditary trustee stated: "We have never had any problem before. But these thieves are professionals. Local persons would not do this. It is the foreign hand. Will the police do the needful and capture the miscreants?"'

Wikipedia had further data available. '*The idol of Avatar 9 is first mentioned in an inscription found in the temple regarding a curse that will accurse whoever removes it.* [citation needed] *Avatar 9 stands on a lotus pedestal in 'samabhanga' posture.* [citation needed]'

Googling 'idol thefts' in general, Hari read of many similar cases. Especially in Tamil Nadu, the menace was of epidemic proportions. Were the same gangs spilling over into Karnataka? But who dared to buy sacred objects that became cursed once they were unlawfully obtained?

He bravely googled on and found that according to online sources Karnataka alone had 3,000 historical temples worth robbing, out of which 90 per cent were likely to be looted shortly if not immediately and around 200 had already been ransacked within the last fifteen years. It was a 500 per cent racket. Just the week before, an 800-year-old Hoysala era Ganapati idol was stolen from Karnataka and a rare Trimurthi Shivalinga had been dismounted by suspected miscreants at the Kalleshwara temple in Maccheri.

It was semi-shocking how a museum in Canberra held in its collections a bronze idol valued at over $5 million stolen from Suthamalli in Tamil Nadu. A gallery in Sydney displayed a tenth century stone Shiva worth a quarter of a million dollars, stolen in 2004 from the Vriddhachalam temple. Hari checked on Wikipedia and found out that Australia was originally a colony of convicts, shipped off from Britain in order to lower crime rates. He wasn't surprised, considering that the Brits themselves had organized the criminal looting of India up to 1947. Various priceless artefacts from Srirangapatnam, plundered in 1799, were flaunted by the Victoria and Albert Museum in London as well as at several other museums around Great Britain.

But it wasn't just the British and Australians who were involved in the racket. A museum in Sweden exhibited a fifth century idol acquired under suspicious circumstances and the Tengapura Durga had somehow ended up in Germany. An art museum in Ohio held a Chola-age Ganesha idol from Sripuranathan, while a museum in Massachusetts proudly displayed a rare nineteenth century Tanjore style portrait worth $35,000, which had vamoosed from India. Two stolen eighth century sandstone idols were in the catalogue of a prominent auction house in New York, valued at $475,000 each.

In Manhattan, there was a certain shop that had been shipping purloined idols worth many millions of dollars out of India for fifteen years, arranging false provenance certificates and ownership documents to clients who demanded such papers. Currently on the shop's website, and on display in their fancy high-street window, was a Shiva-Parvati bronze idol on sale for $8.5 million.

Experts estimated that, on an average, upwards of 2,000 antiques were smuggled out of the country per year, with a total market value of $100 million. Hari calculated that it amounted to 160-170 objects per month or one every four hours. The numbers were unbelievable. Authorities, such as the Idol Wing of the Tamil Nadu police, did their best to stop the menace, as did concerned citizens with civic sense. However, even if temple thefts were highly illegal and totally punishable according to the Antiquities and Art Treasures Act of 1972, which prohibited export of objects older than ninety-nine years, that law did not apply in Australia or in Manhattan. Hari saved the pertinent information to PDF files on his pen drive, as he couldn't afford to take so many printouts, but he felt that the evidence must be stored in a safe place. He kept the pen drive in his back pocket.

Until then, he had never suspected how valuable India's past was. He knew it was great, but that there was so much money in it! His job was clear-cut: somebody had to save history. But where to start? This wasn't going to be as easy as he had made it out to be when he assured the baba that he'd have things fixed in a jiffy. He reread the temple trustee's statement that 'the foreign hand' had its autograph signed all over the affair. Judging from how many millions of dollars foreigners paid for stolen idols, it was a valid point.

However, Hari still suspected that the two visitors, who stayed at the choultry on the night the idol vanished, hadn't been foreigners. Maybe from a Halegudehalli perspective they were – anybody from Bengaluru would seem to be a creature from another planet there. Maybe they were hand in glove with the foreign hand?

He pulled up the photograph of the ledger that he'd snapped with his mobile and scrutinized the names. Criminals rarely knew how to spell their own names. But these were illegible by design, not accident. Only the initials were decipherable: DA and RIP. Hari then recalled something else being said about the two: they had claimed to be in the import-export business. *Export?* A piece of the puzzle fell in place – he guessed what kind of export business they were involved in. Smuggling of precious antiques out of the country.

He summed up the clues: the foreign hand and its lackeys. Bengaluru was a cosmopolitan city with all manner of suspicious aliens living in its nooks and crannies. He'd go and seek them out, one by one. Unlike other people, Hari wasn't xenophobic. But he decided to start with the only Pakistani he knew.

As he emerged from the cybercafé, the long lunch-time lull was off the air and Bangalore had got its buzz back – or maybe it just seemed so, now that he had a heroic duty to fulfil.

He got on his scooter and drove past a banner that said 'Drink and driving awareness campaign: You boose! You croose! You loose!' According to it, the traffic police prided themselves on having booked 62,576 cases against drunken drivers during the last year, which was a record number, especially considering that there were only 6,60,000 vehicles in town – so in a purely mathematical sense, it worked out to one in ten or so preferring to have their pegs in their car rather than in a bar. In turn, it meant that Bengaluru drivers were more drunk than ever before, explaining why such sobering banners had cropped up everywhere.

By the old jail he turned towards the city centre, the erstwhile Cantonment that had been renamed Central Business District in order to make it seem more modern. The jail was where Uncle had been incarcerated. It had been converted into a 'Freedom Park' where Hari used to go with Diamond. He told her colourful stories of his illustrious uncle who took off every weekend after treating the guards to birthday cake laced with sleeping pills. Uncle spent the night out partying with his poet friends and drunk-drove back at 3 a.m., after the police check posts were disbanded but before the prison guards woke up – since Uncle, as a former lawyer, was particular about not getting caught violating section 185 of the Motor Vehicle Act. The guards never suspected a thing even though birthdays shouldn't come more than once a year.

Diamond and he had sat on one of the benches under the shady trees and laid up plans for the future. They didn't do that anymore, it was almost as if the future had come and gone without them quite noticing. Eighty missed calls? He doubted that she was calling to say she loved him.

He drove down Sheshadri Road, keeping an eye on the rear-view mirror. There was no red Padmini trailing him. Traffic was busy and every other vehicle was a bus that bullied scooters to the edges of the road like a bullock swatting flies with its tail. Soon he saw the High Court's red building – where Uncle had fought cases until he ended up in the dock himself and got disbarred. He continued past the State Central Library and steered towards Langford Town.

Hari hoped that Farooqi was alive. He was an old contact of Uncle's and he might provide an opening into the investigation. A resourceful man, he used to be a spy, and nobody quite knew if he worked for India or for Pakistan, or both. But he'd been provided with a brand-new identity and was allowed to stay in the country. He settled in Bengaluru, which in the 1990s bore the sobriquet 'pensioner's paradise'.

The ex-spy ran a Kashmiri souvenir emporium in a back alley not far from the Double Road bus stand, where Hari again dodged several of the ballistic behemoths of the BMTC. He swerved left into a side lane, followed it to its end, then turned again into an even more impossibly cramped back alley until he came to a humble shop tucked away between the Maximum Price Store and the Sweaty Lingerie Boutique.

At the entrance, an ornamental lamp studded with glass pieces in different hues hung from chains of yellow metal. Hari ducked so as to not bang his head on it.

The narrow but deep shop displayed a jumble of artefacts from floor to ceiling. Everything looked a thousand years old: elongated wooden masks, patinated copper statuettes, weathered Tibetan tangkhas. Only an expert could tell, from the discrete smell of turpentine, that few were genuine collector's items and the tangkhas came out of a sophisticated colour xerox machine that printed on cloth. Luckily, most tourists weren't experts.

Although some of the merchandise was old, say ten years, the lion's share was mass-produced. They were then aged by Farooqi's handymen who used chemicals to subtly alter the colouration, hammers to create cracks and bumps, and a metal file to erase the 'Made in China' labels.

Hari had been one of these helpers, way back when he needed to earn during the hard times when Uncle was in jail. Sometimes he had spent days in the workshop, when large orders needed to be filled, but mostly his job had consisted of tipping off Farooqi when tourists en route from Mysuru to Goa arrived in town. Because the shop was so hard to find, customers came through touts and when they saw its secretive location they took it for granted that the antiques were exclusive.

The old man himself was in fine shape, his hair and beard as white as the snow capping K2 and his gaze as sharp as two AK-47s. The main difference was that he wore tiny spectacles on the bridge of his nose.

'Salaam aleikum, uncle-ji,' Hari greeted him.

'Aleikum wassalaam,' said Farooqi and ripped the last morsel of meat from a mutton chop before he chucked the bone in the dustbin. He wiped his hands on a silk handkerchief.

'It's me: Hari.'

'Hari who?'

'Majestic.'

'You don't look like a nobleman. Quite the opposite.'

'I used to work for you when I was nine.'

Farooqi blinked a few times. 'Oh, yes, I remember. You brought many big spenders. My boy, how you have grown! You look nobler than a camel, I dare say. How is your uncle?'

'Sadly demised.'

'I'm sorry to hear. He was a truly good man. It's been a long time since we had those poetry addas. My, how time flies. This is indeed a special day for me to have you step into my humble emporium. Come, have a glass of kahwa with me.' Farooqi showed Hari into a chamber at the back: it was a modern office, two Dell laptops and a laser printer on the desk. Large keys dangled from hooks over it and the only old object was a battered samovar which dated to the war in Afghanistan in the 1980s. Farooqi had got it from a Soviet soldier in return for not shooting him in the gut. Instead, he shot him in the foot. As many times as it took for him to die.

'Uncle Farooqi, you have latest model laptops! You must be doing well.'

'God willing, god willing. One is for use with the Internet, I sell a lot of the stuff on eBay nowadays; the other never goes online so as to protect me from ransomware and hackers. Security agencies routinely implant viruses into comps and phones. The least I can do to show my appreciation is to make it harder for them.'

Furthermore, Farooqi had upwards of fifteen cheap mobiles lined up on the rosewood desk, all in different colours. Hari, who normally carried two, wondered if the spy was reformed or still up to cloak-and-dagger stuff. To Hari's knowledge, only high-level police informants carried that many phones, so he decided to be circumspect about the ATM matter and anything else punishable with rigorous imprisonment. Meanwhile, Farooqi took out a glass jar of green tea leaves from a desk drawer.

'You don't have coffee?'

'It creates urological issues and loose motions. And kidney stones. At my age, one can't risk one's health.'

Hari found health advice that wasn't based on astrology hard to take seriously. Farooqi set out delicate glasses on the desk. Then he rubbed cinnamon bark, cardamom pods and tea leaves between his hands before he divided the ingredients between the glasses. He added dried saffron strands, rose petals, crushed walnuts and almond from silver boxes. He poured steaming water from the samovar over the mix.

Hari tasted. Somewhat okay. Once he had slurped it, the preliminaries were over. He unfolded the page from the guidebook with the illustration of the Ninth Avatar. 'This was stolen from a village temple and I've promised to bring it back.'

'I have lots of similar ones in the shop. For old time's sake, you take any.'

'Not any idol,' said Hari, 'but this same one. I have personal reasons.'

'It's probably old,' said Farooqi and frowned.

'One to two thousand years, give or take.'

'You know I sell fakes. You've worked with me.'

'Correct-u. But what about all these,' said Hari and waved towards the shop – crammed with ritual objects, lamps, semi-nude goddesses, carpets, painted scrolls, 'isn't there anything that is real?'

'What does it mean to be real? Take the lamp at the entrance, how old would you say it looks?'

'Ninety-eight years and eleven months?' he said in an attempt to flatter the old man.

'It came from the factory last week.'

'Doesn't look very modern.'

'But I must follow the law and it says that if I were to sell genuine items, I need clearances for each piece of merchandise in addition to an antiques vending license. Furthermore, if a private person wants to purchase any antique, he must register with the Archaeological Survey and let them inspect the object once in three years. Easier to sell fakes.'

'But wouldn't you earn more if you broke the rules?'

Farooqi refilled his glass with hot water. 'Breaking rules isn't necessarily good for business in the long term. But on the other hand, if you have the patience, take anything in my shop, wait for a hundred years and it too will turn antique.'

'So an idol like this couldn't have passed through your hands or any other law-abiding antiques shop in town?'

'I shouldn't think so.'

That eliminated half of the shops. 'Who deals with these then? I happen to know that it is a big business, so there's got to be *somebody* doing it.'

Farooqi sighed a weary man's sigh. 'Can I do anything else for you?'

'Would you buy a consignment of armpit fans? They're semi-antique and tourists will love them. Besides, my wife wants me to get rid of them, so I'll give you a good price.'

The older man rinsed his mouth with the hot beverage. 'No, but I can offer you a job.'

'What job?'

'International courier. I have many things that need to be transported to many parts of the world. You speak good English. Pick your destination. Enjoy a trip at my cost for old time's sake.'

Hari was tempted. But it sounded shady. 'Why not give me the name of *somebody* who deals in those things and I'll take it from there? It would be cheaper for you than sending me abroad.'

'Ask around and I am sure there are many who will tell.'

'Who?' said Hari, sensing that the old man was unwilling to finger that *somebody*. Even if Bengaluru itself was a city with eleven million people, it often felt as if everybody knew everybody. It made Hari quite sure that Farooqi knew Mr Somebody.

Farooqi took another sip of tea, but his hand trembled.

Hari decided to push. 'Give me a name and I'll pretend I haven't seen you in a quarter century. And if you want it that way, you will not be seeing me for another millennium or two.'

The old man wiped his fingertips on his silken handkerchief. 'By then I'll be dead and gone. God willing.'

'Not even your grandchildren will see me. Unless they need my help. I run a big detective bureau now.' Then he realized that perhaps it would mean bad luck to speak the name of the person aloud. Certain things had repercussions. 'Say the first letter in his name.'

Eventually, Farooqi said, 'There are people here in town who you might want to talk to.'

'Yes, like who?'

'I'm remembering a friend of your uncle's. Who'd you think of if I said U?'

'What, me?'

'S.'

'Me is ... What are you saying, Uncle Farooqi?'

All of a sudden, the bells started clanging. Flashback to incidents from way back: he had been a very small child then. Uncle had taken him along when he went across town for some typical underhand affairs.

The passing of time had added a dimension of myth to that man. Salvatore first appeared on the scene in the 1970s and was believed to be on a secret mission. He was allegedly born in California, at the prestigious Betty Ford Clinic, though his detractors joked that he probably hadn't been further west than Calicut. Lots of people were attracted by his flamboyant American manners, his 'Howdy ho' way of speaking. He was nabbed by the Crime Branch after having worked too hard to seduce one patriotic Anglo-Indian lady by offering a free holiday to Singapore – provided that the nubile lass helped him with his 'cover story' by acting as if they were married, which meant sharing a double room with a single cot. The police registered a case under the anti-Romeo regulation act. With Uncle Mamool as a defence lawyer, it dragged on until the prosecutors found more important things to do and Salvatore got off by posting bail.

'I think I see.'

'You know then where to look,' said Farooqi as he watched Hari's face go through a range of emotions, red and white stripes bursting into a spangle of stars, as he explained that the particular part of town where Salvatore lived was one big treasure trove of vintage furniture and carved doors and window frames that were essentially discarded as trash when bungalows were demolished. One just had to walk the by-lanes of Kamaraj Road to find godowns packed to the rafters with Victorian chairs,

Edwardian tables, Portuguese almirahs, Mogul mirrors, Nizami chests, Japanese transistor radios and a range of knick-knacks that the colonials had collected on tours of duty. Much of it was older than ninety-nine years and so their export was restricted. Owners took the help of the likes of Salvatore to ship antiques in containers custom-declared to be full of garden decoration plaster of Paris gnomes made in Hyderabad.

'Thank you so much, bye-bye and all the very best.'

Farooqi watched Hari with those large warm tea-coloured Kalashnikov eyes through tiny wire-frame spectacles and said, 'You don't need to thank me. Just remember I never spoke to you, not since you were nine years old.'

11

> Going down memory lane makes you notice how you have made progress on all fronts except at home, so it is time to focus on that which matters.

Crossing Bengaluru's city centre usually took half a lifetime. Rush hours lasted months. Top speed peaked at 12kmph. But traffic was on his side today and thirty minutes later he reached the non-vegetarian end of Mosque Road. Briefly, he thought of uploading his feat to the Limca Book of World Records.

Rows of restaurants and bakeries lined the street. Uncle used to love to eat here during Ramzan – the fasting period turned the street into a food festival with stalls selling every imaginable kind of meat. Grills were set up on the pavements, camel humps were cooked on stone slabs and quail deep-fried in buckets of fat. The memories made Hari's tummy growl. Well, no time for non-veg nostalgia.

He took a couple of turns into the by-lanes, past a banner proclaiming that 'Drive Wreck Less, Rather Than Reckless', until the rich aromas of Arabian roasts got left behind. Momentarily, he thought he had lost his mind. Many of the landmarks were no longer there, such as the peepal tree on one particular back street corner. There was a coffee vending machine in its place.

He asked the vendor if he knew of any old bungalows. The guy rolled his eyes as if Hari was a lobotomized langur who could speak. Hari bought an overpriced latte to soup up his mental engine – it didn't taste anything like the filtered chicory brew that the darshinis served up. Times were changing and again Hari worried that he was getting old … a rotten banana was the last thing he needed to become.

When he used to visit with Uncle as a child, in the good old 1990s, this had been a district of charming bungalows, gabled and turreted, with Mangalore-tiled roofs, broad verandas and quaint monkey tops over the windows. The bungalows stood in their own gardens with servant quarters, cow sheds and private putting greens. Now it was block after block of apartments with tiny balconies strung with washing and outside plumbing on mouldy walls. The lanes of Fraser Town were lined with high-rises developed for the yuppies who were taking over.

Then he spotted the last bungalow standing on the block. So discreet that one might pass it by without noticing. The nameplate had a single word on it: *Intelligence*. That rang a bell.

There was otherwise no bell visible, so Hari pushed open the cast-iron gate. It was unlocked. The lawn hadn't been watered. There was no groundwater anywhere near Bengaluru in the hot months of April and May. The trees in the yard were leafless. The dry paint on the veranda pillars was peeling off in sheets.

In the portico an elderly Caucasian male was caught in this time warp, sleeping on a plantation chair. The unshaven face was covered by a film of sweat. His Lacoste T-shirt was inside out; his baseball cap faced the South Pole. There were empty so-called 650ml 'badawallahs' of UB Export on the table.

Hari honked.

Salvatore woke up in a split second. A sawn-off shotgun appeared out of nowhere and was aimed right between Hari's eyes. Impressive.

'Howdy ho! Remember what the good doctor said: Easy does it. Show me your back.'

'Good afternoon, Papa Sal,' greeted Hari as he lifted his shirt to prove he didn't have a weapon tucked into the back of his pants. 'Good to see Papa is hale and hearty.'

Salvatore lowered the shotgun and took aim at Hari's tummy instead. Hari tried not to think too much of what might happen if Salvatore's geriatric finger shuddered. It would surely be bad for digestion.

'And who be you, sonny boy?'

'Hari.'

'Harry?'

'Yes.'

'Harry Potter, like in the stupid books?'

'Not to be mixed up with that Potter. I'm much better. I came to notify you that my uncle, Ontappa Kallappa Mensinkai, is sadly demised.'

'I'm sorry?'

'Yes, me too.'

'And who be he?'

'Alias Mamool, alias "OK".'

Salvatore knitted his brows. His deep exhalations smelt of mothballs. And senility. After having thought for a bit, he put away the shotgun, smacking his dry lips. 'Okay. Sit down and have an iced pint, sonny boy.'

'I don't drink. I drive.'

'So OK was your uncle?'

'Strictly speaking: adoptive uncle.'

'Harry, Harry, wait a minute! Were you that weird little dwarf he used to bring along? By God, you are.'

'I was a kid back then.'

Hari waggled his head.

Salvatore scratched his beard, plucked a louse and squeezed it dead between his yellowing thumbnail and forefinger.

'I watched you play here in my garden, talking to yourself and whipping that fig tree yonder. Son, I always thought you'd grow up to be a gangster, one of those mental ones with a muzzle over his face in jail. *Haarrh*,' he said, and shaped his hand into a claw and tore at the air between them.

Hari took a look at the gnarled trees. He vaguely remembered playing with them. The garden didn't seem to have recovered. He cleared his throat and handed over his visiting card with both hands, Karnataka-style. 'I'm a private detective now. Total VIP, more than world-famous. So, we're almost colleagues.'

'Here's my card in case you need any black-ops done.' Salvatore tossed it to Hari. It gave his various aliases, office addresses in Langley, West Point, Quantico and Guantánamo Bay, and also special qualifications such as *Son of the Founder of Ku-Klux-Klan*.

In the olden days, Uncle Mamool and Papa Sal always had dirty business to clean up, the meaning of which at the time was unclear to Hari, but being an inquisitive kid, he did gradually figure out that the Italian-descended US citizen had been stationed for some purpose in Bengaluru during the turbulent Emergency Years in the 1970s. Officially as a foreign correspondent.

Due to his proximity to the Leftist movement, Uncle had been Salvatore's main informant. That was another enigma. It had never been clarified whether Uncle sold genuine information or disinformation on behalf of the Soviet propaganda office in Bombay.

Then the 'section' Salvatore worked for hit a rough patch when it was found that they were involved in domestic industrial espionage in the USA and on top of that dabbled with foreign policy matters by assassinating politically elected leaders, on occasion toppling sovereign governments of certain countries and invading others. It was seen as inappropriate behaviour.

Commissions were set up in the US and the morale among covert staff hit rock bottom. Thousands of field agents were laid off. Salvatore was, supposedly, one among them. These things were set up to be deniable, so the 'Bangalore station' remained forgotten.

However, for Salvatore none of this mattered. He lived on in the fancy bungalow that had been bought with American tax money. It was believed that he had been instrumental in fuelling the city's 1980s gang wars by supplying smuggled guns and ammo. He watched Hari thoughtfully and swigged his beverage. 'Sonny boy, how did OK die? Gimme a name and I'll have the son of a bitch bubble-wrapped and air-lifted to Guantánamo before the sun goes up tomorrow.'

'Once CIA, always CIA, eh?'

'Lower your voice or I shall have to cut off your tongue and feed it to the rats.' Salvatore stared wildly about the gardens, as if sting reporters lurked in the bushes.

Hari remembered something that Uncle used to say: how the CIA model had always been to take useless psychos and turn them into killing machines.

'Sorry Papa. It was a silly accident. Uncle stepped out of a restaurant, but wasn't aware of the sewage pit outside and took the plunge headfirst.' It was a sad demise considering how Uncle had just been released from the detox facility where he had been cured of chronic alcoholism. On his way back to CD Road, he had stopped to celebrate with a small peg.

'No shit? Let's get the guys.'

'No foul play suspected,' Hari clarified. It was one of those pits the Sewerage Board randomly dug up. They forgot to put up a barrier and by the time Uncle had fully recovered from his sobriety spell it had gotten dark. Since the streetlights weren't working on that particular stretch, he was found only the following morning. He was taken to the ICU at the nearest hospital, which was the one from where he had just been discharged, and code blue was announced. Doctors gave him chest compressions and he was hooked up to a defibrillator. The treatment broke his ribs. When reddish Old Monk froth came out of his mouth and nostrils, they declared him dead and stuffed his orifices with cotton before applying tincture to his lips to shut them for good. The cremated body was then couriered to Puncherwallah Complex where Hari found it in a box.

Hari immersed the ashes in the Main Drain ghat in the slum. For the next thirteen days, he kept bottles of Old Monk outside Puncherwallah Complex and every morning they were empty.

'I'll update the relevant secret docket. We have lost a fine agent. On a more personal note, I shall miss OK.' Salvatore looked grim and vulnerable at the same time: his short-sleeved

Lacoste hung loose on his shoulders. The belt, with the buffalo-shaped buckle, had been pulled tight and yet the khaki shorts almost fell off when he stood up to open the icebox and uncork another beer with his teeth. An incisor broke off and slid into the bottle. 'Aw shit, not again,' he said.

'You've got to see a dentist,' said Hari. 'I know a good one, he'll give you a discount.' And Hari would collect a commission.

'Nah! I anyway plan to get rid of all my teeth before I die.' Salvatore guzzled. 'Cheers to OK.' As an afterthought, he opened a pouch of Haldiram's mixture and offered a fistful to Hari. 'On the face of it, it may look to you like an accident. The Russkies used such tricks. Might well be them, since he turned his back on the KGB.' Some may have thought Salvatore pathetic and Hari could have told him that the KGB had ceased to exist in 1991 when the Cold War ended (and their director was then made president of Russia), and that's when Uncle stopped receiving money from them, but listening to Salvatore hold forth on KGB methods reinforced Hari's belief that he knew something about something. Salvatore pointed to a yellowish shrub, 'That there is *Gelsemium elegans*, it's native to India, pretty to the eye but deadly for the body. It's also known as heartbreak grass. I stole some from a KGB doctor's garden. He was sent here to develop new, undetectable, biological methods of poisoning. Suppose somebody is a whistleblower like that Snowden, if he'd been a Russian citizen they'd have dipped a ball in its juices.'

'Is it so?'

'Unfortunately, we at the CIA can no longer do it to Americans because the Congress keeps an eye on us. But the Russkies would get some kid to bat the ball. Seeing it coming at him, the victim instinctively catches it. He gets the residue on his hands. A day later, he collapses from no obvious cause. Here in India, this herb is sold as a homoeopathic medicine against migraine and asthma. I guess that's why those diseases are fairly uncommon here. The patients die.'

'I'm not two-hundred per cent sure I understand the story.'

'What story?' He chucked an empty beer bottle into the garden. Judging from the crash, it broke against another bottle.

'The one you just told me.'

Salvatore rubbed his hands together. 'The moral is that people who ask the wrong questions sometimes die.'

'It is possible that Uncle asked for one Old Monk too much. That happens.'

'Everybody can make a mistake, but if you're smart you turn that into an advantage. My ancestor from Genoa in Italy, whom you may have heard of – in Italian we call him Cristoforo Colombo, but he is better known as Columbus – was on his way to India one day.'

'Oh, I didn't know.'

'Even he didn't know, because he made a basic navigation error so he ended up in America by mistake. That's why he's famous today, even if it was all a mistake. If he had come to Bangalore … he'd have been just like me.' Salvatore opened another beer with his rattling teeth.

'I had no idea that Columbus was looking for Bengaluru. Churchill too lived here. Everybody wants to come here.'

'The sun always shines on those who deserve it, son.'

It echoed something that Hari had been brooding over, and the fact that he was no discoverer of new worlds, the most unlikely person to ever travel abroad, saddened him. Anyway, it usually rained wherever he went. Taking an optimistic view, bad weather protected him against skin cancer. He felt a fresh mosquito bite on his leg and as he bent down to scratch it, he saw a bandicoot scurry past with a grilled chicken carcass.

Salvatore burped and continued: 'Is there anything at all I can do to help you?'

'I was wondering ...'

'Of course, I should have asked you earlier. You want work? I can use an odd-job man 'round the house. Can't pay, but you wouldn't spit at a plate of free food, would you now, son? I think I have leftover chicken from yesterday somewhere in there. Hungry?'

'Thanks, but no thanks, Papa. I have a full-time professional job.'

'Oh yes, you told me. Good for you.' But his voice betrayed regret.

Seeing all this decay surrounding the man, Hari was unable to shake off the feeling that he was in the presence of a piece of heritage that would soon be gone forever, to be replaced by another apartment block.

In those days, the outer cast-iron gate had always been locked from the inside. When he and Uncle would get there, a tiny sliding window opened in the compound wall and a guard confirmed their identities and that they indeed had an appointment with 'sir'. Oversized dogs would always be barking.

There was generally a row of white Ambassador cars in the yard, some with red beacons. A retinue of servants kept the egg pakoras coming and pegs flowing. Sometimes Hari sneaked into the drawing room and admired the floor-to-ceiling bookshelves filled with souvenirs from around the world. The TV with a satellite antenna was one of the first privately owned in Bengaluru and beamed cricket games between the Windies and the Kiwis, or CNN News with updates of the world situation. Much war in the Middle East, a typical American concern, was being discussed here over smuggled bourbon.

Now that he stared into the dim drawing room, it seemed as if the bookshelves were empty. Hari asked, 'How about yourself? You're well, Papa? Still in business?'

'Little of this, little of that, son,' said Salvatore. 'This economic liberalization has been a spanner in the works so to speak. Nobody's willing to be overcharged for smuggled whisky when they can go, at their convenience, to any shop and pay through their noses. Besides, in this new cashless society nobody has black money to spend on fine beverages.'

'I heard the antiques sector is thriving, but.'

'Ah yes, selling something?' Salvatore had him pegged right away as a player.

'Want to buy a thousand armpit fans in original boxes? They're like iPhones but more useful in a hot climate like ours. And they'll be antique within ninety-nine years.'

'I doubt.' Salvatore eyeballed him, 'Is that why you came?'

'No Papa.'

'Then what are you after?'

'I was hoping to find a particular something.'

'So buying, then?'

'Not so much buying as retrieving.'

'I'm all ears for the next five seconds. Then I'll load the shotgun.'

'The Ninth Avatar.' Hari put the page with the sketch of the idol on the table. If the old spy turned out to be the thief, he might become hostile. And in that case, Hari wasn't sure of how to proceed.

'Nope, can't help you. Back in America we have a saying: "In god, we trust." But I don't personally touch gods, even if I trust them. It brings bad luck, you know.'

Hari was prepared to believe him. If he had the item, he would have said so before finishing Hari off with a shot to the back of the head, mob style. 'Gang goes around to rural temples where they don't have CCTV and takes anything movable. Heard of them?'

'I don't do business like that. Who were they?'

'Nobody knows. I only have some initials of their names, RIP and DA, and they call themselves businessmen but look like thugs. Mean anything to you?'

'Of course.'

'Is it so?'

'Heh … "Rest in Peace" and "District Attorney" … classic mafia codes. These days there are so many players. Stopped dealing with young turks, the risk of getting slashed with a machete while waiting at a zebra crossing is too high. I take it they're brash kids if they're so audacious as to leave initials. You'll find them bragging about it in some bar.'

It did occur to Hari too that most likely they'd be the kind that boasted about heists, but the problem was that there were 2167 bars and stand up liquor counters in Bengaluru, far too many to check them all. 'Who does business with suchlike?'

Salvatore scratched his beard and another louse fell out, but before he killed it, it jumped into the furry area below his throat like Indiana Jones into the jungle. 'See, son. I have this feeling.'

'What feeling?'

'That I must ask you if you're sure you want to meet somebody who might not be good for your health?'

'Those people I meet all the time.'

Salvatore nodded. 'Fine. There's an old MI6 agent who trains rowdies, used to stay over in Cooke Town. It was some British covert project to hinder the Indian independence movement.'

'That's like prehistoric times.' It sounded as if Salvatore spoke of somebody who lived a century ago, when India was ruled by pinkies such as Churchill. He had expected more specific information. But if, on the other hand, the Brit was around the corner it might be worth the trouble. 'He's still there?'

'Double-0 agents retire at forty-five, but he's gone private and has a couple of bad boys in his service. Must be in his eighties at least. Ever worked for him?'

'No. Why'd you ask?'

'Crazy people to do crazy things.'

'So, tell me more,' said Hari tactfully.

'You know how these Brits are.'

'They eat Marmite?' Hari once helped a Scottish tourist track down the last jar in Russell Market, left behind in 1947 when the colonials went home. It had been mouldy, but the tourist was thrilled – yeast and mould were more or less the same thing.

'Turd preserve.' Salvatore rinsed his mouth with beer.

'Tell me about this Brit.' One thought bothered Hari: How many foreign hands was he going to have to shake before he handcuffed the right one? It seemed as if all retired spies in Bengaluru were blaming each other. The Pakistani sent him here, this American sends him to the next agent. A wild goose chase?

'He's got bad teeth.'

'I might be able to connect him with a better dentist. Who is he?'

'Name's Doug Maddox. He deals in anything that fetches a fistful of rupees.'

'So where do I find him?'

'They say he built a posh villa in Sri Lanka or Jamaica, but I happen to know he still comes here often. Because of his "presumed" vast knowledge, he's freelancing as a consultant for auction houses in London. He rents godowns around Kallapete, I believe, but mostly operates out of guest houses – cops are on to him so he moves from lodge to lodge, always the cheapest, uses rooms to store stuff, Sir "Fred Friendly" he calls himself.'

'Sir Friendly?' echoed Hari.

'Alias Jack O'Bedlam when he claims to be sent by the IRA, Dan McDruff when he uses his Scottish identity, or Father Blessing when he pretends to be a missionary, or Parkinson Sahib when he tries to impress people. Alias Brandy Darling when he goes to Koshy's to drink.'

So many aliases. Hari felt envious.

'Thanks Papa, I'll go and ask him. I know Kallapete.'

'No son, that's exactly what you're not going to do. What I didn't tell you is that he was one of the biggest covert agents in British history with 366 confirmed kills according to the dossier. The boys in his service will wring your neck. I don't doubt your courage, but his boys weigh about fifteen to twenty stone per head.'

'Is that the size of their brains then?'

'Witty, are you?'

'All muscles then?' asked Hari to clarify.

'Son, the main reason you should worry is that he's afraid of going to jail. Anything he perceives as a threat is dealt with …'

'How?'

'With deadly force.'

'How do I approach him then?'

'If you find him, meet him in a crowded place. Never turn your back on him.'

'I'll make a mental note about that.' But he doubted that it would be feasible. Turning your back on somebody was a necessary prerequisite if you were running for your life.

'Now sonny boy, if you'll excuse me, it is time for me to continue my afternoon meditation. My guru-ji tells me to meditate on an arrow and a target.'

That was the prepare-for-your-next-rebirth exercise. With a tinge of melancholy in his tone, Salvatore added, 'You go ahead and have a nice day.'

'Bye-bye, Papa Sal, and all the very best with your arrow. I hope it hits the target,' Hari said as he left the spy to bask in the remains of the sunlight that filtered through the dead trees in his garden. He'd be extra careful when he met the Brit, if he found him.

12

> Work issues leave you frustrated, but a chance meeting with an influential person is likely to give you an advantage.

The municipal BMTC terminal was known as Mezestic Bus Stand after the now demolished Majestic Talkies which once stood nearby. It was the heart of Bengaluru. It was also its intestine and, some crude foreigners said, its most unmentionable body part.

It was where people arrived by the busload with their soft-focus ambitions. Tourists too got off the long-distance buses, emaciated by dysentery, rushing madly around the platforms to find a lavatory. For city dwellers, this was their main transport hub – wherever they came from and wherever they had to go, it involved an inevitable change at Mezestic and a brief scuffle with pickpockets, attention-diverters and other tricky species that inhabited the platforms, until they escaped into the air-conditioned confines of the metro trains that ran under the bus station. It was also where losers, after using up whatever money they had brought with them, were seen in the evenings waiting for the last homebound bus.

A lucky few made the station into their livelihood and never left the platforms, such as 'Pusher Prasad', who dealt in inferior charas, spurious ecstasy and recycled opium, or the dwarf who sat inside a tin box and sold papers chronicling city days and nights – the juicy stories of scandals and vandals. Hari picked up *Hottu-Hottu*, a steaming tabloid that gave an overview of what went on when decent people took naps and miscreants, antisocials and rowdy-sheeters were awake.

Hari had spent his growing-up years loitering at the station, keeping an eye out for potential customers. Tourists in need of rooms. Latent shopaholics who might require Kashmiri handicrafts. People never knew what they wanted until they met the right tout – and that was usually Hari. He felt at ease here, where one disappeared in the milling crowds. He sat down in a canteen and ordered coffee and studied the tabloid. He needed to defraggle his brain.

The tabloid was better updated than the Internet and the ink so fresh that it came off on his fingers. There was no mention of arrested temple looters, nothing on a smuggler don going by the name of Maddox. One story was about how the police were looking for aluminium cylinders claimed to be nuclear bombs. *Brilliant*, thought Hari as he wondered what to do with the sample cylinder Doc had given to him. Then he noticed that a freelance reporter, Naanu Gotillamma, had filed a news item about how 'ex-detective Hurree Mezestic' had agreed to do a tell-all interview but absconded by the time the reporter reached his office, so one could assume that 'the selfsame aforementioned Mr Mezestic' was the mastermind behind the recent crime wave bamboozling the banking sector. An inside job, she wrote.

Hari plugged his phone charger into one of the sockets and contemplated speaking to Diamond, but whenever he moved his finger towards the speed dial with her codename, 'Number 1', he hesitated. He desperately wanted to have good news for her, something better than being implicated in a 'recent crime wave'. Besides, she herself had given him a deadline until Monday. So, he started making calls.

His nervous system was hardwired with a comprehensive list of the area's lodging houses and dormitories. The mathematical component of his brain sorted them by location, comforts (attached or common bath; number of cable channels or no TV), by room rate or phone number. If he was involved in the idol theft, Maddox was bound to have left a trail. He started from the bottom, price wise, and worked his way up.

'What do you want?' said the man who answered the phone.

'A very good afternoon to you too. Is this the Kama Boardless?'

'Who wants to know?'

Kama Boardless Lodging House doubled as a brothel, so one had to speak in riddles. 'The one who's trying to call you.'

'And who are you then?'

'This is Churchill speaking.' The colonial Prime Minister had spent his youth in Bengaluru and so was highly likely to have sired some illegitimate children in town, thought Hari and tried to sound British.

'So what?'

'I'd like to leave a message for one of your guests, my great-grandson, a pucca English gentleman, but since I was born in 1874, I'm so senile that I forgot his room number.'

'Can't help you,' said the voice and the phone was slammed down.

Hari pressed the redial button, changing his voice into a booming register. 'Yo bro, I'm calling long distance from Nigeria. Don't cut me off, bro. I wanna discuss a very important business opportunity.'

'What business?'

'To cut a long story short, bro.'

'Yes, cut it.'

'Bro, I'm an old sinner and have caused lots of harm to people, including one of your guests.'

'That's a bad idea.'

'I realized now only. I sent him a fake email regarding tax refunds. I may not be able to meet and greet every single soul I cheated, but I'm doing my best to track down as many as possible. So now that I've found his whereabouts at your luxurious spa resort, halleluiah, the Almighty will lessen my burdens.'

'Why should I give a damn about your problems?'

'Plus, there's a finder's fee of thirty per cent for yourself, bro. Any Englishman staying with you?' said Hari who knew that if one spoke fast enough and used a lot of fancy words, people had no time to analyze what one was saying. They were likely to think that if something sounded wrong, they themselves had misunderstood it. And if you peppered your talk with references to money, everyone was bound to get interested.

However, not always. There was a sceptical silence on the line. 'Yo there, bro?'

'What's his name, this English personality?'

'Doug Maddox. The last name is spelled M-A-D- ...'

Before Hari had completed the sentence, the answer came, 'No guest by that name.' Maybe the hotelier had fallen victim to Nigerian frauds too many times and knew that one must be wary.

'Bro, he sometimes uses his pet name. How about Sir Friendly?'

'*Friendly* with whom?'

'Maybe it was Darling.'

'I'm not your *darling*. Don't you know the name of the person you want to speak to?'

'Yo, five hundred per cent for sure, it is Parkinson Sahib.' It complicated matters that the man went by so many different aliases.

'You're wasting my time and time is cash.'

Stingy type.

'Can I leave my number and you call me if he turns up? To compensate for wasting your time, I'll transfer the finder's fee in advance if you send me your bank account number and PIN code.'

Before the phone was slammed down this time, he gave his mobile number. He made many calls. Everybody told him to stop bothering them. But generally, since there were mentions of money, they took down his number, just in case.

That was that. After having made dozens of dud calls to cover the shady lodges he knew, he had used up the currency on his prepaid card. He concluded that Maddox wasn't in town. In which case, the Briton had nothing to do with the idol theft. He played with the urea-flavoured fennel seeds in the dish that held the billing slip before he put money down. Low on cash again, he needed business.

Then his phone started ringing manically. Maybe he should pick up and speak to Diamond? He felt sorry that he hadn't even washed the dishes like promised. But it was an unknown number. He hesitated. It could be the enforcers from the bank or one of the hoteliers wanting to get a share of the Nigerian money. But when he took the call, it was the voice of a woman on the line.

'He-hello?' she said hesitantly.

'Yes, tell me?'

'I'm standing right outside.'

'Is it so?' *What was going on?* Hari did a 360 degree in the canteen, but saw no woman with a mobile. For a moment, he worried that it was somebody he had scammed in a previous lifetime. Ghost call from hell?

'Yes. But your office is closed.' The voice was edgy. 'It says it is open twenty-four hours.'

Oho, he thought, *a prospective client?*

'Ah yes, but have you ever heard of IST?'

'Indian Standard Time?'

'Indian *Stretchable* Time! Get it? It's meant to be funny.'

'But it's an emergency.'

This sounded serious. He changed his tone. 'We are, of course, at your service and thank you for dialling our call centre hotline. Your call is important to us. How may I redirect your call?'

'I must speak to somebody.'

'That'll be me then.'

'In person.'

'That is also possible. Right at this moment our agency is conducting a major stakeout, so if it is totally urgent I request you to take a right outside our office and walk down the alley.

You will see a small kiosk selling coffee. Parcel a cup for me to cover the first appointment fee. Then you go straight from there.'

'Towards the bus stand?'

'Highly correctly. That is where the operation is taking place.'

'But ... perhaps I shouldn't disturb.'

'Don't hang up, we're simply waiting to nab a certain lynchpin behind a recent crime wave against digital banking.' His prayers for business were about to be answered. 'I'll take fifteen minutes off.'

'If you're sure about it.'

'My coffee break is anyway starting right now. There's fourteen minutes left.'

'Won't it be dangerous?' Her trembling voice sounded sexy like some heroine in a movie.

'My lady, coffee is dangerous for geriatrics with urological problems, loose motions and kidney stones. As long as you're in the flower of youth, you will be in no danger whatsoever. Besides, the bus stand is swarming with our field agents. It is the four-hundred and twenty per cent safest place to be in Bengaluru.'

She showed up minutes later. He recognized her from the takeaway coffee she was carrying in a flimsy plastic cup, treading gingerly down the ramp from the foot-over bridge. Dressed in a richly synthetic bright sari, she had a big round tikka above her nose and was older than he had expected. Probably almost forty, but still hot.

'There you are,' he said and pressed his palms together. 'My good self Mister Majestic or Hari if you wish to be less formal. How may we help you?'

'We?'

Hari nodded at the dwarf selling tabloids and then at a foreigner scurrying off a bus and towards the loos. 'For a civilian, it is impossible to tell who is a detective and who is not, for as they say, it takes one to know one.' He summoned up the biggest smile.

She handed him the coffee and he downed it in one go. No coffee could beat Coffee-Anand's when it came to sugar levels.

'Let's sit down,' he suggested and led her into the canteen. 'I am sincerely regretful that nobody was at the office, because it would have been such an honour to host you there, rather than here. This is not quite our style, but we're engaged in a colossal operation so every staff member is on round-the-clock duty. Even that fellow who plucks the dishes off the tables is with us. You wouldn't know by looking at him, but he's trained to kill using a dirty teaspoon. Isn't it unbelievable?'

'Yes, it is quite incredible. Can't he use a clean one?'

Her skin had a wheatish flush that suggested she might have been drinking palm toddy in her teens as she grew up in some village, followed by arranged marriage and a move into the city to which she had never adapted.

'It wouldn't be the same thing. Now, now, don't take tension, I know exactly how it feels. Your husband is cheating on you for the third time, is it not?' That was usually the case when a woman consulted a detective. First time, they forgave, second time, they thought something was wrong with themselves, then they declared war. Triplex would enjoy tracking a cheating husband and taking snaps. He could thus be re-hired on a freelance basis. Things would get back to normal again.

'No.'

'How is that possible?'

'He is a pure vegetarian actually.'

'Is that the problem?'

'No, but I read about you in the paper.'

'Today?' said Hari almost biting his tongue off.

'No, about a year or two ago. You were a hero in those days.'

'The newspaper editors feel that people like me are an inspiration to mankind,' he said and waggled his head modestly, though it thrilled him to be able to bask in the rays of yesterday's sun.

Unexpectedly, the woman sobbed into a handkerchief. Many people were in denial about their auntyhood. Ageing wasn't easy to accept. Then she started the upload. 'My name is Tulsi and I live in the Main Drain Semi-Slum. My husband is Bisi Sambaranna.'

That meant they were neighbours. He now recalled seeing her in a standard-issue nightie outside a hut. She'd dressed up because she was coming to see him, her hero. Suddenly he felt sorry for her. 'Despite the pressure on our services, we want to help the common people, so do tell me what your problem is, Aunty.'

'Yesterday gold polishers knocked on the door and offered to clean my jewellery at an affordable rate,' she sobbed and Hari had an uneasy feeling that he knew what he was going to hear next. 'Since my daughter's wedding is coming up, I took out the jewellery from the Godrej steel almirah. All of it. Because she's marrying a suitable boy who has a green card and a job in California, and is the correct subcaste. I'm usually not such a fool.'

'No Tulsi Aunty, I didn't think you'd be. What language did they speak?'

'In bazaar-Hindi they told about a new vegetarian cleaning powder. So I thought they knew what they were doing.'

For sure they knew. He'd heard of gangs that travelled from faraway places to perpetrate scams in Bengaluru, but aloud he said, 'Tell me more.'

'I swear, I kept an eye on them as they put my gold ornaments in a copper vessel with the powder and sealed it, then I gave them their fee and sent them off. They didn't touch the vessel again. They told me to wait five hours before opening it. Since I knew that the ornaments were in it …' She went silent.

'How did you know?'

'It rattled when I shook it and I locked the vessel safely in the almirah.'

'Then what happened?' He guessed the answer, having been a scamster himself, but he was a detective now, so he had to ask.

'You won't believe, but when I took out the vessel, it contained ordinary pebbles. My gold worth two lakhs was gone!'

'I can't believe it,' said Hari. She had described a known modus operandi. Why, similar cases were reported in the newspapers day after day, yet gullible housewives fell for the trick. After analyzing sufficiently, he said, 'That surely is the strangest thing I have ever heard.'

She put her hands to her face. 'Sir, I've learnt my lesson and, in the future, I am going to be more cautious. But will you help me get the ornaments back? If my husband Bisi finds out, he will get gallstones, what with the dowry we're already paying. Our savings will be gone.'

Hari rocked back on his plastic chair, detective ishtyle. 'We shall look into the matter, Missus Tulsi. Our basic fee is fifteen thousand per week.'

'You're a people's hero,' she said and sank down to the floor, bending to touch his toes with her tear-stained hands. Other customers stared disapprovingly at Hari, who they presumed had said something inappropriate to the respectable woman, maybe blackmailed her.

'Aunty, there's no need to massage my feet.' They were too sore from the cigarette burns he had received from the enforcers. 'We'll do the job, don't worry.'

'I don't have that kind of money, sir. Please, I will be eternally grateful.' She sobbed and more people turned to stare.

He found it hard to deal with weeping aunties; he was used to hardboiled criminals. 'Not to worry, Aunty. We shall do the needful and retrieve your valuable ornaments.' Then he remembered that he was broke. 'We require a deposit of only a thousand for the first seven days to cover expenditure.'

'Sir, that's my grocery money for the month,' she said and blew her nose in his toes.

'Okay. We'll make adjustments ... a hundred will do,' he bargained on her behalf. He'd always been a poor businessman. 'As for the fee, we may waive it, if you do minor chores for us.'

'Is it something immoral or anti-national?'

'No, not at all. We're a bit understaffed at the moment, but no scary things involved. Let me revert back to you on the selfsame matter.'

'Thank you.'

'No mention.'

'I mean it. You're a good man.'

'Saints and prophets are usually good.' He took leave of her, wished her all the best and as a precautionary measure he left the bus stand – the woman had created a scene and one never knew what might trigger off riots hereabouts. The smallest things resulted in ten buses being burnt and any flimsy rumour led to a skull being crushed. He crossed Dhanvanthri Road through the underpass, where video pirates and other petty merchants flaunted their stock. Might the pirates be working for Triplex? The other shopless vendors sold electrified tennis rackets that sizzled mosquitoes, disco globes for home parties and similar crazy stuff, and perhaps they too were part of Triplex's commercial empire.

Hari emerged in the dusty bustle in the alley that connected the tunnel to CD Road, lined with umpteen seedy bars, mostly the stand-up and guzzle variety serving travellers who needed one for the road before they boarded their buses, and informative banners with cautionary messages such as: 'If you know you are driving to your death, would you still drive so fast?'

Somewhere here he might find the gang of jewel thieves. After topping up his phone with whatever coins he had left, he put the word out on the scamster network's WhatsApp group, which linked local conmen. Hari had technically quit the profession, but liked to stay in touch, go for trade meets and reunions. He soon got a handful of suggestions about where to look for outsider scamsters – none of the tip-offs was too specific because ratting without pay didn't make sense. One came from a legendary old-timer, Shanty Ram the 'social worker', who suggested that Hari drop by and have an evening meal with him. 'See you at Majestic Hotel … 7 minutes.'

Majestic Hotel, which was around the corner, was older than Hari but was named after the same cinema hall. It was one of those hotels with no rooms. It dated from 1971 and opened early which made it convenient for rowdies who needed omelettes and Horlicks after a busy night of rowdy-sheeting. Hari knew that

Shanty Ram always went there to have his meals of rich ghee rice and spicy mutton fry. As he stepped in, he spotted Shanty Ram alone at a table full of tin plates.

'It is good to see my young friend Majestic in Majestic Hotel,' joked Shanty Ram, sucking out the marrow from a bone. Back in the day, Shanty Ram was the undisputed king of scamsters, starting out with cheque book fraud and from there graduating to organizing unauthorized charitable blood donation camps but selling the produce to hospitals at inflated rates. Hari had heard rumours that his heyday was past. Local people had caught on to his tricks and he hadn't moved on – he wasn't into skimming, spoof websites and registering fake domain names. But somehow, Ram was still eating mutton on a daily basis and judging from the fact that he wore two toupees, in different colours, he fancied himself a true bigwig.

'Long time no see, macha. You look like you haven't had a drink in days.'

Did he know that Hari had had to stop having fun? But aloud Hari wisecracked about it, 'Is my face that ugly?'

'No-no, I mean that you actually look healthy, you've put on weight and all. What will you eat? There's keema paratha. My treat.' Some gravy had splattered on Ram's khadi kurta.

'I'm trying to be vegetarian,' he said and settled for masala rice and gudbud for dessert, though he knew that for the nuttiest gudbud one had to go to the coast. Where he had never been rich enough to go.

'Sorry about your uncle.'

'Shit happens.'

'He was one of the stalwarts. I remember that day when he started a riot in the courthouse. Anyway, I hear you're pretending to be a law-abiding citizen. I must have misheard some malicious rumour that your enemies are …'

Hari hoped that he had no more enemies that he could count on his own fingers, toes and orifices.

'No, it's true. I've gone over to the other side. I'm a private detective.'

'That's why I got piqued when I saw your WhatsApp message. What's up?'

While they ate, they analyzed different gangs and their varying operational models. Some dressed like policemen and stopped women in the street to warn them against chain-snatchers. They'd get their victim to remove gold chains, tie items safely in a handkerchief and send the scammee home – only problem was that the handkerchief, when untied, turned out to hold worthless metal pieces marinated in snot. Such gangs were trained in Mumbai and acted filmy-ishtyle. Other gangs from the north showed people a laptop and offered it cheap; scammees went to take out the money from the ATM and when they returned the laptop was packed in a reassuringly heavy computer box, but back home, upon opening it, they'd find a brick.

Tamil gangs were attention-diverters, performing the classic 'you dropped currency notes' trick outside banks and, as the victim picked up a few tenners from the ground, the gang sped away with the victim's cash-filled briefcase. Andhra gangs dealt in fake gold ornaments. The crimes often remained unsolved because after doing a number of successful scams, the conmen took the train to another town. It was harder for people like Shanty Ram, who belonged in town and couldn't honestly leave. That's why local scamming was a loser's business.

Hari mentioned that Missus Tulsi claimed this particular gang spoke bazaar-Hindi.

'Hindi, she said, did she?' asked Shanty Ram and then he mentioned a gang from Agra staying in the dormitory at the not-so-discerning Kama Boardless Lodging House. 'I bet they're not here to build another Taj Mahal. I have been seeing them for a week now, when I do my rounds to collect protection money.'

Hari scratched his hair, it was high time to change the oil. Why wasn't he surprised? Agra, the capital of gem scams. He'd heard of gangs from there. Suave and persuasive, especially those who had been trained near the Taj Mahal, which was a gemstone hotspot due its tourist trade – tourists happily bought worthless glass replicas of the Kohinoor diamond. And the Kama Boardless was a favourite haunt of low-budget crooks. Perfect fit. 'Thanks. It must be them.'

'When you bust their balls, tell them I said hi. By the way, do you need money?' asked Shanty Ram and laid ₹1,000 in soiled tens and twenties on the table.

'What's this for?'

'I heard you have two girls and even a wife. Must be costing a bomb.' Shanty Ram suggested that Hari join him as a junior bhai: he didn't see any difference between a private detective and a hired torpedo. He collected 2 per cent cuts from business operations, but some, like the scamsters from Agra, refused to give the 'cultural donation' to Shanty's socio-religious charitable trust. In such circumstances, Shanty could find use for an underling. He bragged that he had recently moved into a barsati in tony Sadashivnagar, because whenever a cinema hall was torn down and a mall was built, the 2 per cent meant big money to the bhais, which meant more spicy mutton for Shanty Ram, whose ambition it was to become the biggest don and stand for elections. But for that he needed enough henchmen to capture all the poll booths. 'Business is going up, but I'm getting too old to walk around and threaten people with dire consequences. I want somebody with me whom I can trust. Would you like to eat meat every day?'

Apparently, he hadn't listened when Hari told him about his vegetarian aspirations. Hari rolled his head sideways.

'Macha, why don't you take service as my porki?'

'Like in Challenging Star Darshan's movie?' asked Hari.

Porki had been a big hit years back. Due to its choreographed fight scenes, it completed a hundred days in the cinemas on CD Road (Hari and Triplex saw it every night), and it was even dubbed into Bhojpuri. The film's priceless climactic fight, where goondas flew out of windows, took three weeks to shoot. About half of the budget had gone into that one scene. Hari smiled, 'It was full ticket's worth.'

'Ya macha. We'd make a great team.'

'Let me think about it,' said Hari. They both knew it almost certainly meant no, which probably was a very bad decision on Hari's part.

'Take the money before I change my mind. '

Hari pocketed the wad of cash. He was flattered about being compared to Challenging Star Darshan, but sometimes you had to make the wrong choice in life to reach the right goal.

13

You're geared towards success but there is no success without perspiration, so sweat it out.

The entrance to the nondescript Kama Boardless Lodging House faced HM Road in the block between 3rd and 6th Cross roads. In the reception area, a TV played filmy songs. A sepia picture of a wedding couple on the wall was daubed with fresh vermillion paste. A black and white picture of an elderly version of the same man, with the face hand-coloured in pink, was garlanded, but the jasmine flowers had withered years ago into a brown string.

A dark corridor led deeper into the building and a steep staircase climbed to the first floor which had an upper veranda facing the street. The desk was unattended. The rate posted on the grooved felt board was ₹149. A lone man was busy sweeping the floor. In his fifties, he was dressed in shorts and a tattered uniform jacket that missed most of its buttons.

Hari stretched out his hand. 'It is a pleasure to meet you. I am an NRI.' The easiest trick in the book was to sound pompous and people who had an inferiority complex always accepted whatever you said. The caste system worked that way.

The sweeper turned to Hari without looking him in the eyes.

'My good self room boy Victor.' Judging from the name, he was Christian.

'Myself co-director *Harry* Majestic.' Hari's name, when pronounced as Harry, also sounded Christian. A bond was forged. Hari ceremoniously folded a ₹10 note that he tucked into Victor's breast pocket. As a strategy, it was the best: tip first and expect good service after. The other way around rarely cut it in these parts. 'Would you be kind enough to see if you have any outsiders staying?'

'You're looking for the Mad Dog? The manager said some asshole had … sorry … a gentleman called.'

Hari's first instinct was to scold him, but then the bulbs started flashing under his eyelids.

Mad Dog? Ah, Doug Maddox!

'Yes, yes, Doug. Ah yes, "Mad Dog" for sure,' Hari said in an easy voice signalling that he and Maddox were, basically, childhood friends. What a karmic coincidence. Hari waggled his head vigorously. 'Tell me.'

'You told the manager that you wanted to return his money?'

'Correct-u. There's an opportunity for you too to make a bit of coffee money,' said Hari and stuffed another ₹10 note into the room boy's pocket.

'Mad Dog was a good man. He always gave generous tips. I'd never take money from his friends.'

'Okay, you can give back the tips if you like.' Hari was playing his cards right and had been upgraded to a friend. Or perhaps the Mad Dog had more friends on Facebook than one could have guessed. Then the one significant word registered. 'Was?' he echoed.

'He's dead.'

'Ayooh, how it happened?'

'He collapsed a few days back here in the lodge. On the first-floor veranda.' Victor nodded upwards. 'This one came and took him to that place.'

'Oho. But which this one and that place are we talking about?'

'Uh. This one ... *ambulance* to hospital. Never came back.'

All hospitals in the neighbourhood weren't pure veg. Patients didn't always survive. 'You're surely sure?'

Victor shrugged. 'Since he was taken away, he hasn't paid rent, so manager Obiraya sir will empty his room. Sell the things to recover dues. After you called, he went to fetch the scrap dealer. I thought I must inform you.'

So the hotel manager knew that Maddox's room contained things that must be gotten rid of.

'Oho, good thinking, Victor. And you're saying that my dear old family friend Mister Doug is in the hospital morgue? Thank you for intimating me, your teamwork spirit in this matter is appreciated. Tell your manager that I'll settle the bill for Mister Doug's serviced apartment.' Hari made a quick calculation: seven nights cost ₹1,043 which meant that he almost had the weeks' rent covered with the money Shanty Ram had given him, but on the other hand, he could try a bluff first. 'I will also carry some necessities for him. Clean underwear. In case he isn't fully dead, yet. Sometimes the hospitals save people by curing them instead. So I may have to go through Doug's luggage. Okay?'

It took Victor a minute to process the data upload, which explained why he hadn't advanced to any deputy managership. 'Obiraya isn't back.'

'But let's not waste time, it may be a matter of life and death. You must be having a spare key? I have many impossible missions to complete.'

In the event, Victor's loyalty to Maddox won and he led the way up the stairs to the street-facing veranda which was lined with yellow doors numbered from 201 to 212 and 214 to 222. Victor unlocked the padlock on 205. The door next to it bore the sign: 'Kama Dispensary & Gent's Gynaecologist: Consult All Kinds Virility Problems.'

The room was about five feet by six. The walls bare, no shelves or cupboards. Most of the space was taken up by a metal cot with a mattress darkened by sweat. Instead of a table there was a low stool with an ashtray and a stack of cigarette packs of an old-fashioned brand, Charminar. Below the stool were empty quarts of cheap Bagpiper whisky. Victor switched on the mains and the fan blasted away so hard that papers stacked in a corner fluttered around and were about to escape through the open door and fly into the street. Hari quickly bent to pick up the papers and glimpsed a suitcase under the bed.

'Sure this is the room?' He had expected something somewhat posher.

'Yes.'

He sat down on the cot. The papers were printouts of medical tests: many values were in bold, way above the upper limit of the reference range. BP was 200, cholesterol as if he'd been eating six-egg omelettes daily, his liver was barely alive. The name at the top was given as Parkinson Sahib, ninety-four years. Hospitals and diagnostic clinics hereabouts didn't ask for IDs as long as one paid cash. Hari smiled his broadest smile at Victor: 'Lord Doug was a great man, once.'

'I know, he often told me about his years in service.'

'What did he say?' asked Hari and picked up a copy of the *Lonely Planet* guidebook from the floor. It looked like a pirated edition. He observed that many of the pages about temple towns in Tamil Nadu were missing. When he flipped to the Srirangapatnam section, the description of the Halegudehalli village was torn out. He compared the tear with the page found in the temple. It was a perfect match.

'That it was very important.'

'Yes, but times change and what was important yesterday isn't very important today. Unless, of course, it turns into an antique.'

Victor didn't react. The words were too complex.

'Did he ever tell you about his current business ventures?'

'No, mister. I'm a room boy.'

'But he tipped handsomely?'

'I used to mail things on his behalf.'

'I see. What?'

'Small packages. Sometimes bigger.'

'Did he send anything in the last one week or so?'

'Mad Dog had been ailing for a month, so he hadn't been up to much.'

'Oho.' So the statue hadn't been sent off by post. Hari leaned down and studied the suitcase under the bed. 'Say Victor, this might take longer than expected.' He became officious again. 'Do you have a dormitory where I could book myself a cot? I may need to stay around and take care of Lord Doug's affairs.'

'I can find out if there are vacancies.'

'And it is quite dusty here. You may want to notify housekeeping so that Doggie feels welcome when he is discharged from the hospital ... if he isn't fully dead.'

That would give Victor enough to deal with and Hari sufficient time to rifle through the Brit's belongings. As soon as he heard Victor go down the stairs, he pulled out the suitcase from under the cot. It was the only possible place where the idol could be hidden. His luck continued as he found it unlocked. He rummaged through the sets of shirts with '00' monograms, fancy ties, boxer shorts, silk socks covered in fine layers of fungus. Nothing valuable, no idols or other religious objects.

Next, he considered whether to cut up the mattress. He swept his hand across it. No statue-sized bumps. So, if the idol was with Maddox, it had to be with him in the hospital. He became aware of steps outside and pushed the suitcase back under the bed. Victor returned.

'There is one vacancy in the dorm. The five others are rented by people from Agra.'

'What kind of people?'

'Quiet people who don't make trouble. Except they take rum in the evenings.'

'I'd love to share accommodation with happy rum aficionados from Agra. It is a beautiful town with fine architecture.' He'd never been to Agra – and knew nothing about it except that the Taj Mahal was there and it was a good scene for touting, especially if one was employed by a gem dealer. 'I'll make a move then and get going to the hospital. I see these are important test results and without them the doctors may administer the wrong medication.'

'You can't just take his things and go.'

'Don't worry, I know what I am doing.' He pretended to verify the medical records. 'I shall quickly go and come.'

He pushed another ₹10 into Victor's breast pocket and the room boy let him take the papers. In the street, Hari bought a bunch of flowers from a pushcart vendor and a quart of Bagpiper from the booze stall next to the lodge. 'Operation Idol' was about to enter its final, climactic stages, and Hari had to come up with a Plan G for how to end it. He decided to improvise. He called up Missus Tulsi and told her that she'd get her jewellery back if she helped him a bit, instructing her about the basic theory of the bad cop, worse cop routine. She'd seen movies, so she knew what he talked about.

Being paranoid like all ex-spies, Maddox had checked himself into the hospital under the name Parkinson to avoid detection by authorities who might scrutinize hospital records. Hari had spotted the same name in the medical test result.

The fake name game. Of all these old spies that he'd been meeting, none of them wanted to shoulder the responsibility for what they had done. It struck him as tragicomic that this old boys' network – if it could be called a 'network' – had been dumped in the gutters of Bengaluru.

'Terminal case,' the pretty Malayalee nurse stated as she led Hari and Tulsi down the corridor to the semi-private ward that Maddox shared with one rowdy and one goon. People like them were antisocial and knew little English apart from trade argot such as 'I'll kill you, bastard,' so as long as Hari, Maddox and Tulsi stuck to polysyllabic English they wouldn't understand much.

'Mad Dog' Maddox had cirrhosis of the liver. The trembling ninety-four-year-old Briton was hirsute like a weed-infested construction plot that needed a full vegetarian Malleshwaram shave, which included nostrils and ears, and possibly other body parts, too. His skin was bright pink with lesions, the whites of his eyes were green, his moustache was snot-encrusted, and he snored feebly, so he was alive. His situation made Hari recall what the baba at the temple told him – *crime brings its own fatality with it.* Meaning all bad guys die at the end of the plot.

The nurse woke him up by gently touching his arm.

'Huh?' Maddox said and farted. How had these Britons ever managed to rule India?

Hari set down the flowers on the night table next to the bed. As soon as the nurse turned her back to them, he pulled open the table drawer and slipped the Bagpiper inside. As he did so, he examined its contents: it contained medicines, no idols. 'Something to sip. Anything else you miss? I see you have all manner of medications here.'

'Bagpiper ...'

'Yes, of course: Number 1 selling beverage!'

'I used to love it, innit. But I don't drink anymore.' His accent was British public school, the kind you heard on the BBC. 'You are not any of my kids.'

'Nope. This is Missus Tulsi. Say hi to the uncle.'

'Hi Uncle,' said Tulsi.

'So who are you?' He coughed up bile into a spittoon.

'Harry, the name is Harry.'

'Speak up, laddie. I'm a trifle deaf.'

Hari shouted. 'Just like Potter but way better.'

The old man crinkled up his face and then it went blank, like a TV being switched off. 'Who is Potter?'

'You haven't read Harry Potter?' said Tulsi. 'You must be highly stupid.'

Wrong number, this generation gap was wider than the Palk Strait. Never one to give up, Hari decided to see what the Briton might confess on his deathbed. He reminded himself that the clinching evidence had been the torn page from the *Lonely Planet*. So without missing a beat, he said, 'I'm sorry if I disturbed your death throes. Trying to be humanitarian. God save the queen.'

Maddox whispered. 'Are you from the church?'

'Something like that,' said Hari.

'Like what? Speak up, laddie. Take a seat while you're at it.'

'I keep meeting Victor at the Rice Memorial Church on Sundays and he told me about your malfunction.'

'Fun while it lasted.'

'How are you holding up?'

'It'll be over soon.'

'If I had a liver, I'd have gladly donated it to you.'

'Why, that'd be kind of you. You must be a good sport.' Maddox was a total Englishman, down to the stiff upper lip – although it was stiff from dried snot more than any cultural idiosyncrasy.

Hari chose his next words with care, 'Would you like to come clean?'

'What's that?'

'Anything to confess, goods to declare?'

'Yes, but I'd have to kill you if I told you, innit.'

'Prefer to take your secrets with you to the grave?'

The old Briton was silent for a minute, as if debating with himself whether to declassify anything, then the upper lip became less stiff as he desperately excavated his left nostril. 'It may sound stupid, but I never thought I would die.'

'That's how it has to happen before you can move forward.'

Maddox looked at Hari with hope in his eyes. 'What about that liver of yours, laddie – is it for sale?'

'It was stolen.'

The Briton showed his disappointment by farting dirtily.

'There are lots of thieves around,' said Hari. 'Ask Missus Tulsi for example.'

She nodded purposefully.

'Who is she?'

Hari decided to play hardball. 'She's an undercover policewoman. Yeah, so let's be honest with each other. What can you tell me about the Ninth Avatar?'

'Beg your pardon?'

'It's not a Hollywood movie sequel, it is a statue.'

Tulsi looked puzzled, but lectured the old spy, 'The gods, not just your Christian one, expect you to own up to your sins.'

She was too good. Hari might hire her permanently.

'What sort of statue?'

'Well, it's one of the usual gods,' said Tulsi.

'God number nine to be precise,' Hari added.

'What about it?'

'It was stolen last weekend from a temple in Halegudehalli, about a hundred kilometres outside town.'

'So what am I supposed to know about it?'

'Everything.' Hari knew he was bluffing because he hadn't got a finger up the nostril right then. Only those who didn't know how to hide their secrets had fingers planted up there.

'I can't even get out of this bed.' But the spy was getting agitated.

Tulsi wagged a finger. 'Just because you're bedridden doesn't mean that you're free of guilt.'

But out of respect – Maddox was much senior to Hari and also a white man and besides he had been nicknamed Mad Dog and Hari loved dogs, rabid or not – Hari didn't call him an outright liar. Instead he said, 'You used to be a major fence, big player in stolen artefacts.'

Tulsi added, 'But he may be mistaken. You don't look so big now.'

'I'm not sure if I should take that as a compliment.'

'Doubt if it was meant as one,' said Hari. 'In your colonial days, you got away with looting, but it is not 1799 anymore.'

Maddox leaned over and coughed into the spittoon. 'No offence taken. You're an okay kid, Potter. You Anglo? Am I your daddy?'

'I don't know.'

'You don't know your own father?'

Hari shrugged. He'd in fact never met his father. 'It's a long story. You might not live to hear the end of it. Though I can visit you again in jail and tell it in episodes. By the way, my mum is cooking the food there so if you were my "daddy", you'd be reunited with her soon.'

'Yes, she's the jail cook,' Tulsi played along.

'I hear the upma is scary. If you don't talk to us, Missus Tulsi will arrest you in a jiffy and you'll go there. But as you're anyway about to die, I'm thinking why waste tax-payer money to put you in an overcrowded cell?'

'No point,' said Tulsi.

Maddox nodded slowly, again burrowing a finger up his nose – a sign that something truthful might be spoken. 'I'd prefer to spend my last days in freedom and I hate upma.'

'You should eat it with pickle,' said Tulsi. 'Strong pickle.'

'Doesn't help. I tried.'

'So how shall we play this?' said Tulsi.

'What if I say that I perhaps know which statue you're talking about?'

'I'd say I'm glad you can still make sense of things.' Then he added as an afterthought, 'I never liked upma either. So maybe you are my dad.'

'Well … if I tell you, will you make that lady cop go away?'

'Depends on what you tell us,' said Hari.

'You tell me first. Who fingered me?' Maddox demanded and pulled the pinkie out of the nostril. It started to sound like a typical cold war trade-off, tit for tat and butter for fat. Even in his present condition, he was plotting the next move in the Great Game.

Hari eyed the ceiling.

'Was it Salvatore? Did you know I used to hang out with Ian Fleming? Met him in Bombay in the 1950s. Nobody ever wrote anything about Salvatore.' Then, somewhat bitterly, he added, 'Fleming bought himself a villa in Jamaica for the money he earned on my story and look where I ended up.'

'I have no idea what you're talking about.' These foreigners. They were so devious. But he'd look up the Wikipedia for that Fleming-Lemming if it turned out to be important.

'Then who? Come on, Potter. I don't have much time left. Was it the Pakistani?'

Spies were a suspicious breed. Even as he lay dying, the game continued. Hari got a brainwave and pretended to spill the beans. 'Have you heard of R-I-P?'

That silenced the old spy. His trembling finger sought its way into the nostril and sunk itself in all the way to the knuckle. He was displaying an honest emotion.

'Sorry, that was insensitive. I mean, do you happen to know anybody whose name has those initials?'

'R-I-P?'

'Yes. That's how I found your tracks.' As proof, Hari showed the torn up *Lonely Planet*, which Maddox seemed to have used like a mail order catalogue to direct his thieves to ancient temples. He waved it before Maddox. Tulsi also waved a hand although she seemed less sure about what was going on.

'You're talking about the hitman who operates out of Kallapete?'

'You know him then? I knew it.' Playing hardball had been the right strategy. Now and then the dirty laundry had to be washed.

Maddox chewed his unstiff lip, but it didn't take him that long to get started now that the balls were in the air. 'It was me that taught him how to kill, how to speak the Queen's English, and he's double-crossing me. I'll kill the bastard.'

Hari could have informed the old foghorn that the great Chanakya codified the basics of spycraft 2250 years before MI6 hired its first double-0. India was always two millennia ahead of the West.

'Naughty boy, huh?'

Maddox brooded. Then he laboriously continued. 'Will you help me, Potter?'

'At your service twenty-four-slash-seven. Our weekly rate is …'

'I don't have that long left, but you can make things easier.'

'How?'

'All this talk about upma is driving me mad. So first of all, I would like a proper ham sandwich. But you have to get the bread from Albert Bakery, the meat from Bangalore Ham Shop, the cheddar from Nilgiris, and homemade mustard from Lusitania Cold Storage.'

The price for the information seemed affordable, but Hari also did make a note of the fact that the spy lived fully in the past – none of those shops was younger than fifty years and the sandwich sounded totally colonial. Once he got the confession, he'd just buy the bugger a Maggi-noodle stuffed grilled Chinese sandwich from the nearest street vendor. 'Okay, if I agree to that, will you tell me?'

Maddox nodded. 'I'd do anything for an honest-to-goodness ham sandwich. What I know is the following, innit.'

'I'm listening.'

'They promised they could lay their hands on any idol.'

'So your old chum got it for you?'

The confession followed. 'I'd heard that it's supposed to ensure safe passage into the next life. Possible other health benefits, too, like curing liver cancer. So I asked them to get it for me. Heck, I already knew from the medical tests that I was dying. So long shot, but I thought possessing the idol might save me or at least ensure that I'm reborn as myself.'

This bugger was more likely to be reborn as a public urinal. The city needed more of those than of these foreigners, thought Hari, but kept his big mouth shut.

'If I give you its whereabouts,' said Maddox, 'can you bring the statue here along with that ham sandwich?'

'I don't deal in stolen goods.'

'Before you return it to the temple, let me just see it once.' His rheumy eyes beseeched Hari as he started digging his nose again. 'If they managed to steal it, it should be in Kallapete, in a godown belonging to Paisavasool Exports. You wouldn't believe your eyes if you saw all the loot stored there.'

Hari could believe. Kallapete bazaar wasn't a place where one brought tourists, unless they were of the less discerning kind. More of a centre for fencing stolen goods, wholesale. 'You're sure?'

'I'm sure I'm dying.' Maddox looked around the room. There was a medical monitoring machine with a grey LCD screen next to the bed. It beeped once. Then there was silence. And then it beeped again. 'That's the only thing I am sure of.'

'Okay boss, thank you, bye-bye, and all the very best.'

'You'll come back?'

'If the idol wills so,' said Hari.

Tulsi added, 'Hello and goodbye.'

14

> Expect increased activity on the professional front so don't take undue tension and furthermore you should speak with loved ones about certain issues.

'That was exciting,' said Tulsi.

By the time he had treated her to a cup of chicory at the stall outside the hospital, reassuring her that this was a breakthrough in the case regarding her stolen jewellery, the sun had begun to set with the speed of light, as it always does in a city without horizons, where a sunset rarely gave you the time to reflect on what you'd been up to all day.

'So is he the one who plans the crimes?'

Hari dodged the question.

'Karma catches up with even the biggest fish,' he uttered philosophically, preoccupied with his own thoughts. He regretted that his staff had been fired. AC Gaadi and his rickshaw would have been handy right now if he were to assault the godown of the crooks. But Diamond wouldn't approve of rehiring Gaadi.

Besides, he ought to call her and check how things were on the home front – but if she asked him about where he was going to spend the night and found out that he had booked a cot in the infamous Kama Boardless, she'd think he was about to embark on some no-good naughtiness.

'What's the next move?'

'Just planning it.' The best plan in the world would be to have the best plan in the world, but if that wasn't possible one had to make do with whatever.

'Is there anything else I can help you with?' asked Tulsi. She appeared enthusiastic, but it would be too risky to bring her along.

She had performed well during the interrogation, but this he had to do alone. This was potentially dangerous.

'No, go home and boil the ghee rice for Bisi Sambaranna and your daughter. So that she's fat and healthy on her wedding day and will breed many grandchildren for you.'

'Do you have children?'

'Yes, but not enough.'

Before heading into the bazaars, he visited Chaddi Dost who ran a fancy goods shop south of K. G. Circle. Hari borrowed a cigarette lighter made to look like an automatic handgun. It was the right size, the right weight, and Chaddi's lighters were often used in B-movies. The only way to tell that it wasn't a gun was if you pressed the trigger – a bluish flame spewed out of the muzzle instead of bullets. Chaddi let him have it against a ₹750 deposit and he'd get half back upon return of the lighter. That pretty much depleted Hari's cash. He had a tenner and a coin left.

He knew roughly where the Paisavasool Exports godown stood in the maze of old Bengaluru. He rode his scooter through happening streets that specialized in pre-dinner snacks at this hour, until he came to a shadier zone where people kept off the streets after dark. When he stopped to ask for directions, they avoided giving straight answers but said things like 'right-u left-u', while it would later turn out that 'full straight-u' was the correct route. One old woman told him that the godown was next to where there had once been a liquor shop that lost its license due to agitation by local housewives. Eventually, he arrived in an area of town where two plus two could become three or five, but never four, and the shops dealt almost exclusively in stolen goods – TVs, DVD-players, mobiles, scooters, motorbikes, cars, the usual stuff that was easily recycled.

Somewhere off the main road, he turned into a narrower street where houses stood cheek by jowl; it was a by-lane that according to his phone's GPS didn't exist. As the crow flew, it wasn't distant from reality – yet a planet apart.

The shut liquor shop was identifiable by two reformed alcoholics squatting on the front step, sharing a cigarette in disbelief that their watering hole was gone. However, there was no evidence of any antiques warehouse.

The next-door building had a bluish nondescript mud wall without windows and a sturdy double door in hardwood, built to withstand attacks by elephants. On the wall were posters for Kannada film releases, adorned with armed rowdies and slogans in English, nonsense phrases in the language of cool: 'No One Has Invented The Condom For Their Guns They Are Deadly Dangerous!' If this was the godown, he ought to have brought a bulldozer, rather than a fancy cigarette lighter.

He kept riding and studying the surroundings carefully but did not see any other building that might conceal the godown he was searching for, and so he stopped his scooter half a furlong up the road, where a row of wrecked cars lined the street. One had a bumper sticker stating 'Love is like a Chinese mobile, no guarantees', which was a direct reminder of the twenty-first century and it made him feel a little safer. To minimize risks, he parked so that his scooter faced the street, rather than the kerb, under one of those helpful traffic police banners: 'If you don't have traffic-sense, you will find yourself in ambu-lense.' It would make for a faster getaway in case he had to run. He paid an urchin with a wild Bob Marley hairdo his last ₹10 to see to it that his bike wasn't dismantled, with the promise of an additional tenner if the girl herself refrained from selling it off on Alibaba to some filthy rich Shanghai-based collector of hero memorabilia.

He tucked the cigarette-lighter-handgun inside the waistband of his jeans, against the small of his back, and hoped that it wouldn't self-ignite. He walked back keeping his eyes wide open and circled the suspect block on foot. Most of the backstreet houses were residential. Except for a factory for stitching purses and vanity bags. Hari peeked in through the door that had been kept open for circulation, yet sweat hung like a dripping rag in air that was fluffy with lint. The unit seemed to exclusively employ children; nimble-fingered for those little plastic pearls that had to be sewn on to the handbags.

After completing the round, he sat down with the reformed alcoholics outside the shut bar-cum-booze shop. It had to be the building next to it – with the thick mud walls, robust door and violent film posters – that was the thieves' godown. He decided to watch it for some time, while he chatted up the old-timers.

'Had your beverage?'

'No hard drinks, our missuses won't allow.'

'Right, right, I know. I'm also married.'

They told him about the fun they used to have. Hari gathered that the toothless old-timers hardly ever left the street. When he asked about the sweatshop round the back, he was told that the kids came from elsewhere. The industrialist rented them, via agents, for ₹3500 a month and they worked from nine in the morning to nine in the evening, and the rest of the time they were locked up, slept on the floor and watched Bhojpuri films on DVD. They didn't go to school as far as the old-timers knew. Hari filed away the data and made a mental note of the pertinent detail that the employer could be prosecuted under the Child Labour (Prohibition and Regulation) Amendment Act of 2016 and also the Juvenile Justice (Care and Protection of Children) Act of 2000.

At least the kids should be allowed to watch Kannada movies and learn the local culture, and see the non-dubbed version of *Porki*, the three of them agreed. That led to a discussion around the 1995 superhit movie *OM*, which Hari had re-watched the night before. 'Coma, Coma Prema,' sighed one of the old men.

Idling was a non-fishy activity for men hereabouts, making it the perfect cover. Had he appeared to be busy with anything whatsoever, such as staking out the godown, people might have thought that Hari was up to no good. When a motorcycle-borne policeman rode by on his leopard-spotted Cheetah bike, he didn't even turn his head in Hari's direction.

Then luck struck. Two gents exited from the suspected godown and padlocked the door. The first, who displayed more authority due to his blazing red eyes, was flashily dressed in non-imitation leather pants, judging from the squeaking sound they made, black T-shirt, gold chains with little dangling guns, Mohawk hairdo, moustache, red shoes (if he kicked somebody to death, blood wouldn't show) and by and large he fit the description that the baba at the temple had given. Hari also thought he may have seen his mug on the rowdy-sheet at the police station. He was almost sure that he had.

He was followed by a flunkey, not quite as rakish as his boss but a giant with thick arms covered in skull and crossbones tattoos. The main difference between the two of them was that while the first rowdy wore real gold, the second one wore plastic gold. It wasn't easy to tell the difference, but as an ex-bank watchman Hari could smell that the first one was probably beloved by the gods, the second in a karmic limbo. His wrap-around Ferrari sunglasses were almost certainly pirated, his leather wristbands were made of Rexine and he wore multiple nasty piercing studs in his forehead. Like small horns. If one got headbutted by him, one's face would be pockmarked for life. His sideburns looked like they had been painted to his face with ink and his moustache was phenomenal: easily the biggest that Hari had ever seen outside a cinema screen. Hari knew him – and made him out as one of the thuggish toughies who rowdy-sheeted in the Main-Drain Semi-Slum.

'Who are those distinguished gentlemen?' he asked with a quiet nod at the men getting into a SUV parked in a no-parking spot across the road. It looked like the same car that had almost run him down the other day, outside the police station. It was a strange coincidence. But then life itself was utterly weird. 'Look a bit … dicey.'

'Slightly criminal,' one of the old-timers volunteered.

'So not fully?'

'They only do half-murder.'

'Half?'

'They tried to kill one man, but he survived.'

The reformed alcoholics lowered their voices. 'The boss is known around here as Ripper, alias RIP,' said one, the other adding, 'His assistant is called Deadlyappa. Nobody fools around with them.'

'I see.' Hari made a mental note to be cautious if he had to fool around. Not that he planned to do anything so stupid. RIP and DA – or 'Deadly Appa' – matched the entries in the pilgrim's choultry guestbook, so he knew he was on the right track.

These, then, were the two who had gone to Halegudehalli last weekend and taken the idol to sell to Maddox. Maddox hadn't got it, because he was in hospital, which meant that it still had to be in their godown – reasoned Hari. Selling stolen idols wasn't easy, unless you had a buyer ready. You couldn't just stand before any stall in a mall and auction it.

The thieves left in the SUV which meant that they were going some distance away. It was past eight, so if they had drinks before dinner they'd take at least until 11:30 p.m. when regular bars shut or 1 a.m. if they went to a five-star hotel. If they didn't indulge in drunk driving, they might be away all night. Meanwhile, the godown remained unguarded. If somebody had stayed behind, they wouldn't have locked it up.

Hari turned to the two ex-alcoholics who had entertained him with colourful stories about their backstreet. 'So I'll take your leave then. Got to go and do the needful. All the very best and bye-bye.'

After stepping around the corner, he rang Sub-Inspector Pushpa. 'Had food?'

'I was about to, so this had better be good. Any new information you wish to share about the ATM heist?'

Hari regretted very much that she was sitting before a hearty uneaten dinner, but maybe she could parcel it? He shared the tip-off that a sweatshop exploited children and that right then would be a perfect time to raid it.

'I'm on the way.'

'Can I have my non-offender certificate back?'

'Let us see.' Her career ambition was to become a Joint-Commissioner – so she avoided answering questions that might harm her career. Hari heard the slop-slop sound in the background as she poured her curry back into the tiffin carrier.

A while later he saw the Lumax blues of her Bolero flashing. Sub-Inspector Pushpa busted the illegal unit along with five constables. It was a proper raid.

None of the employees was more than fourteen years old. Many were half that age. There were thirty-four children, including nineteen girls. The owner turned out to be none other than Hari's old friend Shanty Ram. He was led out of the premises to a waiting police jeep. To play it safe, Hari loitered in the background. Neighbours came out to see what was going on and Hari disappeared in the throng, like any non-descript vagrant. It was an art to be able to look useless, which he had mastered to perfection during his earlier, somewhat criminal years.

Pushpa set about calling her contacts at the Labour Department, the anti-human trafficking unit of the Criminal Investigation Department and an official from the nearest remand home, Mamta Madam, who made it her business to rescue children in peril. Mamta had tried to rescue Hari when he was younger, but given up – a hopeless case was a hopeless case.

Hari wasn't going to stay around until Madam came. Or for Shanty Ram's gang, if they turned up to take charge.

However, he felt good about having done his proper deed for the day and the fact that he had declined Shanty Ram's job offer earlier. The children would be taken to a shelter, get food and clothing, and in due time they'd be sent back to their native places. He asked Pushpa if she minded him stepping inside. 'Don't mistake. Just want to clarify doubts.'

Without a word, she looked the other way. He sneaked in. The sweatshop had unpainted concrete walls, save for the back wall, which was made of bluish mud. The godown would be directly behind it, he had calculated. The owner had crammed in many small tables and stitching machines, because his workers were so tiny. It was possible to produce thousands of purses in a day. Hari felt somewhat cynical about capitalism and its promises.

He went upstairs to Shanty Ram's office where the constables were packing files into cardboard boxes. Hari greeted Ropu, Ramboswamy and other cops he knew by name. Ramboswamy congratulated him on his marriage and asked why he wasn't on honeymoon. Ropu, who knew Hari was married already, asked if he had become a bigamist. Hari simply rolled his head sideways (which basically meant anything), wished them the very best and bye-bye, and nobody paid much attention to him – to them he was an untrustworthy person who would snitch on his own friends for the price of a masala dosa.

There were shelves with the usual commendations and diplomas celebrating Shanty Ram's affordable products. What Hari found most unsettling was that the office had no religious images on its walls. His own office, which he had inherited from Uncle Mamool, had pictures of every god and godman, including demigods down to cricket players to cover all bases. But not these people. It was a place where godlessness ruled.

Hari climbed up on the rooftop terrace, where Shanty grew potted flowers and had set up plastic chairs and a foldable table. There was a bar in one corner of the roof garden, with the usual gangster beverages: Khoday's rum and Royal Stag whisky.

From the roof, he glanced down into the alley and saw that the neighbourhood had gathered to watch the spectacle of the local big shot getting busted. It was hard to tell if a riot was going to follow or not. But it was likely. This was Bengaluru after all, India's riot capital. And Shanty fancied himself the biggest bigwig hereabouts.

Hari went to the side of the terrace that overlooked the Paisavasool Exports godown, which consisted of a courtyard surrounded by storage rooms. Despite the dim light, he saw that it was empty of people – just as he expected, since he had seen them lock it up from outside. Timber had been stacked in a corner, by the look of it poached and smuggled sandalwood. On top was a fat sculpture of Queen Victoria lying on her back as if on a pyre. It had gone missing from Cubbon Park a month earlier. Stealing statues seemed to be happening on an industrial scale here.

He found a tool shed on the roof. It contained various implements for fixing problems on the factory floor. There were no crowbars, but Hari picked up an axe and a hammer that might come in handy. Getting down to the godown roof wasn't going to be a problem, he determined. These old buildings being low, it was a short drop. He jumped.

Once he landed and rolled over on the roof, it occurred to him that it might be harder to get back up again. But first things first: he had to locate the idol, steal it back and set life straight by worshipping it. There was no going home without it. He lay still and listened for movements from downstairs. When he didn't hear anything, he got up and checked the courtyard again – still nobody there except the queen of England. The statue was massive. So he slid over the roof's edge and landed on top of her, then climbed down to the ground.

He fumbled about in the dark until his pupils dilated sufficiently for him to see his way around. The godown consisted of storerooms with padlocked doors. One room had a door that consisted of a metal grille and so he started with it. Shining his phone torch through the bars, he saw a floor of red earth in a space roughly 200 square feet in size. It looked like a disused wrestling pit. His uncle was in the habit of visiting places like it and gambling away all his money. Then he noticed that the iron gate was unlocked. He pushed it open.

Hari removed his shoes before he stepped in. Wrestling pits were considered to be sacred spaces, temples for a religiosity in which wrestling was worship.

He looked around but found only ancient stone dumbbells and iron cudgels, a 100kg neck weight shaped like a donut made of stone, and sweaty langootis hung from nails. There were no cupboards. No hole in the wall that could hold a stolen idol. The red earth smelt of muscles, nose bleeds and tears. Hari dug it up in a few spots but found no buried treasure, just traces of panic, mortal aggression and broken teeth.

No idols except for one cut out from a calendar, nailed to the wall. A table in a corner had a television set and a stack of betting chit-books. On the walls were sheets of paper with data about cricket and horse-racing match-fixing schemes. So, on top of everything else these people were bookmakers. He walked out into the courtyard to explore the other rooms, which were more likely places to store stolen goods. Only trouble was that he'd have to break into them, which meant breaking laws. Then again, a detective had to do what a detective had to.

There were two hardwood doors facing the courtyard, securely locked. One had three padlocks on it, which was a dead giveaway. If there was anything valuable here, it'd be behind that one.

He made sure nobody was watching from any of the rooftops before he set about getting the locks off. Luckily there was a halo of ambient noise around the area – the usual prayer calls and bell-clanging of a couple of different religions combined with the honking of evening traffic and the police raid in the backstreet with its accompanying racket. Nobody would notice his hacking. He hoped.

The locks may have been brand new and the door and its frame were rock solid, but the screws that held the hinged hasp and its staple in place were rusty due to the dampness of the mud walls. He smashed the axe into the wood above the hasp. He hacked till, little by little, the wood gave away. Once he had created a big enough gap he forced the peen of the hammer into it and wrenched until the metal strap broke loose.

Then he attacked the next lock, repeating the process.

After it came off, his mouse elbow, compounded by the usual carpal tunnel syndrome, began acting up. Surfing in cybercafés, dreaming of being a hero, didn't exactly prepare one for this. But now that he'd started, he had to finish and get out before the thieves returned. Because he wasn't going to get a second chance.

Ignoring the fatigue in his aching arm and shoulder, he went on hacking with the axe. Even if it took him the whole night, he'd break down every single door in the godown. With renewed energy, he worked on the third lock. At last, the final hasp came off and the three locks hung limply from their shackles. He pushed open the heavy door and found the switch for a single naked overhead bulb.

When the creaking died out and the light stopped flickering he was totally freaked out. The storeroom was full of skeletons that grinned at him with yellowish teeth. Each was laid out on a piece of canvas on the mud floor. It was shockingly inauspicious.

15

There are masses of messes to clear up before you are free from certain worries and fears that have begun to seem like permanent features in your life.

He *ought* to turn, run and get out, far away from there. But it was too late to shut the door and pretend that he hadn't seen what he saw.

A privately run mortuary? No, hardly. It took an effort to stop his hands from trembling. Grave-robbing, he figured. But who would rob a graveyard? Lunatics or scientists? That must be it, lunatic scientists!

Then he spotted an article from a news magazine pasted on the wall and it had an image of a skeleton, with arrows pointing at different parts and the applicable rates. It was highly illegal to loot graveyards, but according to the magazine, business-minded people who understood science did it because there was big money in it. Medical schools around the world needed skeletons. According to the article, foreign buyers paid upwards of $3,000 for a good one: a skull alone fetched $1,200 if the teeth were intact, a hand was worth $200 and a pelvic bone $190, but a vertebra was a bargain in comparison at $43 only. These thieves were nasty. Here were skeletons worth lakhs of rupees!

But he saw no stolen idol. After having looked around, he left the skeletons to rest in peace or whatever they were up to and went to the next locked door. It had to be where the religious artefacts were kept. The storeroom seemed to be the larger of the two. It could well be filled with idols, but with luck he'd be able to identify the right one.

He was tired, his arm ached. But it was nearing midnight and he'd soon have to be mindful of noise levels, so better to get this over with. He slammed the axe into the wood. Again, it was slow going. Despite the age of the doorframe, it was durable and the rusted nails had merged into one rough substance with it. But fortunately, this had only one padlock.

As he hacked away at it, he noticed with a sense of pride that he was getting good at breaking and entering. He chuckled. Because it was almost funny. Here he was breaking into a thief's storeroom. Maybe he should switch careers and become a burglar of burglars. It ought to be a safe job – thieves couldn't report a theft to the police – in case he needed to rethink his career as a result of the unfortunate ATM heist.

The hasp came off and he kicked the door open, hero-style. He located the switch. Again a naked bulb shone down from the ceiling. He got the second rudest shock of the night. No stolen idols here either. The chamber was completely empty. The blue walls were bare. The mud floor was red, smooth. He had taken for granted that the idol would be there, that he'd grab it and go. But nothing was going according to plan tonight. For sure, plans were meant to be adjusted to fit the way things went, rather than being followed – especially if one was a flexible, winner type of personality.

He scratched his coconut-oily hair. Had it been there and then removed? But he saw no traces of it. How to find out? He took another round of the building to see if he had missed anything in the other rooms, but couldn't bring himself to dig among the bones, and no, there was not even the smallest alcove in the walls, no secret trap-door in the earthen floors.

When he stepped out into the courtyard, he heard noises from the gate. He hoped it was just some passers-by making mischief by committing nuisance. *But no!* Somebody was unlocking it. *Blasted!* They were coming back. He thought of the only possible hiding place: the wrestling pit. He hurried inside. By reflex he left his rubber sandals at the door. Then he quickly dug a hole in the dirt about the size of a shallow grave, lay down, and shuffled soil back over himself. He didn't cover his face – just smeared the reddish mud on his cheeks and chin and hair.

As he lay there, it occurred to him that what he ought to have done was climb atop the bulky statue of Queen Victoria on her sandalwood pyre and try to jump up on the roof. But it was too late now, as a gang of drunks staggered in. They were in a cheerful mood, laughing fearlessly at the police who were raiding just around the corner when there were so many stolen items here, right under their noses.

Then one of them observed that the storerooms had been broken into and the doors were gaping wide open. That one was Ripper, or RIP, the boss type. He was accompanied by Deadlyappa and a third man, who, as far as Hari could make out through the iron bars, was a really big wrestler type, at least twice as big as the gigantic Deadlyappa: muscles lathered in Ayurvedic oils, probably 150 kilos overweight, no neck, crew-cut hair, a broken nose and cauliflower ears. When he turned his head, Hari noticed that one of his ears had been half chewed off. Perhaps somebody had mistaken it for gobi manchurian?

They all stopped laughing. No better way to spoil a rowdy-sheeter's mood than to break into his godown.

As RIP crossed the yard, the creaking of his leather pants was totally ominous. He cursed in the choicest blasphemous language until Hari's god-fearing ears felt red hot, as if somebody had stuffed chillies into them. With his heart hammering in an unfathomable staccato rhythm, pumping excess blood to his brain, Hari employed his analytical skills in order to think his way out of the predicament. He made observations regarding the two gangsters' previous incarnations. RIP had not been a prawn in his past life but everything spoke of a barracuda: especially the fishy hairdo.

Deadlyappa, the pierced bodyguard with all the skull and crossbones tattoos, said: 'Somebody's been here.' He was a slow thinker. Previous incarnation: a buffalo.

RIP's baggy eyes turned into two bazookas searching for a target. 'It's some cheeky thief. To break into a master thief's godown!'

As Hari peeked out from where he had buried himself, his calculator brain flashed odds for his survival, ranging from low to microscopic to all bets off. This wasn't a street scene in which he could melt into the crowd like an innocuous bystander.

'My godown!'

'Maybe they were trying to rob you, Ripper.'

'Somebody is going to die for this.' RIP didn't see the rationale in the old adage, 'what goes around, comes around'.

The strapping third fellow was watching silently. He was dressed in a langooti, which was the traditional fighter gear. He did a few Bruce Lee moves, kicked a brick in half. It vanished in a puff of dust.

'We should teach them a lesson, Ripper,' said Deadlyappa, and glanced into the wrestling pit without spotting Hari.

'He'll receive more than a lesson in good behaviour. He's going to get his neck chained to a jute sack stuffed with discarded car batteries and sunk in the sewage nullah as a warning to others.' Alcoholics always blamed other people. They never saw their own errors. It lay in the nature of their sickness. Hari had grown up with an uncle who was like that. Nevertheless, Hari didn't want to end up in the drain. In these hot months, it had almost dried up and it would take ages to drown properly.

'What did he steal?'

'That's the strange thing. Nothing seems to be missing.'

'That is strange, Ripper.'

'But he left his chappals,' said the wrestler, who had spotted Hari's sandals.

'That's even stranger. Why would he?' said Deadlyappa.

'Maybe he wants to fight me,' said the wrestler.

Hari almost screamed like a castrated banana, then didn't because the noise would have given his position away. It dawned on him suddenly. Of course, it was midnight game time. They were going to put on a fight with illegal betting now that the bars were shut. Hari should have known it the moment he discovered the wrestling pit. It didn't smell as if it was disused at all, it smelt of fresh blood and leaked bone marrow and droplets of brain tissue.

The wrestler had come anticipating a regular night of breaking spines at $43 apiece and now he'd get to crack Hari's as a bonus.

What to do? If he stayed where he was, they'd find him, and if he was forced to defend himself in a life-and-death match, he'd get a first class pummelling and then end up six feet deeper than he currently was under the wrestling pit's red earth surface ... or worse, in the skeleton collection. But the wrestler didn't come inside. Instead he took up position by the gate, just by Hari's sandals. He was a formidable road block, if Hari tried to make a run for it. But the exit was temptingly close.

He wondered briefly why there was only one – wrestlers usually fought in pairs. Then he focused on vital matters. What about a Plan H? Nothing clever came to mind. The only possible plan that he could think of was to do something really stupid. If he acted fast, gambled with the highest stakes and bluffed it might just work. He counted on the element of surprise, which should give him an almost 50 per cent chance of making it out of there alive.

So rather than hide and die, Hari jumped up.

And then he ran towards the wrestler.

The man had planted his feet wide apart – at least some twenty-five feet apart – so it should be possible to slide under him, pistol-whip him on the private parts and roll out through the gate. Hari galloped straight towards him and hoped that he'd freeze when he saw the fake handgun that Hari waved in the air. Unfortunately, he didn't stir. Plan H wasn't working. The wrestler had quick, professional reflexes. Instead of backing off, he swung an arm and a huge fist hit Hari in the face like a sledgehammer – the blow was so powerful that he flew like a crumpled-up-and-chucked potato chip bag in a cinema hall during the climactic fight scene.

He landed on his back in the wrestling pit and the lights went out.

Hari's brain rebooted. He knew who he was. But, where was he? His brain felt totally numb in a way he hadn't experienced since he had stopped sniffing glue in his late teens. Three big men were walking in his direction. He held something in his hand. It appeared to be a gun. He raised it.

'Stop, don't come closer.'

'Who are you?' some bossy type asked.

'Wrong question. The question is: what am I *doing* here?' Because that's what Hari felt like asking himself. He lay on his back in a kind of sandpit. In front of him were three men who did not look like his friends. He knew his friends well: Triplex, Doc and Gaadi. Where were they? Who were these? His short-term memory had been reset.

'Okay … so what are you doing here?'

'Yes, that's what I just asked you.' Hari was feeling dizzy and what he wanted to do, more than anything else, was to puke up his dinner.

'Let me guess then. I think you came here to get yourself killed. Are you ready to die?' asked the bossy type.

'Is it necessary?'

'Yes, because you broke into my godown. It is not done.'

'Oho! I didn't know it was your godown. I must have mistaken it for somebody else's godown.'

'I don't like trouble.'

'Neither do I,' said Hari and felt relieved. 'So, what can I do to fix it?'

'Take the punishment.'

'So charge me under Section 295-A for hurting your sentiments.'

'What were you trying to steal?'

'I can ... explain everything.' He tried but couldn't come up with a handy lie. He couldn't exactly remember what he was doing there. His head was aching too much.

'You better or you die.'

'Is there no alternative option?' It was a legal phrase that his uncle had taught him to use as and when it was required.

'Put away the gun and come out of there.'

'No, you come in here if you dare and I'll take care of you,' said Hari, who felt strong like Knockout beer with the gun in his hand.

But the boss turned his back on Hari and spoke to the wrestler.

'Thalemamsa, I'll give you a grand for his head. Just pull it off gently,' he said and threw two ₹500 notes on the ground.

Hari's negotiating position was of course somewhat awkward. They were three and blocked the only way out. The man who had multiple piercings in his face was swinging a heavy motorcycle chain covered in thick grease. Hari levelled the weapon at the wrestler's balls.

'But he has a gun,' Thalemamsa pointed out, his watchful eyes tracking Hari's every motion.

'Correct-u. Give me an excuse and I'll do target practice!'

'What excuse?' the cool-as-curd wrestler said, as if he were counting the odds for whether Hari might put a bullet between his legs or not.

'Any will do!'

'I'm sorry, I need money. I have five kids to put through school.'

'That is a noble ideal, but I can pay more for my own head,' bluffed Hari.

'How much?'

'My skull is worth at least a thousand American dollars, or about seventy times more in Indian rupees, give or take.' Where did he get that figure from? He tried hard to remember. It was as if he had recently read it somewhere. On a price list. *But where?*

'He's lying, I'm paying no more than three K for it,' said the boss. 'But don't break his skeleton. Looks reasonably well proportioned, though a little scrawny. If we bury him in the pit, worms will clear the flesh off his bones in two months. Then, once we sell his sorry bones, you'll get half of the profit as a bonus, Thalemamsa.'

Who was this man, who saw business opportunities everywhere? If a living person could have his skeleton stolen, then what was this market economy coming to? Hari faced the one called Thalemamsa. He tried to think of a way to break the stalemate. He said, 'You don't have to wait two months for your money. I'll give you anything you want tonight.'

'Right now?'

'Tonight itself. Name your price. Will one lakh do?'

'Where will you get that kind of money at this hour?' asked Thalemamsa, but he seemed interested in a deal.

'I've got a private ATM in my office.' Hari was speaking from the top of his head, but he also did recall having had an ATM installed recently in his corporate headquarters. Or had he dreamt it?

'Don't listen,' the bossy one said. 'Just kill him.'

'Why don't you do it?' said Hari, but he wasn't thinking laterally, the alpha male had taken control. The same problem afflicted many men. 'Come fight me if you have the balls of a bullock or don't … if you only have chicken balls.'

'Chickens don't have balls.'

'Don't change the subject,' said Hari and changed the subject back to one he was more comfortable with. 'I came here peacefully.'

'With a gun?'

'As it turned out I was justified in doing so.'

'So what are you going to do? Shoot your way out of here?'

'I'm warning you that I know how to use this one.' To prove his point, he aimed it at the ceiling and squeezed the trigger. There was no blast. Just the feeble hissing as a bluish flame spewed out of the muzzle.

The three of them stared. Then the bossy one laughed.

'I propose that we resolve matters in a gentlemanly way,' said Hari quickly. 'May I light your cigarettes?'

No reply.

'Don't tell me you're all non-smokers.'

The bossy one turned to the other two. 'What do you think, boys?'

'I have a suggestion,' said the one with the motorcycle chain.

'I have ears,' said Hari.

'Why don't we make him wrestle for his life?'

'Good thinking, Deadlyappa. But what if he wins?'

Where had Hari heard that name before? He vaguely remembered having gone for a pilgrimage. Had he and this Deadlyappa character been travelling together? No, it couldn't be.

'He won't,' said Deadlyappa and whipped the air with the motorcycle chain.

'Okay, you fight, we invite some friends to bet, and if you win, you get ...'

'I'll get three wishes, right?'

'What wishes?'

'Don't worry, like your colleague says I'll probably lose.' Hari was being strategic. He tried not to involve his male ego. Male ego was one of man's weaker points, if he had to be honest to himself.

It had often occurred to him how women always seemed to have an advantage because they lacked male egos. Would his wife, for example, ever be in a situation like this? Hardly. Suddenly he recalled having a wife. His memory was being defraggled. 'I'm famous, so if you kill me, you'll also become famous.'

The boss thought for eight seconds.

'Three? I suppose that is only fair. But if you're so sure of losing, why play at all?'

'I can bet on my own loss, which will take care of my family's future when I'm dead and gone.'

'Makes sense even if it means you must be insane, I suppose.'

Hari got up. They shook hands.

Since the drinking dens had closed for the night, it didn't take long to invite a bunch of compulsive gamblers – they were all connected on WhatsApp. A late-night fight was a treat. The chance to win extra drinking money for the next evening was a bonus. Half a dozen gentlemen tied up their loin cloths and spread themselves out along the wall of the wrestling pit to have a good view. They squatted on their haunches.

Hari noticed that some of them called the bossy type RIP. Sounded familiar. Again he started having flashbacks. There was a temple and nine gods … avatars? But shouldn't there have been ten? There always were. Was one missing? Or maybe he was just getting religious in anticipation of his own death. It was a known fact that people often turned to god towards the end of their lives. The earth was cool and sticky under his feet.

Then RIP announced the fight. 'This thief who insulted me wants to get three wishes fulfilled. To give him a fair chance, I'm letting him keep his gun. It'll even out the odds, so kindly place your bets.' RIP chortled, he didn't let the gamblers know it was only a cigarette lighter – it was his way of rigging the match. After collecting the wagers, he continued, 'To get all three wishes, he'll fight three of my best men.'

Hari was shocked. That wasn't the deal. Thalemamsa entered, he had oiled his naked upper body and arms and smelt like the world's biggest coconut. With him came another huge wrestler who was introduced as Mudde and who looked like one of those movie villains who could take uninterrupted pummelling forever and wouldn't die until the last reel of the flick. The third fighter was Deadlyappa and he was whipping the air with his motorcycle chain.

But it was too late to back off now, when the pit was filled with punters who wanted to see him bleed, and more betting money was already being collected by RIP. Some of them actually betted on Hari's survival, which gave interesting odds. When RIP asked if Hari wanted to bet, Hari said, 'Will you let me bet on credit?'

'Dead people get no credit.'

'Oho, is it so?'

The wrestlers and Deadlyappa circled him. Mudde was an old school wrestler who came close until he stood in front of Hari. He started jumping up and down on the spot, making threatening moves and doing the yogic 'hooga chakka, hooga-hooga hooga chakka' breathing exercise. Hari wasn't exactly sure of the meaning of the chant, except that chakka meant jackfruit in his wife's native language, Malayalam. He now knew what a jackfruit must feel moments before it is dismembered into juicy pods. There was no use waiting for that to happen, so Hari tried the cinema ishtyle karate kick that AC Gaadi had become notorious for. But his leg was too short – or alternatively, the wrestler stood too far away. His foot fanned the air before the wrestler's tummy and then nothing. The wrestler grabbed him by the foot and tossed him over the shoulder. Hari's cranium hit the ceiling and broke the light bulb.

The wrestler let go and Hari thumped down on the ground. He heard his spine rattle, the way loose coins rattled in one's pocket. But it didn't break. Luckily, the earth was soft. That saved him the $43 it would have cost to buy a new one. However, his cranium felt like it may have shattered, he had crushed glass in his hair and his brain felt mushy, but then again, the head wasn't the most important body part in action films, he reminded himself. With the bulb broken, it got dark and disorienting in the pit, but the spectators switched on their phone torches.

Hari was in the limelight, so he crawled up again.

'Next time you do that you will surely regret!'

The wrestler did it again and the second time Hari hit the ceiling, his brain splattered all over the place. The audience gasped: 'Wah! Wah!' They were getting their money's worth.

The brain matter tasted bitter. Maybe it was the coffee he'd been drinking during the day. But suddenly it was as if the two pulped halves of his brain reconnected and he could see clearly, his temporary amnesia gone. He headbutted Mudde straight in the langooti and the man's sensitive private parts that were as soft as aloo bondas got flattened so hard they felt – against Hari's forehead – like crumbled Maddur vadas. The man howled from the pain.

Hari got up and shouted, 'Stop this!'

'What, giving up?' he heard a voice say.

'No, but I need to think.'

'What is this nonsense?'

'The Ninth Avatar!'

'What's that?'

Hari knew then what he had to do. He wasn't going to die today. It seemed an unlikely decision, considering the situation, but even if he made the wrong choice – when karma so obviously wanted him to die – it was worth giving karma a chance to better itself.

'Wrong question. Here's my first wish, tell me: where is it?'

'You haven't earned your wish yet.'

'Okay, let us see about that.'

Moving as fast as he could, Hari brought the fake gun down with a crackling snap on the face of Thalemamsa who, panting heavily and angrily, was standing and waiting for the fight to continue – and his turn to take on Hari. The metallic butt of the weapon crunched his nose. His nostrils turned into two red fountains.

'You broke the rules!' Thalemamsa yelled. The fleshy remnants of cartilage dripped off his face like the olfactory organ of a clown who, trying to repair a mixie, amateurishly had forgotten to switch it off before looking down too deep into it.

'No, I just broke your nose. And there's only one rule that I know of.' Hari had more important things than wrestling rules to worry about. He smashed the gun hard into Thalemamsa's skull, because like some English uncle called Darwin had said on Wikipedia, the unfit never survive for long. Nature has its own way of dealing with losers. But these people had probably not read about Darwin on Wikipedia, so instead Hari quipped, 'As the American philosopher Clint Eastwood once said, men must do what they must. And if it means that I have to kill, I will.'

'So fight,' said Deadlyappa, prepared to step in and whip Hari with the motorcycle chain.

'Let's hear what he wants for his wish first,' said one of the spectators.

'Yeah, give him what he wants, Ripper,' said another one of the punters. 'He's already brought down two of your wrestlers.'

'What nonsense are you talking?' asked RIP.

'I'm bringing greetings from Doug Maddox. Name rings one or two bells? Maybe even three or four?'

RIP exclaimed, 'The mad English hero.'

'But the dog is dead,' said Deadlyappa.

'Wrong. Maddox is in hospital. And he sent me here on an errand. One thing has to be done before he takes off to where the sun doesn't shine. That'd be back to Britain, I suppose, and maybe some old family tomb.' All of them were listening now. Hari went on: 'Okay, so we're all friends of Uncle Maddox. Right-u?'

'The Mad Dog,' whispered one of the spectators. Obviously, the Englishman was something of a living legend among gamblers, racketeers and other worthies of the city's underbelly.

'Did you have to break in here to tell us that?' said RIP.

'A proper misunderstanding. Maddox wanted me to pick up a thing that belongs to him and since you were out of station, I had to act in haste. No time to waste, he may off-hogaya any minute as you know. So here it comes: where is the Ninth Avatar?'

'What avatar is he talking about, Rippu?' said an elderly, fat man in the audience.

The mobile torches turned to shine on RIP's face.

'I've no idea what the madman is going on about.'

'Idols are part of our heritage and irreplaceable, so not for sale. But last weekend you stole one from a temple near

Srirangapatnam. You meant to sell it to Mister Doug,' Hari went on.

'You robbed a temple?' said the fat man, who looked like some friend of Shanty Ram's with all his gold chains and big rings on his fingers and a huge toupee.

'Careful with what you accuse people of,' said RIP who was beginning to see where this was going. 'You're talking about that ugly little statue?'

'Ugly or not, that's what I'm talking about.'

'It was just a job. The Mad Dog looked for "antiques". It means stuff you can't get in souvenir shops. This one he read about in an English book.'

'So you think you're actually innocent, because you're too stupid to pull of such a heist on your own,' said Hari.

Some of the spectators laughed.

'Shut up! I told him there's any number of idols waiting to get stolen. It's enough to go to the nearest village temple. No watchmen, day or night. Ridiculously easy, you walk in and take what you see.' He was a braggart.

'Oho, is that so?' Hari led him on.

'But he wasn't after any random statue. Mad Dog gave a page from a book about a particular one. He promised us fifty K. So we went and got it. It was just lying around. We didn't harm anybody or do anything bad.'

Hari sensed movement to his left and jumped aside when the motorcycle chain whipped the air where he had stood a nanosecond earlier. He did a half turn and slammed the gun-muzzle straight into Deadlyappa's mouth, smashing the front teeth, and pulled the trigger.

Deadlyappa stepped back but Hari followed and kept pumping in fire with the lighter until there was smoke and a burnt smell coming from Deadlyappa's ears. It was the ear wax turning into adulterated ghee. He was somewhat surprised by how much power the fake gun gave him, but then he adjusted to the situation and screwed the muzzle deeper until he could play ping-pong with the tonsils.

'I'm too sorry, but I think my gun has lost its condom. You like non-veg? Brain fry? They say one can go on living with half a brain as most people use less than half of their IQ anyway,' Hari went on as the flame was sucked right into a vacuum within the thug's head.

RIP eyed his hitman with contempt. Deadlyappa sobbed. Even big boys cried when their brains got pistol-fried. The punters were cheering.

'So let's get on with it,' said Hari. 'Then what?'

'Mad Dog died. That's what happened. We were told so when we went to his lodge to deliver it last Saturday.'

'Well, he hasn't fully died yet, but he soon will. Lots of people in Bengaluru suffer from cirrhosis of the liver, it's normal in a city where happy hours last almost all day.' Hari did his best to sound solemn. 'Anyway, the idol must be handed back.'

'To whom?'

Hari thought strategically. 'To Mad Dog … and then to the temple. Saves you the embarrassment and improves his rebirth options and you can claim your reward. Full jackpot.'

'Foreigners aren't reincarnated, they go to hell,' said a scholarly type in the audience.

RIP added, 'Anyway, none of this is my fault. If the dog had been at the lodge instead of playing dead in hospital, he'd have got it. But I didn't want to sit around with it. Too hot to handle. I'm a religious man.'

'But you have a godown full of stolen dead people.' Hari couldn't believe what he was hearing.

'Is that true, Rippu? Are you the one who's been doing grave robbing in town?' said the politician type, seeing a conflict about to blow up.

'This little fool is lying. I trade in medical supplies for schools and suchlike. It's proper business.'

'What about the idol?' said the politico who wasn't that concerned with dead people, since they anyway weren't going to vote. 'Is it with you?'

'Of course not. Some tourist bought it the very same day for five K.'

'Five thousand for our country's irreplaceable heritage!' said Hari. 'Even my skull is worth more than that. That's sacrilege five thousand times over.'

'I should have asked for more, shouldn't I?' RIP said sheepishly. 'It's worth a lot or you wouldn't have broken into my godown, no?'

'Try five million dollars and you're closer. Who was the tourist?'

'Damn it,' said RIP who realized he had lost an opportunity to become a millionaire.

'Shame, shame on you,' said one of the punters.

'Should we try to find the client and renegotiate?'

This man, thought Hari, seemed determined on wrecking everything: first by stealing the idol and then sending it off to a foreign land. What could one do if a bunch of idiots ruined their own heritage? He looked around at the audience. The beams from the phone torches where straying, the focus had been lost. Hari took advantage. 'Unfortunately, we live in a men's world where violence and greed are the only languages that are universally understood. I personally think it's wrong. What do you feel?'

There was a murmur of approval.

Hari prepared to bolt and run.

That's when it started to go terribly wrong. As he backed towards the exit, Thalemamsa jumped him. The fellow had recovered from the face-busting bull's-eye from Hari's pistol and felled him in one go. Hari was totally dying with the wrestler squeezing his throat in the crook of his arm. The other arm locked Hari's gun hand. Hari wished that his fake gun was real.

'Kill him softly,' said RIP. 'We can use the skeleton.'

Recovering from the brain-frying, Deadlyappa got visibly excited about the prospect of ripping Hari's skeleton out of his skin. He circled closer while looking for a suitable limb to tear off. The other wrestler, Mudde, was also getting his balls back and bolstering himself with that yogic 'hooga chakka, hooga-hooga hooga chakka' mantra.

Hari struggled, but to no avail. He was trapped. Deadlyappa sank a foot into his gut. The foot was heavy, it went in deep.

RIP spoke to himself, 'Wonderful, wonderful.'

Thalemamsa took hold of Hari's $1,200-head in order to twist it like a bottle cap. Hari thought: *God, tell my wife I loved her muchly.* He spent the next nanosecond meditating on an arrow heading for its target, which was the best thing to do during the last moments of one's life.

'Careful! An intact skeleton is worth more than loose parts, Thalemamsa,' interrupted RIP's sharp voice by the time the wrestler had twisted Hari's head some 720 degrees. Temple sacrilege and grave robbery and rigged wrestling matches – everything was about earning another tainted rupee.

That command made his men stop what they were doing. RIP was acting brave now, with Hari down.

'Get off him, Thalemamsa. I'm going to flog him myself.'

Suddenly there was a loud sound and RIP fell down on his knees. His head tilted forward. Then he dropped down dead next to Hari.

Behind him stood the backstreet politician holding one of the ancient stone cudgels. It was smeared with blood.

'What did you do that for?' asked Deadlyappa.

'This little thief was only supposed to fight the three of you. Not Rippu. I came to watch a fair match. I'm not going to stand around and let anybody torture somebody. Especially since that somebody turned out not to be the real thief. Rippu is the thief here.'

Then he threw the cudgel to Hari who caught it – it was heavy, but in one fluid motion he continued swinging it in a wide arc behind his head and smacked it right into Mudde's reproductive glands. Mudde toppled over with a castrato howl and without waiting or breaking the pendulum motion, Hari swung it again anticlockwise, following its force in a gravity-defying move that whacked Thalemamsa's face, and whatever was left of lips and nose flew helter-skelter, splattering the walls with a pinkish goo, and finally the cudgel hit Deadlyappa's big toe with such power that the bone inside it broke with a loud crack. Deadlyappa hopped around on one foot. His other toe remained smashed like a cockroach on the ground, pinned down by the ten-kilo-cudgel.

'Bastard, I'm going to kill you!'

Hari scrambled up. He had made a couple of new enemies for life. He stared wildly at the onlookers, but none of them moved.

'I may be a bastard, that is fully true and fairly correct, but I have a mother like everyone else. Don't insult her. When she gets out of Parappana Agrahara Jail she'll spank you.' He spoke like they did in the movies.

The fireworks display paid off. The backstreet politician started clapping his hands and the rest of the audience followed suit. The art of warfare was subtle. Much could be achieved by merely invoking one's mother. At times, more than by actual violence, thought Hari.

'That's a true hero's spirit,' said the politico. 'I think it is obvious who the winner is. And who lost.'

'Who is the winner?' asked Hari since he wanted to be sure that the wrestling match really was over.

'This is the loser,' the politico said and kicked RIP who begged for mercy and Amnesty International's helpline number to be dialled. So, he wasn't fully dead. This was what was called a half-murder then. 'You better pay up, Rippu.'

'If he doesn't, I will,' said Hari who was too happy to remain alive. 'I have a private ATM.'

'And you have two more wishes,' said the politician.

'I wish to leave and look for that missing idol and bring it back to the temple where it belongs.'

Some of the men applauded.

'And third wish?'

'I wish you all the very best, and bye-bye,' said Hari and beat a respectful retreat. But he'd be back. The empty storeroom had given him an idea. He must bring the ATM machine, put it in that storeroom, lock it and then tip the police off. Perfect planning. That way he could legitimately claim a 10 per cent finder's fee. When he came home with one lakh in his tiffin carrier, Diamond would be happy and forgive him.

On the whole, everything had gone okay in there. The scooter waited where he had left it, but the urchin who guarded it refused to let him take it until Hari gave her another tenner as promised. Which he didn't have.

'Give me a break,' said Hari. 'It's past your bedtime.'

'If you don't pay me I'll put you to bed, old fart.' The evil little girl brandished a barber's razor to reinforce her threat.

Hari gave her the ₹750 lighter and took off. The urchin was a born winner.

16

Put your best foot forward and be ready to go that extra mile.

The night wind licked his face like a friendly puppy as he rushed his scooter up alleys that were almost empty. It cooled him down and he realized how close to death he had been back there.

It was too late to go home. The door would be bolted and he'd wake everybody up. Instead, he drove to his office in Puncherwallah Complex. Nobody was awake on CD Road, not even the guards outside the ATMs. There was no red Premier Padmini as far as he could see. Perhaps they assumed that only an idiot would be caught twice at the same location. Then they didn't know Hari.

He walked up the steps, unlocked the office and sat down at his desk. Back at work again, the hero redeeming himself.

He now knew who had instigated the theft of the idol, stolen it and fenced it, and he also figured the information was worth nothing if the idol had left India in the luggage of a tourist who had no idea how valuable the souvenir was. The idol might sit for years on a souvenir shelf, practically lost for good unless its true value was realized. He stared into the wall by the door, but it held no answers.

The moral so far was that there was little moral left in this Kali Yug. The end of days lurked around the corner. He turned his chair and stared at the wall. On it, the pictures of gods looked down on him. Movie stars, cricketers and of course Uncle's photo fringed by burnt incense sticks. He missed Uncle's demented, opinionated yelling, which always followed his customary evening 360ml peg of rum.

Hari had practically grown up in this office. As a puppy, he'd slept in an empty liquor box by the door, stuffed with old newspapers and sawdust. Those had been untroubled, happy days. He touched his ribs with a hesitant finger, but there wasn't acute pain – only a throbbing ache. A painkiller should fix it. He pulled out the desk drawer. The only thing in it was the aluminium cylinder that Doc had given him and which, as it happened, didn't contain anything of value. He played idly with the cylinder. He was tired.

But, he had another case to solve. Tulsi's lost jewellery. It was nearing 2 a.m. and there was only one place to go. It was walking distance.

Though Hari banged on the door and woke him up, Victor was all smiles since Hari had tipped him well the last time they met.

'I'll need that one,' said Hari.

'Which one?'

'That cot.'

Victor gave him an inquiring look. 'You should wash off that mud from your face. But water just ran out.'

'Doesn't matter.'

'And you look like you need a doctor.'

'I'm fine, had a merry night with the boys in the wrestling pit. How much?'

'How was the dog?'

'Just fine. It was wagging its tail. Really looks forward to coming home here to his doghouse. Missing his master, in fact. That would perhaps be you. So how about that dorm?'

'Twenty-four rupees for twenty-four hours.'

'One rupee per hour, that's a decent rate. I'll need a cot until dawn. Five rupees should suffice. You happen to have a fiver to lend me until the banks open in the morning?' said Hari, conveniently ignoring the fact that he had no bank account, just a stolen ATM.

'Banks will be shut tomorrow. Full state-wide bandh with rasta roko pre-announced and minimum fifty buses will be burnt.'

'Oho, why?'

Victor explained the political turmoil in the state due to the frequent ATM heists; Hari hadn't had time to follow the news. An immediate demonetization was expected to follow shortly.

'Is it so? Lend me twenty then?'

Because of the earlier tip and the possibility of a repeat, Victor agreed. Hari offered Victor an armpit fan as a safety deposit.

The ground-floor dormitory had bunk beds against three of the walls. One was free. A sorry mattress. You dealt with it by sleeping with your clothes on, as if on a pavement, but softer.

Hari rested uneasily with bedbugs mistaking him for chewing gum. When he swatted the mosquitoes, he ended up boxing his own ears. Unable to sleep, he counted his troubles. One, two, three and so on. The main mission was to set his marriage straight, but first he needed to worship one particular idol. And if that one was lost, how was he to succeed?

He could, of course, ignore the whole matter, but he'd promised the villagers he would bring it back. He had to figure out where it had ended up and do something about it. Spread the word in the hotels that he was searching for a tourist who had been seen hereabouts. If the foreigner rented a room in the Majestic area, he'd find the tracks. They'd have xeroxes of passports. It was just a matter of persistence.

The others snored. He noticed empty bottles in the trash bin and playing cards on the table. Celebrating their loot or gambling it away?

When morning broke, the men got up one after another, lighting cigarettes and packing their stuff. Addressing them in English, Hari told them what he'd heard from Victor, that the entire city would be shut down for a day.

'What bandh?' asked the leader of the group, the only one out of the five who spoke good English.

Hari explained it was one of those regular-as-clockwork all-Karnataka strikes that one organization called in response to another, to counteract the one supported by their political opponents, opposing a remark by somebody regarding something about an ATM guard's dereliction of duty which was expected to be the last drop that would lead to a final collapse of the rupee. Unfortunately, two bandhs didn't cancel each other out. Unless one wanted to participate in the mandatory stone throwing and bus burning, the thing to do was to remain indoors until 6 p.m. The gang leader turned to Hari. 'So how do you know everything about the strike?'

He was probably only in his forties, but gave the impression of being much older because of his missing teeth. Hari informed him that he had arrived by the 12510 Guwahati Express which had been running fourteen hours behind schedule due to Maoist trouble at New Cooch Behar. 'Got into town early today and had to walk from the station in the middle of the night. Nobody wanted to drive me even though I offered to pay fifty-double the meter.'

They had been on their way to buy unreserved tickets for the morning train to Chennai. Hari touted another option – an evening train and they'd sleep nicely, saving on one night's accommodation. Why not take dinner together as soon as the strike was over? Hari knew where one got the best aloo parathas for forty bucks, and also aloo gobi.

They were from Agra, all right. Having worked as a confidence man, he easily befriended them. The thought of potatoes decided it. Nobody from Uttar Pradesh could resist an offer of a free aloo meal.

'Me, I'm a travelling salesman. Unique invention, the armpit fan which sells like hot cakes thanks to the climate collapse. Cashing in big time. And you?'

He handed out free samples to break the ice. Due to load-shedding, the ceiling fan wasn't working. It was the hottest month in Bengaluru since 1931 and although it was only 39 degrees outside, it felt like 49 inside. The fans were soon running in every armpit. Their names were Amar, Akbar, Anthony, Aflatoon and Afghanikababwallah. Hari guessed the names were fake. He couldn't quite put his finger on how, but he knew that everything about them was fake.

They were dressed in nylon pant-shirts, except Akbar and Afghanikababwallah, who wore cotton pyjama outfits.

'So what's your business in town?'

'As you must be knowing, Agra is the centre of gem trade. But because everyone can't go there, we come where people are. We'll be off to Chennai. There's lots of jewellery there to be polished.'

Polished off, thought Hari cynically. He knew then that he had his men – for how many jeweller conmen from Agra could there be in town at any given point of time? Surely, they had some form of trade union or WhatsApp group that helped them divide the territories and avoid overlapping, just like the tech-savvy Bengaluru crooks had. It was now simply a matter of getting them to hand over the jewellery. But aloud he said, 'Time pass?' He indicated the deck of cards on the table. 'I'm a hopeless gambler, my wife always complains when I lose the grocery money ... so don't try to raise the stakes too high.'

They started a game of teen patti with one-rupee stakes. He won some, lost more, and as they got friendlier with each other the inevitable question popped up, 'So by the way, what's your salary as a travelling salesman?'

Amar eyed Hari as if calculating how much they could fleece him for.

It was late afternoon and Hari was putting lots of armpit fans and promissory notes into the kitty, whetting their appetites until it was time to strike. By then he owed them ₹37,692 plus GST. People had been killed for less.

'Usually enough to get by. Business is business and unpredictable. My good self, I have one more thing to sell, but it is worth a fortune. So I'm thinking if I close that deal, I'm set for life.' He was preparing for the kill.

'Which is?'

'Which is hush-hush. Damn it, I'm out of cash.'

'So what do we do about it?' There was a hint of menace in Amar's question.

'Have you seen this before?' He ignored the hostile vibe and pulled the aluminium cylinder out of his jhola. None of them had. Excellent. 'This is my big secret. Don't tell anybody.'

'Want to put it in the kitty?'

'This is not to be gambled away. It is built to withstand any kind of impact. Know what it contains?'

Of course they didn't. Besides, they were busy squeaking as the fans ripped out hairs from their armpits.

'Ten crore worth of red mercury.'

'Is it some kind of chilli powder?'

Hari lowered his voice. 'It's what you make bombs out of.'

'What kind?'

'Any you like, nuclear, atomic, dirty.'

'That's heavy stuff,' said Amar, reaching out to touch it.

'Easy,' said Hari, but let him feel its heaviness. 'Imagine the world's biggest tandoor in which we all get cooked. No armpit fan will cool you after that.'

'How did you come by it?'

'The usual way. A separatist group in the Northeast obtained it from China years ago in order to blow up the railway between their parts and mainland India. They procrastinated until it was too late. Nowadays everybody flies in and out of Guwahati, except salesmen like me who must carry lots of samples. So they sold it to me at the railway station there.'

'And you're saying it is worth ten crores?'

'That's the MRP if I can find a buyer. I'll bargain, because I got it cheaper,' he made sure it sounded as if he were boasting while he actually waited for one of them to make the first move. Traps worked best if the victim was allowed to walk into it by choice. He pretended to study the cards in his hand with a troubled face.

'How much did you pay?'

'Two lakhs only.'

'How come you got it so cheap?'

'See, these things can't be sold through advertisements in the newspapers. It is a market where transactions are conducted when the opportunity knocks.'

Amar appeared to have doubts. 'If you have such valuable merchandise, why stay in this dump?' He passed the cylinder back to Hari.

'Spent my cash on this, thinking I'll get at least one crore but then there's this strike and the threat of the rupee taking a plunge and anyway I couldn't get a rickshaw to my usual fence in Kallapete. With the bandh I can't afford to run around, suppose ruffians waylay me? They'd blow up the entire bus stand and all the buses in town. This was the first safe place, inhabited by good decent people like yourselves, that had a vacant cot.' Hari gave logical answers to dispel doubts. 'It was nice getting to know you, but maybe it is time to go find a buyer so that I can pay my gambling debts to you all.' He shoved the cylinder into his jhola.

'Wait a minute,' said Amar with an eye on the credit slips Hari had put in the kitty. The jewel cleaners debated among themselves in a type of Hindi that Hari found hard to follow. Finally, Amar turned to Hari, 'We know one fellow in our native place who wants to blow up the Taj Mahal.'

'Why?' said Hari, who couldn't understand why anybody would destroy their own heritage.

'He wants to become a terrorist.'

'Oho, I see. Then he really needs some of my red mercury. How much will he give?' Ideal buyer of a fake nuclear bomb.

Amar made a call standing in the corner.

The rest watched over Hari.

The phone conversation ended and Amar's tone was sweeter when he returned to the gambling table. 'He has offered to pay you four lakhs twenty thousand; you stand to make a profit.'

'I can't go to Agra to meet your buyer. Shouldn't I just give this to my man in Kallapete and pay back my gambling debt in an hour's time?'

'We'll give you three and a half lakhs' worth of jewellery. And you get the remaining money as soon as we collect it from him. That's our final offer.'

Amar's terrorist friend had probably offered more and Amar planned to take out a hefty commission for himself, judging from his eagerness.

'From where will you get it? You're nothing but jewel polishers.'

The other four gang members all nodded towards Amar. He took out a bag with a wrist sling from under his pillow. From it, he brought out a blue velvet pouch.

'We also buy and sell second-hand jewellery.' He emptied its contents on the table: a pile of gold chains, bangles and earrings. Hari's hunch was that it constituted Tulsi's savings.

'It looks like it might be worth max two lakhs.'

'I suggest you make a trade.' A challenge hung in the air. Amar's voice was cold despite the heat in the dormitory. The five of them watched him guardedly.

'Oho, it is stolen, isn't it? If I take it from you, you don't have to risk fencing it in Chennai. That's why you want to get rid of it fast?'

'Look here, be reasonable. If we want to, we can take your bomb for free. We're five, you're alone. What do you prefer?'

Hari pretended to inspect the gold critically. 'I'll have to get it evaluated by my contact in Anchipete gem bazaar before you decamp. You hold on to that.' He gave them the empty cylinder and pocketed the pile of jewellery. 'If it isn't worth minimum three lakhs, I'll come back for my red mercury.'

Hari walked off thinking: *the things idiots do for a quick buck!*

The duplicate bandh had been peaceful. Shopkeepers were rolling up shutters. Things were going well – he'd recovered Tulsi's gold, he planned to shift the ATM machine to the godown in Kallapete during the coming night with the help of AC Gaadi and offer him one third of the finder's fee, after which he'd tip off Pushpa and she would have to give him back his non-offender certificate, and then he only had to retrieve the idol, put it back in the village temple, worship it nicely, and all would be fine. He was beginning to feel optimistic.

Immediately, one thing occurred to him. Doc had a scanner. It was worth a try. The cybercafé had its door shut, but Hari knew that Doc slept inside so he banged. Doc opened. His neck was still in a brace. 'Majestic, your wife is hunting you. Keeps calling. She's real worried. Soon she'll hire detectives to track you down.'

'She can hire me then.'

'You must call her.'

'Did it sound urgent?'

'Uh, she thought you may have met with an accident and maybe were in coma in some hospital.'

'My phone broke the other day. I haven't had time to tell her.'

'Want to borrow mine?'

'What are you looking like that for?'

'I told her I have been seeing you around and she was freaked out that you hadn't called home.'

'Oho. I think you better give me your phone then.' Walking to the far end of the veranda, he dialled Sub-Inspector Pushpa because he had had a brainwave. Their relationship had thawed considerably after the previous night's bust and a medal for gallantry was coming her way. 'Hearty congratulations. You deserve it, Aunty. Speaking of which, I hear you're interested in fake red mercury.'

He didn't complain about her grabbing the medal that was rightfully his; as a police informer his fate was to never gain glory.

'You have information?' She was stunned at his resourcefulness.

'Maybe. If you're not too busy doing the needful, talk to five gentlemen – they go by the aliases Amar, Akbar, Anthony, Aflatoon and Afghanikababwallah. They're hiding at the Kama in HM Road. Know the place?'

'It's that brothel.'

'It is like a hotel for brothers, so yes, if you want to play with words. Anyhow, catch them before they take the next train to their native place, Agra, where they plan to blow up the Taj Mahal.'

'How do you know this?'

'I have my informers. One mister Victor told me he overheard them plotting, but don't bother trying to locate Victor. He's a top-secret guy, not easy to find unless you know his Hotmail ID. I heard they have a cylinder with or without explosive matter in it and enact god knows what other immoral schemes.'

'Sounds like it could be the people we're hunting for. Drop by for a coffee on the house.'

'No mention,' he said, offed the mobile and focused on his next duty. He'd call Diamond later. There was a time for everything and right now wasn't the time for love. And later was always a later problem. Doc helped Hari scan the *Lonely Planet* page with the black and white image of the idol. He saved the sketch to one of the hard disks. On Google, he uploaded the picture to the page for image searches and clicked Enter.

It took 0.15 seconds before he got the result: 12,800,000 hits. *Hmm*. There was something fairly commonplace about the exclusive idol. He sat back on the rickety chair, preparing to spend the rest of the year at the cybercafé.

The topmost fifty or so had a likeness to the stolen idol, but already towards the bottom of the first search page any striking similarities tapered off and images became more varied. Any type of oriental statue entered the fray. All the results weren't statues either – some images were printed on undies, woven onto doormats, and one was of a liquor bottle in the shape of an old monk. 'Total blasphemy,' he mumbled.

However, the first dozen or two were in the ballpark. Seated figurines, legs crossed, one hand held up in blessing, palm out, elongated ears. When he checked the details in the accompanying text boxes some were labelled Chola, so he figured he'd count those out – he distinctly remembered being told that the idol was more Gupta than Chola.

He checked dates for when they had been uploaded. One recent digital snap was more or less exactly like the sketch. Except it was a colour photograph. It was greenish, with a hint of purple. He enlarged the thumbnail and studied it more closely.

This photograph matched the drawing, every which way he looked at it. He tilted his head to get a different angle. The way the sculpture held its hand. The almond shaped eyes with yellow diamonds. Then he counted the folds in the lunghi – everything was correct. He found up to eleven identical unique features and similarities, ranging from a wart on the sole of one upturned foot and shaving cut marks on the cheek to a chewed finger nail. More importantly: no contradictory details. It couldn't be a coincidence.

'Got you,' he whispered as a smile played on his lips. Amazing – the statue had been stolen so recently and it was already online, waiting for a buyer.

He clicked to the page where the image was hosted, expecting eBay or Alibaba or something similar to open up. Instead, he was transported to a remote country called Sweden in a part of the world known as Scandinavistan, a city by the name of Gothenburg, and a curatorial news blog at some stolen antiques shop that called itself the World Culture Museum which announced having acquired, that same week, a new exhibit to please the art aficionados of the town: 'The Lucky God of India.'

The Lucky God of India? How audacious. Should he email their helpdesk and ask them to kindly courier the idol back? *Would they?* He googled for more data on Wikipedia and found that those people, traditionally, had been Vikings who plundered and raped everybody who was anybody, including monks in British monasteries. Whoever they met was turned into a blood eagle – which meant that the spine was chopped and the lungs were ripped out to make the victim look like a bird. The Viking thugs had colonized America 492 years before Salvatore's great-grandfather Columbus tried to do it. The Swedes had even made an attempt to colonize India in 1733. It was a short-lived colonization of a single village, Parangipettai in Tamil Nadu, perpetrated by a dozen sailors who were scared off into the jungles by the British and the French who were busying themselves in the lead up to the 1799 battle of Srirangapatnam and total ownership of India.

So according to the webpage, a Swedish woman working at the museum had come and looted what was left unlooted in the 1700s. *Hmm.* Like all other colonialist countries, they'd hardly send back any loot. He read through the blog again. An exhibition of stolen art was to open at the World Culture Museum end-May and run for a month. It wasn't clear how the sale was to happen, but probably it was an auction – it usually was, in these cases. He had to make it in time for that, before the idol was sold off.

He went to Google maps and keyed in the museum address in Gothenburg. It was 8,901 kilometres away from his present location. The how-to-get-there-directions came to fifty pages and included a lengthy trek through the Hindu Kush Mountains and the warning 'use caution – may involve sections not suited for walking'. Google estimated it to take 1,724 hours on foot.

He'd have to check with Pandit Pundit. Maybe there was another god he could worship instead, to get his luck back on track. Because this was perhaps one god that had left Indian shores for good.

17

> Venus being your main planet, you may be lucky in love and unlucky at gambling – but despite that you can count on winning a romantic foreign holiday for one, though not necessarily in this lifetime.

'Hari is a loser,' said the naughty parrot.

'I'm a little busy today,' said the illustrious Pundit. He had less and less time for Hari's troubled life.

'Please guru,' Hari pleaded, 'I need your wisdom.' It felt as if, somewhere along the line, his existence had peaked and got jinxed. He refused to vacate the visitor's chair until he had related everything that had passed since their last consultation – the worst chain of events possible, yet Pundit remained unperturbed, as if he had known all along. In the background, the occult parrot cackled about some money Hari owed it, a baseless allegation which Hari did his best to ignore.

'... and so, to cut a long story short, guru, a supari killer in a red Premier Padmini is stalking me, my wife is angry and the idol you told me to take darshan of is in a shop in a random country called Sweden. And my friends have unfriended me.'

'Unfriended?'

'Yes. All of them.'

'What does "unfriended" mean?'

'What it sounds like.'

'Then that is part of ageing. Get used to it. The only prediction I can give today is that it will always get worse before things improve.'

'But I'm already thirty-three years old and nothing is improving.'

Pundit made an esoteric gesture and a lit cigarette appeared in his hand. He offered it to Hari, 'You need medication.'

Hari took a drag and the fag calmed him down. 'Isn't tobacco bad for health?'

'It is veg, so preferable to non-veg and if your current life is a tragedy, its carcinogenic side effects will help you get reincarnated faster. Besides, with my blessings the ash will turn into vibhuti, so daub it on your forehead.'

'Will that solve everything?'

'No, because I doubt that you will be a man in your next life.'

'Oh no! Will I be a woman? But what will happen to my marriage? I don't think Diamond is into lesbianism.'

'Don't worry, you will hardly take rebirth as a lady.'

'Thank god.'

'You're welcome. You will, maybe, become a quadruped.'

'But that is terrible. I'll have to live in the jungle.'

'Yes, so carry mosquito repellent. But four legs are useful there. You will keep balance.'

'Hari is a loser,' said the parrot.

'Is there nothing I can do about it?'

'If you really want to get rid of all your troubles, you have to do as I said and take the darshan of the Seventh Avatar.'

'Ninth, you said before.'

'Yes, that's exactly what I said. So, go to wherever the Ninth is and do what you must.'

Hari blasted his astrologer silently. If he had advised him about the Seventh Avatar, which was not stolen, from the beginning, his troubles would have been over by now. 'How is that possible?'

'Are you questioning me?'

'Well … no. But guru, how to know for sure?'

'It is written on your forehead.' Hari's white-clad neighbour wasn't merely an astrologer but also a face reader and theological scholar. He had cracked the Da Vinci code, when the book was first published by the CD Road book pirates, by counting the missing pages and multiplying them with a random auspicious number selected by the parrot. The solution to the code had turned out to be 420.

'But I have never seen any writing there.'

'That's because the letters turn upside down in the mirror, so you can't read them yourself. But to my farseeing eyes, it is like a tattoo in Braille.'

'Oho, is it so?' Hari pictured how his whole future was nothing but a tattoo. He had no option but to follow what was written. He made a mental note to xerox his forehead and double-check what it said there. 'Sorry guru, but isn't there any other avatar closer by I could take the darshan of? Like that number seven you just mentioned.'

'Mostly when people ask me that question, they already know the answer they wish to hear, merely wanting me to confirm they're right. That kind of people should go to the charlatans who sit on street corners.'

'But …'

'Hari is a loser.'

'The parrot has a valid point. You were born a nincompoop and shall die one unless the gods intervene. Look at this as a divine intervention, then. You must battle the demons that live in Sweden, a country known for suicides and blue films, like Eisenhower wisely said,' Pundit boomed, getting into his act.

'Is there no other way out?' Hari ducked the saliva rain that splashed in his direction.

'Does what I say sound funny? Is my prophecy somewhat unclear? Are my profound words wasted on you?'

'No, I hear you loud and clear.'

'So hence I am not a joker like you.' Pundit was peeved. 'Destiny is tattooed on our skins and there's no way you can remove it.'

'Guru, all the very best and bye-bye, I'll send you a foreign postcard.' Hari pretended to pay the parrot the usual consultation fee, grabbing a ₹100 note instead. In spite of everything, it was just a stupid parrot.

Either he'd have to spend the next ten weeks walking day and night, by which time the exhibition would be over, or he would have to stop robbing petty cash from parrots and raise more substantial resources.

Flying was the best alternative. If he had been a parrot he could have flapped his wings. But the cheapest air tickets were in the range of ₹50,000 if he wanted a return, which was necessary if he was going to bring home the idol. Breaking open the ATM wasn't an option if he was going to help Sub-Inspector Pushpa find it intact in the godown and get rewarded by the bank. He couldn't pawn Tulsi's jewellery without destroying her marriage and her daughter's future. So somehow he had to find a big amount of cash … and fast.

Then there was the matter of the visa. A visa wasn't unattainable if one had a passport – it was simple to forge an invitation letter and a hotel voucher. But there was the passport matter. Had his uncle, the notorious master forger, been alive, he'd have manufactured an almost genuine passport with a visa of Hari's choice in an afternoon with the aid of quality paper, kerosene, a raw potato and a laminating machine. Now he had to fix it in some more proper way.

The right way was out of the question, because getting a passport was tricky unless you were born with one. To begin with, since he didn't have a birth certificate, he was ineligible. His uncle had once explained that he'd first need to approach the court to seek an order from the magistrate to obtain a 'No Objection Certificate' which enabled the municipal authorities to issue (should they so wish) a birth certificate. However, the municipal fellows always sent the court order back to the court for verification. That procedure alone took six months. Once he got the verified certificate, the process included a further police verification of that verification, which took another twelve months. And this wasn't the time to be scrutinized by the police. Not when he already was under the scanner for the ATM heist.

Besides, he needed to be in that foreign country in time for the exhibition, before the idol moved on to its next destination, which might turn out to be the vault of an unscrupulous collector. Then he had another idea: Plan I.

Once again, he drove up Mosque Road. On the way, he picked up a small gift, figuring it'd help improve Salvatore's moth-bally smell: a ₹59 tube of Old Spice shaving cream.

Salvatore blessed him for visiting so soon again and invited him indoors. No shotgun threats this time. His face was covered in a film of pre-monsoon sweat and he was wearing the same Lacoste T-shirt as last time, but now it wasn't inside out. *Did these foreigners never clean themselves or their garments?*

The dining room hadn't been dusted in a long time and the chairs had their padding repaired with duct tape, but with that the home improvement had ended. Hari wondered what he had found so posh about this place when he was a child. Now he saw it for what it was: curry-stained table cloths and plastic roses in booze quarts. They took seats at the table. A grilled chicken peeked out of a jungle of beer bottles.

'Let's break bread, sonny.' Salvatore finished saying grace.

Although he had promised his astrologer to stick to vegetarian food like cigarettes, he relished the wings and leg pieces that he was given. He said, 'Last time, you asked me if there was anything you could do for me.'

'I wouldn't remember.' Salvatore held the limbless carcass in both hands, pressed it into his face and sucked the skin off.

'I'm not asking you for anything much.'

'Don't be stupid. What point is there in asking, if not for too much?'

'Do you happen to have any blank European passports left, Papa Sal?' He figured that with a European Union passport, he needn't go through the rigmarole of applying for a visa. Fake visas were so easily detected these days when airport officials were connected online with migration authorities.

'What'll you want it for?' said Salvatore and dipped his face into the belly of the carcass, slurping as he sucked out the spare parts, kidney and liver.

'Short holiday in Sweden.'

At that Salvatore burped and smiled a greasy smile. 'I tell you, those *bella biondinas!* If I was two generations younger, I'd have come with you. You're going to have fun, kiddo.'

'I never have fun, I'm married.'

'In Sweden, every second blonde is a divorced single-mother eager for steamy romances with dusky Romeos.' Salvatore wiped grease off his cheek with the back of his hand. 'Take it from me. I'm half Italiano, am I not?'

Hari did the maths. If 50 per cent of them were divorced, it provided too good odds for falling in love. Triplex would have played those odds gladly. But Hari refused to give in to temptation. 'Oho, Romeo was Italian originally?'

'So was Casanova. Ours is a country of romantics. Funny that you bring this up. You know, I never saw myself ending up a Bangalorean, always thought I'll go to some sedate place like Sweden to die in a do-it-yourself coffin from IKEA.' Salvatore waved his bony hand at the windows, where the view was obscured by the surrounding apartment blocks. 'It's not too late yet. Builders try weekly to buy me out and pack me off. One offered to set me up in a retirement community in Arizona. Private plunge pool, but I knew that as soon as I signed over the property he'd tie a sack full of old car batteries around my neck and sink me in Ulsoor Lake. Maybe I'll come with you rather than getting killed over this house.'

'I think I've met that man who ties batteries around necks.'

'I had to chase him out with my shotgun. Can you believe it?'

'Yes.' Hari could believe anything when it came to real estate matters in Bengaluru and the jute sack with car batteries was a standard way of dealing with inconvenient customers.

'You see, I kinda like to sit on my veranda and drink UB Export all day.' He lifted a bottle to his lips and gulped down golden liquid. 'They don't have beer like this in the States. I'll tell you a story.' Salvatore made the chicken carcass sit up on its bum on the table. 'Sonny boy, have you heard of the Beatles?'

'Like cockroaches but smaller.'

'Actually, they were big, some said they were bigger than Jesus. Anyway, John Lennon flew down to meet his guru in ... let me see ... the year '72. From New York City, he brought me a case of Budweiser, thinking that I didn't have anything to drink. It is an awfully pissy beer. In fact, I had infiltrated the hippie movement and so John and I first met in Rishikesh in '68 and hit it off. I used to roll reefers laced with LSD. He slept on that couch in the corner and we smoked a lot. And I told him.'

Salvatore went silent, his eyes fogged over with remembered hashish smoke.

'Told him what?'

'I said, Johnny boy, listen to me. Don't go to New York. You stay here, play your hippie songs at Koshy's, and live peacefully.'

'Why?'

'They didn't want influential youth icons who understood politics. Those were the days of Vietnam. They wanted Muppets to be icons. The FBI had a dossier and asked me to report who John met here in India, so I knew from my colleagues that they were going to get rid of him. First deport him, but that didn't work because he could afford good lawyers. And we know what happened next.'

'What?'

'He was exterminated eight years later ... like a cockroach.'

'Oho, that's too bad.' Hari didn't understand the story. Working as a spy it seemed one could faff endlessly and be drunk half of the time. Though if that was all spies did, then a large part of Bengaluru (the male half of the population) counted as secret agents.

'So, what I mean is you got to be careful there in Sweden. Don't play Russian roulette with Bofors cannons.'

'I'll try not to. So how about that passport?'

Salvatore got up and walked to the bookshelf. 'Let me see, I have unused Italian passport books somewhere here. My old Cosa Nostra contacts send me complimentary ones now and then, should I decide to return to the old country. I keep selling them when I'm short on cash. Here, one is left.'

'How much?'

'Gimme enough to buy a beer or two.'

It had dark red covers and nothing but the serial number punched into it. Hari could add any photo and name he liked. And Italians looked a bit like Indians, so pretending to be Italian should be easy as cake. 'Thanks, Papa Sal. I owe you big time and I'll transfer the beer money into your account.'

'It's okay for OK's sake. I don't see much of a future for passport rackets anyway – with these new biometrics, if you don't match what the computers say, you're done for. But you can always take a chance, only sixty per cent of all passports are screened against databases, so you stand a forty per cent chance to make it through. But I hope you'll come back and share a meal with me once in a while.'

Old spies were so happy with so little, thought Hari. Though, on the other hand, Salvatore was quite drunk. Drunks tended to be happy, sentimental and trusting.

'Came back for more of my famous kahwa?' Farooqi said as he chopped the almonds with a dagger against the pad of his thumb, adding, 'For a moment, I seriously thought I'd seen the last of you. But bad news never comes in single postings.'

Hari had forgotten about his promise to never return. At the Kashmiri souvenir shop it was closing time, but Farooqi seemed as pleased as Salvatore had been to receive a visitor. At least there were no bullets flying out of his Kalashnikov eyes.

'You offered me an international courier job and that I can pick my destination. Business is dull right now, so I'd like to give it a go. Then I swear you'll never see me again.'

'You people,' Farooqi laughed. 'Just like your uncle. Where do you want to go?'

'I need a ticket to Sweden.'

'Sweden, is it?' Farooqi scratched his beard. 'And why?'

Being a quick thinker, Hari recalled something he had heard in passing. 'This thing called IKEA has great do-it-yourself stuff. I was thinking that they maybe need an Indian middleman.'

'You don't know that they've opened a shop in Hyderabad?'

'Yeah, of course, so I thought that they may want a local man in the B'luru.'

'It's doable.'

'Does that mean yes?' said Hari.

'Incidentally, my wife's third cousin's nephew studies chemistry over there.'

'He does?'

'My wife has hundreds of relatives.' As he spoke, Farooqi went to a steel cupboard, unlocked it and dragged out a brown suitcase. A brand new American Tourister made in Nagpur. 'Here's the deal. If you take this to him, I'll pay for the return ticket *and* throw in pocket money.'

Hari checked the suitcase. 'What is it?'

'A suitcase … you need one, don't you?'

'But boss, what's *in* it?' The question was relevant, because from what he could see it was empty – which made no sense at all.

'Whatever you put into it.'

'You want me to carry an empty suitcase?'

'It doesn't have to be empty,' said Farooqi as he patted the lining. From the steel cupboard, he took out what looked, to the unaccustomed eye, like pouches of vacuum-dried MTR brand instant idli mix. 'Luggage allowance is thirty kilos, I need five of that. Pack your things, go safely and meet my wife's relative. He will exchange it for another identical but completely empty suitcase. Sounds good?'

Too good. The idea of some unknown substance in his luggage made him think of certain truths: a family to return to and take care of, for example. An idol that wanted to get home to its temple. It was hardly going to be a matter of transporting idli batter to the relative, but some other kind of powder. Every day he read in the online papers about drug hauls at the Bengaluru airport, from where passengers smuggled out ephedrine and ketamine painstakingly concealed inside mixer-grinders. A 5kg consignment could be worth crores. 'What happens if I'm caught?'

'Nothing.'

Hari slapped his forehead for emphasis. 'Treat me like you'd treat a grown-up.'

'Nothing serious, I mean. They don't award death penalties there. Their jails are like our two-star hotels: a private room, clean sheets, full board, and then you're deported at their expense. Think of it as a bonus holiday.'

It was incredible how attractive Farooqi made it sound.

'Let me think about it.' But he already knew the only possible answer. 'So, if I carry that, you'll pay my ticket?'

Farooqi sipped his kahwa. 'That's the idea.'

'That is far too generous of you.'

'What are friends for?'

'That's what I always say,' said Hari and went along with the game since it was his only chance. 'Thanks for the suitcase. It'll be good to carry winter clothes in. I heard their winters last most of the year.'

'It is May, so almost summer over there I heard from my relative. We're skyping,' said Farooqi and nodded at one of his Dell laptops. 'I'll let him know that he should expect you tomorrow.'

Hari downed the last of his kahwa in one shot. Well, that had been quick. Now he had to get the passport fixed. He leaned back in the chair and played with the empty tea glass.

'Anything else?'

'Uncle ... passport.'

'You don't have a *passport?*'

'I almost have one. You're one of the best fixers in town and I need you to fix this for me.' Hari put it on the desk and opened it up to the blank ID page and then he pointed at his own face. 'Put me there. Biometrically correctly. You have the right machines to make it ninety-five per cent real.'

'Perhaps I do. How come Italian passport?' said the Pakistani, feigning ignorance.

'Need-to-know basis.'

'So what details should I put in it? Your name?'

'I was thinking of avoiding that.' One never knew, but there might be a Red Corner Notice in the airport computer system due his problematic lifestyle. 'I need a fake name.'

'What name?'

Hari hadn't thought that far, but then he remembered something that Salvatore had said about respectable Italians.

'Romeo.' That should be convincing, to be named after a national icon.

'Any last name?'

'Yes, Casanova.' It had the right ring to it.

'Very imaginative and sounds Italian enough.' Farooqi browsed the virgin passport. 'This also requires an entry visa into India, if you wish to exit the country. And an immigration stamp. Lots of work.'

'But you can fix it if anybody can.'

'That's the sort of stuff I do, but what if they ask you to speak Italian at the immigration counter?'

'Pizza-pasta, Romeo Casanova is fully fluent in native tongue,' he said, cocksure as an uncooked spaghetti. 'If you give me whatever pickles from home and idli batter you want to send abroad I'll take it and pack it,' said Hari and reached for the suitcase, but Farooqi pulled it back to his side of the desk.

'No need. Go get your clothes, come back in two hours and meanwhile my assistants will prepare the suitcase.'

'I wouldn't want to inconvenience them.' Hari put his hands on it, but Farooqi wouldn't let go.

'What are employees for, if not to make life easier, what?' Farooqi smiled back and keyed in something on his computer with his other hand. He aimed the YouCam at Hari. 'What's your mobile number?'

'Uh ... there's no currency left on my prepaid.'

'I need to be able to reach you at all times. Give me the number and I'll top it up with talk time.'

The laser printer started humming as it spat out Hari's air ticket. Things were moving faster than anticipated. What had seemed difficult just hours ago was suddenly happening and he wasn't sure how he felt about it. As Hari drove homewards, he got busy plotting. He'd empty the suitcase on the way to the airport, then claim that whatever had been in it was missing by the time he reached Sweden. Who could prove the truth? Farooqi wasn't personally going to stitch methamphetamine wrapped in marijuana leaves into the lining. He'd have one of his helpers do it, so that fellow would be equally suspect. Plus, every suitcase handler at airports en route.

Now came the harder part.

'Do you want supper, dear?' Diamond said as she wrapped her arms around him in their bedroom. The kids were asleep and Diamond had been busy watching a popular talkshow where the host on a nightly basis out-shouted and insulted his studio guests, so he sneaked into the bedroom. But she followed. Strangely enough she wasn't screaming at him. 'I was so worried.'

'Already ate.' He kissed her ear and it tasted of honey and salt.

'Where? And you have so many bruises.'

'An old business partner of Uncle's. I went over to let him know Uncle passed away and he was so devastated that I had to keep him company over dinner and then on the way I was burping so much that I fell off the scooter and the back wheel ran over my face.'

'You could have called.'

'I didn't want to disturb you. You were watching something interesting on TV.'

'Hari.'

'Yes?'

'We need to talk.'

'Honey, there's nothing to worry about, I swear on my next reincarnation as a quadruped. I'm here, am I not?' he said and caught a tear running down her cheek with his tongue, loving that sweety-salty flavour of hers. 'There, there.'

'But according to the papers you're suspected of having stolen that ATM. And now on TV they are debating whether security guards provide security or insecurity.'

'Who says I did anything wrong?'

'The neighbours read it in *Hottu-Hottu* and they are going to riot and burn a bus tomorrow. I can't begin to tell you how humiliating it was. And frightening – one fellow with scars on his face and bad burns has been asking about you.'

'When?'

'He was sitting in a red Premier Padmini in the lane. People thought he was a pervert so the local political activists accosted him. Before they beat him up and burned his car, he asked about you and showed his gun.'

'Good they beat him up fully. I'm innocent.' Stuck in denial mode, he said, 'I am trying to fix everything. Just wait.'

'Don't you see that you must quit this dangerous business? For your daughters' sake, if nothing else. What if you're gunned down? They'd become semi-orphans.' She was relentless.

'Nothing will happen.' He looked around their homely and cosy bedroom; they had experienced so much pleasure on that cot. Maybe they could have some quick enjoyment before he left?

'Didn't you hear what I just said? That man was armed. Or what if they break your fingers and you can't telephone me for help?'

'That only happens in non-Kannada movies.' He didn't mention that lately he'd been beaten to pulp on a daily basis. He concluded that this wasn't the time to rekindle romantic embers. 'What, honey?'

'You lost one million rupees that you were hired to guard and then you basically admitted doing it in that newspaper interview!' She sounded unnecessarily upset about it.

'The interview never took place, because I never met that journalist. So, I'm not so sure I made a fool out of myself.' He threw a loincloth into a plastic bag.

'But it says in the paper that you spoke to her on the phone, they even gave your number in the article.'

'How am I supposed to have spoken to journalists when my phone is broken?' At that moment came the dart-hits-the-bull's-eye ding that his backup phone made whenever he received a message. 'Oh, now it is working again.' He checked. It was from the airline, confirming that his flight was on time, at 3.40 a.m. 'Sorry honey, I've got stuff to take care of.'

'All lies!' She took a step back and placed her hands on her hips: always a dire portent. One could say that she wore the pants and he wore the loincloth. 'Fixing this and fixing that. Knee-jerk trouble-shooting when it's already too late.'

'I'm not so *sure* I'd put it that way.' But for the first time in maybe forever, he felt that a wife came with specific disadvantages.

'Nowadays you're never *sure* of anything.'

'What do you mean?'

'The best thing about being ignorant is that you're the last person to know.' If she hadn't been pregnant, he could have sworn it was PMS. Their past quarrels were being repeated almost word by word, with Diamond blaming him for not living in the real world or something such. But he was out there every day, while she watched people shouting baseless claims on TV. But maybe it was because he always worked and she ended up caring for the kids that her mind had been distorted by talk shows. So really, he couldn't blame her. Then she added, 'Do you think you can remain on the board of Diamond Majestic Investigations Private Limited after this?'

Habitually, she got the name of their agency wrong, it ought to be Diamond *and* Majestic Investigations (Pvt) Ltd. He tested a gentle, 'But I'm your husband, honey.'

'Don't mix up our personal and professional lives.'

Only now he noticed that her face was slathered with layers of cold cream against which her eyes were like two red-hot potato bondas.

'Honey, but I started the agency.' He rolled up two more loincloths and dropped them in a plastic bag. He was undertaking his first international mission as a professional investigator. Once he returned victorious, she'd be happy again, like when they had got married. He smiled reassuringly. 'Make me coffee will you? I've had a couple of terrible days.'

'People trust women, not men, and rightly so.'

He did a quick mental scan of their marriage so far. She had demanded full-fledged partnership and he had been happy to sign over the company in her name. Taking into consideration that she had no criminal record, it was a decent strategy.

They went into the kitchen. She boiled the milk and squeezed decoction out of the filter. 'Are you going somewhere?'

How did she guess? Maybe there were telltale signs. Like how his tail drooped between his legs. Or the way he had been digging out fresh nylon shirts and flashy pants from his side of the wardrobe? 'It's a job trip.'

'Who sanctioned the permission?'

'I'm using up my casual leave.'

'To that temple town again? Have you become superstitious?'

He was shocked at how she knew of all his goings and comings. He had taught her too well how to be a perfect detective. Very soon after their marriage, the hotline between Sub-Inspector Pushpa and Hari included a download link to Diamond and everything hush-hush that the police knew about him was known by his wife too.

'A little more far-far. I'll go and come.'

'Where's that supposed to be and what's it supposed to mean?' she asked as she handed him his coffee.

'Lovely coffee. I can only enjoy the coffee made by you.' He also thought that it might well be his last proper filter coffee in many years if he ended up in a foreign jail. 'Anyway, I'll just be out of station for a day or two …,' he hesitated, not sure of her geographical sense, '… in a town called something like Gautampuri.'

'Never heard of it,' she said. She was so beautiful with her hair messily tied up as if thoughts were exploding out of her mind.

'It's on the wrong side of Pakistan. You won't even notice, honey. Would you like a Scandinavistani burkhini as a souvenir and we'll take a beach holiday as soon as I get back?' A white lie might sometimes be preferable to a dark truth, just like Hercules white rum was to Old Monk dark rum in certain cocktails.

He watched her lips. They quivered. He glimpsed the chipped tooth, which was one of the reasons they had fallen for each other, or so he loved to think. He had himself lost a tooth in a fight once. But right then the fact that they were both defective didn't help. The cold cream was being washed off her face by sad tears.

'What are you going there for?'

'Scandinavistan is an interesting country, famous for having failed in colonizing India and despite that they made the Volvo which rules our bus stands. And they're starting an IKEA in Hyderabad. I'll take you there, honey. We can buy a posh cot.'

'Don't lie. You're going to leave me,' she said, jumping to conclusions. She was crying so hard that her eyes had turned into monsoon clouds. The tears splattered Hari's face.

'What you're saying is patently untrue. I shall revert immediately. This coffee is too good. It must be the extra chicory.'

'I've sacrificed everything and you ... and you're dumping me like a used rag. Or what am I supposed to think when they say in the papers that you robbed a million rupees and then you abscond from the country?'

'But honey ... how can you say such mean things?' There was a Mammootty poster on the kitchen wall: her Malayalee film hero was combing his moustache with a machete. Hari touched his own moustache ... it drooped. 'I love you.'

'What you love is trouble.'

'I hate trouble.'

'Is this how you deal with it? By running away?'

She had cornered him. Their voices had also grown louder and Ondu peeked into the kitchen.

'Children,' said Diamond, 'wake up and smell the chicory.'

'But honey, I've already put my thumbprint on the dotted line. You always say that we must be more professional. If I fulfil the mission, it'll restore my reputation. People will forget what the newspapers say about me. Our agency will get big contracts.'

'As if! I *know* you. We may as well file for *divorce*. Then off you go.'

That was what Pundit had advised him to do and the one thing he didn't want. He was amazed to hear it from her as well. For sure, they had had minor disagreements, but never filed any FIRs against each other or mentioned the 'D' word. But she had changed since they had first hooked up; her idealistic worldview had shattered many times over and her illusions had been unaccountably lost. He rinsed his mouth with the dregs of the now-bitter coffee.

Diamond appeared to be looking for something hard and heavy. There was a pressure cooker in the kitchen sink. He worried that she might press his head down into it and put it on full boil.

'Why wouldn't I return home? I love your coffee,' he set the tumbler down on the counter and worked on humouring her and smiled at the kids – one, two, and the third in her belly: the four important people in his life. 'I'll bring back Swiss chocolates for each and every one of you.'

He grabbed the plastic bag with his nylon pants and neon T-shirts, and loincloths, whatever little he owned in the way of garments. Couldn't afford to miss the flight or Farooqi would crack his male body parts with a nutcracker and mix them in his famous kahwa. Her voice echoed behind him. 'I haven't finished speaking to you.'

When they got married, he'd been fascinated by her voice – grated jaggery mixed with silken dates and sugarcane juice – and he had therefore taken to calling her 'honey', a natural pet name for her. But over the years, he realized that her given name was the most appropriate. She was a tough cookie: 99 per cent diamond, a single per cent candy-coating.

'I have a meeting with the visa fixer. Pause it right there and I'll listen to the rest later.'

'Will you be back for breakfast?' A tinge of anxiety suggested that love still existed as a possibility.

'I'll try my best.' If he told her he was on his way to the airport right then, she'd smash his skull with the pressure cooker for sure.

18

> A foreign tour might suit your mood or if not that then spiritual journeys – in other words you can trip into outer space or inner space.

He loved her so. But marriage was beginning to feel like being locked up inside a booby-trapped suitcase, he thought as he watched how the villages lining the road had fused together into one endless stretch of dhabas and malls. The highway was spectacularly unclogged at that time of night and the travel went faster than expected. Way too fast for Hari's liking – he would have wanted the driver to obey the traffic police-issued banner on the roadside: 'Better be Mister Late, than to be Late Mister.'

Apart from his marriage, he couldn't stop thinking about the American Tourister suitcase. *Might it be a bomb?* If it was made of recently bought red mercury, he should be safe. But his Plan J of removing the contraband from the suitcase and selling it to Pusher Prasad, who hung out at the bus stand, before boarding the airport bus had come to nought when Farooqi arranged a car with one of his wife's innumerable nephews driving.

Hari chatted to alleviate his own nervousness, but the nephew replied as if they were on SMS or Facebook; unsmiley, thumbs down, unfriend.

The suitcase and his wife weren't the only problems. There was another concern that he had never felt before, which grew more acute the closer to Kempegowda International Airport they got. What happens to a fish when it is taken out of water? It dies fully. On his own street, on CD Road, he was Mr Majestic, the undisputed king. Well, others would dispute it. But he himself never did.

Before he had time to conclude that line of thought, the Maruti slid up the curving ramp of Trumpet Flyover leading off the Hyderabad Highway. The inauspicious road sign that stated 'TERMINAL' suggested a slow and painful death (he'd encountered the double-meaning of the word in his online language course: 'being in the final stages of a fatal disease'). These were the thoughts that ping-ponged inside his skull, giving him a headache.

Within another few minutes he made out the gleaming passenger terminal up ahead. The car rolled to a halt in front of it. Hari got out. The nephew gave him the suitcase. The plastic bag with his clothes had fit easily inside, yet the suitcase was remarkably heavy. Should he dump it in one of the waste bins? But the nephew followed a few steps behind.

Bad situation, he thought as they came up towards the security cordon. Odds were stacked against him. Any number of things could go wrong.

'Are you sure they won't detect that the passport is fake?' he said, trying to make small talk and avoid the unavoidable.

'We're not amateurs.'

'But what if ...'

'The person at the check-in counter only has thirty secs on an average to screen each passenger. Take two Calmpose and act as if you're not flying for the first time and nothing will go wrong.' He handed over the pills to Hari and made him swallow them. 'If they ask you anything, stick to your cover story and don't get nervous.'

Hari wanted to linger at one of the coffee outlets and have a last cuppa of filter chicory, to ward off the evil feeling that once he stepped inside the terminal, things would never be the same again. But coffee might make him jittery and enhance his doubts. He really should abort the mission and go home. Live happily ever after and see his kids grow up. He thought of faking a heart attack. But the nephew was in a rush and pushed him towards the entrance. The guards verified his travel documents and he was let through. They didn't notice that his passport was forged.

Turning to glance over his shoulder, to glimpse India for the perhaps last time, he saw the nephew touch his middle and forefingers against his own eyelids, then wag them at Hari. The wall was of glass and he kept track of Hari's progress so there was no instance when he could have opened the suitcase to remove whatever Farooqi had put in it. No option but to walk up to the check-in counter. The airline personnel treated him nicely on account of his EU passport. The uniformed lady glanced at it for barely a few seconds before giving him the boarding pass. The suitcase, placed on a black rubber conveyor belt, disappeared out of sight.

As if in a weird dream, he walked through the vast air-conditioned departure hall to the escalator that took him to the immigration counters. Every single passenger was thoroughly scrutinized, as if they knew that somebody was leaving the country with a fake passport. If the officials thought anything was amiss, they'd search his luggage for sure. He closed his eyes and prayed until the tourist behind him nudged him forward. It was his turn to walk up to the counter. Twelve steps. One more.

Thirteen. Bad number.

'Chicory aayita?' he greeted the uniformed official, who had an imposing grey moustache.

The man stared at Hari's face and then at the passport and browsed through it. 'This is an Italian passport, but you speak good Kannada.'

Oho, Hari had forgotten. He should have thrown in a few Italian words. He said, 'Macaroni? I was adopted from here but mistakenly grew up in Pizza, in the region of Pasta. I then reverted.'

'For what purpose?'

'To look for my intellectual roots.'

'What does that mean?'

'It has to do with the brain and the soul.'

'According to the arrival stamp, you entered three months ago. Where in India have you been?'

'Bengaluru only. It is the nicest city in the world. There is no chicory like the local chicory.'

'And where are you going?'

'Why?'

'Answer the question and address me as "saar" from now on.' Despite the fancy passport, the official had pegged Hari as a slumdog. *Remarkable*. He browsed through the passport once more. 'Your destination?'

'Sweden, sir, as it says on the air ticket. Is there a problem, sir?'

'Switzerland, why-u?'

'It is the land of hillocks, functioning clocks and edible chocolate, sir.'

'Who will you visit in this one?'

'To be honest with you, I don't want to go.' He realized that the best strategy was the reversed plan: because whatever he wanted, the official was going to deny.

'Why?'

'I'd rather stay here and drink coffee and raise a family and live happily ever after, so if you would kindly detain me on any flimsy pretext until I miss the flight-u, it would be the best-u.'

'Is it so-u?'

'It is-u.'

'Happy journey-u.' Bang, the official stamped his passport with the exit stamp. He handed it back to Hari, already aiming his eyes at the next in line.

Hari approached the customs line where he spotted a notice. 'Foreign as well as Indian nationals departing from Kempegowda International Airport are required to ensure that they are not in possession of any prohibited goods, which includes antiques older than ninety-nine years, sandalwood except in handicraft form, or Indian currency exceeding ₹25,000. Any violation may result into confiscation of goods, arrest and prosecution.' But the notice didn't mention pure Afghani heroin, ketamine, ephedrine or other drugs, so he felt safe. Somewhat ironically, after customs he came to a duty-free shop where whisky was much costlier than on CD Road. Totally dubious brands such as Johnnie Walker (which was most popular among adulterated boozes) cost five thousand bucks. Back on CD Road, you got a full bottle of Original Choice for ₹206.

He thought of parcelling vadai for the trip, because tourists he had met claimed that there were none in Europe. Now he realized his error. In the middle of the night, people were having sit-down meals at joints with high-end names such as Malgudi Tiffin Centre, buying idlis at dollar rates. These were some other kind of travellers than the ones he was used to meeting-and-greeting at the bus and railway stations. Nothing was cheaper than ₹50, not even the coffee. He decided not to eat or drink until he came home to CD Road again, unless he found food at Indian rates somewhere along the way.

Boarding started half an hour before the departure time predicted on the ticket. Everyone seemed to know what to do and an endless queue formed at the gate before he could blink. At least five passengers had cleverly arrived in wheelchairs to get onboard ahead of the others. Hari made a mental note that the next time he flew, he too would go by wheelchair.

The line snaked into a tunnel and at the end of it, he was inside a congested tube full of chairs, almost like a crowded BMTC bus – and it took him a few seconds to realize that this was the aircraft that was going to take him abroad. He had expected air travel to be seven-star, this wasn't even semi-deluxe. He sat down in a free seat and somebody came and told him he was sitting in the wrong one. *How was he to know?* He whipped out his phone and dialled up Triplex. Finally, he got an answer. But Triplex didn't sound particularly happy about hearing Hari's voice. 'I'm watching a viral YouTube-clip with Baba Sehgal.'

'You'll never guess where I am.'

'In jail again?'

'I am on an airplane going to ...' He had to stop to think. Triplex wouldn't have heard about Sweden. 'Switzerland.'

'That's a good one, Majestic. You drunk, you skunk?'

A cute woman in a nifty suit came to his seat. 'Please switch off your cellphone, sir. You need to listen to the security announcement.'

'Huh?'

'We're ready for takeoff.'

Hari held out the phone to her, 'Repeat that last part. Triplex doesn't believe me.' Wow, he was going to have incredible stories to tell Triplex about the stunning air hostesses he met on this trip.

Puzzled, she obliged. 'We're ready for takeoff. Switch it to flight mode, please.'

'Where's the rush? I need to make another call.' He was thinking it'd impress his daughters if they heard him speaking from the air, but the hostess was adamant.

'Sir, you may switch on your phone again once we reach our destination. For the time being, please keep it on flight mode,' she scolded him, but smilingly.

Was she flirting with him? Interestingly, the plane moved softly – there were no potholes on this airfield. Things shook and the seat tilted back. Through the little window next to his seat, he saw a web of orange streetlights shrink away in the distance. Was that ...? No, it couldn't be! But it was ... *how small the city was!* The nice air hostess wheeled a trolley to his seat, 'Sir, anything to drink?'

'Too costly, you must give a discount.'

'It is complimentary.'

'Meaning?'

'It is included in the air ticket price you paid.'

But he hadn't paid for his ticket. *Free booze?* Hari couldn't believe it, must be bootlegged Johnnie Walker.

'So, would you like something from the bar?'

He shook his head. This was not possible, they were cheating him. He had stopped drinking, but they tried to ruin him. 'I don't take hard drinks.'

'How about coffee?'

Now she was making an offer he couldn't refuse. He asked for six cups and belted them down in quick succession before she had a change of mind. He didn't have to pay. It was the weirdest thing that had ever happened to him. Another trolley came down the aisle. *Free food.* Here he thought that there were no free lunches in the real world, but first he got coffee and now pulao with peas, roti and curry with paneer. The portions were small compared to Suleiman's canteen, so some cheating was involved.

Late in the morning, local time, he saw an unpopulated country of green forests and blue lakes through his window. The plane landed without crashing.

When he walked towards the immigration barrier, he noticed long lines of passengers stuck at the 'Non-EU' counters. So, he chose one that said 'EU'. The uniformed woman inside the glass booth took his passport. Not unexpectedly, she was a blonde.

'Romeo Casanova?' she sighed and her voice sounded lovesick.

'That is my good self.'

'I feel I have heard that name before.'

'For sure, I'm more than world famous.'

'For what?'

'For my pizza and pasta. I'm a celebrity chef.'

'Do you own a romantic little bar in Italy, perhaps in a cobblestone alley and that has been featured on TV?'

'Actually, it is a global multinational chain. I'm launching an outlet here in your country. You're welcome to the inauguration.'

'What is it called?'

He didn't even think before he spoke. 'Maccodonaldi.'

'I think I've heard about that one. You should make pizza with moose meat. It is our national animal.'

'That's a sooper plan. I'll cook the moose in a tandoor for better flavour.'

She thought for a bit.

'Can I have your autograph?'

And then he was waved through. Leaving India had been hard, entering Europe was easy. He followed the other passengers who seemed to know where to go. Standing at the luggage carousel his toes were cold. Couldn't his suitcase come so he could get out of there and into the sunshine? Other passengers got their stuff, filled their trolleys and walked off. There were a few suitcases lolling on the conveyor belt, pushing at each other, but none of them was the brown American Tourister.

Then the carousel stopped spinning. The conveyor belt came to an abrupt halt. The evil temperature went up by several degrees and his toes got hot.

Had he missed something? Then it dawned on him. It must have been detected at an X-ray checkpoint. The friendly woman at the immigrations desk had probably chatted him up in order to delay him, while they opened it. They'd be watching him to determine if he worked alone or had an accomplice. The baggage hall was emptying fast. The last straggling passengers filed towards the customs barrier. He followed, trying to blend in. A man in uniform was silently examining the passengers and Hari noticed him because of the dog. He liked dogs. Dogs liked him.

Hari stopped as there was something sticking to his sandal. It was his luggage tag with the fake name, 'Romeo Casanova.' He pretended to tie his shoelaces – though he of course had no shoes – while he removed the sticky tag. Bending down, he spotted a tottering grey-haired man dragging an American Tourister suitcase towards the green channel. It was brown. It was Hari's. Whether he was suffering from Alzheimer's or not, that man was stealing his lunghis and nylon shirts! The thief had removed the luggage tag, but it was unmistakably the same suitcase.

Actually, it was maybe all for the best. This was the moment to act slyly. He'd let the man carry his suitcase through customs, jump him outside and steal it back. A white man like him would hardly be stopped by customs officials.

Hari followed, closing up surreptitiously.

Right then the sniffer dog started pulling at the leash. The luggage thief slowed down. Hari slowed down even more. The dog moved forward and the thief started to turn, as if he needed to go to the public toilets at the far side of the hall. But the dog trotted up and laid its paws on the suitcase. The thief had no idea what he had got himself into.

Hari walked through the green channel and left the arrivals hall with nothing but the clothes he wore – a bright nylon shirt, a pair of shiny polyester pants, rubber sandals and fake passport, mobile phone and 500 Swedish rupees in his pocket, which was what Farooqi had given him towards expenses. It was enough to buy about 200 portions of idli-vada and filter-coffee according to his calculations, so it should last him through the trip.

Then he got a bad shock when he got outside.

There was a bus that said 'Göteborg' in front. Hari asked if it was going to Gothenburg, too.

'Same thing,' said the driver, evidently used to strange questions.

'Oho, that is too good, so how much?'

Bus tickets were 95 local monies and he had to redo the maths a few times. *₹700 for a bus ticket?* 'Make it cheaper. I'm a foreign tourist. I'm good for economy.'

'I don't decide the price,' the driver said and drew off with an almost empty bus, instead of offering Hari a discounted seat.

He decided to walk and save money. The road the bus drove away on should technically lead into the city, so he followed it on foot.

The air tasted fresher than on CD Road. There was plenty of greenery. The pavement was unbroken. No potholes in the road. But it was extremely cold, despite Farooqi's claims that it would be summer in Europe. The situation wasn't looking good at all. Unless he turned into part of the permafrost, Farooqi's relative would surely give him the jute sack treatment for having misplaced a fortune's worth of illegal drugs.

19

You may feel anguish about people misunderstanding you, so be careful of what you say.

A long exit way passed cargo terminals and it was similar to Bengaluru's airport but in reverse. *Everything was the opposite here! Where were the people and other sentient beings?* Back home the road would have been full of humans, cows, pigs, goats, bowel movements, normal things.

Trees lined the road instead. In Bengaluru, although there was the odd wild banyan and a few domesticated coconut trees, and, of course, a few parks, the nearest jungle was in Burma. Here trees grew all over and nobody had cut them down. *How come?*

He passed a McDonald's next to a petrol pump. Efficiently, cars and humans got nourishment at the same time. Hari had always thought of it as an Indian luxury restaurant. He went inside, thinking of parcelling spicy potato burgers in case he had to walk far to get into town. But the menu was strange – no McAloo Tikki™ or McSpicy Paneer ... *fake McDonald's or what?* He decided to wait until he found real Indian food.

He continued walking. He spotted one car, far away. Other than that, he only saw trees, trees and more trees. Like the end of the world. He took a selfie to MMS to Triplex, standing in the middle of the driving lane with his phone raised, when the car – in the opposite lane – slowed down and honked.

Photos were perhaps not permitted near the airport. Hari put away the phone, waved at the seedy-looking Viking descendant driving the ramshackle Volvo, and stepped to the edge of the road. He had read up on Vikings on Wikipedia. They were essentially rapists who spoke in runes but pretended to be international businessmen. This had been their homeland once, he thought, so surely old Vikings lurked in these forests. He continued in the direction he thought the city would be.

Minutes later, a car slowed down next to him. It was the same Volvo. It must have turned and followed. Rolling alongside Hari, the side window opened. The driver leaned out. '*Hallå där blatten.*'

Hari waggled his head noncommittally, he didn't understand runes. The Viking uncle went on speaking gibberish. Hari gestured, twisting his hand the way it was done back home when one meant to say no. The Viking didn't get it. Hari thought: Control-Alt-Delete. But there were no Esc buttons on the keyboard of reality.

He worried that he had, by mistake, entered some kind of male red-light district. Prostitution always happened near railway stations and bus stands. Maybe here, in this well-to-do country, the red-light area was the turn for the airport. Sex tourists could go and come quickly. *Was the man a local tout?* One of those who hung around transport hubs and talked people into doing what they oughtn't, in which case they were almost colleagues. The man switched to broken English. '*Höh*, don't you know how to speak? I don't get why you're here in the first place, if you don't understand dogshit.'

'I am a tourist.' Hari walked on, the car rolled slowly beside him. 'I'm sorry if your language is called dogshit. But I like to speak with dogs.'

'*Höh*?' the man said. 'Where are you from?'

'Italy.' Sticking to his cover story.

'What are you doing so far from home?'

It struck him that this man acted too authoritatively to be a tout, but he might be a local politician. Hari clarified, 'I am on a sightseeing tour. I have a European Union passport.'

'You don't look so Italian to me.'

'I'm sorry if my looks disappoint you,' said Hari, although he couldn't explain to himself why he should feel apologetic about his good looks.

'You look more Syrian or … Pakistani.'

The man was wide off the mark, about 1,500 kilometres at least, but his observation scared Hari. Even 1,500 kilometres was too close for comfort.

'I'm a *bona fide* Italian chef,' he insisted.

'And you're looking for spaghetti here, *höh*? But you understand, in Sweden you cannot walk on highways. Only cars, get it?'

'Oho, is it so? I was wondering why there were no people in the streets, but thanks for telling me.'

'So why do you go on walking?' He steered closer until his Volvo forced Hari out on the shoulder of the highway.

Was the Viking going to do to him what his ancestors had done to innocents around the world? Exercising caution,

Hari said, 'I missed the bus from the airport, so nothing to do but walk.'

'Where are you headed, *höh*?'

'Into town.'

'Hop in and I'll give you a ride.' He opened the passenger door. Hari took one more step, to get around the hood of the Volvo. 'It's far, you can't walk that far. *Höh*, *höh*. Not in those sandals. *Höh*, where's your luggage?'

'I travel light. I have the EU passport and so according to Wikitravel, I don't require a visa.'

'Let me guess. You've come here searching for blonde women?'

Was he a pimp?

'I have enough women at home, thank you muchly.' Hari stepped back, but the entire road was fenced in so he couldn't make a run for the forest.

'Get into the car before you regret it. I was just diagnosed with prostate gland disorder. Otherwise, I don't pick up hitchhikers. Was feeling a bit low, wasn't I?'

Hari didn't bother to explain that he hadn't been soliciting a ride and saw no connection with the man's prostate, but got into the car since there was no other option. Crumbs of a million pizza crusts, burger meals and half-eaten finger chips littered the floor. The Viking was dressed in worn rubber boots and a raincoat, but on a closer inspection, Hari was sure of that all-too-familiar smell. The telltale signs were there. The dyspeptic looks. The paunch. Hung-over eyes. Bacon lips. Unwashed hair peppered with dandruff. Undercover, but 3,000 per cent cop. Hari almost guessed the cop's diet, too. Maybe because pizza had destroyed his health, he had developed an aversion towards Italians?

He flattered the cop. 'Love your tie. It is unusual. What do you call it?'

It was made of a black leather string and had a grinning skull with crossbones on it.

'I call it the hangman's noose. Want to know why?'

'Not really.'

'I believe in justice.'

'That is wonderful,' said Hari.

'Welcome to Sweden. My name is Barsk, Herman Barsk.'

'It seems like a lovely country. I'm Romeo Casanova, my good self.'

'It is the hell on earth.' Barsk lit a cigarette and pressed down the gas. 'But it might improve, they're going to turn the airport into a big tourist destination with funny things. It'll be called Airport City. They will have many pizzerias. You should come then, it'll be just like home for you, *höh, höh.* Do you have airports in Italy? Look, this here is Brörrödsmotet,' he said indicating a highway bridge that the car was passing.

Much as he tried to, Hari couldn't see anything that distinguished the place. 'Why is the road fenced in?'

'Because of the goose.'

'Goose?'

'Yes, it mashes the cars. It is horny.' It sounded as if the local goose was like the Indian elephant in mating season. Barsk let go of the steering wheel and made a demented gesture with fingers splayed. 'You haven't heard of it? King of the forest.'

'A bird with horns?'

'Our national animal isn't some stupid bird.'

'Oho, you mean the *moose*?' He remembered what the flirty blonde at the airport's passport counter had said.

'Sorry, what am I saying? Yes, the moose. There are so many that we must shoot them all once a year.'

'Sounds horrible.'

'Not at all. We eat them. Yum. Man against moose.' The cop gave running commentary as they drove into town. 'Also, we have another kind of fence that protects against the noise that cars make. *Höh*, in Italy you must be used to noise. But let me give one piece of advice: here we shut up. We're also the highest taxed people in the world.' The only noise was the constant blabbering. *Yet they had to soundproof their roads?* He thought he smelt liquor on the cop's breath.

'Is there anything else I can show you?'

'Yes, the World Culture Museum.'

Barsk slammed on the brakes. 'Culture?'

'Yes, they sell old things. You know: culture.'

'You said *culture*?' Barsk was digging for something in his armpit and there was an edge of stainless steel to his voice.

'It basically is the same thing as civilization. Have you heard of it, here in your native place?' Maybe culture wasn't part of the Viking lifestyle.

'Whenever I hear that word, I do this,' said Barsk and pulled a gun from inside his raincoat.

'Oho.'

He cocked it and waved the gun in Hari's face. 'The drain on tax money, and those hippies who pretend culture is important, is nothing less than a national scandal. Are you one of those?'

'No, constable sir.'

'*Höh*? You called me constable?'

'Yes, constable.'

'How did you guess?' A car behind them honked, but Barsk showed his middle finger in the rear window.

'Takes one to know one.' Hari had nothing to lose by bluffing. 'So, as one colleague to another, where is that so-called museum?'

'Do you have a gun?'

'No, I'm on a study tour to learn exotic cooking. I work in the police canteen.'

'And you want to see culture?'

'Yes, have you heard of the World Culture Museum?'

Barsk spat out the driver's window and stepped on the gas again.

There were more and more buildings now, so Hari surmised they were approaching the city proper. Barsk stopped the car at a large five-street-junction where trams and buses halted. A tree grew out of the concrete, around which was a circular bench where a lady sat with a toddler. Next to it was a squat small building, a shop of some sort. 'This here is the Crossroads. Where you get off.'

'Is it a famous local spot?'

'Here in town, everybody knows it.'

'It is very scenic.' In truth it wasn't, but for a public square and a transport hub it was uncommonly clean. Of course, Hari knew what 'crossroads' meant. In India, it was a crucial stage when people made important decisions that affected their future careers. But he had also read on Wikipedia that for Westerners it was traditionally the place of executions (before electric chairs were invented so that people could get executed more comfortably indoors) and was, therefore, the best place to sell your soul to the devil, who hung around to collect wrongdoers.

'And there's your museum.'

The building Barsk indicated stood on the far side of the junction square: a huge, concrete box. There was a hint of steel wool in Barsk's eyes now. 'I hope you won't be doing anything that might land you in trouble here.'

'No such plans, constable.'

'Because if you give us trouble, I'll give twice as much trouble to you.'

'That is very generous of you. If you come to Italy, I'll reciprocate and take you on a guided tour. Bye-bye and all the very best.' He opened the car door and slipped out.

Barsk called out after him, 'Listen up, Pastaface, I'll be keeping an eye on you.'

Hari stepped away quickly from the car. The Crossroads was surrounded by brown-brick buildings five or six storeys tall and with red roofs. The World Culture Museum stood about 250 metres away, an architectural monstrosity. It wouldn't be that easy to break into, not like some old godown in Kallapete. Stealing the idol back might turn out to be trickier than expected.

It was like being in some kind of virtual reality. He'd seen pictures of Sweden on Wikipedia and Google Maps, but here those pictures were not computer simulations ... it was all real.

A small park lay up a slope on the right side. A good vantage point. The square had a convenience store open from 6 a.m. to 11.30 p.m. that sold sandwiches, cigarettes and SIM cards. To prove his honesty and save his neck, Hari wanted to call Farooqi and inform him that a kleptomaniac had stolen the suitcase at the airport and got busted by customs. The girl at the store counter greeted him the moment he got close. '*Hej!*'

'Prepaid SIM for my semi-smartphone, please.' He showed off his Nokia Asha.

'*Ja-ja*,' she said and switched to English. 'We have that.'

'Which is the cheapest?'

'*Ja-ja*,' she said, 'then it would be this start packet.'

'How much, please?'

'*Ja*, 199.'

'I'll take ... how much was that again?' He could not believe his ears: ₹1,500 for a SIM. He must have misheard. 'Can you make it any cheaper?'

'How do you mean?'

'*Swalpa* discount *maadi*.' For a moment, he was back in Bengaluru, where you were expected to bargain when people quoted ridiculous rates. Even the Frenchman at Srirangapatnam had demanded a discount on the food and eventually walked off without paying anything.

'Sorry, I didn't get that.'

'You have to reduce the rate.'

She mulled it over. '*Jamen*, you can also buy this mobile phone which includes a SIM and you get free calls, free SMS and free surfing.'

'But I already have a phone.'

'It's the best for you, *ja*. It is less, only 195.'

Less to buy a phone with SIM, than SIM without phone? In India, you didn't get a phone cheaper than a SIM, particularly, if the phone came with a SIM in it. Then he got it: she was trying to cheat him. He didn't understand the trick, but recognized a typical 420-scam punishable in India. And so, he said, 'I'll compare and come again.'

Unlike shopkeepers at home, she didn't call him back with an improved offer. Now that he was becoming aware of what a big fraud this convenience store was, he saw the absurd rates on the price tags: a sandwich was the equivalent of ₹195 (as compared to ₹20 at home), a newspaper was ₹400 (against ₹5). The store sold machine-made coffee and a small one was ₹150! Coffee-Anand gave a full tumbler for ₹5 to regulars, ₹10 to foreign tourists. Maybe these were tourist rates?

Next-door, inside the waiting hall for tram passengers, was a competing coffee kiosk called Espresso House. They had chai but it was almost ₹280 and a coffee was marginally cheaper at ₹200. But the tiniest sandwich was ₹425! Hari staggered out and collapsed on the bench that circled the lone tree in the square. An un-Swedish-looking woman sat there with her baby, surrounded by big paper shopping bags full of junk. She didn't spare him a glance when he leaned his face in his hands. She rattled her paper cup at passers-by. He realized that she belonged to a team, with two young men. One of the boys peddled magazines, the other sat on the ground, weaving baskets. They were professional beggars.

He felt the ground move under his feet. He had supposed that the money he carried would last for weeks, but it dawned on him that it was barely enough to buy twenty-six small coffees. And he drank at least twelve per day to keep his vital functions in working order.

He could only buy coffee on an emergency basis. And the emergency wasn't far off. His phone made a noise and when he checked, it had hooked itself up to some local network, so apparently his prepaid SIM worked here. He keyed in an SMS to Farooqi.

'Reachd but prob. Suitcase lifter@airport. Drug squad sniffer dog alert. Chased by undercover cop. Kindly transf money 2make up 4loss of garments c/o ur nephew.'

The single SMS cost more than he'd pay for two hours at a cyber café in Bengaluru! He had fresh missed calls from Diamond, but didn't dare to call back because of international roaming. He got up and walked down the street, past a Thai eatery, two Japanese sushi places and an Italian restaurant that only took cards, no cash, but an eatery named Holy Cow gave him hope until he peeked at the menu card in the window and realized it was a steakhouse specializing in beef items – total sacrilege – and he finally spotted an Indian vegetarian canteen where the dish of the day, palak paneer with chutney, was ₹600. He just didn't have the right kind of budget for this country.

He could go without food for a day or two, that he was used to, but sooner or later his body would need coffee to function.

The World Culture Museum lurked before him. He did a loop around the back, and found a parking lot and a bicycle stand. Through a forty metres long display window he looked down into a cavernous exhibition hall where statues stood on pedestals and icons hung on the walls. From that distance, it wasn't possible to make out if any of them was the Ninth Avatar. But that must be where the stolen idol was kept. Save for all the glass, it was a bunker-like structure, dull colours, probably a sophisticated alarm system, forbidding. Even Parappana Agrahara Jail looked more welcoming.

He had mistakenly expected it to be a regular shop for stolen goods, like the Kallapete godown back home. It turned out to be an actual museum. On the façade, above the main entrance, was an illuminated advertisement for the upcoming exhibition: 'The World of Lucky Gods.'

First of all, he had to stake the place out. There was no fee to enter, so he walked into a large open foyer with blindingly white walls, light-brown wooden floors, much concrete and a lot of glass, which gave the building an almost transparent feel. The main exhibition hall was locked, but upstairs he saw a display with photographs from Afghanistan.

He tried to act inconspicuous, but his rubber sandals kept making a flip-flopping noise against the wooden floors. A woman in black walked past him in the corridor outside the galleries. She looked vaguely familiar. She caught his eye and said something. He smiled and nodded, but had no clue what she was going on about. He hadn't taken into account that people were going to speak without English subtitles, unlike the pirated Ingmar Bergman DVDs. She climbed up the stairs to the fifth floor, which apparently held the offices. She seemed to work there, then. *Was she the one who had blogged about the Ninth Avatar?*

Atop a broad wooden staircase, across the foyer, was a terrace canteen. The staircase was pompously wide. The chairs were bucket style, neither Rexine nor semi-deluxe. There were strange decorations on the walls, which he presumed to be art, or maybe not, who knew? According to the menu displayed on an electronic screen, a coffee was nearly ₹200, which was beginning to seem like the regular rate around here. His hands were trembling from severe withdrawal symptoms.

People walked in and out of the canteen, but lunchtime was over and he took a seat at an empty table as far as possible from the counter. Shivering from the coffee craving, he observed the routines around the building, and deliberated on whether to buy coffee or not. Then his mobile dinged. A businesslike message from Farooqi that signalled a definite shift in their relationship:

'Expekt u 2 rekover sootkase content. Spik 2 wifes 3rd nephew re lokal needs inkl jute sack & kar batteris. We have agriment & u now I now where u live, bastard.'

No more free kahwa, that was for sure. He wondered whether to warn Diamond, but she was an ex-nurse and could perform vasectomies blindfolded. As he was brooding over Farooqi and the fact that there was no more cash coming his way, and hence no coffee, he spotted the woman in black who had spoken to him in passing. She stood at the food counter. Her black hair had reddish roots. Waiting for the cashier to total her bill, she eye-balled the cafeteria. Their pupils slammed into each other again. It was brief, but it was one of those soul-sucking moments. Or maybe it was just the mug of coffee on her tray that made him feel so.

She turned back to the cashier and finished her transactions. She carried her food tray and came towards him. She stopped at his table. '*Hej, är den här platsen upptagen?*'

He vaguely guessed, from her tone, that the runes meant something – perhaps a question whether the seat across from his was free. But the cafeteria was pretty empty, so she could have sat down anywhere.

Her tray held a slice of pie with creamy filling oozing out of it and a porcelain mug of coffee. She was wearing a black T-shirt, the text of which was made three-dimensional by her boobies. Hari speedread the message – which stated that somebody called Kafka didn't have much fun either – and then he turned his attention to her face. Her earrings were silver hoops. She had freckles. She smiled. So he nodded and smiled back.

20

> You are likely to meet with strangers, so be creative in your efforts and don't take decisions based on emoticons.

'Sorry, you must be one of the Syrian refugees. I should have known that you won't speak Swedish. Just arrived in the country?' she said as she switched to English and set her tray down. 'Mind if I take a seat?'

'I'm waiting for somebody.' In fact, he had waited for the right moment to make contact with her. But he was unprepared for this: she had come straight to him!

'Your English is good.'

'I'm not from Syria.'

'My bad. I noticed you were interested in the exhibitions. A new one opens next week on Friday. Do come.'

'Do you work here?'

'Sort of.'

'As what?'

'I've been temporarily hired to curate the exhibition. It's been complicated, but also very rewarding.'

'What complications?' he queried.

'Well, I find that I don't know enough about anything.'

'Is it so? But if you put together the exhibition, aren't you supposed to know everything?'

'No, you see, nowadays curating is more about feeling the vibes that objects send out and asking pertinent questions. The idea is not to provide answers, but make the viewers think for themselves. Because how can we know for sure anyway?'

'What vibes are those?'

'A special vibe that things have. It is hard to explain. But you know it when you feel it.'

'Then you might as well exhibit almost any vibrator?' It sounded flaky to him. That wasn't Hari's idea of a museum.

'Any piece would not give *me* the vibe. The vibe has to be … *deep*, you see.'

'I see. It seems *very* interesting.' He decided to play his cards close to the chest. Next Friday was a long way off. Before then he wouldn't get darshan of the Ninth Avatar unless he could slyly get access to it through this lady. 'It's an exhibition of … exactly what?'

'Idols from around the world.'

Before he could ask another question, his phone rang. He checked the screen. It was Diamond. The timing was odd, almost as if she knew that he was chatting with a good-looking Swedish woman.

'Is it your … date? She's late?'

'I'm a bachelor.'

'Ah ... I see ... aren't you going to answer?'

'Wrong number.' He didn't know how to explain to Diamond that he was in a canteen with a lady who was so clearly coming on to him with her talk about vibrating objects. 'Besides, got to take off ... I have a meeting to rush to. I think I am in the wrong café.'

'Okay, it was nice talking to you.'

'Same-same,' he said. She had basically invited him to the exhibition. Mission objective fulfilled. Now he needed a Plan K for how to dupe her into parting with the idol. 'Bye-bye and all the very best.'

To begin with, he must make living arrangements for ten days or so. A budget room within walking distance. If he found one where breakfast was included, he'd stuff his pockets with bananas and survive all day. He walked far and wide – but there wasn't anything akin to Kama Boardless Lodging where dorm beds cost ₹1 an hour.

His phone dinged. A message from Diamond. 'Tried calling. Where R U? Will UB home 4 dinner? I'll fry mackerel 4 U. I bought rich plum cake 4 dessert. Sorry 4 yesterday. Went wrong. Dint mean what I said.'

What to say? That he had unaccountably flown to Sweden? No, not possible. He simply had to sort things out quickly and go home before the mackerel fry got cold and she became angry again.

Evening.

For dinner, he bought a chocolate bar at the convenience store. He tried to bargain, but the girl said, '*Ja*, no discount.'

It cost him a little over ₹100, but there were peanuts in it. As he sat on a park bench, nibbling slowly, it resulted in a feeling of a not-completely-empty tummy. If he ate one chocolate bar per day, he'd spend ₹1,500 on food for two weeks. Homeless people, including the woman and the two boys who had been begging and peddling at the Crossroads, crept up the slope of the park. He followed and picked a sleeping spot away from them in the bushes. It fulfilled his main requirement: it was free. With the World Culture Museum down the road, he'd have access to restrooms in the daytime.

The sun didn't set until after 9 p.m. and even then, it didn't get fully dark. He found it disturbing that there was no proper night. In the end, he slept with his hands covering his eyes, dreaming about piping hot vadai with spicy sambar gravy. He heard noises from the square, people making merry late into the night. Those must be the rich who didn't have to go to work the following day. A little before midnight he woke up frozen and took a walk. It was 5°C according to the neon digits glowing on the board on the wall of a building next to the square. It was the coldest he'd ever experienced. The convenience store was closing and he thought of buying a hot coffee, but resisted the temptation. Maybe he'd treat himself to a cup for breakfast.

The others lived among the bushes in homes made of cardboard, tarpaulin and bin liners. They were also awake, boiling hot soup in tin cans. Hari chatted them up and they turned out to be Romanian. They shared some soup with him. The woman he had seen down in the square, whose name was Candelia, knew English and told Hari that she and her baby daughter were spending the summer holiday in Sweden, but planned to go home when autumn came and she hoped to get a job. She was a certified Montessori teacher. If this was the summer, then Hari didn't want to know what a European winter was like. Candelia asked him what he was doing being homeless so far from India.

He told her that he was a former ATM watchman who had lost the ATM which resulted in an unfortunate chain of events. She didn't press for details.

He slept again under his bush. There was slight rainfall in the wee hours. He woke up soaked to the bone, his feet like lumps of ice. His throat was sore, his nose runny and his ears hurt, and he wasn't sure if he'd survive this until the exhibition opened. He was impressed by how the Romanians handled the hostile climate. Light came by 4 a.m., sunrise was at fiveish and by 6 a.m., the golden blob was already up in the sky. He shivered on a park bench, waiting to thaw. Then the day began with a trickle of noise, not like back home with a tornado of temple chanting, wailing prayer calls, assiduous tongue scraping and throat clearing.

A woman walked her puppy in the park, the first animal he'd seen. The dog sniffed at his toes and she threw a coin at him. He got a bit shocked, but then he thanked her and pocketed the tenner. It was worth something like ₹75. The beggar identity was a good cover. He'd melt into the background. Two more coins and it'd buy a mug of hot coffee. The convenience store was already open and the coffee must be brewing. Gradually vehicles and people passed through the square. Soon he had collected three coins. It was a great beginning for his second day in the country.

At lunchtime, he went to the museum canteen to celebrate with coffee. From its smell, he could tell there was no chicory in the brew. He added so much sugar that it became like sweet porridge. Just as he had finished his cup, he saw the black-clad woman again. She was buying lunch on a tray. And she recognized him. Hari smiled his friendliest tout-grin. He was prepared this time.

Again, she walked up to his table. 'How are you today? Do you mind?'

'Oho please, take a seat. Take two.'

'Thanks, you're not expecting company today?' She seated herself across the table from him. 'Where are you from then, if not Syria?'

His smile was the biggest in Bengaluru, it encircled his entire head twice around, almost chopping his brain off. He thought for a nanosecond whether to use his cover story, but then again if he told her the truth, or suitable parts of it, they might find an excuse to discuss the exhibition's stolen Indian components. So he said, 'India.'

'Yeah? You don't say ...'

'You've heard of India?'

'I almost hoped you'd say that, because you look a bit Indian.'

'I thought I looked *fully* Indian.'

'Yes, I mean – of course. I love India. I tasted such sweet coffee there. Can I buy you a cup?'

His karma was too good. For sure, she had announced that she had taken possession of the stolen idol and its whereabouts on her blog, which had led Hari to this museum. So it hadn't been that hard to track her down. Sweden was a well-organized society where a detective didn't have to run from pillar to post. But now she had walked straight into the trap by sitting at his table. In India, a lone woman would never accost a single man the way she did.

He rolled his head sideways. *But why so tongue-tied?* Hanging out on CD Road, he loved chatting up random foreigners, but for the first time he found it hard to come up with the words. Fish out of water. *What do they do – suffocate?* And get fried in coconut oil.

'Is that a yes or a no?'

'As you like. I take sugar.'

She went back to the counter and fetched him a mug of coffee. She also brought a pile of sugar cubes on a saucer for him. He said, 'So you have gone to India?'

'My god, it was hot. But it was also very … how should I put it? Colourful,' she said and nodded at his neon T-shirt. She herself wore a black T-shirt and black jeans. She grinned. 'Ours is not a colourful country like your India.'

He'd noticed – without really paying attention – that most people out there on the streets wore muted grey, brown, dark blue. Once you thought about it, it was striking how colourless everything was.

She worked at her pie. 'Want some?'

'No, I'm too overstuffed. Resting tummy and digesting. Forgot to bring my antacids. How's the exhibition work going?'

'We'll have a Bollywood-themed party on the opening night. Do come. It's a funny coincidence to meet you here.'

'Very funny. My name is Harry.'

'Harry doesn't sound Indian.'

'My fully proper good name is Hariappa Romeoswamy Casanovajee. I sincerely do hope to see your exhibition before going back.'

'Hey, maybe you can be the chief guest at the inauguration and give a talk on the ancient glory of Indian culture. Do you know a lot about it?'

'Maybe I do. I am very interested in gods.'

'My name is Barbarella. Nice to meet you, Romeo … uh, Harry. Your country is incredible.'

'Isn't it?' he said.

'I remember the saris. And the scents of spices. Cardamom is my favourite. And cinnamon. The gurus, too, but I didn't have time to hang at any ashram. Just saw them on cable TV. I wish I had a guru to teach me the immortal wisdom of nirvana. Do you have one?'

She was talkative and inquisitive, so naturally he wondered if she may have been an Indian in a previous lifetime. If she had been, then her earlier incarnation may have been as a flaky paratha. Not the most intelligent life form on the planet.

'Surely I have. In India, everyone has at least two. Without guru, man is lost. With one guru, you're half lost. With two, you're okay. So you went on holiday?'

'A research trip.'

'Research, oho?'

'Preparing all this, yeah.' She cut off some pie with her spoon and nodded in the direction of the exhibition hall. 'Finding out about this and that. But I'll look for a guru next time I go.'

'A husband can also be like a guru. Did he go with you?'

She shook her head.

'He allowed you to travel alone? No issues?'

'I don't have a ...' She smiled that ironic smile of hers. Then shrugged. 'Yeah.'

'Oho, what happened? He passed. I'm so sorry. Hence you are wearing black only?'

'No ... not at all. There was just no poetry in the relationship anymore, only limericks.'

Although from an academic point of view, Hari didn't understand the words, he got the meaning.

'It is the saddest story I ever heard.'

'No big deal. We just stopped seeing eye-to-eye. After he got prostate gland disorder, he changed. Anyway, yeah, let's talk about something fun instead.'

Prostate gland disorder? Was it possible that she had been dating the undercover cop – Herman Barsk? Hadn't he said he'd been diagnosed? Was that why he hated culture? Because she had dumped him? This was getting too much for Hari. So he gladly changed the subject, 'Are there any interesting exhibits in your exhibition?'

'Many. It's about different religious objects and how they can be good for you. When I was in India I accidentally came across one of the nicest pieces. You won't believe, yeah, but it was sold to me by a man who came up as I was strolling in a bazaar. He claimed it was a hundred years old and had to sell it because his father died, to buy the sandalwood for the pyre, you know. I thought he was bluffing, that it was some kind of newly manufactured copy made to look old. You know?'

'Did it vibrate?'

'Well, I hadn't seen anything quite like it in the souvenir shops. Of course, I bargained. Got it for a song,' she paused, as if thinking back.

'There may be unscrupulous people involved in such affairs.'

'Tell me about it.'

'But I can take a look and verify if it is real. Shall we go to the exhibition hall?'

'It's not in the building.'

So locked up in a bank vault, perhaps. Then she showed him her mobile and on the screen it had a photograph of the Ninth Avatar. 'This is it. Experts on Asian art at the university here felt that it might be a genuine antique. Perhaps a thousand years old! Can you believe it? As if it was meant to happen. What is it that you call it?'

'Karma.'

'Yes, it was that!'

'That happens a lot in India. Everybody gets what they deserve. Next time you come, you will too.' End up in jail for smuggling, he thought to himself. At some level, it also meant that she was innocent; she hadn't known that she was abetting the looting of national heritage – which legally complicated matters. But aloud he said, 'So you had luck with the gods?'

'Yeah, now I feel sorry that I bargained for it. It's as if I cheated that poor seller. He just wanted money and ended up selling me an actual treasure.' But she didn't sound regretful.

'Oho, that's the most amazing thing I ever heard.'

'Isn't it? It was like it was meant to be the centrepiece of my exhibition. But enough about me, let's talk about you. By the way, do you have family here in Sweden?' she said, starting to question him, which he felt somewhat uncomfortable about.

'No.' The only contact details he had were of Farooqi's wife's relative, in whose house he was supposed to sleep on a mat on the floor, but since he had lost the suitcase and whatever contraband it had contained, he thought it best not to get in touch. Then there was that jute-sack business. 'Not here.'

'But in India? Somebody told me you're a billion people. How many of those are you related to?'

'None, I'm an orphan.'

'I see. Do you have children?'

'No.' He didn't know why he lied, it just came out that way.

'Oh yeah, I forgot – you said you were a bachelor. And what brings you to Sweden?'

'Business.'

'What kind?'

'Unfinished.'

'That sounds mysterious,' she said and Hari made a mental note that he shouldn't alert her to any of the dicier aspects of his mission – such as burglarizing her museum and stealing its main attraction.

'It is simply business. Products to import to India, now that our consumer economy has surpassed yours. Not that interesting to talk about.'

'Oh, I must tell you that we don't produce anything in Sweden anymore. Our souvenirs like Dalecarlian horses and Sami handicrafts and ABBA albums are made in China. Even the Volvo car plant is owned by the Chinese. So you must go there if you want something Swedish worth importing. What products are you planning to buy from here?'

'It's a business secret,' he said as he finished the coffee. 'I don't want to bore you with it, but IKEA is opening a shop in Hyderabad and I have to fix the fixing. Hence, I'll take your leave. Thank you for the coffee. Bye-bye and all the very best.'

She smiled that ironic smile. 'Bye then. And see you, yeah?'

She took out a tablet computer and started reading. He wondered about the feeling he was getting. He wished that he was more like Triplex, a man who didn't know the meaning of the word 'bashful'. He'd have seduced the woman and made her hand over the idol as a love token.

While waiting for the exhibition to open, he went around begging in the streets like the other non-Swedes did. It was an affluent town where every second shop was a restaurant. There were wellness centres aplenty run by certified yoga healers, and many takeaway coffee bars. Home decoration shops sold Buddha statues and he contemplated buying one, rather than robbing the museum. But the statues cost a bomb. It'd be cheaper to steal the right one. Whenever he collected enough coins, he went to the museum and had a mug of coffee. In the late afternoon, the canteen was quiet and he could sit and enjoy the warmth for as long as he liked.

One day, the third after his arrival, he saw the Viking cop Herman Barsk in the square. Hari hid behind some bushes up on the slope. Barsk went into the World Culture Museum. When Hari thought about it, he recalled having seen the battered Volvo loop around the square the day before. Was he suffering from persecution mania or was the cop snooping? From then on, he avoided spending too much time at the museum.

His homesickness was strongest at night when he curled up under the bushes and thought of how much he missed his wife, kids and mackerel fry. Whenever bad thoughts entered his mind, he reminded himself of the mission objectives: it helped him to stop bothering about the chill which iced his bones. When he froze too much he walked around in the park to build up body heat and chatted with any Romanian beggar that happened to be awake sniffing glue. He connected with them better than he connected with the Swedes. Candelia told him there were second-hand shops where one could buy almost brand-new clothes. She had noticed that he always wore the same outfit. When he found one such shop he discovered that it was still too expensive for him – a pair of pre-owned pants were almost ₹500 and for that amount one could get two new pairs in Bengaluru. Or two and a half cups of coffee in Sweden.

Sitting with the Romanians, he heard shouts in the square. The Swedes, who were so quiet and focused in the daytime, turned into noisy Vikings at night. He asked Candelia about it. She said they were dangerous when they got drunk and it was better to not make contact with people after dark. One local man had threatened to throw acid on the beggars if they didn't go back to Romania.

Another day, across the cafeteria, he spotted Barbarella. Face tilted down, she spied on him through falls of hair. He nervously turned away, as if she had caught him out. Then *she* sat down at his table *again*.

'Hello there, mysterious stranger.' She smiled. 'Mind if I sit?'

There were, as always, several empty tables in the canteen. He waggled his head.

'Meaning yes? Harry, wasn't it?' she said as if tasting his name between her luscious lips. She had two sandwiches and two coffees on her tray. 'Would you like one? I see you here every day, but you never eat a thing.'

'I'm on a diet. The Bollywood crash diet. One is not supposed to eat anything but bananas. But lots of them. Many different kinds of bananas. However, only before five in the morning.'

'How interesting, maybe we can serve bananas at our Bollywood theme party then, if it continues until the break of dawn? Please, help me with this. I bought two ham-and-brie subs thinking that I was hungry, but I'm not. And take one coffee, too.'

The sandwich was stuffed with creamy cheese and cold meat slices, so not really like eating hot curry with homely pickles.

She went on, 'How long will you be here?'

'Until it is done.'

'I see. Are you enjoying your stay?'

'The thing I regret to say is I miss vada and sambar, or even north Indian dal fry would do if it came with hot rotis, I mean: lentil curry with flat bread.'

'That's all?'

'And gobi manchurian and perhaps Suleiman's goat brain fry, though I am a vegetarian.'

'Fried brain, yeah?' She sounded amused. 'So where do you reside in Gothenburg?'

'I put up around the corner. I have a nice view over the museum.' Self-consciously, he studied his rubber slippers.

At that, she looked at him kind of strange. 'Yeah, so that's why you've been sitting here every day? I wondered. So, you're staying at Gothia Towers? That's a luxurious hotel. And you say you work for IKEA?'

He waggled his head, she was asking too many questions. 'What I'm doing for them is 80 per cent legal. Which reminds me that I have a lunch meeting back at the lodging and boarding house,' he said in order to vamoose before she exposed him as a fraud. Rule one in the college of fraudulence. 'Bye-bye and all the very best.'

'Lunch,' she called after him.

'What's that?'

'How about lunch any day when you don't have another meeting?'

'I'm terribly busy. Every day,' he emphasised.

'Squeeze me in, yeah. Dinner tonight?'

He stopped and plotted. Was it a good or a bad idea? Did she suspect that he had been sent to steal back the Ninth Avatar?

'I insist. I know an Indian restaurant where you get your curry and those other things. And my treat, please. When I went to India, in every souvenir shop, yeah, they gave me free chai. But, you know, I didn't have enough time to find a guru. Maybe you can help me.'

'Sometimes it takes a lot of work to find the right guru. But it is preferable to finding the wrong guru.'

She listened attentively. He decided to play along. Besides, the mere thought of real food made the offer hard to resist. And for free, too.

'Shall we meet in front of the entrance at seven tonight, yeah?'

'Okay,' he said. As he climbed down the wide staircase to the foyer, he brainstormed furiously. Had he tricked the perpetrator into stepping into his trap or was he being entrapped – or had he just agreed to go on a romantic date? Plucked out of his circumstances, his social milieu, he realized how much he was defined by his living environment, the people around him, and CD Road itself. This journey to the West was showing him aspects of himself that he'd been hitherto unaware of. Back there, he was married, a good father, a respectable hero. Here, he was nobody, a beggar – and somebody else was taking shape within him, taking over. How he missed his advisors. Pandit Pundit would surely have had something to say on this matter. Triplex would certainly advise him to do the exact opposite.

Going down the broad stairs of the canteen, he turned and saw Barbarella. She blew him a kiss. No, she was blowing her nose in a paper napkin delicately. He caught his balance and walked straight into the Viking cop.

'Oops. Mister Herman. How is your prostate gland today?' By the time he stopped himself, it was too late. 'I mean general health, career and love life?'

'Mister Capricciosa, well-well. Finally caught you.' Barsk smelt of stale cigarettes and yesterday's souring beer binge.

'It's Casanova actually.'

'Whatever, do you happen to be related to the great opera singer Castrato?'

Strange Freudian slip.

'Why?'

'All of us Swedish cops love opera with our pizza.'

Hari thought for a moment about running, but that might make the situation worse. First, he wasn't 1,000 per cent sure if the civilian cop was stalking him or Barbarella, but if he was her ex-lover, the situation could turn ugly.

'*Höh, höh*. Shall we continue our conversation from that day?'

'For what purpose?'

'I'm keeping an eye on you. What did you speak with that woman about?'

'Just some guest at the canteen, who asked if she could have my table after I was done.' Hari played it down.

'Don't bullshit me.'

'Please go ask her yourself.' The moment the cop climbed up the steps to confront his ex-girlfriend, Hari would make his famous disappearing act – maybe even fly back to India with the next available plane. Or if there were no flights, he'd flap his arms until he reached Punjab and then simply walk down the Grand Trunk Road.

'You come with me,' said Barsk.

He meekly followed.

21

There are going to be problems and you're going to be given the choice to do or die.

Barsk walked him out of the safety of the building and without a word he continued round the back of the building. Hari followed.

'Where are we going?'

'*Höh*, I can't put my finger on it,' Barsk said.

'On what?'

'What you're up to?' he said, giving Hari the uncomfortable feeling that he was close to being arrested. 'What's your business in that museum? I went inside the other day and saw nothing of interest.'

'Their coffee is too good.'

'No, it ain't. Instant coffee is better.'

Behind the museum was one of those grey parking lots that Hari had gotten used to seeing everywhere. Cars were so well provided for that he found himself wishing he was a small car rather than a human, maybe one of those electric models. Then he could park himself anywhere and, instead of starving, plug his nostrils into an electric socket.

'Somehow I can't believe that you're an Italian ... or a cop for that matter.'

Neither could Hari believe that the middle-aged human wreck that was taking him towards the rickety old Volvo was a cop. The rest of the country was in such tiptop shape and this product of extensive inbreeding amongst local constabulary had tagged himself onto Hari for no reason ever since he had got off the plane. Just his luck. Then an ominous thought struck him: *Was Barsk a narc?* Was he investigating Farooqi's suitcase case? It would explain his presence near the airport the day Hari landed. 'I may not exactly be a cop.'

'What's that supposed to mean?'

'I often work with them as a dietician to help them lose weight.'

'But you're here on holiday you say, *höh*?' He unlocked the Volvo and shoved Hari into the passenger seat. Barsk sat on the driver's side and grabbed a flagon from under the seat. It had no label, but Hari feared the worst. 'Cat got your tongue?'

Hari waggled his head. 'No cat, prefer dog. Am I under arrest or something?'

'Not necessarily, unless you feel that I should arrest you. Should I?'

'On what grounds?'

'You tell me. Are you from Syria?'

He had heard that one before. Suddenly, he couldn't be sure if Barsk was a conman enacting some nefarious 'fake cop targeting tourist' scheme. He suspected it was too late, and risky, to ask to see Barsk's badge.

'We keep an eye on people coming from Syria. The town is crawling with jihadists. One of those terror travellers, are you?'

'Not at all ... I just travelled here to enjoy myself.'

'Don't lie. Your idea of fun is to ram a truck into innocent bystanders, *höh*? What mobile phone are you using?'

'Why, a nice Nokia, I believe it is a local brand.'

'It's a bloody Finnish phone. Show it to me.'

Hari did so: a basic semi-smartphone model produced for the Indian market.

'You're lucky. Had it been a Nokia 105 RM-908, I'd have had no choice but to arrest you. There is one more thing you can do to clear your name, Mister Noodle-hair.'

'What does my phone have to do with anything?'

'The 105 RM-908 is the model favoured by terrorists. One of those and a pressure cooker is enough to make a bomb.'

'Well, so I must be innocent then.'

'Prove it.'

'Like how?'

'Like have a drink.' From the glove compartment, Barsk took two paper cups and from the flagon he poured an oversized drink of clear spirit that could only be described as a maxed-out Patiala peg.

'I don't drink.'

'Why not?'

'It is a matter of principle.'

'You can if you are who you claim to be.' Barsk himself stuck to instant coffee. He mixed two spoons of powder and poured water from a thermos flask in his paper cup. 'Confiscated that from a smuggler down by the harbour, *höh*, good stuff.'

'You're not having a peg with your cuppa?' said Hari.

Barsk shook his head. 'It would create problems.'

'You don't even take milk in your coffee?'

Barsk repeated the headshake. An avalanche of dandruff showered over Hari and whitened the coffee in Barsk's paper cup.

'Are you a recovering alcoholic? My uncle was one too, until he died from the recovery side effects.'

'I'm Swedish and we never recover.'

'How do you mean?'

'We call it being "dry alcoholic" if we delude ourselves about having recovered. I'm a "wet" one, but can't risk it during working hours. If they put me through a breathalyzer test, I'd lose my job.'

'Oho. That'll surely reflect badly on the force. I think I'll also stick to coffee.'

'*Höh*, do you now? But I want to see you empty that bottle and show me that you're not a terrorist.'

'Is it necessary?'

'You've never had a drink in Syria?'

'I've never been to Syria.'

'So all I'm saying is prove it. Bottoms up.'

'Why would that prove anything?'

'It proves that you're not one of those non-drinking fundamentalists coming here to blow up that museum. Not that I'd bother. Art, all fake. Literature, all lies. But if you drink up, I won't have to take you in.' Barsk lit a ciggie. 'Your choice.'

Hari touched the brimming paper cup to his lips. He was wary of drinking with drunkards. Even more if the drunkards were cops. But he saw no alternative. He had read online about the West's global war on terrorism and didn't want to end up in some camp where non-whites got tortured. If proving oneself to be an alcoholic was what it took to survive in Sweden, then .... he downed the beverage. The liquor burnt his throat and hit his tummy.

'Very tasty.'

Barsk poured him another and relaxed. 'I don't mean to offend. But take one more.'

'No problem,' said Hari, as the moonshine ate into his innards. It was so potent that he felt his own heartbeat through his asshole, then a faint rattle as if he were about to shit in his pants, and finally the booze fumes exited as a sneaky fart that licked his underpants. This booze had the same uric-acidic texture as Old Monk, which used to be his uncle's favourite beverage, rum so vile it surprised him that the bottles it was served in hadn't already died of cirrhosis.

Barsk sipped his coffee. '*Höh*, didn't mean to behave like a racist, but one can't be too cautious. I am the last person in the world to distrust another person because he happens to be of the wrong colour. But these days, you can't trust anybody, not even yourself. But I think you're okay.'

'You do?' That was a relief.

'Also, until now you haven't been picked up by security cameras buying a pressure cooker. The secret service keeps tabs on who buys them. Shops automatically red-flag customers, especially if they have Muslim names like yours, Mister Ravioli.'

'Oho, I didn't know they are used only for bomb-making here. In my native place, we boil rice in them.'

'Be that as it may, if you had bought one, I'd have had orders to take you down.'

'Why?'

'If you did anything suspicious like use the pressure cooker.'

'Oho, even if I only boiled rice in it?' Hari was pretty sure the Viking cop was delusional. His wife used pressure cookers all the time and nobody had taken her down. 'That's the only thing we use them for at home.'

Barsk stared at him for a few beats. Then he appeared to relax. 'Our city used to be paradise on earth when I was a kid, *höh*, but now it is a multicultural hell full of beggars, pickpockets, prostitutes, gangsters and football hooligans. Nobody goes to church. *Höh*, I saw on the telly that the troubles in the Middle East are spreading this way. And we don't want to deal with that on top of everything.' The booze settled within Hari and his skin glowed, so he nodded politely as he listened to the rant, which wasn't uninteresting per se: it taught him a lot about Europe's mental health status. 'Nothing wrong with foreigners otherwise, except that one can't trust you. The way you dress, rubber sandals and all, I couldn't help but draw my conclusions. I got limited time left to save the world – health issues, you know. *Höh*, so I figured if you were one of those terrorists and I bagged you, it'd have been nice.'

'Boss, that would have been wonderful.'

Barsk had another instant coffee. Hari wondered how long it would be before he could excuse himself. But the cop went on about his prostate, then about his diabetes, and finally about his wife leaving him. 'She refused to kiss me at the wedding. We were barely married for two weeks before she met somebody else,' he said as he stared with his maniac eyes into Hari's face. It was hard to sit close to him, because his teeth were in a third-world condition and his breath smelt of untreated cavities. No wonder his wife had second thoughts.

'I too have some trouble with the wife. Have you remarried?'

'Planning to get a dog, cheaper maintenance.' Barsk toasted him with his coffee and Hari felt obliged to down another gulp. 'If I do, I'm going to call it Bobby. Bobby, get it? Like the British coppers.'

'Dogs are nice.'

'Want to see my gun?' Barsk pulled the Sig Sauer out of his armpit. It looked sweaty.

Hari reached out to touch it.

'*Ajabaja*, no feeling! You're not allowed to finger everything you see. It can get you into trouble,' said Barsk. 'Instead of staying at a hotel, why not crash at my place? You can use the sofa. Ever since my wife left me I've been ... lonely.'

Barsk had to get back to work and drove off after giving Hari his address. The key would be under the doormat. Hari thought about it for a moment, but decided to rather crawl up the slope to his bush – he was badly drunk – but they all looked the same, or maybe he was seeing double. In the thick undergrowth, he found a nest of cardboard and slipped into a deep coma. He awoke with a serious headache and a random Romanian fretting over him sleeping inside the wrong cardboard box.

It was ... bedtime? Hard to tell in this country where the sun barely set. Hari checked the clock on his phone. Past seven. No time to lose. He rushed down to the museum entrance. It was locked. At first, he didn't see her, then he noticed two women smoking one cigarette at the corner. He rubbed his eyes and they merged into one single woman. With two cigarettes, one that she handed him.

'Hello,' he said and pretended to be sober. The best way to do so was to keep one's mouth shut. But it wasn't in his nature. 'What a lovely night, right?'

She looked him up and down as he brushed grass and dirt from his neon tee, which wasn't as clean as it had been on the day he landed.

'I take it you don't have a bicycle?'

He shook his head. At which it nearly fell off from his shoulders. No, he was missing something else ... his balance. He held on to the wall. 'Sorry, had a stressful afternoon so I didn't have time to steal one.'

'Steal?'

'Borrow, I meant. I mean, rent.'

'Maybe we can do this another time. You look unwell.'

'No-no, boss, I'm *fine-dine.*' He did an appropriate mudra which mesmerized her like a swaying cobra.

'Then let's go to Masthugget,' she said. 'Have you been there yet?'

Hammers and tongs were at work on the cogwheels of his brain. 'Is it a nice place-space?'

'That's where the cool hangouts are, yeah. I know one Indian bar. Their food is really spicy. You're gonna love it.'

She left her bicycle at the museum and they took a tram. They sat at the rear. Despite dizziness, Hari understood they were going to some Majestic type of area where there were Indian bars. He anticipated a feeling of normality, of bazaars and noise and the flavour of homely edibles. As he watched Barbarella, he thought to himself: *she's beautiful.* Then he thought to himself: *I must not think so.*

'I saw you meet up with your business contact at the museum. You guys had a "wet" lunch?'

'It is possible,' said Hari and she smiled.

'I wasn't sure if you were making things up when you spoke about doing business. A bit shady, that IKEA guy.'

'Oho, super-shady middleman. Let's not talk more about dirty business.' Hari found grammatical sentences containing polysyllabic words hard to put together. He desperately needed coffee. There should be coffee at the Indian restaurant, with 60 per cent chicory and too much sugar. He relaxed and dozed off.

At some point, she shook him awake. 'Hey, we're getting off here!'

Hari was too slow to react and by the time she pushed him towards the doors, they shut in his face. Bengaluru buses never shut their doors. Even when they moved one was allowed to get on and off, he explained to her.

'This is Sweden,' she said.

'Okay sorry, I thought we were going to some Indian neighbourhood where things might be normal.'

'It's all right; we'll get off at the next stop and walk back.'

They reached a large square where a lot of people milled about. It had a fountain with sculptures to remind people of Sweden's glorious colonial past. She said, 'This here is called the Iron Square. It used to be a bit of a downmarket area, but now it's gentrified and nice.'

'Even our slums are developing,' said Hari.

Though not like this one. Almost every building had a fancy bar on its street level and people drifted from one to the next. Some sat in pavement cafés, shivering in spite of being wrapped up in thick quilts, and drinking cold white wine and chilled beers. She walked him to a quiet side street not far from the tram stop. There was a red brick building across from a parking lot.

'This is where I live. Maybe you'd like to wash yourself ... before dinner?'

'Very good idea.' He hadn't washed himself properly since he left home. He asked, 'But won't your reputation suffer?'

'Why would it?'

'If the neighbours see a stranger entering your apartment.'

'Yeah, no,' she burst out laughing. 'I don't have much of a reputation to worry about.'

'Oho.' He wondered if she meant what he thought she meant.

Her apartment was huge ('I share it with an aboriginal didgeridoo player who is on tour back home in Australia,' she said and he wondered what that meant), but cosy with an oriental rug on the floor, a glass-topped dining table and several antique carved wooden chairs, sari cloth hanging from the curtain rods, sea shells and crystal stones on the window sills. She lit a perfumed candle that gave off a faint odour of cardamom. On the coffee table, an Oriental manuscript, richly illuminated with *Kama Sutra* figures, lay open. She took him to the bathroom. He sobered up during the shower. Afterwards, he found that she had laid out a dark grey shirt and black jeans on her double bed. The socks and black leather boots felt odd on his feet, but, on the other hand, his toes didn't freeze.

She was smoking in the kitchen. An exhaust fan over the oven was whirring. 'They don't allow smoking really, too many allergies ... as if inhaling my second-hand smoke might lead to gluten intolerance in the building.'

'Oho? Is it so?'

'But smoking on the balcony is too damn cold. I think you've been wearing the same clothes for ...'

'As it happened, my suitcase got stolen.'

'I'll put them in the laundry.'

They turned the corner of the house, past a shop with strange mannequins in rainbow-coloured tees that said, 'Being Straight Is Not Normal', and walked down a back street until they reached the promisingly named Mummy-ji ka Thali Pub which was a tidy place with a big window facing the street, five tables and a bar counter. 'Here is where I go when I don't feel like cooking,' she quipped. 'But this is a bar street patrolled by Nazis, so it's better you don't come on your own.'

There were fancier eateries in Bengaluru and many streets where you didn't have to die, but he didn't mention that. When they were offered the menu, Hari waved it away and ordered spicy churmuri chaat, a plate of idli-vada, and six filter-coffees. He urgently needed to feel flavours in his mouth. He explained to Barbarella that vada were 'deep-fried savoury donuts, the greatest delicacy' but it turned out that a plate of vada was something like ₹1250.

He immediately cancelled the order.

'Eighteen-rupee set dosa?' he tried.

'You could go for the vegetarian Taj Mahal special thali,' suggested the waiter.

They ended up having Barbarella's favourites, tandoori king prawns, palak paneer and garlic naan. She ordered a bottle of red wine to go with the food.

'Atmosphere is calm here,' commented Hari, who had gotten used to the evening noise from the Crossroads. 'How thoughtful of you to buy clothes for me!'

'No worries. They're my ex's.'

'Oho, meaning?'

'Ex-partner's.'

'Oops. Won't he get angry?'

'He's not coming back. Besides, I paid for them.'

The partner's clothes fit him, but wearing a stranger's briefs weirded him out. Hopefully, they had been washed in disinfectant or he too might get infected with prostate gland illness.

'So no family?'

'My ex has the kids, mostly. We were never married, really. Just one of those things that happened.'

To make small talk, Hari continued, 'So the … uh,' he was about to say bastards but corrected himself in the last moment, 'kids don't see you much. That must be hard.'

'They come visit me sometimes, but they live on another planet.'

'Oho, which planet is that?'

'It is called Counter-Strike. They want us to go for some championship in Tokyo, but I can't afford it. Why travel so far just to play a computer game? When I have enough money, I'd rather go back to India and find myself a guru who can guide me to nirvana. I'm a bit wild myself.' She giggled.

'So what does your, eh, ex-non-husband do? Can't he take them to Tokyo?'

'He gets sickness benefit from the state.'

'Wonderful. Is he a cop?'

'No, a literary critic. You could say he's policing the writers, yeah. Why don't you tell me about yourself instead?'

'My uncle raised me. His family were peasants.'

'What kind of animals did they keep?'

'Mosquitoes.'

'What on earth for?'

'They bred them and milked them, and sold the produce to blood banks at hospitals.'

'Oh? But I thought you said that you didn't have any family?'

'It is hard to explain. But yes, he is fully dead.'

They were alone in the small restaurant, except for the one waiter at the cash and takeaway counter and a chef by the tandoor. He had travelled across half the world in pursuit of this woman and now she had – what? – taken him out for an Indian-style date in the local version of the Majestic area.

But once he tucked into the grub he was in a heaven where the gods engineered godly things. There was mango pickle, too, and everything was wonderful. He regaled her with stories of his heroics, described the genuine Indian dishes he'd treat her to when she came to 'the B'luru' next.

A Bangladeshi couple walked in and chatted with the cashier in Sylheti. They parcelled tandoori paneer.

Then she and he were alone again, and she talked about her student years. It turned out that Barbarella wasn't her original name. She was plain Lydia and had moved to town from a small place up in the north, to study theatre. She wanted to become a director 'like Ingmar Bergman'. So in order to further her career, she changed her name from the grandmotherly Lydia to something more dramatic: Barbarella. Unfortunately, her career never took off, so she opted to work as a part-time helper in an art gallery. She had an aptitude for that because now she had a project-based employment at the museum. If all went well, she might get a permanent job.

Everything was perfect until, towards the end of the meal, Barbarella happened to look out through the window and into the gathering dusk. 'Oh damn, not again.'

'What's wrong?'

Under a street lamp on the other side stood a bald man in leather jacket and jeans.

'Is that a friend of yours?'

'Not exactly,' she said and frowned over the wine goblet. 'I wouldn't call him that.'

'Shall I take care of that man?'

The doorbells jingled.

'*Hej* Lydia,' he said as he came to the table. He exchanged a few words in runes with Barbarella and evil eyes with Hari. He was quite impressive in his rough outfit, shaved skull with a tattoo across it of a Swedish flag which was bright blue with a yellow cross, and a great Viking beard.

She replied with fewer words. Hari guessed the meaning of some – like 'Indien'. Then the man faced him. 'So you're from India?'

'Approximately.'

'My name is Jesper Knödelbödel. Remember that name. And what the hell do you think you're doing?'

'Meaning?'

'Those there are my clothes you're wearing. And that's my wife you're having dinner with.'

'Jesper, for fuck's sake, I'm not your wife, I've never been and will never be. I may be the mother of your children, but we were a mistake. We've gone over this. Please leave.'

'I haven't finished speaking to your new "special" friend. Did Lydia tell you that I backpacked in India in the 1990s?

Whereabouts are you from?'

Hari was about to say Bengaluru, but changed it to 'a place near My-sore', pronouncing the town's name the way tourists did and because he knew that town was more popular with tourists.

'Oh yeah, been there.' Jesper pulled up a chair.

Barbarella got up from hers.

'We're leaving. Come, Harry.' She went to the cash register to take the bill.

'Yes, you go Harry,' Jesper mocked. He followed them to the counter and ordered an Indian Pale Ale and told the waiter to put it on Barbarella's tab. She didn't object.

'Cool down,' said Hari as parting words to Jesper and then he scooted out through the door, after Barbarella.

Jesper stayed back, nursing his beer.

'So that was your, eh, non-husband?'

'He's the biggest asshole on earth. I'm sorry about that,' she said. 'Jesper has problems.'

'What's his problem?'

'Me. I suffer from commitment phobia. I hate clingy people.'

'Oho. Do you want me to go back there and take care of him?'

'No, let him take care of himself.' They walked in silence to her house and he thought of the long way he had to go to get back to the Crossroads, only to crash in the bushes. But she said, 'It's too early to call it a night. Come upstairs for a nightcap?'

'I have duties.'

'How about tea then? I can make chai with cardamom flavour; I bought the spice mix in India.'

'Sorry, I prefer coffee.'

'I got an espresso maker for Christmas from my parents. How do you like your coffee?'

'With milk.'

'It heats the milk too, so I can offer you a frothy cappuccino.'

It was an offer he couldn't refuse.

22

> Spiritual pursuits come to the forefront, so keep your mind clean because if dirt enters it you may face trouble.

She asked him if he preferred soy or oat milk with the coffee. She didn't use cow's milk and Hari liked that thought – an act of kindness towards cows. But then she explained that it was due to allergies that nobody drank cow's milk in Gothenburg. It sounded as if there was something wrong with the karma here. He sat on the sofa, planning how to get her to take him to where the Ninth Avatar was stored, whether it was in some vault under the museum or at the university being examined by experts. Preferably ASAP. Although he didn't want to sabotage her exhibition, because she was good-hearted and he had truly enjoyed the meal, he had no choice.

Pouring herself a big glass of rosé wine with a slice of orange in it, she lowered the ceiling light with an advanced electronic dimmer and put on Ravi Shankar's otherworldly ragas –

she streamed them from her phone that she plugged into a docking station.

'In India, we have pirated CD records,' he uttered in order to have something to say. 'There used to be cassettes when I was a child.'

The coffee was too good, with plenty of hot milk that diluted the decoction suitably. She sat down next to him.

'That is so retro!' she said. 'I think you're a saint jay si!'

'Uh, what?'

'Sing yes? I heard about these in India. I met some at the Villa Pottipatti hotel in Bangalore ... they came from America to take initiation.'

'Ah, you mean sannyasi?'

'Yes, that's them. You've got to tell me everything.'

'Meaning?'

'Somebody must have given *you* the sacred initiation.' She poked a manicured forefinger into his chest.

'Ah yes, the saint's name is Sri Pandit Pundit-ji.'

'Sir Funny-funny, what a lovely name. And he must have an ashram, then?'

'Yes, indeed.'

'What's it called then?'

'Ah, it is known to pilgrims as Sri Puncherwallah Complex. Many tourists come from Hollywood to visit it.'

'You know what I'm going to do? I'll start saving right away so that I can go to this Sir Funny-complex Ashram and join it and give up this earthly life. You know, we don't have holy men here in Sweden.'

'You don't?'

'Being a priest here is like any job, technically even atheists can apply for the position ... if they need a job.'

He couldn't believe what he was hearing. 'But how do the gods feel about that?'

'Nobody asks them. People believe that god can't feel because he doesn't exist in the first place. Only humans can feel god if they think they feel his vibes. It's a private thing.'

'But that's total blasphemy. So how about the female gods? Are they also being treated like nothing?'

'We don't have any.'

'That's undemocratic,' said Hari.

She stared at him for a blink. 'So explain how this guru thing works.'

'It is basically very simple.'

'I thought it was complicated,' she said and downed her wine, then refreshed her glass from the bottle she had kept on the coffee table. Drops of wine splattered on the copy of *Kama Sutra* and Hari averted his eyes from the nude figures on the page. He noticed that each move Barbarella made gave her slacks an ever increasing wedgie and her boobies beckoned him.

He tried to sound pompous. 'Essentially, when we surround ourselves with material objects, we form *attachments*, which lead to desire, self-deception and madness. Humans are self-destructive. So my guru helps me with that.'

She played with his shirt buttons. Though strictly speaking, they were Jesper Knödelbödel's buttons and she had paid for them, so he couldn't say no. 'And how does he help us understand our attachments to other *people*?'

'You see, all humans are variations of yourself. So to know another, like your mother, you only need to figure out who you are. The rest will follow.' He sipped on the delicious coffee and felt happy to chat with Barbarella. She didn't question everything he said. Unlike his wife. He was already regretting that he'd have to betray Barbarella.

She beamed at him triumphantly and undid one of Jesper's shirt buttons. 'I couldn't help noticing that you've been around a lot.'

'Oho, me? Around where?' *Now what?* Perhaps there were CCTV cameras in the museum canteen.

'Around me. Practically every day. Admit it.'

He waggled his head noncommittally.

'You often come to the museum, as if you had some special interest ... an *attachment* perhaps.'

'Meaning?' He inched away.

She took a swig and moved closer. 'I think you've been watching me, checking if I'd make a fine disciple, my guru.'

'Uh, yes. Of course, I have.'

She whispered hoarsely, 'I find you attractive too.'

'God's love is attractive.' He took a deep breath and blurted it out, 'Since I am a spiritual type, I was curious about the Indian idol you told me that you had found.'

'Oh guru! Would you like to see it?' she said, overjoyed.

'Well, if you insist.'

'I'd love to have your opinion on it. It'd mean much to me, since you are my guru now.'

'Is it so?'

'Yeah, I must write about it in the press release on Monday, but I don't know much about the mythology surrounding that kind of idol. It'd be good to have an interesting story about it, so that the exhibition gets a lot of write-ups.'

'In that case, it shall be my honourable duty to help you. Shall we proceed to the bank vault then?' he asked, glad that they'd be distancing themselves from the sofa.

She held up a hand, palm facing him, and, after another sip, walked across to a bookcase in the corner. No, she didn't walk – she sashayed like a ramp model. She unlocked a drawer and took out a small object, about as big as a thumb. It looked familiar, but for some reason he had expected it to be bigger.

'What do you think?' She handed him the idol as if one could touch it with one's bare hands. 'We tentatively identified it as a miniature of excellent north Indian craftsmanship. But what I don't understand is how it came to be in a bazaar in south India.'

Did it really vibrate or were his hands trembling? Despite its diminutive size it was surprisingly solid. The features were finely drawn, the statue itself was verdigris green, but he also spotted the yellow jewels in the eye sockets. He had thought it was going to be a bulky sculpture that'd fill a suitcase – but it was pocket-sized. No wonder it had been pilfered easily from the temple.

He had to go about this cleverly. He weighed every word. 'Actually, it is correct that it was made in north India proper and, hence, was transported to the south about one thousand years back, give or take a year or two.'

'How can you tell?'

'See, in those times, there was much turmoil in the north. So we have a legend of three saints who followed the voices of gods.'

'Yeah, we also have a legend of three holy men. But they chased a star.'

'That sounds like sci-fi, but these were real. Recently, I met a baba who told me how this sacred idol was kept hidden from invading idol-breakers. Dressed up as beggars, they rode on second-hand camels for many days through deserts and braved storms in the mountains, until one day they reached a place outside B'luru. A lovely temple had just been built – so the three sacred men moved in with this one.'

'Yeah?'

'I think it may be the same one.'

'But how did it end up with that fellow in the bazaar?' She peered down into her glass.

'There's only one possible answer and I think you too know what I mean.'

She became very severe.

'As a rule, we obtain things through trusted middlemen. Nowadays, for example, one wouldn't dare to buy objets d'art from Syria. The militants there turn their heritage into a source to fund wars. One Syrian came to me recently and offered to sell a stone tablet from 8500BC. Can you believe that?'

There were many things he could believe. He knew laws were toothless when it came to international heritage smuggling despite the UNESCO prohibition against illicit trade in stolen cultural property that he'd read about online.

She asked, 'So do you think the seller stole this … god?'

'That would make possession of it illegal and you'd be liable for prosecution next time you set foot in India. The Interpol would in that case already have issued a Red Corner Notice. Have you spotted any mysterious men outside your apartment or the museum?'

'No, but …' She stared at him.

'Very good then, nothing to worry about.'

'Yeah, but I think I'll go to the police station tomorrow and hand it in anyway, if you suspect it is stolen. It might be the safest thing to do.'

That would also be the end of it. He quickly added, 'No-no, don't do that.'

'What for?'

'The baba told me that after the big battle of 1799 there was a lot of looting. Hence, it is likely that an ancestor of the seller stole it over 200 years ago. Maybe his grandfather was a camp-follower who snatched whatever he could lay his hands on.'

'That still means it's stolen.'

He had to think up a Plan L. He improvised. 'Yes, in a way but so long ago that the period for prosecution would have expired. What matters is the curse.'

'The curse?'

'The gods predict disaster for any mortal who attempts to remove their images from sacred dwellings. It may cause delusions that endanger your mental health or that of visitors at the exhibition, leading to divorces and maybe even suicides. Have you had strange dreams lately?'

She continued staring at him, her tongue flicked across her moist lips, and then she cast down her green eyes and took a quick sip of her wine.

'I knew it,' he said.

'So it is an unlucky god? And I wanted to call the exhibition "The World of Lucky Gods" and now you say that anyone who sees it will fall sick.'

'There is a remedy,' he added. 'Once we cleanse it, it will be a lucky god. The bad luck will end up with the man who sold it to you, because it is the person who uses it for monetary gain, the one who has attachment to the material world, who will suffer the most. It is also important to note that until it has been purified, you should not show it to a living soul.'

'I let the experts at the university see it. What about them?'

'Please do not count them as living souls any longer.'

She gasped. 'And I've seen it.'

'Don't worry, I'm here and I'm a certified hero. My guru taught me how to remove curses.'

'Could you do it?'

'Sure, I can fix anything and also give it a thorough cleaning so it'll look brand new when you exhibit it.' He recalled the scam that had been perpetrated on Tulsi by the jewel-cleaners from Agra and thought it could work here, too. Besides, he did genuinely worry that the curse of the Ninth Avatar might strike Barbarella. She had been good to him. And the only way to protect her would be to take the statuette away from her, he rationalized.

'What equipment do you need?' There was something endearingly childlike about her.

He used that as a lever to tilt her mind upside down. 'Special herbs. Turmeric powder. Plastic boxes.'

'I have Tupperware. And there's a spice jar in the kitchen.'

'Sooper, and I can go tomorrow morning and collect the herbs.' He had seen all kinds of things growing in the park near the Crossroads. He'd come back and swipe the statuette – perfect.

'That'd be great,' she agreed.

He thought so too and he now had his Plan M in place for how to make a clean getaway. From now on nothing could go wrong. He excused himself to visit the bathroom, texted Doc his passenger number and asked him to log on to the airline website and alter the booking, prepone the flight home. He'd go back as soon as the statuette was in his hands and then rescue his marriage.

He stepped out of the bathroom and found that Barbarella had changed into flimsy silk pyjamas. She poured herself the last dregs from the bottle and toasted him. 'To your health, my guru.'

She seemed to be in a romantic mood.

'I hope you don't think I'm a loose woman, but I put in a diaphragm.'

He quickly googled his mind and recalled having read about female contraceptives. He blushed. She misinterpreted it.

'Okay, come on,' she said. 'We're both mature and consenting.'

'Come where?' Hari heard his own heartbeat – a kind of hoarse techno rhythm with minor arrhythmia. It sounded familiar, it was the soundtrack of a movie item number. *Coma, Coma … Prema.* He was torn between conflicting emotions, one of which was represented by a one-mile erection that tented his pants.

'I'll be a tiny bit frivolous tonight for your sake,' she said. She removed the push up bra and her boobs fell into his hands.

This was a necessary step for his development into a superior human being, resisting temptation and all that. But flirting a little with a foreigner was perhaps a small sacrifice to make for the greater common good, he convinced himself. When in Gothenburg, you didn't do as a South Indian did. He squeezed.

'Let me make one thing clear,' she said, tipsily. 'Don't think that you're the one taking advantage.'

He removed his hands from her chest and hid them behind his back. 'Please don't mistake, I was trying to check if you have a pure heart.'

'Don't be sorry. When I travelled in America I heard worse pickup lines.' With that, she threw herself on top and started touching him inappropriately. *Bad, bad*, he told his brain but his eyeballs bounced out of their sockets and suckled on Barbarella's wine-red lips. This wasn't necessarily love, but sometimes a man had to do what he had to.

Morning after. He had a steaming cup of cappuccino before his nose. This was nicer than waking up huddled under a bush surrounded by snoring Romanians. But mentally, once the gears started clicking, he was in a worse-off state. What a polished gem his wife was in comparison with this single mother who was estranged from her own kids. Together with his wife, he'd experienced so much true love. This was like eating broiler instead of desi murgh. He had been unfaithful for the first – and last – time. But for the first time since he got married, he had been very drunk. That explained it.

So, on closer inspection, it was one of those you-know-exactly-what-kind-of-mornings when the brain smog hung low and every thought sounded like a burp. He checked his phone and noticed that in the drunken euphoria of last night he had sent an SMS to Triplex, bragging about how much XXX-fun he was having. He regretted it now. 'Don't you have to go to work?'

'It's Sunday. Sundays are for special breakfasts.' From the freezer she took out a carton of strawberries.

'Oho.' Her silk pyjamas was transparent in the light from the window and instantly he felt physical activity going on in his own body.

She returned to the bed with a bottle of champagne that she uncorked and she threw frozen strawberries in each glass. He decided to play it by ear. Aloud he said, 'The auspicious muhurat for Yogic practice is one and a half hours before dawn and unfortunately, we missed it.'

Today, he was too sober to fall in love again. However, on her insistence, he accepted a glass of the fizzy beverage. Already with the first sip, the sour champagne bubbled up through his tear ducts. As a breakfast, ice-cold strawberries in champagne was a tad disappointing: he'd have to download recipes and teach her to cook dosa. He said, 'Rather than wasting a beautiful day in bed, why don't we practice austerities? Speaking of which, don't forget to launder my clothes, so that Mister Jesper can get his garments back.'

'You're so full of awareness.' She hugged him. 'I'm so lucky to have met you.'

What was he doing? he asked himself as they kissed. Here he was acting as if there was something going on between the two of them. He pulled away. *Behave yourself*, he told himself.

'What happened?' she said.

'Let me go and collect the required herbs with a clean soul while you do the laundry,' he said and got dressed and escaped with a pounding heart.

He could explain away a mildly flirty infidelity case or at least Triplex would pooh-pooh a fling, but a repeated offence was a different ballgame that meant crossing a border that should not be crossed. As soon as the door shut behind him, he told himself not to go back in there. Ever. It was the curse of the idol, leading him astray. He'd rather sleep with a hundred Romanians in the bushes than spend another night in Barbarella's bed. On the other hand, if he walked away, his journey would end in failure. He had to have that idol.

A man accosted Hari in the stairwell. Hari thought he'd seen him before, but couldn't immediately place him: bald with a tattooed skull, big bushy beard, eyes wild as if he hadn't slept all night, dressed in a heavy leather jacket.

When Hari was about to push open the street door, the man blocked his way. 'Excuse me.'

'Yes,' said Hari.

'Harry, isn't it?'

'Yes, I'm quite famous.' Right then there was a lot going on inside his head.

'Let's have man-to-man talk, shall we? Old Beefeater Inn on the corner has Guinness on tap. They'll be opening about now. How about you buy me one?'

'I'm a teetotaller.'

'What's that supposed to mean?'

'I don't drink.'

'You looked merry yesterday.'

Part of his blackout from the previous night cleared and he recognized the literary critic with the prostate disorder. Back home, a cuckolded husband would have pulled out his machete, but this wilted lover wanted a free beer. On second thought, there was no need to complicate the situation any further. He deliberated whether to take up the peace offer and buy that Guinness and be quits with Jesper. How much would it cost? 'Jesper, was it?'

'Listen, you know what first went through my mind when I saw you with her at the restaurant? I made calculations.'

'Oho, is it so?' Hari had guessed it: mentally the man was a pocket calculator. He himself was always making calculations for various odds and reincarnation options, too, so it piqued his curiosity.

'I noticed from your way of eating that you're right-handed, so I have to block that arm first, then punch you in the spine to break it clean off. You'd be gone for good.'

The wrong man to go out and have a beer with. But aloud he said, 'That's advanced thinking. But a vertebra is worth forty-three dollars only as long as it is unbroken.'

'I don't necessarily have to break it if you stay away from her, you hear.'

'But she's just a friend.'

'Allow me to laugh. She cares for you as little as she cares for me. She's naive and egoistic, she's not a woman – she's a world war. That's why she threw me out. She'll discard you too when she has had enough.'

Hari waggled his head and offered sound logistic feedback. 'Surely she'll get angry if you break my spine. I suspect it'll destroy your chances of winning her back.'

Jesper started breathing heavily.

'A friendly warning, next time I see you leave her apartment, you watch out.'

Hari walked off. Probably best to avoid this man … pretend he didn't exist. In the street, he felt safer. There were other Swedes, not a lot of them, but the occasional one who might intervene if the ex-partner went ahead with breaking his spine. He saw a green area uphill to the right. There'd be grass and flowers there.

23

> Think big, act bigger and the results can be spectacular.

It was beautiful in an ugly way. He'd never seen anything like it in India. It had large green salad type leaves at the base and a big yellow flower with a soft cushion at its centre. When he broke the stem, milky goo oozed out of it. Perfect. They grew abundantly, too, so he collected a bunch before he headed back to the apartment, hoping that things had cooled off.

'These are common dandelions,' said Barbarella, in a fault-finding mood since he hadn't consented to romance in the morning.

'In my native place, they are called "soma". The juice has magical properties,' he bluffed. Why did women always get so irritated with him?

'Yeah and I've heard one can brew wine from them and get pissed.' She had uncorked another bottle.

He used her mixie to prepare a potion from the dandelions and asked her if her ex-partner was dangerous, or if he'd ever threatened her, and she lay back on the sofa and talked. 'Sorry about yesterday. God, that was embarrassing. Jesper isn't such a bad person. When he stalks me, I think he thinks that it proves he is showing concern. He's dyslexic, but no other major problems, none that I noticed immediately.'

Dyspeptic? That would be like Hari's uncle. 'Good he's not bad.'

'He dreamt of overcoming it, you could say, to become a writer and put down all his life on paper and make it into a bestseller.'

'One should fight one's weaknesses.'

'True. But nobody wanted to publish his autobiographical novel in twelve volumes because he forgot to use the spell-checker. So his published writings are book reviews. Bitter, yeah. Whenever he felt the pressure of not having a career he got weepy and wanted to be hugged. But I mean, I can't be his mother too, can I?'

'No, and I wouldn't want to be his father.'

'So yeah, he shaved his head, got himself a tattoo and acted macho, hanging out with people who hate foreigners. He saw it as his mission to destroy authors, especially if they had non-Swedish names and were translated into Swedish, butcher their books and make them stop writing. I told him that one can't sabotage other people's work just because one has mental problems. Also, he threatened to throw acid on those beggars near my workplace. For my sake. To clean up the country.'

'Oho?'

'When he was diagnosed with the prostate disorder, he became so weird that I had to break up our relationship. He didn't take it well.'

'So sorry to hear.' It was strange that a woman could do something as drastic as chucking her man out, even if he was a lunatic. Hari was used to being pushed around at home, but in the end, he was the man of the house. 'Where do you keep your plastic boxes?'

She handed him a set in different sizes. Perfect. Then she added, 'By the way, I called some of my friends.'

'For what?'

'For the ritual. I want them to meet my new guru.'

Uh-oh. So, he was going to have to do his great vanishing act before witnesses?

It was pure improvisation from then on.

Barbarella insisted on draping the room in white satin bed sheets. She placed an inflatable mattress by the far wall on which Hari was to sit in the lotus position. Bare-chested, he wore one sheet dhoti style to fit the picture. He'd seen enough holy men in real life, so he crossed his legs and held his hands in mysterious positions with the fingers pointing every which way. His beard was about a week old, not a full guru beard, but sufficient.

Barbarella changed into white jeans and a knitted white top. The friends came on the dot, most of them dressed in white and each was given a glass of white wine; some brought their own boxes of wine with taps on them. They were all women, seven or eight of them. They sat on the floor, a few giggled; others were quiet and aimed their eyes at him.

Momentarily, Hari felt inadequate to the task of performing whatever exorcism they hoped to see.

Barbarella welcomed them in the runic language and he understood that it was he who was being introduced from the choice of words – 'indisk visdom', 'global jetset guru' and 'mirakulös'. Then Barbarella switched to English. 'So I hand over the stage to Guru Harry Romeo, principal disciple of Sir Funny.'

His mouth went dry. He started hesitantly, 'Greetings. I come from another planet. Sorry, I mean another plane of existence. I have passed through many lives.'

A girl with spectacles interrupted him. 'Pardon me, Harry, but we've heard that you're from the IT capital of Asia. We expect you to be different from the standard gurus. More with-it, digital savvy, but you don't have a Facebook fan page.'

'You googled me?'

The girl nodded, she was holding up her phone and filming him. He got even more self-conscious.

'Yes, I am different from the proper gurus. I am my own Facebook, just look at my face and see how it is like an open book with my sacred destiny tattooed in Braille on my forehead.' He exhibited his teeth in a massive smile that pulled the corners of his mouth almost up to his eyebrows as he inserted ideas like computer viruses into their source codes.

While letting his motor-mouth spout catchy phrases favoured by his astrologer, he showed them the magic trick based on the scamster model. He tucked the idol amongst the pureed dandelions, put the flower salad in the smallest Tupperware box, sprinkled turmeric (he called it 'vegetarian gold powder') and chanted the item song 'Coma, Coma Prema' from the gangster classic *OM*. He made sure to display the plastic box to them – it was transparent and the flower arrangement remained visible, although one no longer saw the idol.

He then rolled layers of clear tape around the small box and put it inside a medium-sized box, together with more dandelion salad and turmeric. That box was taped and inserted into a larger box, and so on until it was impossible to make out the innermost one. Then he gave the set to Barbarella with the instruction to store them in a dark, cool place and open them after twenty-four hours – one box at a time with a wait of one hour's mantra-chanting before the next. She went and put it into the fridge. He announced, 'Now you have seen the ritual and hence you are blessed. Go home, cured.'

One of the girls said: 'Aren't we also supposed to learn a secret mantra that we can use when we are in need?'

'Yes, imprint this mantra on your minds: "*Swalpa* adjust *maadi*." You can chant it in your own bathrooms.'

'What does it mean?'

'Ah, it is a philosophical concept from my native place.'

'And how does it translate?'

'Sort of being humane.'

'And when do we use it?'

'For example, if the bus is crowded.'

'Does that help then?'

'Something like that.'

'Is there life after death?'

'Yes, two-hundred per cent guaranteed.'

'Are you sure?'

'No.'

'Why do you say that there is then?'

'Because …,' he was about to say that his wife didn't think so and increasingly he found that she was always right, but then he thought strategically. 'Because sometimes, if we're good enough, we can hit the jackpot and go for nirvana.'

'Are you for real?' said another woman who seemed to be getting frustrated with his evasive answers.

'Mostly, when people ask that question, they already know the answer they wish to hear,' said Hari quoting something that Pandit Pundit used to utter. He had spent many years listening to his prophecies, so he knew what to say and when. 'Or does my divine teaching sound amusing to you? Do I look like a joke?'

'No,' the woman hesitated. 'Yes, I mean.'

'Make up your mind. It is important that we strive for clarity in our muddled puddles of thought. I hope the rest of you heard me loud and clear. Or are my profound words wasted on you Western pagans?'

'Not at all,' they said.

'Let's be happy about it then,' he proclaimed, happy that he had managed to sneak the Ninth Avatar into the folds of his satin sheet dhoti. *How much more happily can things work out?* They'd be bound to swear that they saw him put it in the box, if there was a police investigation.

'About what?' said one of the girls who had giggled before, but was now sternly aiming her phone camera at him.

Hari waggled his head sideways. He remembered that the bartender at his favourite CD Road bar was the convener of a laughing club. 'About our ability to enjoy togetherness. Why don't we laugh together as much as we can? You must understand this: what we do is more important than what we do not do, but it is easier for us not to do what we ought to do, and instead do what we should not.'

'Excuse me, but what are you saying?'

'Just that laughing together is the opposite of acquiring self-destructive karma.'

There was a long moment of total silence. Then one of the giggly girls burst out laughing. Whether it was at what he had said or pure mass-psychosis was hard to tell, but soon the whole room was in an upbeat mood. Everyone laughed until they coughed up wine through their noses. Some started to dance in an esoteric manner, impersonating elves or perhaps garden gnomes, and threw their bras in the air. When they calmed down, one of them said: 'Harry, through your deep wisdom, you are making us feel healed.'

'Yes,' he said, because 'yes' was always a good word to start a sentence with, 'but that's because you don't have sufficient wisdom in your own country. Always seek quality before quantity, instead of acting sad over being divorced single mothers.'

Suddenly they went quiet again and he received a few hostile glares. He may have said something wrong. He went into damage control mode. 'I don't see any husbands accompanying you. But the world has room for everybody, as long as you can laugh, so don't worry, remarry. Got it?'

Some stood up politely to give him a standing ovation.

'Any questions?'

'Do you have a Twitter handle so that we can re-tweet your wisdom?'

'Such a divine evening,' said Barbarella. 'My friends liked you.'

'How do you know?'

She showed him their Facebook updates on an iPad and his stunt was all over the World Wide Web, with snaps of women raining bras on him. A video clip on YouTube had been viewed 301 times. *Oh no, Diamond mustn't see this.*

She was pensive, too. 'Must you go back to India?'

How did she know that he had preponed his ticket? Had she checked his phone messages?

'Who said I'm going?'

'The first time we met you said ...'

'I say many things. The wise listen to what they want to hear.' Better prepare her for the inevitable. 'I'd love to spend many incarnations with you. But how can I stay? This is a strange country.'

'Where there's a will, there's a way.'

'They don't serve cheap vadai in the restaurants,' he said and smuggled the idol under the pillow.

She didn't notice because she was busy googling on her iPad. 'Hey, if I learnt how to cook the way you like it, would you stay?' she said after she found an Indian food importer who sold instant vada mixes online. She told him of an earlier 'friend' of hers, a Bangladeshi chef, who after applying for a residential permit and, getting rejected, was contacted by a freelancing official from the Migration Department who offered help against a cash consideration – a special consultation fee, he called it.

'Back home, we call that a bribe.' He felt inexplicably jealous at the thought that she'd been friends with some Bangladeshi.

Barbarella shrugged.

'But it worked for him. For 55,000 Swedish crowns that man fixed everything for my friend, who is now part owner in that restaurant where we had dinner yesterday. He was given a Romanian EU-passport because it can be difficult to tell the difference between a Romanian and a South Asian.'

'I don't have that kind of cash.' Besides, he had a somewhat forged EU-passport already. Not that he intended to tell her.

'Can your business partner lend you?'

'Who?'

'That shady guy from IKEA who you met at the museum.'

'I'll surely ask.'

'Then I might decide to marry you.'

Hari got so shocked at the thought that he didn't know what to say.

It was 4 a.m. according to the alarm clock on the bedside table and light outside the window. Back home, the days were approximately of the same length no matter the time of year. About twelve hours light, twelve dark. Here the bizarre sun came up much before it was due. According to what his astrologer had told him, it was ungodly if the sun crossed the horizon before the night was over.

Barbarella snored. It was Monday morning and she'd have to go to work soon. Then he'd make good his escape. He watched the minutes tick away on the clock's display, waiting for the time to go home.

He should have returned to sleep, but there was something about the long days that threw him out of gear. As if he wasn't meant to be in bed. In a sense he wasn't, not in this particular bed. Combined with the feelings he was developing for Barbarella, he felt confused – about the sun, love, food habits, but, above all, about where he belonged. Had he been a Swede in an earlier lifetime and now come back home?

Back in Bengaluru, he had often felt like a fossil. But meeting these real-life dinosaurs, the surviving Vikings, he realized that his life was still an unwritten film script. The final reels had not yet been canned. He could do what he liked. The preponed flight was taking off at noon, but if he wished so he could delete the SMS ticket from his phone. For when he was prevailed upon to stay, only part of him wanted to leave. Other parts had other ideas. Besides, Barbarella had already downloaded recipes for gudbud as well as majige huli.

He reached for his phone to check the timing on the ticket back to Bengaluru – where his uncle was dead, his mum was in jail, his wife didn't understand him, his children recognized the sound of his flip-flops but not his face because he was always working, and his friends thought him a weakling. There'd be the enforcers sent out by the bank to welcome him back and what were his chances of survival if RIP, Deadlyappa and the big wrestlers joined hands with them, and Farooqi and all his wife's nephews? Too many problems, simply too many.

Meanwhile here, now that he had a soft bed to sleep in, he liked Sweden. The cold wasn't bothersome as long as one stayed indoors. There were many good things as compared to CD Road. For several days, he hadn't been pummelled. Even Barbarella's ex-partner had merely attempted to talk him out of seeing her rather than actually breaking his spine. His finger moved towards the 'delete message' button.

He sat up abruptly. *What was he thinking?* Barbarella slept peacefully wrapped in her satin sheets, but Hari got restless, pulled on the borrowed clothes and stepped out for a walk. He was going to go around the block to clear his thoughts, but he kept his mobile, passport and the idol in his pocket just in case he decided not to return to Barbarella. *Was he losing his mind?*

He shuffled down to the end of Plantage Street, to a wider road that had trams running in the middle of it. There was no traffic at this hour, only empty tracks. He tried to get a feel for the area: could he see himself living here? The street was lined with grills and it seemed that these Swedes weren't vegetarians. Maybe it was because he had been a Viking in a past life that he found it hard to adjust to vegetarianism in the present life?

He studied the menu posted outside one and found that they charged 492 local monies for a T-bone steak. He'd have to get an income if he stayed.

There were no Swedish restaurants in Indian cities, as far as he knew. Here he noticed signboards like Bombay and Maharani, even Namaste Nepal, so he knew this was ground that Asia would conquer one day. Had his presence a deeper meaning? If he stayed, he might well become the official Mr Fix-It of Sweden when Indian territory and economy expanded to engulf this town, too.

Despite the skies being bright, everything was shut. The morning sun warmed the right side of his face. He came to the square where they had got off the tram. It had a fountain and neat public toilets, but was empty of people. Ahead, he spotted cranes and ships, and a harbour.

Since he didn't know how to swim, he turned right towards where he saw trees. Coming from Bengaluru, he enjoyed parks. The greenery stretched along the water's edge, into the distance. A woman cycled down the bicycle lane. He heard her shout '*hej*!' and then she was gone. He walked past a sports bar, a fishing goods store and a tattoo parlour, then across yet another parking lot to a canal with boats anchored along the quay.

Was life offering him a second chance?

Was the clean canal a suitable final resting place for the Ninth Avatar? He'd taken its darshan, which had resulted in his finding love together with Barbarella, and now the avatar could go its own way. He took out the statuette from his pocket and dangled it over the water.

But there was the matter of what the baba at the temple had said. The words echoed in his memory: 'For whomever it is with, it'll be a curse.' And now it was with Hari. The curse might shadow him forever. No, he had promised to return it, so he pocketed it again. He could courier it back to Halegudehalli.

Yes, that was a perfect solution. He walked on, in his mind saying goodbye and all the very best to his many friends. Triplex, who always got him into trouble. But he had good sides. Triplex was sensitive, intelligent and emotional. He only made occasional lapses, such as when he masterminded the ATM heist.

Gaadi, who fought with him whenever he was in a foul mood and kicked him around when they stole the ATM, was mad, but in a good way. What about Doc? Doc was a bore, but he'd miss the free Internet he got on eternal credit. On the other hand, Doc was a finicky pedant who nitpicked. One could surely live without that.

Diamond? As he tried to think of his wife, his thoughts kept reverting to Barbarella's milky skin and freckled face, green eyes and the red roots of her black hair. Being with Barbarella was like undoing everything that had gone wrong in life. *Should he stay or should he go?* But if he stayed, he'd have to give the idol back to her. He had other doubts too. He hadn't told Barbarella that he was married and had two and a half children. How would she take it? What about his own family? Would Diamond accept bigamy? He stopped on the side of the canal. Was he lost?

He had walked a considerable distance in deep contemplation, but he was able to reconstruct the walk in his mind: along the canal, before that across a square with a fountain. He'd conquer this city, too, and be its king, just like he was Mr Majestic back home. It was time to return to bed and another breakfast of champagne and strawberries. Yes, that was the solution.

Then he heard some noise.

The strip of greenery widened into a large park. He made out a main street, a bridge crossing the canal and grand buildings. There were loud voices. Curious, he went to get a closer look at what the Swedes were up to – because at the Crossroads he'd heard them shout at night, but never gone down to check what it was about. If he was to stay, he should know the truth about the Viking descendants.

He came to the main street at the end of the park and started to cross it when he recognized it as the grand boulevard where, on the steps of a theatre complex overlooking a big square, he'd been sitting and feeling lost on one of his first days in the country. There was a smaller square at this end of the boulevard. Some thirty youths were facing each other in it. They seemed to belong to different groups, but all wore baggy jeans, hooded jackets. Some were Swedes judging from their pork-coloured skins, others had darker complexions. They were in their late teens, too young and well-dressed to be rowdy-sheeters. He didn't feel threatened, so he stopped to watch.

When one boy staggered in Hari's direction, he saw that his face was bleeding. Others felled that one with a severe trashing, using broken bottles, wooden sticks and paving-stones. A gun went off and one of the kids went down, clutching his leg. A youngster with a roaring chainsaw came running straight at Hari.

It took a few seconds to make sense of the mayhem, because he was looking for the cameras, the lights, and the director to apply to for a cameo role. But it wasn't reel. It was real. Turning to run back across the street, he smashed into a car. It braked with a squeal. Hari stopped to catch his breath, hands holding on to the steaming hot engine bonnet. He could have got killed. Then he saw it was Herman Barsk's battered Volvo, with Barsk in the driver's seat, and it was too much for his brain to handle. The cop was really following him. Hari did a namaste and walked away, he didn't want to get involved in street fights or arrested in this strange country.

He looked over his shoulder. Barsk got out of his car and spoke into a walkie-talkie, brandishing his service pistol to keep the rioting youths at bay. He fired warning shots into the air.

Hurrying to Barbarella, to safety, his thoughts clarified like butter. By the time he entered Plantage Street, his heartbeat relaxed, and he patted the pocket where the idol was. He'd been lucky. The avatar was on his side. Closer to her building, he saw three bald, bearded men outside the front door in identical leather jackets, jeans, army boots. Hari said, in an affable voice, 'Good morning, Jesper. You're up early.'

Jesper held out a hand as if in greeting. Hari was about to pump it vigorously when he noticed there was something in it. First, he didn't see what exactly it was, but then Jesper flicked a switch and a blade appeared with a clicking sound.

It was a stiletto.

24

Since you've not followed the advice given, there's nothing good in your horoscope today, sorry; also, no auspicious time this time.

Jesper pointed the knife at Hari. 'I'd like my clothes back.'

'Let me step inside and wash them first,' said Hari in order to avoid stripping in the street.

'And my wife.'

'Yes, I'll scrub your missus, too.' Hari had been about to argue that she wasn't Jesper's wife, but a free woman.

However, the odds were unfavourable. Three of them and he was alone, so the mathematical formula read ☺±☻±☺☺, which meant that two of them could backstab him while he faced off with the third. He didn't see another soul in the street. Perhaps he should have let Barsk arrest him at the scene of the street fight on whatever trumped-up charges. Too late to run back. He checked if flattery could defuse the situation. 'Speaking of garments, you're nicely dressed. Colour coordinated.'

'We're in a band.'

'Oho, live orchestra?' He suspected they wouldn't let him off the hook so easily, but there was no harm trying to fake a friendship, as his uncle used to say. 'You play instruments or do cinema playback?'

'This here is Spearman on guitar …'

'I also go to dance school,' said Spearman.

'… and the big guy is Månsson, who beats the hell out of the drums.'

'I have brain damage,' said the big guy.

'And I play the bass guitar. Our band is called The Rapists.'

'Oho?'

'Yes, originally, we thought we should be known as The Racists, but my wife thinks it sounds politically incorrect.'

'Yes, I can see why The Rapists sounds less political.'

'It's an anagram.'

'What does it mean?' said Hari, who loved finding out new, strange words.

'That you can scramble the letters and get a different word.'

'Such as?'

'Therapists. You understand that as a literary critic, I am really good with language. We play traditional Viking music and our biggest hit is called "We're Not Intolerant But Foreigners Go Home To Wherever You Came From", which you must have heard on Spotify. It's downloaded a lot.'

'I'll download it and trade autographs with you. All the very best and bye-bye.'

Without a warning, Spearman did a high ballet kick with his army boot and the blow landed in the middle of Hari's face. He reeled backwards in a fountain of nose-blood, crashed against the wall and then slid down to the pavement like a rag. He blacked out thinking that while Barbarella had told him how docile Jesper was, she'd forgotten to warn him about Jesper's friends.

When he came to, Hari noticed Jesper bending down to rip his face off.

The stiletto in his hand was closing in to give Hari a clean shave. No, he wasn't intending to leave his moustache in this godless country! He reached for Jesper's beard, to pull him off balance, but Jesper moved back.

Hari gazed around dizzily. His face was wet, probably with blood. It kept pumping out of the nostrils. Pain would come.

The three skinheads formed a triangle around him. Nobody else was out at this hour. Nobody'd hear if he screamed.

'Bastard, I'm going to kill you,' said Jesper and squatted to pin Hari's feet down against the pavement.

When Hari sat up, Spearman rammed his toes, encased in a steel capped boot, so hard into Hari's head that he hit the pavement again. Then he grabbed Hari's arms, pulling them back and setting down a foot on each hand. His combat boots had hard soles. There was some kind of deja-vu involved here. It made him recollect his nightmare with the two enforcers. *Was life coming full circle with death?* But that time he got away. *Surely such happy endings happened no more than once?*

Or maybe history repeated itself like reruns on TV? As the big guy Månsson set down a boot on Hari's tummy, preparing to stomp on Hari's intestines until they were comprehensively mashed, Hari was reminded of the fighters at the ancient wrestling pit, who wished to flog him and sell off his skeleton. That time too he had managed to run. *So such happy endings did happen twice?*

Could he wish for a third repeat? This time, however, with Spearman's boots pressing firmly on his hands, and Jesper holding his feet in place, he could not move, and didn't see how he'd get out of the mess. He learnt something important there and then: his fantasies of settling in Sweden were futile. He didn't belong among barbarians like these modern-day Vikings. If he survived, he'd fly back to India, to his ancient and hallowed civilization, and return the idol to the temple where it, and he, belonged. His plan to stay back had led to an instantaneous karmic dip.

'How about we go and have that beer instead, Jesper?' said Hari. 'I think I can afford to treat all three of you. I can also tell you this interesting story about how you Swedes tried to colonize India in 1733. Want to know how it ended?'

'You should have listened when you had the opportunity.'

'I'm all ears. Don't I deserve a second chance?'

'Pub's closed,' said Spearman and pressed down his boots on Hari's hands until the finger bones crunched.

'Google the YouTube video from yesterday. You will see that I was giving an inspirational talk in your missus's nest and nothing fishy happened. See it for yourself to know the truth.' The wisdom that he preached about happiness and enjoyment, rather than negative attachments, might change Jesper's standoffish outlook.

But Jesper wasn't into peace and happiness. 'This is what is going to happen,' he said. 'I'm a reputed literary critic. If I think that your inspirational talk sucks, we'll teach you a lesson that you'll remember until you die.'

'Do I jump him or what?' asked Månsson.

'Hold on a sec, he shouldn't die before we teach him the lesson.' Jesper pulled out his iPad. It was the same model that

Barbarella had, so Hari guessed she had paid for them both. Either she was too kind or she had got a package deal. Jesper went online and played the clip from the day before, in which Hari got the ladies to remove their bras. Then he aimed the camera lens at Hari. 'You're not getting the Nobel Prize for Literature on the basis of that.'

'Maybe for peace?'

'Maybe for shutting up because I'm tired of listening to you. You don't belong here in our culture.'

Hari's hands hurt when Spearman ground his boots into them. So this was the last sensation he was going to experience?

'Or how about we kill you and make you shut up,' said Jesper, acting tough.

'But can I choose?'

'Choose what?'

'Between shutting up and dying, I prefer the former,' said Hari. 'Shutting up seems a good Plan N.'

'Plan what?'

'N, it is one of the last plans in the textbook. One last thing before I shut up –'

'You're going to stop talking or I'll make you. Hold it right there. I want to upload this. Okay, Månsson: jump when I say so.'

It was at that moment Hari understood how dangerous and difficult the world outside India was. Having a rhinoceros-sized skinhead pulp one was the worst of worst-case scenarios. A light morning drizzle washed Hari's face. God had made up her mind and she was sobbing.

Månsson prepared by breathing heavily. Earth's gravity must have exerted a phenomenal pull on his beer belly. Hari's only hope was that he'd be too heavy to lift off the ground. He regretted not having taken out travel insurance. He'd need to have the two halves of his body stitched back together after this. But of course, he might also end up a viral YouTube star. He smiled at the camera, making the best out of the situation.

'*Hallå där, köttbulleboys*,' came a voice from down the street.

Hari recognized that bellowing tone. It was Herman Barsk. The cop stood feet wide apart, his raincoat filling up like a sail in the morning breeze, looking like a bat that had overslept and missed his midnight blood feast.

'Don't interfere, bum,' said Spearman. He spoke in the runic language, but Hari, who was used to foreigners, made out the essence by analyzing the tenor of his voice.

Spearman barely finished the sentence before the Sig Sauer was in Barsk's hand: 'Or what will you do about it, *höh*?'

Silence. Nothing happened.

Barsk said what sounded like: '*Höh*, don't tell me you sissies haven't been through this before. Line up against the wall. Resist and I'm going to stuff apples in your mouths and do target practice.'

The musicians appeared confused, the way one might be if one lost the sheet music in the middle of an opera. But they obeyed the command. After all, they did dress in uniform-like clothing, so orderly conduct was to be expected. It was a relief for Hari. He wriggled his fingers – circulation was coming back. No bones broken.

'Mister Lasagne, thank your lucky stars that I decided to keep an eye on you. Now what is this about, *höh*?'

'I have no idea,' said Hari.

'Shut up, I wasn't talking to you. I asked our home-grown amateur fundamentalists,' said Barsk, and did something obscene with his Sig Sauer on Spearman, who sang in falsetto. Barsk switched to runes again. Whatever it was that he told them, the three didn't dare to move after that statement of intent. Barsk switched to broken English. 'Okay Lasagne, you get up and walk slow and easy towards my car. Door's open. And don't look back. I don't want witnesses.'

'Please, don't leave us with him,' pleaded Jesper. 'If you're a good man, Harry, drop your charges and keep my wife.'

'Sorry, got to go. All the very best and bye-bye.' He had no intention to take a place in the line with the three musicians, whose swan song was about to begin. He wondered if people here were reincarnated tragically and died as soon as they managed to ruin their healths.

He heard them beg for mercy, but didn't peek over his shoulder. He sat in the passenger seat of the battered Volvo and used his hankie to stop the nosebleed by twisting it tight and stuffing it up his nostrils. The car floor was littered with scrunched up paper cups that smelt of stale coffee, which perhaps explained why Barsk had been so trigger-happy back there. He heard cries. Minutes later, Barsk slid into the driver's seat and holstered his gun. It was not smoking and Hari had heard no bullets fired.

'Scum.' Barsk threw a stiletto on the rubber mat on the car floor. Then he pulled the hooch bottle from under the seat and passed it on to Hari. 'Help yourself. I don't drink between 6 a.m. and 6 p.m.'

'Yes, you told me so.'

'Lately, we've had trouble with gangs in town. There was a major fight reported from Avenyn and as I was on my way there, who did I see if not you? I work to nip the vermin in the bud, so I decided to follow and see where you were going.'

'Why?'

'*Höh*, in case you were one of those terror-tourists after all.' He started the engine. 'But as it turned out you're an average loser.'

'Oho, that's exactly what a magical parrot once told me. So you have a valid point.' He wasn't going to argue with the mad cop. Besides, his bruised lips hurt when he spoke. 'What do they fight about, these gangs?'

Barsk talked as they drove. At the main street corner, he gave way to a tram and then turned right and away from the direction of the city centre. 'How do I know what these people think? Love affair gone sour, somebody flirted with the wrong girl. Then that has to be avenged, the avenge has to be revenged, and so on: homicide, double-homicide, triple-homicide. I don't mind them killing each other, but innocents get hurt when there are shootouts in restaurants and public parks. Bloody UFOs. Some of them control drug trafficking in their neighbourhoods – incidentally, a big bust was made at the airport about a week ago, a brown suitcase full of ephedrine from India, which may have a connection to the gang war this morning. But most of them are into it for the fun ... entertainment violence, *höh*. There's no honour among criminals anymore. When I was a rookie cop, we'd often find the killer crying on the doorsteps of the police station. Not so anymore, no regrets. Doesn't feel like Gothenburg any longer, more like the Middle East.'

'I'll report that to *Lonely Planet*, the travel guidebook I write for.'

'Shall I give you another piece of my mind?' Barsk tapped a military rhythm on the steering wheel as they came to a large forested area which made Hari think of home, of Cubbon Park. They took a steep left up a road climbing a ridge to a hospital complex. 'This here is the Sahlgrenska University Hospital, where you may have spent the rest of your holiday if I hadn't stepped in.'

'Oho, nice hospital. Too bad I'll have to give it a miss.'

They drove through winding streets until they came down a slope and Hari recognized the Crossroads ahead. Barsk rambled on, 'How about I drop you at the same spot where I found you and you get the hell out of here as soon as possible? Take the next flight back to Pizzaland? And live happily ever after.'

'Can I think about it and let you know?' Hari was missing Barbarella's soft hugs. In a short time, he'd gotten used to them. Very few hugs awaited him at home.

'Not negotiable.'

'I thought so.' It was destiny then.

It seemed like Barsk had emotions, for he added, 'Now that you're on these guys' death radar, you are pretty much a walking stiff.'

'Why didn't you arrest them?'

'For what?'

'They were being naughty.'

'They'd get away with a warning. Unless they killed you first. And I didn't feel like watching that happen. So, I thought I should save your sorry skin. Seeing that you're a guest in our country.'

'Ya boss, great idea.'

'Thanks. You're not drinking?'

'I'd prefer coffee at this hour.'

'Why didn't you say so? Thermos flask is under the seat and there are cups and instant coffee in the glove compartment.'

They were on the highway to the airport. There was time for coffee to cure his headache. He mixed the coffee powder – there was no milk or sugar, he'd have to guzzle it black. 'So boss, why did you decide not to arrest me then for fighting with those guys in the street? I mean, if you want to get rid of me.'

'No particular reason,' said Barsk.

They sat in silence for some time, then Barsk added:

'*Höh*.'

Hari knew within the third of a second that something or the other was bothering the veteran cop. 'Even then, I'd be interested in knowing.'

'It'll sound crazy.'

'Tell me more.'

Barsk hawked and spat out the window. 'Don't push your luck.'

'I don't feel too lucky today.'

'*Höh*. Okay, because of a dream.'

'About me?'

'Before I first met you and that's weird.'

'Is it so?'

'Then I saw you near the airport – straight out of my nightmare.'

'Oho? So I was in the nightmare?' Hari felt proud of having insinuated himself into somebody else's dreams.

Barsk coughed and lit a cigarette. 'Sometime back, I dreamt I was wearing a strange kind of costume, sort of in-between a suit and a short-sleeved shirt, and uncomfortable synthetic pants. And rubber sandals.'

'We met in the dream?'

'You could say I was busy torturing you.'

'Torturing me? How come?'

'Money. I stubbed out cigarettes on your feet. I told myself to stop, that Swedish cops don't torture suspects, but it was as if I was under hypnosis.'

'Oho, by mistake you mistook my feet for ashtrays, is it?' He tried to make sense of what he was hearing. It was universally acknowledged that nothing comes out of nothing. But something came out of something. He could have informed Barsk that what he described had happened just recently. He still had burn scars from the night at the bank construction site. Was it a coincidence – or was there a spiritual connection between the two, as if the same scriptwriter had scripted the biopics of their lives? But he saw no need to upset the cop. The man was troubled enough.

'I decided to cut down on smoking the next morning.' He took a deep drag on his cigarette. 'The dream ended with my trousers catching fire. Next day I was diagnosed with prostate disorder. So when I saw you, I almost shat in my pants.'

'I'll reimburse you for the dry-cleaning bill, if you send it to my office in Italy.'

'Oh, don't bother.'

'That's the least I can do. But why didn't you tell me before?'

'I decided, when you turned out to be real, to keep an eye on you. Figure out if I'm going insane or not.'

Hari could have told him that he was, obviously, quite nuts, but he decided to keep a diplomatic silence. Throughout his foreign expedition unknowable forces had directed him and what Barsk said about the dream encounter reinforced that belief.

'Can I help with that?'

'Yes. See to it that you get out of the country before anything awful happens between us.'

'Oho, it is too good of you. But I'm sure it was a strange dream you had. You don't seem insane,' he lied.

'You lie like a cuckoo.'

Hari didn't know what to say. Until then the drive had been through forested landscape and Hari poured another black coffee every few minutes until he started missing his antacids. Then they turned off the highway and into the airport area with its vast car parks. The fantasy of settling with Barbarella in Sweden faded. He still had Farooqi's banknotes in local currency because he had lived thriftily on begged coins, leftovers and gifts. In hindsight, he could have spent his remaining budget on taking Barbarella out for a thank you lunch. It felt wrong to leave without farewells. And he could have shared some money with the kind Candelia and the other Romanians. Perhaps he was going to miss Herman Barsk too. He'd have wanted to hold a speech. Like heroes in the movies. But this wasn't a movie. So he asked, 'Will you write a report on this?'

'Not sure there's anything to report. Tourist came. Tourist got mixed up with the wrong people. Tourist went home.' Barsk smiled for the first time.

'But if you did, you'd mention me?'

'Why should I? You're a nobody who got in the way. And hereby your sightseeing is over. Once you're inside that terminal building, keep walking until you're on your plane and don't ever come back.'

'But what if I ...'

'Why would you want to die?'

'Right. Good point.' Hari finished his coffee. The departure time was merely hours away. He said, 'In that case, bye-bye and all the very best.'

'Got your things?'

Hari waggled his head.

'As I recall you didn't have anything when you landed. Not even a gun. I didn't ask why and I don't give a shit, unless you cause trouble. But you have your ticket, *höh*?'

'I travel light.' He had what he needed, the Ninth Avatar was in his pocket along with his passport and the SMS ticket was on his Nokia. But his eyes caught Barsk's tie made of a leather ribbon and with the grinning skull. 'Can you do me one last favour?'

'*Höh*?'

'With all due respect, I've been fond of your tie ever since we first met.'

'Yeah, I noticed your moronic stare.'

'Would you consider giving it to me as a farewell gift?'

'Why would I?'

'If you do, I assure you that you will never ever see me again.'

'Take it,' said Barsk, handed him the ornament and drove off.

Hari discarded the grinning skull. To smuggle the twice-stolen idol out, he knotted Herman's string tie around the thumb-sized idol's neck and then he made a larger loop around his own neck. Perfect. He figured that if he wore the idol as a necklace, like any old lucky charm, and as long as it was in full public view, nobody would notice that it was a stolen antique.

He walked into the terminal thinking that he'd done things that he perhaps shouldn't have, but it was good that he did what he did, rather than not do anything at all. He completed the check-in and security, and waited for the boarding announcement. Airport staff did react to his smashed-up face, but he told them his car had run into a moose. It was normal over here.

Pre-monsoon, so he saw no stars, but as the plane dipped towards Bengaluru he made out street lights and vehicles moving about down there.

At 3 a.m., the Bengaluru airport was forlorn, like a shopping mall that some international corporation had misplaced. Hari walked past the luggage carousel. He carried a plastic duty-free bag with gifts for Diamond and the kids. He had used up the leftover Swedish money to buy Swiss chocolate at the airport.

He wasn't stopped by the custom's officers: there were too many passengers coming with trolleys full of flatscreen TVs from Singapore and vodka from Moscow. Besides, there was no law against smuggling archaeological artefacts back into the country – it was merely prohibited to take them out.

Despite the late hour, or maybe it was very early, a bus was leaving for the central bus stand. *Home.* He stopped for a minute to take in the smell of the air itself. It was so different from the frigid air of Europe. It was lukewarm despite being in the middle of the night, rich like his wife's armpit and beery like a cheap dive bar at closing time.

Sweet home, he completed the thought and was going to touch his forehead to the tarmac if it hadn't been for the bus starting to move and threatening to crush his skull under its wheels. He jumped on and zoomed in on another fellow, about his age, and took the seat next to him. To prove his cosmopolitanism, he addressed him in English, 'You're going to Majestic bus stand?'

'That's where this vehicle is going,' said the traveller, yawning for effect.

'Listen, if you need a cheap room for the night, tell me. I have connections. But listen, where do you come from?'

The fellow yawned again and said nothing.

'My good self, I went to Sweden and came back just now only. Saw some cool stuff over there. Ran into a moose. It's a big animal that destroys cars, so they have to fence in the roads. Can you believe it? It is like the Indian elephant but with horns. It would never fit into a tandoori oven.'

Gradually he managed to engage the traveller in a conversation that lasted all the way into town. He worked as an engineer and told Hari about the Emirates, while Hari uploaded stories from Sweden in return – the Crossroads, the World Culture Museum, the Indian food, the ladies – and a few other passengers got into the spirit and shared anecdotes from Manchester and Berlin, and they had hearty laughs about weird foreigners. Only one of them argued that punctuality may have some practical use aside from the auspicious moments as per the stars. The rest felt that the foreign obsession with punctuality was just that: an overrated virtue indicative of an inherent inability in obsessive-compulsive savages to accept things the way they were.

Then Hari told them about his job as a detective and enlightened them about the fact that in only 20 per cent of all cases worldwide, when clients suspected their spouses of cheating on them, were they wrong. The remaining 80 per cent were right. As the bus drew in at the platform, Hari looked forward to many new clients now that he had sown seeds of suspicion – through his patented nine-point scheme for how to be sure one's wife had been unfaithful. More than one would surely reach home and notice signs of infidelity, and then they'd hire his services. Besides, the engineer from Qatar took on Hari's offer about a reasonably priced hotel.

'If you're staying for longer, I'll arrange PG-accommodation. But hotels here in Majestic are any day better than putting up at the Taj. Good to avoid dicey non-veg and the loose motions you get in five-star lodges. Why take tension?'

At that hour the streets were desolate, so the engineer was grateful for a guide. The express bus to his native place, Chikmagalur, wasn't leaving until about noon. Hari pocketed a commission from the Kama Boardless Lodging once the engineer got his key to room 205. Maddox had checked out for good and his ashes were in an urn in the reception, with an invoice addressed To Whom It May Concern.

'Victor, you take good care of my bosom buddy.'

Rather than driving his scooter to Halegudehalli straight away, he now wanted to go home and spend a few days with his family, settle matters with Farooqi (if possible) and get rid of the incriminating ATM machine in his office. The idol was thousands of years old and another week away from its abode was not going to hurt.

25

Every dog has its day.

Unlike abroad, there were traces of life in the muddy alleys – not only in the form of piled-up garbage but also that hard-to-put-one's-finger-on yuck that oozed up from cracks in the pavements as if the city sewers suffered from gastric ailments. *How he had missed these normal things in that antiseptic country!* Of course, he had been away for less than ten days, but considering what he'd gone through, it amounted to a lifetime's worth of hallucinations.

Plan O was to beg Diamond for forgiveness, so that she wouldn't feel sorry about him going abroad without her. He'd do it kneeling and promise her a vacation in Nandi Hills. Being in love with Diamond was hardest on the kneecaps.

As he wanted to avoid stumbling on one of the semi-broken steps and breaking his bones, he climbed cautiously up the dimly lit stairs. He stopped when he was almost at the first floor, from where he could see that their nameplate was still in place: 'Diamond Majestic Family Abode.' So she hadn't shifted from Cyber Villas in his absence.

The doorbell had been broken ever since they moved in and the landlord wouldn't pay for fixing it, nor did Hari feel that he should fix the landlord's broken property, and anyway in the daytime the door was open, what with the kids running in and out, so there was no need for a doorbell. Except now.

When he was about to step up to it and bang on the door, he noticed an unusual smell.

He froze. What was it? Menthol smoke.

It made warning bells go off in his head like an anti-virus software detecting malware in the modem. He tiptoed down the steps again.

Something was wrong. This called for an investigation into the matter and as usual, being a 24x7 operating detective, he was the right man in the right place and at the right time.

Time for Plan P. He rounded the slum building's corner to where a series of water pipes ran up the side. He had never scaled walls before, only fallen from rooftops. He grabbed a water pipe that seemed firm. Like any dog, a detective had to learn new tricks, so he hauled himself up by placing his feet on the clips that connected the pipe to the wall.

Adrenaline kept him going. That and a strong sense of worry. When he reached the window to the landing one flight of steps above their first-floor home, he could see the glowing tip of a cigarette just an arm's length away. Faint moonlight seeped in, menthol smoke seeped out. A semi-sleeping man sat and smoked on the topmost step. The glow moved closer to a face and then as the cigarette was inserted between the lips and the smoker took a deep drag, it illuminated his face for a second.

It was the same man – Kelasamadi, alias Mental Menthol, with those nasty burn scars on his face. He had shaved off his hair. His eyes were big and aglow with the fire of hatred. Hari could guess what it was about. Payback.

Because Hari had climbed so quietly up the dark steps and stopped before he reached the door, Mental hadn't noticed him.

As his night vision improved, he saw the long on the floor next to Mental. If Hari had made any noise in the stairwell, his head would have been rolling downhill by now. He felt his blood curdle into onion raita, hot and cold at the same time. What about Diamond and the kids? He was about to spit at Mental, and abuse him roundly, but held back. The reason he sat and watched the door had to be simple – he had not gone inside and killed Hari's family. The probable cause was not kindness, but that he didn't want to alert Hari about the trap.

'I'm tired of this,' mumbled Hari and lowered himself down again. 'I should live in an ashram, like old men do.'

But in his mind, Plan Q took shape. A single thought kept churning: *kill all crooks.* Kill them as many times as it took to stop them from being reborn again. Then he abandoned the idea of extreme violence as a stupid one and thought of Plan R.

He needed to plan this final operation well. He was going to retire after this, so it had to be good. He walked to his office, brooding like a monsoon sky minutes before an outbreak. Here he had been prepared to come back as a hero and restart his career. He'd return the idol and receive a government citation and … Plan R was moderately violent, but it also had to be cancelled. He had to save his family first. He unlocked the padlock and threw open the office door. Back to square one.

He turned his eyes to the pictures on the walls, of saints and gods, movie stars and mahatmas, and asked himself what they'd have done in his place. He didn't get a coherent reply. They had never faced the same situation, they offered no Plan S.

Instead, as per a new plan – Plan T – he started carrying out the armpit fan cartons. He'd have to get rid of them. It was time to get over Uncle's death. Time to stop thinking and start acting. Finally, he unearthed the ATM machine. He SMS-ed Farooqi. 'Sorry about everything. I am ready to pay back for the untoward loss incurred by you. Go to Uncle's old office immediately and you will get full compensation.'

He pocketed the gold jewellery from the desk drawer, the only valuables in the office apart from the ATM, left the door unlocked so that no crook would have to break down the door, climbed up to the roof and lay down there – the air was warm as urine and smelled like a cocktail of rum, beer and port wine, unlike the chilly frigidity of Scandinavistan, so he started drifting off to sleep. It had been a tiring journey.

But his eyelids snapped open every time he shut them. *Were his miseries never going to end?* A possible Plan U was to invite Mental Menthol to go with him on a drinking binge to the seedy bars of Magadi Road, on the western outskirts, where unclaimed corpses were found so often that people had stopped noticing, spike his beverage with *Gelsemium elegans* – the so-called heartbreak grass from the CIA garden – and add one more corpse to the pileup. That'd teach Mental to 1) stop harassing innocent people and 2) not try to chop off Hari's head and that 3) kindness is preferable to wickedness.

Bad plan with too many ifs and buts. Then eventually he lost count of all the things he wanted to teach the crooks of CD Road, tiredness took over and he started snoring softly, happy to be back home in a familiar world. He only woke up because of the racket CD Road traffic made and the first burning rays of the nuclear sun that was about to turn the Deccan summer sky into an atomic furnace. He ate some of the duty-free chocolates for breakfast and got down from the roof.

As he expected, his office door was ajar and the ATM missing. It was simple mathematics: tell a crook where to find money and consider it stolen. Hari had known these things since childhood. For a man with a wife who had many nephews, shifting the ATM out of Hari's office had been a piece of cake.

He called up Farooqi while he waited for Coffee-Anand to show up with his steel wire basket full of piping hot coffees in tall glasses. Hari was going to buy them all and request Anand to go get six more. The old spy picked up immediately as if he had been waiting for the call.

'Hari, my young friend. When will you be dropping in for kahwa? I'd love to hear about your holiday in the West.'

Clearly the peace offering had been accepted, because the voice was warm and kind again.

'I keep my word. Besides, I prefer coffee.'

'Okay.' There was a moment's silence. 'But it is always such a pleasure doing business with you. Whenever you want to take your family for a foreign holiday, let me know. I'd be glad to help out.'

'I'll think about it.'

'You think far too much, you always did. Anyway, thanks for this. A little cash always comes in handy.'

'No mention. But you may thank me even more if I tell you that the police are on their way and you need to hide the ATM machine once you've emptied it of cash. And I know the perfect place to hide it.' Hari told him of the sweatshop in Kallapete bazaar and which ought to be shut down and abandoned, and from the roof of which they could drop the empty machine into the yard belonging to Paisavasool Exports. Nobody would find it there. 'Bye-bye, and all the very best.'

'Wait, before you hang up, Hari, there is something that you may need to hear.'

'What?'

'You know that American fellow, who was a friend of your uncle?'

'What if I do?' said Hari and made sure to stay in denial mode in case the news was bad.

'Anyway, they found him.'

'Who?'

'Fire brigade. He had fallen into Ulsoor Lake.'

'Was it an accident?'

'They think so, because he had by mistake tied a sack full of old car batteries to his neck and they think due to that he fell into the water.'

'Oho, he probably wasn't as smart as you would be if you got that ATM into Kallapete immediately,' said Hari and disconnected the call.

Once morning broke and businesses opened, an even better idea, Plan V, took shape and Hari climbed downstairs to the alley at the back of Puncherwallah Complex, past the 'Beware of Vehicle Lifters' sign. But there he found his scooter gone. The stray dogs stared at him with disappointed eyes. He hadn't fed them for a long time, so they had let a vehicle-lifter steal his scooter. *Revenge – so this was what it felt like? To hurt others? How much fun is that?* There was a voice inside his head, speaking pompously, and involuntarily his hand went to the idol that hung around his neck – *was this Plan V? God's Plan V for him? Was this the Ninth Avatar's way of showing that what goes around, comes around?*

If he waited until the garage opened, he'd be able to buy the scooter back from his landlord Puncherwallah, who was the town's biggest dealer in stolen vehicles. But he wasn't sure he wanted to return to the past. He had to move forward without bitterness, with steadfastness of mind.

He walked homewards, mumbling: 'There'll be an end to existence, but unless that day is printed in red letters on your Bangalore Press calendar, there's no point taking tension. The time we spend on earth, from birth to death, is a constant journey and those who believe in improving themselves are absolved of unnecessary burdens, which makes the walk light.'

It was early, but when he came to the Main Drain Semi-Slum to implement Plan X or whatever it was – by now he was losing count – he found Tulsi with broom in hand, clearing the street to draw a flowery rangoli in front of her hut.

'Good morning, Missus Tulsi,' he greeted her. 'Had your coffee?'

'Oh, how nice to see you,' she said. 'Just about to make, would you like a cup?'

'I'd love to,' said Hari and pulled the velvet pouch with her jewellery out of his pocket. 'The investigation took longer than expected, so our bureau wouldn't say no to a small bonus.'

She put down the broom and eyed him strangely. 'But don't you know?'

'Know what?'

'The police nabbed them. They came to my neighbour's house and, having heard what happened to me, she knew they were up to no good.'

'Is it so?'

'She locked them in her bedroom. And I got my jewellery back. Worth crores.'

'What are you saying?' said Hari and weighed the tiny pouch in his hand. 'Are you, I mean, positive that you got the right jewellery?'

'I am.' Maybe she got some other jewellery that was worth more than hers, and now didn't want her own back. 'We'll sell them and build a house in Mysuru for my daughter.'

'Oho, will you keep coffee in a thermos flask for me?' was all that Hari could muster up as he turned to walk away with some two lakhs worth of gold in his pocket. First he thought of giving the jewellery to his wife as a peace offering. Then he got a better idea – Plan Y. He'd catch a bus leaving for Mysuru via Srirangapatnam, one of the 5.1 Chanel LED DJ Music Party Lazer Show buses that showed nice Real-Star Upendra movies, and he'd have fun. He knew the owner from his touting days and would surely get a small discount. Putting the idol back where it belonged might solve everything in a best-case scenario. But first he'd take care of a few small things.

Standing around the corner from Cyber Villas, his slum home, he called up the junior bank manager, Kitnewallah, who was in charge of the bank's contacts with hitmen and enforcers.

'This is Hari Majestic from Diamond and Majestic Investigations Private Limited. Name rings a bell?'

'I told you not to call us, until we call you.'

'Sorry about that, sir. I just wanted to check if your security experts have cracked the case? Because I have.'

'You have?'

'Do I have to go on repeating every word? Do you want your ATM back or not?'

'What do you want in return?'

'Nothing.'

'Is that a trick question?'

'No, I'm just being professional.'

Kitnewallah did some calculations. Hari could hear an adding-machine chew paper in the background. He didn't know such old-fashioned implements were still in use. 'You may be eligible for a bonus on your next salary.'

'Thanks, but I really don't want my job back. I have more important things to do in life.'

'What can be more important than working at our bank?'

'Watching my three kids grow up. Take notes, because I don't have time to waste on you and I'll only say this once …' He gave directions for how to find the godown of Paisavasool Exports. 'There are some highly crooked export businessmen holed up there and whom your security experts may enjoy taking care of.' He was about to say 'torturing', but didn't want to hurt anybody's sentiments. 'I don't wish to plant criminal ideas in your head, but if this was America, they would have been sunk in a pit full of wet cement before they had time to blink.'

Knowing how substandard the enforcers were, the criminals' toenails were almost certainly going to be sticking out if future customers looked closely at the floor of the vault at the new bank complex on CD Road. But that was the bank's problem.

It didn't take very long. Fifteen minutes later, Hari spotted Mental Menthol coming out from Cyber Villas, carrying the long, again wrapped in newspapers. It was enough to see him head in the direction of Kallapete. Plan Z had worked. He climbed up the steps with the duty-free bag full of chocolates. Their door was open.

'Honey,' he called out, 'I'm home.'

In the event, he divided the gold jewellery into three piles – one to pawn and take Diamond on a holiday. Another to take his old friends for a treaty treat of unlimited Old Monk. And another third for the gods. Gods loved gold. Any god was more interested in those who had the gold to provide them with nice things.

Once their second honeymoon – that took them via Nandi Hills to Mangalore on the coast where they ate lots of gudbud and then IKEA in Hyderabad, where they bought another baby cot – was over, and Diamond stopped chastising Hari for the many errors he had committed during the previous weeks and lifetimes, and she and the kids had returned home, Hari travelled to Srirangapatnam, from where the only way to get to Halegudehalli, unless one had a vehicle, was on foot. He was on a pilgrimage, so he walked.

A man on a bicycle caught up with him. It was the village constable Smaranashakti, who had been mad before, but said hello now. 'So, you're back?'

'Yes,' said Hari.

'That's good of you. We haven't received many pilgrims lately.'

Hari grinned. 'But you will soon.'

The constable was only somewhat tipsy, he'd spent the night in a useless ancient armoury ruin that had once belonged to Tipu Sultan on Srirangapatnam island, where he and his friends made merry, undisturbed, reminiscing of glorious days.

'But you can't party in a historical monument!' said Hari. Recent events had made him appreciate history and heritage. 'They are our heritage.'

'That's what they tell tourists. And they do their best to make it harder for us to use it. Just the other day, they shifted it a hundred yards thinking that we might not find it in the dark.'

Hari had heard of the gigantic exercise to move Tipu's armoury. It was in the news. It was necessitated by the expansion of the railway tracks at the local station. He shook his head. Smaranashakti protested: 'But what else are we supposed to do with monuments if we don't put them to good use?'

He suggested that they share a pot of freshly tapped palm toddy to cement their friendship. Hari could have told him a thing or two about the importance of preserving heritage, but let it be. Smaranashakti offered Hari a ride.

'Thanks, but I think I need the walk,' said Hari.

The moment he saw the temple's gopuram towering up ahead, taller than the roofs of the village huts, he knew that things could only get better.

A few days later it was possible to read the following short item in the newspapers, though if one had blinked, one would have missed it:

'It is reported by our special correspondent in Srirangapatnam that the nearby Halegude Temple, which had been looted by mischief-mongers earlier in the month, has regained its purloined idol. Srirangapatnam Police constable Smaranashakti Kaledukondiruvavanu confirmed that an unknown pilgrim had left the idol in the donation box along with a significant treasure of gold jewellery which would suffice to buy CCTV cameras for the temple, so as to ward off future untoward incidents, and also upgrade the visiting facilities with a ticket booth so that foreign tourists would be encouraged to contribute to the upkeep.'

Acknowledgements

Although most people in the world might wish that there would be a character like Hari Majestic, a hero for hire who sets everything straight without making any profit, he is unfortunately fictional. And so are the other characters in this novel. Even the temple described in it doesn't exist, but the problem with idols being stolen is a genuine cause of concern. A newspaper report I read the day after I had finished the first draft of this book stated that: 'To those who make a lucrative business in stolen antiques, the ancient temples in Karnataka are a soft target. According to the Crime Records Bureau under the State police, in the last fifteen years, smuggling rings have robbed no less than 200 historical temples and monuments of their precious antiques. They have also vandalised many sites while raiding them for hidden treasures.' One reads such news almost weekly. So, the idea for this novel came from actual cases in which heritage was looted by ruthless merchants of antiques, combined with the thought that someone should write a modern response to the nineteenth century novel *The Moonstone* by Wilkie Collins, in which three brave Indians travel to England to retrieve a sacred object stolen by a British soldier after the battle of Srirangapatnam in 1799.

Thanks to Anjum Hasan, always my first reader, and Shruti Debi, my trusted agent, and the heroic Sushmita Chatterjee, my brilliant editor at Pan Macmillan India. Further thanks for lending assorted helping hands, inputs and outputs, to Clare Arni, Dave Besseling, Jan-Erik Pettersson, Pradeep KS, Srinath Perur, Stellan Wahlström and Sudarshan Purohit; and, last but not least, to Mette Wiik and Per Fång with family for hospitality during my research stint in Gothenburg (Sweden), and thanks to Lotta Lekvall and Johan Mikaelsson for special assistance there.